GIANT'S BREAD

Mysteries

The Man in the Brown
  Suit
The Secret of Chimneys
The Seven Dials Mystery
The Mysterious Mr
  Quin
The Sittaford Mystery
The Hound of Death
The Listerdale Mystery
Why Didn't They Ask
  Evans?
Parker Pyne Investigates
Murder Is Easy
And Then There Were
  None
Towards Zero
Death Comes as the End
Sparkling Cyanide
Crooked House
They Came to Baghdad
Destination Unknown
Spider's Web*
The Unexpected Guest*
Ordeal by Innocence
The Pale Horse
Endless Night
Passenger To Frankfurt
Problem at Pollensa Bay
While the Light Lasts

Poirot

The Mysterious Affair at
  Styles
The Murder on the
  Links
Poirot Investigates
The Murder of Roger
  Ackroyd
The Big Four
The Mystery of the Blue
  Train
Black Coffee*
Peril at End House

Lord Edgware Dies
Murder on the Orient
  Express
Three-Act Tragedy
Death in the Clouds
The ABC Murders
Murder in Mesopotamia
Cards on the Table
Murder in the Mews
Dumb Witness
Death on the Nile
Appointment with Death
Hercule Poirot's
  Christmas
Sad Cypress
One, Two, Buckle My
  Shoe
Evil Under the Sun
Five Little Pigs
The Hollow
The Labours of Hercules
Taken at the Flood
Mrs McGinty's Dead
After the Funeral
Hickory Dickory Dock
Dead Man's Folly
Cat Among the Pigeons
The Adventure of the
  Christmas Pudding
The Clocks
Third Girl
Hallowe'en Party
Elephants Can
  Remember
Poirot's Early Cases
Curtain: Poirot's Last
  Case

Marple

The Murder at the
  Vicarage
The Thirteen Problems
The Body in the Library
The Moving Finger

A Murder Is Announced
They Do It with Mirrors
A Pocket Full of Rye
4.50 from Paddington
The Mirror Crack'd
  from Side to Side
A Caribbean Mystery
At Bertram's Hotel
Nemesis
Sleeping Murder
Miss Marple's Final Cases

Tommy & Tuppence

The Secret Adversary
Partners in Crime
N or M?
By the Pricking of My
  Thumbs
Postern of Fate

Published as Mary
  Westmacott

Giant's Bread
Unfinished Portrait
Absent in the Spring
The Rose and the Yew
  Tree
A Daughter's a Daughter
The Burden

Memoirs

An Autobiography
Come, Tell Me How You
  Live
The Grand Tour

Plays and Stories

Akhnaton
The Mousetrap and
  Other Plays
The Floating Admiral†
Star Over Bethlehem
Hercule Poirot and the
  Greenshore Folly

* novelized by Charles Osborne   † contributor

Agatha Christie ®

writing as
Mary Westmacott

Giant's Bread

HarperCollins*Publishers*

HarperCollins*Publishers*
1 London Bridge Street
London SE1 9GF
www.harpercollins.co.uk

HarperCollins*Publishers*
1st Floor, Watermarque Building, Ringsend Road
Dublin 4, Ireland

This paperback edition 2017

9

First published in Great Britain by
Collins 1930

A catalogue record for this book is available from the British Library

ISBN 978-0-00-813144-9

Set in Sabon LT Std by Palimpsest Book Production Limited,
Falkirk, Stirlingshire
Printed and bound in Great Britain by
CPI Group (UK) Ltd, Croydon, CR0 4YY

MIX
Paper from
responsible sources
FSC™ C007454

*To the Memory of
My Best and Truest Friend
My Mother*

CONTENTS

PROLOGUE

It was the opening night of London's new National Opera House and consequently an occasion. Royalty was there. The Press were there. The fashionable were there in large quantities. Even the musical, by hook and by crook, had managed to be there—mostly very high up in the final tier of seats under the roof.

The musical composition given was *The Giant*, a new work by a hitherto unknown composer, Boris Groen. In the interval after the first part of the performance, a listener might have collected the following scraps of conversation.

'Quite divine, darling.' 'They say it's simply the—the—*the*—latest!! Everything out of tune on purpose . . . And you have to read Einstein in order to understand it . . .' 'Yes, dear, I shall tell everyone it's too marvellous. But privately, it does make one's head ache!'

'Why can't they open a British Opera House with a decent British composer? All this Russian tomfoolery!' Thus a peppery colonel.

'Quite so,' drawled his companion. 'But you see, there are no British composers. Sad, but there it is!'

Agatha Christie

'Nonsense—don't tell me, sir. They just won't give them a chance—that's what it is. Who is this fellow Levinne? A dirty foreign Jew. That's all he is!'

A man nearby, leaning against the wall, half concealed by a curtain, permitted himself to smile—for he was Sebastian Levinne, sole owner of the National Opera House, familiarly known by the title of the World's Greatest Showman.

He was a big man, rather too well covered with flesh. His face was yellow and impassive, his eyes beady and black, two enormous ears stood out from his head and were the joy of caricaturists.

The surge of talk eddied past him . . .

'Decadent—morbid . . . neurotic . . . childish . . .'

Those were critics.

'Devastating . . . too divine . . . marvellous, my dear . . .'

Those were women.

'The thing's nothing but a glorified revue.' 'Amazing effects in the second part, I believe. Machinery, you know. This first part "Stone" is only a kind of introduction. They say old Levinne has simply gone all out over this. Never been anything like it.' 'Music's pretty weird, isn't it?' 'Bolshy idea, I believe. Noise orchestras, don't they call them?'

Those were young men, more intelligent than the women, less prejudiced than the critics.

'It won't catch on. A stunt, thath all.' 'Yet, I don't know—there's a feeling for this Cubist thtuff.' 'Levinne's shrewd.' 'Dropth money deliberately thometimes—but getth it back.' 'Cost . . .?' The voices dropped, hushed themselves mysteriously as sums of money were mentioned.

2

Those were members of his own race. Sebastian Levinne smiled.

A bell rang—slowly the crowd drifted and eddied back to their seats.

There was a wait, filled with chattering and laughter—then the lights wavered and sank. The conductor mounted to his place. In front of him was an orchestra just six times as large as any Covent Garden orchestra and quite unlike an ordinary orchestra. There were strange instruments in it of shining metal like misshapen monsters, and in one corner an unaccustomed glitter of crystal. The conductor's baton was stretched out—then fell and immediately there was a low rhythmic beating as of hammers on anvils—every now and then a beat was missed—lost—and then came floating back taking its place out of turn, jostling the others.

The curtain rose . . .

At the back of a box on the second tier Sebastian Levinne stood and watched.

This was no opera, as commonly understood. It told no story, featured no individuals. Rather was it on the scale of a gigantic Russian ballet. It contained spectacular effects, strange and weird effects of lighting—effects that were Levinne's own inventions. His revues had for long been proclaimed as the last word in sheer spectacular sensation. Into this, more artist than producer, he had put the whole force of his imagination and experience.

The prologue had represented Stone—Man's infancy.

This—the body of the work—was a supreme pageant of machinery—fantastic, almost awful. Power houses, dynamos, factory chimneys, cranes, all merging and flowing.

Agatha Christie

And men—armies of men—with Cubist robot faces—defiling in patterns.

The music swelled and eddied—a deep sonorous clamour came from the new strangely shaped metal instruments. A queer high sweet note sounded above it all—like the ringing of innumerable glasses . . .

There was an Episode of Skyscrapers—New York seen upside down as from a circling aeroplane in the early dawn of morning. And the strange inharmonious rhythm beat ever more insistently—with increasing menacing monotony. It drew on through other episodes to its climax—a giant seeming steel erection—thousands of steel faced men welded together into a Giant Collective Man . . .

The Epilogue followed immediately. There was no interval, the lights did not go up.

Only one side of the orchestra spoke. What was called in the new modern phrase 'the Glass'.

Clarion ringing notes.

The curtain dissolved into mist . . . the mist parted . . . the sudden glare made one wish to shield one's eyes.

Ice—nothing but ice . . . great bergs and glaciers . . . shining . . .

And on the top immense pinnacle a little figure—facing away from the audience towards the insufferable glare that represented the rising of the sun . . .

The ridiculous puny figure of a man . . .

The glare increased—to the whiteness of magnesium. Hands went instinctively to eyes with a cry of pain.

The glass rang out—high and sweet—then crashed—and broke—literally broke—into tinkling fragments.

The curtain dropped and the lights rose.

Sebastian Levinne with an impassive face received various congratulations and side hits.

'Well, you've done it this time, Levinne. No half measures, eh?'

'A damned fine show, old man. Blessed if I know what it's all about, though.'

'The Giant, eh? That's true, we live in an age of machinery all right.'

'Oh, Mr Levinne, it's simply too frightening for words! I shall dream of that horrid steel giant.'

'Machinery as the Giant that devours, eh? Not far wrong, Levinne. We want to get back to Nature. Who's Groen? A Russian?'

'Yes, who's Groen? He's a genius whoever he is. The Bolshevists can boast they've produced one composer at last.'

'Too bad, Levinne, you've gone Bolshy. Collective Man. Collective Music too.'

'Well, Levinne, good luck to you. Can't say I like this damned caterwauling they call music nowadays, but it's a good show.'

Almost last came a little old man, slightly bent, with one shoulder higher than the other. He said with a very distinct utterance:

'Like to give me a drink, Sebastian?'

Levinne nodded. This little old man was Carl Bowerman, the most distinguished of English musical critics. They went together to Levinne's own sanctum.

In Levinne's room they settled down in two arm-chairs.

Levinne provided his guest with a whisky and soda. Then he looked across at him inquiringly. He was anxious for this man's verdict.

'Well?'

Bowerman did not reply for a minute or two. At last he said slowly:

'I am an old man. There are things in which I take pleasure—there are other things—such as the music of today—which do not give me pleasure. But all the same I know Genius when I meet it. There are a hundred charlatans—a hundred breakers down of tradition who think that by doing so they have accomplished something wonderful. And there is the hundred and first—a creator, a man who steps boldly into the future—'

He paused, then went on.

'Yes, I know genius when I meet it. I may not like it—but I recognize it. Groen, whoever he is, has genius . . . *The music of tomorrow . . .*'

Again he paused, and again Levinne did not interrupt, but waited.

'I don't know whether your venture will succeed or fail. I think succeed—but that will be mainly because of your personality. You have the art of forcing the public to accept what you want them to accept. You have a talent for success. You've made a mystery about Groen—part of your press campaign, I suppose.'

He looked at Sebastian keenly.

'I don't want to interfere with your press campaign, but tell me one thing—Groen's an Englishman, isn't he?'

'Yes. How did you know, Bowerman?'

6

'Nationality in music is unmistakable. He has studied in the Russian Revolutionary school, yes—but—well, as I said, nationality is unmistakable. There have been pioneers before him—people who have tried tentatively the things he has accomplished. We've had our English school—Holst, Vaughan Williams, Arnold Bax. All over the world musicians have been drawing nearer to the new ideal—the Absolute in Music. This man is the direct successor of that boy who was killed in the war, what was his name? Deyre—Vernon Deyre—He had promise.' He sighed. 'I wonder, Levinne, how much we lost through the war.'

'It's difficult to say, sir.'

'It doesn't bear thinking of. No, it doesn't bear thinking of.' He rose. 'I mustn't keep you. You've a lot to do, I know.' A faint smile showed on his face. '*The Giant!* You and Groen have your little joke all to yourselves, I fancy. Everyone takes it for granted the Giant is the Moloch of Machinery—They don't see that the real Giant is that pigmy figure—man. The individualist who endures through Stone and Iron and who though civilizations crumble and die, fights his way through yet another Glacial Age to rise in a new civilization of which we do not dream . . .'

His smile broadened.

'As I grow older I am more and more convinced that there is nothing so pathetic, so ridiculous, so absurd, and so absolutely wonderful as Man—'

He paused by the doorway, his hand on the knob.

'One wonders,' he said, 'what has gone to the making of a thing like the Giant? What produces it? What feeds it? Heredity shapes the instrument—environment polishes

7

and rounds it off—sex wakens it . . . But there's more than that. There's its food.

> 'Fee, fie, fo fum,
> *I smell the blood of mortal man*
> *Be he alive or be he dead*
> *I'll grind his bones to make my bread.*

A cruel giant, genius, Levinne! A monster feeding on flesh and blood. I know nothing about Groen, yet I'd swear that he's fed his Giant with his own flesh and blood and perhaps the flesh and blood of others too . . . Their bones ground to make the Giant's bread . . .

'I'm an old man, Levinne. I have my fancies. We've seen the end tonight—I'd like to know the beginning.'

'Heredity—environment—sex,' said Levinne slowly.

'Yes. Just that. Not that I have any hopes of your telling me.'

'You think I—know?'

'I'm sure you know.'

There was a silence.

'Yes,' said Levinne at last, 'I do know. I would tell you the whole story if I could—but I cannot. There are reasons . . .'

He repeated slowly: 'There are reasons . . .'

'A pity. It would have been interesting.'

'I wonder . . .'

BOOK I

Abbots Puissants

CHAPTER 1

There were only three people of real importance in Vernon's world: Nurse, God and Mr Green.

There were, of course, the nursemaids. Winnie, the present one, and behind her Jane and Annie and Sarah and Gladys. Those were all the ones that Vernon could remember, but there were lots more. Nursery maids never stayed long because they couldn't get on with Nurse. They hardly counted in Vernon's world.

There was also a kind of twin deity called Mummy-Daddy mentioned by Vernon in his prayers and also connected with going down to dessert. They were shadowy figures, rather beautiful and wonderful—especially Mummy—but they again did not belong to the real world—Vernon's world.

The things in Vernon's world were very real indeed. There was the drugget on the nursery floor, for instance. It was of green and white stripes and rather scrubbly to bare knees and in one corner of it was a hole which Vernon used surreptitiously to make bigger by working his fingers round in it. There were the nursery walls where mauve irises twined themselves interminably upwards round a pattern that was sometimes diamonds and sometimes, if you looked at it long enough, crosses. That seemed very interesting to Vernon and rather magical.

There was a rocking horse against one wall, but Vernon seldom rode on it. There was a basket-work engine and some basket-work trucks which he played with a good deal. There was a low cupboard full of more or less dilapidated toys. On an upper shelf were the more delectable contents that you played with on a wet day or when Nurse was in an unusually good temper. The Paint Box was there and the Real Camel Hair Brushes and a heap of illustrated papers for Cutting Out. In fact, all the things that Nurse said were 'that messy she couldn't abear them about'. In other words, the best things.

And in the centre of this realistic nursery universe, dominating everything, was Nurse herself. Person No. 1 of Vernon's Trinity. Very big and broad, very starched and crackling. Omniscient and omnipotent. You couldn't get the better of Nurse. She knew better than little boys. She frequently said so. Her whole lifetime had been spent looking after little boys (and incidentally little girls too, but Vernon was not interested in them) and one and all they had grown up to be a Credit to her. She said so and Vernon believed her. He had no doubt that he also would grow up to be a Credit to her, though sometimes it didn't seem likely. There was something awe-inspiring about Nurse, but at the same time infinitely comfortable. She knew the answer to everything. For instance, Vernon propounded the riddle about the diamonds and the crosses on the wallpaper.

'Ah, well!' said Nurse, 'there's two ways of looking at everything. You must have heard that.'

And as Vernon had heard her say much the same to Winnie one day, he was soothed and satisfied. On the occasion in question, Nurse had gone on to say that there were always two sides to a question and in future Vernon always visualized a question as something like a letter A with crosses creeping up one side of it and diamonds going down the other.

After Nurse there was God. God was also very real to Vernon mainly because he bulked so largely in Nurse's conversation. Nurse knew most things that you did, but God knew *everything*, and God was, if anything, more particular than Nurse. You couldn't see God, which, Vernon always felt, gave him rather an unfair advantage over you, because he could see you. Even in the dark, he could see you. Sometimes when Vernon was in bed at night, the thought of God looking down at him through the darkness used to give him a creepy feeling down the spine.

But on the whole, God was an intangible person compared with Nurse. You could conveniently forget about him most of the time. That was, until Nurse lugged him deliberately into the conversation.

Once Vernon essayed revolt.

'Nurse, do you know what I shall do when I'm dead?'

Nurse, who was knitting stockings, said: 'One, two, three, four, there now, I've dropped a stitch. No, Master Vernon, I'm sure I don't.'

'I shall go to Heaven—I shall go to Heaven—and I shall

go right up to God—right up to him I shall go, and I shall say: "You're an 'orrible man and I 'ate you!'"

Silence. It was done. He had said it. Unbelievable, unparalleled audacity! What would happen? What awful punishment terrestrial or celestial would descend upon him? He waited—breathless.

Nurse had picked up the stitch. She looked at Vernon over the top of her spectacles. She was serene—unruffled.

'It's not likely,' she remarked, 'that the Almighty will take any notice of what a naughty little boy says. Winnie, give me those scissors, if you please.'

Vernon retired crestfallen. It was no good. You couldn't down Nurse. He might have known.

And then there was Mr Green. Mr Green was like God in that you couldn't see him, but to Vernon he was very real. He knew, for instance, exactly what Mr Green looked like—of middle height, rather stout, a faint resemblance to the village grocer who sang an uncertain baritone in the village choir, bright red cheeks and mutton chop whiskers. His eyes were blue, a very bright blue. The great thing about Mr Green was that he played—he loved playing. Whatever game Vernon thought of, that was just the game that Mr Green loved to play. There were other points about him. He had, for instance, a hundred children. And three others. The hundred, in Vernon's mind, were kept intact, a joyous mob that raced down the yew alleys behind Vernon and Mr Green. But the three others were different. They were called by the three most beautiful names that Vernon knew: Poodle, Squirrel and Tree.

Vernon was, perhaps, a lonely little boy, but he never knew it. Because, you see, he had Mr Green and Poodle, Squirrel and Tree to play with.

For a long time Vernon was undecided as to where Mr Green's home was. It came to him quite suddenly that of course Mr Green lived in the Forest. The Forest had always been fascinating to Vernon. One side of the Park bordered on it. There were high green palings and Vernon used to creep along them hoping for a crack that would let him see through. There were whisperings and sighings and rustlings all along, as though the trees were speaking to each other. Half-way down there was a door, but alas, it was always locked, so that Vernon could never see what it was really like inside the Forest.

Nurse, of course, would never take him there. She was like all nurses and preferred a good steady walk along the road, and no messing your feet up with them nasty damp leaves. So Vernon was never allowed to go in the Forest. It made him think of it all the more. Some day he would take tea there with Mr Green. Poodle and Squirrel and Tree were to have new suits for the occasion.

The nursery palled on Vernon. It was too small. He knew all there was to know about it. The garden was different. It was really a very exciting garden. There were so many different bits of it. The long walks between the clipped yew hedges with their ornamental birds, the water garden with the fat goldfish, the walled fruit garden, the wild garden with its almond trees in spring time and the copse of silver birch trees with bluebells growing underneath, and best of all the railed-off bit where the ruins of the old Abbey were. That was the place where Vernon would have liked to be left to his own devices—to climb and explore. But he never was. The rest of the garden he did much as he liked in. Winnie was always sent out with him but since by a remarkable coincidence they always seemed to encounter the second gardener, he could play his own games unhindered by too much kind attention on Winnie's part.

Gradually Vernon's world widened. The twin star, Mummy-Daddy, separated, became two distinct people. Daddy remained nebulous, but Mummy became quite a personage. She often paid visits to the nursery to 'play with my darling little boy'. Vernon bore her visits with grave politeness, though it usually meant giving up the game that he himself was engaged upon and accepting one which was not, in his opinion, nearly so good. Lady visitors would sometimes come with her, and then she would squeeze Vernon tightly (which he hated) and cry:

'It's so wonderful to be a mother! I never get used to it! To have a darling baby boy of one's very own.'

Very red, Vernon would extricate himself from her embrace. Because he wasn't a baby boy at all. He was three years old.

Looking across the room one day, just after a scene like the above, he saw his father standing by the nursery door with sardonic eyes, watching him. Their eyes met. Something seemed to pass between them—comprehension—a sense of kinship.

His mother's friends were talking.

'Such a pity, Myra, that he doesn't take after you. Your hair would be too lovely on a child.'

But Vernon had a sudden feeling of pride. He was like his father.

Vernon always remembered the day that the American lady came to lunch. To begin with, because of Nurse's explanations about America which, as he realized later, she confused with Australia.

He went down to dessert in an awe-stricken state. If this lady had been at home in her own country, she would be walking about upside down with her head hanging down. Quite enough, this, to make him stare. And then, too, she used odd words for the simplest things.

'Isn't he too cute? See here, honey, I've gotten a box of candy for you. Won't you come and fetch it?'

Vernon came gingerly; accepted the present. The lady clearly didn't know what she was talking about. It wasn't candy, but good Edinburgh Rock.

There were two gentlemen there also, one the husband of the American lady. This one said:

'Do you know half a crown, my boy, when you see it?'

And it presently turned out that the half-crown was to

Agatha Christie

be for his very own to keep. Altogether it was a wonderful day.

Vernon had never thought very much about his home. He knew that it was bigger than the Vicarage, where he sometimes went to tea, but he seldom played with any other children or went to their homes. So it came to him with a shock of wonder that day. The visitors were taken all over the house, and the American lady's voice rose ceaselessly.

'My, if that isn't too wonderful. Did you ever see such a thing? Five hundred years, you say? Frank, listen to that. Henry the eighth—if it isn't just like listening to English history. And the Abbey older still, you say?'

They went everywhere, through the long picture gallery where faces strangely like Vernon's with dark eyes set close together and narrow heads looked out from the painted canvas arrogantly or with cold tolerance. There were meek women there in ruffs or with pearls twisted in their hair— the Deyre women had done best to be meek, married to wild lords who knew neither fear nor pity—who looked appraisingly at Myra Deyre, the last of their number, as she walked beneath them. From the picture gallery they went to the square hall, and from there to the Priest's Chamber.

Vernon had been removed by Nurse long since. They found him again in the garden feeding the goldfish. Vernon's father had gone into the house to get the keys of the Abbey ruins. The visitors were alone.

'My, Frank,' said the American lady. 'Isn't it *too* wonderful? All these years. Handed down from father to

18

son. Romantic, that's what I call it, just too romantic for anything. All these years. Just fancy! How is it done?'

It was then that the other gentleman spoke. He was not much of a talker, so far Vernon had not heard him speak at all. But he now unclosed his lips and uttered one word—a word so enchanting, so mysterious, so delightful that Vernon never forgot it.

'Brumagem,' said the other gentleman.

And before Vernon could ask him (as he meant to do) what that marvellous word meant, another diversion occurred.

His mother came out of the house. There was a sunset behind her—a scene painter's sunset of crude gold and red. Against that background Vernon saw his mother—saw her for the first time—a magnificent woman with white skin and red gold hair—a being like the pictures in his fairy book, saw her suddenly as something wonderful and beautiful.

He was never to forget that strange moment. She was his mother and she was beautiful and he loved her. Something hurt him inside, like a pain—only it wasn't a pain. And there was a queer booming noise inside his head—a thundering noise that ended up high and sweet like a bird's note. Altogether a very wonderful moment.

And mixed up with it was that magic word *Brumagem*.

CHAPTER 2

Winnie the nursemaid was going away. It all happened very
suddenly. The other servants whispered together. Winnie
cried. She cried and cried. Nurse gave her what she called
a Talking To and after that Winnie cried more than ever.
There was something terrible about Nurse, she seemed
larger than usual and she crackled more. Winnie, Vernon
knew, was going away because of Father. He accepted that
fact without any particular interest or curiosity. Nursemaids
did sometimes go away because of Father.

His mother was shut in her room. She too was crying.
Vernon could hear her through the door. She did not send
for him and it did not occur to him to go to her. Indeed
he was vaguely relieved. He hated the noise of crying, the
gulping sound, the long-drawn sniffs, and it always
happened so close to your ears. People who were crying
always hugged you. Vernon hated those kind of noises close
to his ears. There was nothing in the world he hated more
than the wrong sort of noise. It made you feel all curled
up like a leaf in your middle. That was the jolly part about
Mr Green. He never made the wrong kind of noise.

Winnie was packing her boxes. Nurse was in with her—a less awful Nurse now—almost a human Nurse.

'Now you let this be a warning to you, my girl,' said Nurse. 'No carryings on in your next place.'

Winnie sniffed something about no real harm.

'And no more there wouldn't be, I should hope, with Me in charge,' said Nurse. 'A lot comes, I daresay, of having red hair. Red-haired girls are always flighty, so my dear mother used to say. I'm not saying you're a bad girl. But what you've done is unbecoming. Unbecoming—I can't say more than that.'

And, as Vernon had often noticed after using this particular phrase, she proceeded to say a good deal more. But he did not listen, for he was pondering on the word Unbecoming. Becoming, he knew, was a thing you said about a hat. Where did a hat come in?

'What's unbecoming, Nurse?' he asked later in the day.

Nurse, with her mouth full of pins, for she was cutting out a linen suit for Vernon, replied.

'Unsuitable.'

'What's unsuitable?'

'Little boys going on asking foolish questions,' said Nurse, with the deftness of a long professional career behind her.

That afternoon Vernon's father came into the nursery. There was a queer furtive look about him—unhappy and defiant. He winced slightly before Vernon's round interested gaze.

'Hullo, Vernon.'

'Hullo, Father.'

'I'm going to London. Goodbye, old chap.'

'Are you going to London because you kissed Winnie?' inquired Vernon with interest.

His father uttered the kind of word that Vernon knew he was not supposed to hear—much less ever repeat. It was, he knew, a word that gentlemen used but little boys didn't. So great a fascination did that fact lend it, that Vernon was in the habit of sending himself to sleep by repeating it over to himself in company with another forbidden word. The other word was Corsets.

'Who the devil told you that?'

'Nobody told me,' said Vernon after reflecting a minute.

'Then how did you know?'

'Didn't you, then?' inquired Vernon.

His father crossed the room without answering.

'Winnie kisses me sometimes,' remarked Vernon. 'But I didn't like it much. I have to kiss her too. The gardener kisses her a lot. He seems to like it. I think kissing's silly. Should I like kissing Winnie better if I was grown up, Father?'

'Yes,' he said deliberately. 'I think you would. Sons, you know, sometimes grow up very like their fathers.'

'I'd like to be like you,' said Vernon. 'You're a jolly good rider. Sam said so. He said there wasn't your equal in the county and that a better judge of horse flesh never lived.' Vernon brought out the latter words rapidly. 'I'd rather be like you than Mummy. Mummy gives a horse a sore back. Sam said so.'

There was a further pause.

'Mummy's gotaheadacheanlyingdown,' proceeded Vernon.

'I know.'

'Have you said goodbye to her?'

'No.'

'Are you going to? Because you'll have to be quick. That's the dogcart coming round now.'

'I expect I shan't have time.'

Vernon nodded wisely.

'I daresay that would be a good plan. I don't like having to kiss people when they're crying. I don't like Mummy kissing me much anyway. She squeezes too hard and she talks in your ear. I think I'd almost rather kiss Winnie. Which would you, Father?'

He was disconcerted by his father's abrupt withdrawal from the room. Nurse had come in a moment before. She stood respectfully aside to let the master pass, and Vernon had a vague idea that she had managed to make his father uncomfortable.

Katie, the under-housemaid, came in to lay tea. Vernon built bricks in the corner. The old peaceful nursery atmosphere closed round him again.

There was a sudden interruption. His mother stood in the doorway. Her eyes were swollen with crying. She dabbed them with a handkerchief. She stood there theatrically miserable.

'He's gone,' she cried. 'Without a word to me. Without a word. Oh, my little son. My little son.'

She swept across the floor and gathered Vernon in her arms. The tower, at least one storey higher than any he had ever built before, crashed into ruins. His mother's voice, loud and distraught, burrowed into his ear.

'My child—my little son—swear that you'll never forsake me—swear it—swear it—'

Nurse came across to them.

'There, Ma'am, there, Ma'am, don't take on so. You'd better get back to bed. Edith shall bring you a nice cup of hot tea.'

Her tone was authoritative—severe.

His mother still sobbed and clasped him closer. Vernon's whole body began to stiffen in resistance. He could bear it a little while longer—a very little while longer—and he'd do anything Mummy wanted if only she'd let go of him.

'You must make up to me, Vernon—make up to me for the suffering your father has caused me—Oh, my God, what shall I do?'

Somewhere, in the back of his mind, Vernon was aware of Katie, silent, ecstatic, enjoying the scene.

'Come along, Ma'am,' said Nurse. 'You'll only upset the child.'

The authority in her voice was so marked this time that Vernon's mother succumbed to it. Leaning weakly on Nurse's arm, she allowed herself to be led from the room.

Nurse returned a few minutes later very red in the face.

'My,' said Katie, 'didn't she take on? Regular hysterics—that's what they call it! Well, this has been a to do! You don't think she'll do a mischief to herself, do you? Those nasty ponds in the garden. The Master is a one—not that

24

he hasn't a lot to put up with from Her. All them scenes and tantrums—'

'That'll do, my girl,' said Nurse. 'You can get back to your work, and under-servants discussing a matter of this kind with their betters is a thing that I've never known take place in a gentleman's house. Your mother ought to have trained you better.'

With a toss of her head, Katie withdrew. Nurse moved round the nursery table, shifting cups and plates with unwonted sharpness. Her lips moved, muttering to herself.

'Putting ideas into the child's head. I've no patience with it . . .'

CHAPTER 3

A new nursemaid came, a thin white girl with protruding eyes. Her name was Isabel, but she was called Susan as being 'more suitable'. This puzzled Vernon very much. He asked Nurse for an explanation.

'There are names that are suitable to the gentry, Master Vernon, and names that are suitable for servants. That's all there is to it.'

'Then why is her real name Isabel?'

'There are people who when they christen their children set themselves up to ape their betters.'

The word ape had a distracting influence on Vernon. Apes were monkeys. Did people christen their children at the zoo?

'I thought people were christened in church.'

'So they are, Master Vernon.'

Very puzzling—why was everything so puzzling? Why were things more puzzling than they used to be? Why did one person tell you one thing and another person something quite different?

'Nurse, how do babies come?'

'You've asked me that before, Master Vernon. The little angels bring them in the night through the window.'

'That Am-am-am—'

'Don't stammer, Master Vernon.'

'Amenkun lady who came—she said I was found under a gooseberry bush.'

'That's the way they do with American babies,' said Nurse serenely.

Vernon heaved a sigh of relief. Of course! He felt a throb of gratitude to Nurse. She always knew. She made the unsteady swaying universe stand still again. And she never laughed. His mother did. He had heard her say to other ladies, 'He asks me the quaintest questions. Just listen to this. Aren't children funny and adorable?'

But Vernon couldn't see that he was funny or adorable at all. He just wanted to know. You'd got to *know*. That was part of growing up. When you were grown up you knew everything and had gold sovereigns in your purse.

The world went on widening.

There were, for instance, uncles and aunts.

Uncle Sydney was Mummy's brother. He was short and stout and had rather a red face. He had a habit of humming tunes and of rattling the money in his trouser pockets. He was fond of making jokes, but Vernon did not always think his jokes very funny.

'Supposing,' Uncle Sydney would say, 'I were to put on your hat? Hey? What should I look like, do you think?'

Curious, the questions grown up people asked!

Curious—and also difficult, because if there was one thing that Nurse was always impressing upon Vernon, it was that little boys must never make personal remarks.

'Come now,' said Uncle Sydney perseveringly. 'What should I look like? There—' he snatched up the linen affair in question and balanced it on top of his head. 'What do I look like—eh?'

Well, if one must answer, one must. Vernon said politely and a little wearily:

'I think you look rather silly.'

'That boy of yours has no sense of humour, Myra,' said Uncle Sydney to his mother. 'No sense of humour at all. A pity.'

Aunt Nina, Father's sister, was quite different.

She smelt nice, like the garden on a summer's day, and she had a soft voice that Vernon liked. She had other virtues— she didn't kiss you when you didn't want to be kissed, and she didn't insist on making jokes. But she didn't come very often to Abbots Puissants.

She must be, Vernon thought, very brave, because it was she who first made him realize that one could master The Beast.

The Beast lived in the big drawing-room. It had four legs and a shiny brown body. And it had a long row of what Vernon had thought when he was very small, to be teeth. Great yellow shining teeth. From his earliest memory, Vernon had been fascinated and terrified by The Beast. For if you irritated The Beast, it made strange noises, an angry growling or a shrill angry wail—and somehow those noises hurt you more than anything in the world could, they hurt

28

you right down in your inside. They made you shiver and feel sick, and they made your eyes sting and burn, and yet by some strange enchantment, you couldn't go away.

When Vernon had stories read to him about dragons, he always thought of them as like The Beast. And some of the best games with Mr Green were where they killed The Beast—Vernon plunging a sword into his brown shining body whilst the hundred children whooped and sang behind.

Now that he was a big boy—he knew better, of course. He knew that The Beast's name was Grand Piano, and that when you deliberately attacked its teeth that was called 'playingthepiano!' and that ladies did it after dinner to gentlemen. But in his inmost heart, he was still afraid and dreamt sometimes of The Beast pursuing him up the nursery stairs—and he would wake up screaming.

In his dreams The Beast lived in the Forest, and was wild and savage, and the noises it made were too terrible to be borne.

Mummy sometimes did 'playingthepiano' and that Vernon could just bear with difficulty. The Beast, he felt, would not really be waked up by what she was doing to it. But the day Aunt Nina played was different.

Vernon had been conducting one of his imaginary games in a corner. He and Squirrel and Poodle were having a picnic and eating lobsters and chocolate éclairs.

His Aunt Nina had not even noticed that he was in the room. She had sat down on the music stool and was playing idly.

Fascinated, Vernon crept nearer and nearer. Nina looked

at last to see him staring at her, the tears running down his face and great sobs shaking his small body. She stopped.

'What's the matter, Vernon?'

'I hate it,' sobbed Vernon. 'I 'ate it. I 'ate it. It hurts me *here*.' His hands clasped his stomach.

Myra came into the room at that minute. She laughed.

'Isn't it odd? That child simply hates music. So very queer.'

'Why doesn't he go away if he hates it?' said Nina.

'I can't,' sobbed Vernon.

'Isn't it ridiculous?' said Myra.

'I think it's rather interesting.'

'Most children are always wanting to strum on the piano. I tried to show Vernon "Chopsticks" the other day, but he wasn't a bit amused.'

Nina remained staring at her small nephew thoughtfully.

'I can hardly believe a child of mine can be unmusical,' said Myra in an aggrieved voice. 'I played quite difficult pieces when I was eight years old.'

'Oh, well!' said Nina vaguely. 'There are different ways of being musical.'

Which, Myra thought, was so like the silly sort of thing the Deyre family would say. Either one was musical and played pieces, or one was not. Vernon clearly was not.

Nurse's mother was ill. Strange unparalleled nursery catastrophe. Nurse, very red-faced and grim, was packing with the assistance of Susan Isabel. Vernon, troubled, sympathetic, but above all interested, stood nearby, and out of his interest, asked questions.

'Is your mother very old, Nurse? Is she a hundred?'

'Of course not, Master Vernon. A hundred indeed!'

'Do you think she is going to die?' continued Vernon, longing to be kind and understand.

Cook's mother had been ill and died. Nurse did not answer. Instead she said sharply:

'The boot-bags out of the bottom drawer, Susan. Step lively now, my girl.'

'Nurse, will your mother—'

'I haven't time to be answering questions, Master Vernon.'

Vernon sat down on the corner of a chintz-covered ottoman and gave himself up to reflection. Nurse had said that her mother wasn't a hundred, but she must, for all that, be very old. Nurse herself he had always regarded as terribly old. To think that there was a being of superior age and wisdom to Nurse was positively staggering. In a strange way it reduced Nurse herself to the proportions of a mere human being. She was no longer a figure secondary only to God himself.

The Universe shifted—values were readjusted. Nurse, God, and Mr Green—all three receded, becoming vaguer and more blurred. Mummy, his father, even Aunt Nina— seemed to matter more. Especially Mummy. Mummy was like the princesses with long beautiful golden hair. He would like to fight a dragon for Mummy—a brown shiny dragon like The Beast.

What was the word—the magic word? Brumagem—that

31

was it—Brumagem. An enchanting word! The Princess Brumagem! A word to be repeated over to himself softly and secretly at night at the same time as 'Damn' and 'Corsets'.

But never, never, never must Mummy hear it—because he knew only too well that she would laugh—she always laughed, the kind of laugh that made you shrivel up inside and want to wriggle. And she would say things—she always said things, just the kind of things you hated. 'Aren't children too *funny*?'

And Vernon knew that he wasn't funny. He didn't like funny things—Uncle Sydney had said so. If only Mummy wouldn't—

Sitting on the slippery chintz he frowned perplexedly. He had a sudden imperfect glimpse of two Mummies. One, the princess, the beautiful Mummy that he dreamt about, who was mixed up for him with sunsets and magic and killing dragons—and the other—the one who laughed and who said, 'Aren't children too funny?' Only, of course, they were the same . . .

He fidgeted and sighed. Nurse, flushed from the effort of snapping to her trunk, turned to him kindly.

'What's the matter, Master Vernon?'

'Nothing,' said Vernon.

You must always say 'Nothing.' You could never tell. Because, if you did, no one ever knew what you meant . . .

Under the reign of Susan Isabel, the nursery was quite different. You could be, and quite frequently were, naughty.

Susan told you not to do things and you did them just the same! Susan would say: 'I'll tell your mother.' But she never did.

Susan had at first enjoyed the position and authority she had in Nurse's absence. Indeed, but for Vernon, she would have continued to enjoy it. She used to exchange confidences with Katie, the under-housemaid.

'Don't know what's come over him, I'm sure. He's like a little demon sometimes. And him so good and well behaved with Mrs Pascal.'

To which Kate replied:

'Ah! she's a one, she is! Takes you up sharp, doesn't she?'

And then they would whisper and giggle.

'Who's Mrs Pascal?' Vernon asked one day.

'Well, I never, Master Vernon! Don't you know your own Nurse's name?'

So Nurse was Mrs Pascal. Another shock. She had always been just Nurse. It was rather as though you had been told that God's name was Mr Robinson.

Mrs Pascal! Nurse! The more you thought of it, the more extraordinary it seemed. Mrs Pascal—just like Mummy was Mrs Deyre and Father was Mr Deyre. Strangely enough Vernon never cogitated on the possibility of a Mr Pascal. (Not that there was any such person. The Mrs was a tacit recognition of Nurse's position and authority.) Nurse stood alone in the same magnificence as Mr Green, who, in spite of the hundred children (and Poodle, Squirrel and Tree), was never thought of by Vernon as having a Mrs Green attached to him!

Vernon's inquiring mind wandered in another direction. 'Susan, do you like being called Susan? Wouldn't you like being called Isabel better?'

Susan (or Isabel) gave her customary giggle.

'It doesn't matter what I like, Master Vernon.'

'Why not?'

'People have got to do what they're told in this world.'

Vernon was silent. He had thought the same until a few days ago. But he was beginning to perceive that it was not true. You needn't do as you were told. It all depended on who told you.

It was not a question of punishment. He was continually being sat on chairs, stood in the corner, and deprived of sweets by Susan. Nurse, on the other hand, had only had to look at him severely through her spectacles with a certain expression on her face, and anything but immediate capitulation was out of the question.

Susan had no authority in her nature, and Vernon knew it. He had discovered the thrill of successful disobedience. Also, he liked tormenting Susan. The more worried and flustered and unhappy Susan got, the more Vernon liked it. He was, as was proper to his years, still in the Stone Age. He savoured the full pleasure of cruelty.

Susan formed the habit of letting Vernon go out to play in the garden alone. Being an unattractive girl, she had not Winnie's reasons for liking the garden. And besides, what harm could possibly come to him?

'You won't go near the ponds, will you, Master Vernon?'

'No,' said Vernon, instantly forming the intention to do so.

34

'You'll play with your hoop like a good boy?'

'Yes.'

The nursery was left in peace. Susan heaved a sigh of relief. She took from a drawer a paper-covered book entitled *The Duke and the Dairymaid*.

Beating his hoop, Vernon made the tour of the walled fruit garden. Escaping from his control, the hoop leapt upon a small patch of earth which was at the moment receiving the meticulous attentions of Hopkins, the head gardener. Hopkins firmly and authoritatively ordered Vernon from the spot, and Vernon went. He respected Hopkins.

Abandoning the hoop, Vernon climbed a tree or two. That is to say, he reached a height of perhaps six feet from the ground, employing all due precautions. Tiring of this perilous sport, he sat astride a branch and cogitated as to what to do next.

On the whole, he thought of the ponds. Susan having forbidden them, they had a distinct fascination. Yes, he would go to the ponds. He rose, and as he did so, another idea came into his head, suggested by an unusual sight.

The door into the Forest was open!

Such a thing had never happened before in Vernon's experience. Again and again he had secretly tried that door. Always it was locked.

He crept up to it cautiously. The Forest! It stood a few steps away outside the door. You could plunge straightway into its cool green depths. Vernon's heart beat faster.

Agatha Christie

He had always wanted to go into the Forest. Here was his chance. Once Nurse came back, any such thing would be out of the question.

And still he hesitated. It was not any feeling of disobedience that held him back. Strictly speaking, he had never been forbidden to go in the Forest. His childish cunning was all ready with that excuse.

No, it was something else. Fear of the unknown—of those dark leafy depths. Ancestral memories held him back . . .

He wanted to go—but he didn't want to go. There might be Things there—Things like The Beast. Things that came up behind you—that chased you screaming . . .

He moved uneasily from one foot to the other.

But Things didn't chase you in the daytime. And Mr Green lived in the Forest. Not that Mr Green was as real as he used to be. Still, it would be rather jolly to explore and find a place where you would pretend Mr Green did live. Poodle, Squirrel, and Tree would each have houses of their own—small leafy houses.

'Come on, Poodle,' said Vernon to an invisible companion. 'Have you got your bow and arrow? That's right. We'll meet Squirrel inside.'

He stepped out jauntily. Beside him, plain to Vernon's inner eye, went Poodle, dressed like the picture of Robinson Crusoe in his picture book.

It was wonderful in the Forest—dim and dark and green. Birds sang and flew from branch to branch. Vernon continued to talk to his friend—a luxury he did not dare to permit himself often, since someone might overhear and

36

say, 'Isn't he too funny? He's pretending he's got another little boy with him.' You had to be so very careful at home.

'We'll get to the Castle by lunch time, Poodle. There are going to be roasted leopards. Oh! Hullo, here's Squirrel. How are you, Squirrel? Where's Tree?'

'I tell you what. I think it's rather tiring walking. I think we'll ride.'

Steeds were tethered to an adjacent tree. Vernon's was milk white, Poodle's was coal black—the colour of Squirrel's he couldn't quite decide.

They galloped forward through the trees. There were deadly dangerous places, morasses. Snakes hissed at them and lions charged them. But the faithful steeds did all their riders required of them.

How silly it was playing in the garden—or playing anywhere but *here*! He'd forgotten what it was like, playing with Mr Green and Poodle, Squirrel and Tree. How could you help forgetting things when people were always reminding you that you were a funny little boy playing make believe.

On strutted Vernon, now capering, now marching with solemn dignity. He was great, he was wonderful! What he needed, though he did not know it himself, was a tom-tom to beat whilst he sang his own praises.

The Forest! He had always known it would be like this, and it was! In front of him suddenly appeared a crumbling moss-covered wall. The wall of the Castle! Could anything be more perfect? He began to climb it.

The ascent was easy enough really, though fraught with the most agreeable and thrilling possibilities of danger.

Whether this was Mr Green's Castle, or whether it was inhabited by an Ogre who ate human flesh, Vernon had not yet made up his mind. Either was an entrancing proposition. On the whole he inclined to the latter, being at the moment in a warlike frame of mind. With a flushed face he reached the summit of the wall and looked over the other side.

And here there enters into the story, for one brief paragraph, Mrs Somers West who was fond of romantic solitude (for short periods), and had bought Woods Cottage as being 'delightfully remote from anywhere and really, if you know what I mean, in the very heart of the Forest—at one with Nature!' And since Mrs Somers West, as well as being artistic, was musical, she had pulled down a wall, making two rooms into one and had thus provided herself with sufficient space to house a grand piano.

And at the identical moment that Vernon reached the top of the wall, several perspiring and staggering men were slowly propelling the aforesaid grand piano towards the window since it wouldn't go in by the door. The garden of Woods Cottage was a mere tangle of undergrowth—wild Nature, as Mrs Somers West called it. So that all Vernon saw was The Beast! The Beast, alive and purposeful, slowly crawling towards him, malign and vengeful . . .

For a moment he stayed rooted to the spot. Then, with a wild cry, he fled. Fled along the top of the narrow crumbling wall. The Beast was behind him, pursuing him . . . It was coming, he knew it. He ran—ran faster than ever—His foot caught in a tangle of ivy. He crashed downwards—falling—falling—

CHAPTER 4

Vernon woke, after a long time, to find himself in bed. It was, of course, the natural place to be when you woke up, but what wasn't natural, was to have a great hump sticking up in front of you in the bed. It was whilst he was staring at this that someone spoke to him. That someone was Dr Coles, whom Vernon knew quite well.

'Well, well,' said Dr Coles, 'and how are we feeling?'

Vernon didn't know how Dr Coles was feeling. He himself was feeling rather sick and said so.

'I daresay, I daresay,' said Dr Coles.

'And I think I hurt somewhere,' said Vernon. 'I think I hurt very much.'

'I daresay, I daresay,' said Dr Coles again—not very helpfully, Vernon thought.

'Perhaps I'd feel better if I got up,' said Vernon. 'Can I get up?'

'Not just now, I'm afraid,' said the doctor. 'You see, you've had a fall.'

'Yes,' said Vernon. 'The Beast came after me.'

'Eh? What's that? The Beast? What Beast?'

39

'Nothing,' said Vernon.

'A dog, I expect,' said the doctor. 'Jumped at the wall and barked. You mustn't be afraid of dogs, my boy.'

'I'm not,' said Vernon.

'And what were you doing so far from home, eh? No business to be where you were.'

'Nobody told me not to,' said Vernon.

'Hum, hum, I wonder. Well, I'm afraid you've got to take your punishment. Do you know, you've broken your leg, my boy?'

'Have I?' Vernon was gratified—enchanted. He had broken his leg. He felt very important.

'Yes, you'll have to lie here for a bit—and then it will mean crutches for a while. Do you know what crutches are?'

Yes, Vernon knew. Mr Jobber, the blacksmith's father, had crutches. And he was to have crutches! How wonderful!

'Can I try them now?'

Dr Coles laughed.

'So you like the idea? No, I'm afraid you'll have to wait a bit. And you must try and be a brave boy, you know. And then you'll get well quicker.'

'Thank you,' said Vernon politely. 'I don't think I do feel very well. Can you take this funny thing out of my bed? I think it would be more comfortable then.'

But it seemed that the funny thing was called a cradle, and that it couldn't be taken away. And it seemed, too, that Vernon would not be able to move about in bed because his leg was all tied up to a long piece of wood. And suddenly it didn't seem a very nice thing to have a broken leg after all.

Vernon's underlip trembled a little. He was not going to cry—no, he was a big boy and big boys didn't cry. Nurse said so—and then he knew that he wanted Nurse— wanted her badly. He wanted her reassuring presence, her omniscience, her creaking, rustling majesty.

'She'll be coming back soon,' said Dr Coles. 'Yes, soon. In the meantime, this Nurse is going to look after you— Nurse Frances.'

Nurse Frances moved into Vernon's range of vision and Vernon studied her in silence. She too, was starched and crackling, that was all to the good. But she wasn't big like Nurse—she was thinner than Mummy—as thin as Aunt Nina. He wasn't sure—

And then he met her eyes—steady eyes, more green than grey, and he felt, as most people felt, that with Nurse Frances things would be 'all right'.

She smiled at him—but not in the way that visitors smiled. It was a grave smile, friendly but reserved.

'I'm sorry you feel sick,' she said. 'Would you like some orange juice?'

Vernon considered the matter and said he thought he would. Dr Coles went out of the room and Nurse Frances brought him the orange juice in a most curious-looking cup with a long spout. And it appeared that Vernon was to drink from the spout.

It made him laugh, but laughing hurt him, and so he stopped. Nurse Frances suggested he should go to sleep again, but he said he didn't want to go to sleep.

'Then I shouldn't go to sleep,' said Nurse Frances. 'I wonder if you can count how many irises there are on that

Agatha Christie

wall? You can start on the right side, and I'll start on the left side. You can count, can't you?'

Vernon said proudly that he could count up to a hundred.

'That is a lot,' said Nurse Frances. 'There aren't nearly as many irises as a hundred. I guess there are seventy-nine. Now what do you guess?'

Vernon guessed that there were fifty. There couldn't, he felt sure, possibly be more than that. He began to count, but somehow, without knowing it, his eyelids closed and he slept . . .

Noise . . . Noise and pain . . . He woke with a start. He felt hot, very hot and there was a pain all down one side. And the noise was coming nearer. It was the noise that one always connected with Mummy . . .

She came into the room like a whirlwind, a kind of cloak affair she wore swinging out behind her. She was like a bird—a great big bird, and like a bird, she swooped down upon him.

'Vernon—my darling—Mummy's own darling—What have they done to you?—How awful—how terrible—My child!'

She was crying. Vernon began to cry too. He was suddenly frightened. Myra was moaning and weeping.

'My little child. All I have in the world. God, don't take him from me. Don't take him from me! If he dies, I shall die too!'

'Mrs Deyre—'

'Vernon—Vernon—my baby—'

42

'Mrs Deyre—please.'

There was crisp command in the voice rather than appeal.

'Please don't touch him. You will hurt him.'

'Hurt him? I? His mother?'

'You don't seem to realize, Mrs Deyre, that his leg is broken. I must ask you, please, to leave the room.'

'You're hiding something from me—tell me—tell me—will the leg have to be amputated?'

A wail came from Vernon. He had not the least idea what amputated meant—but it sounded painful—and more than painful, terrifying. His wail broke into a scream.

'He's dying,' cried Myra. 'He's dying—and they won't tell me. But he shall die in my arms.'

'Mrs Deyre—'

Somehow Nurse Frances had got between his mother and the bed. She was holding his mother by the shoulder. Her voice had the tone that Nurse's had had when speaking to Katie, the under-housemaid.

'Mrs Deyre, listen to me. You must control yourself. You *must*!' Then she looked up. Vernon's father was standing in the doorway. 'Mr Deyre, please take your wife away. I cannot have my patient excited and upset.'

His father nodded—a quiet understanding nod. He just looked at Vernon once and said: 'Bad luck, old chap. I broke an arm once.'

The world became suddenly less terrifying. Other people broke legs and arms. His father had hold of his mother's shoulder, he was leading her towards the door, speaking to her in a low voice. She was protesting, arguing, her voice high and shrill with emotion.

'How can you understand? You've never cared for the child like I have. It takes a mother—How can I leave my child to be looked after by a stranger? He needs his mother . . . You don't understand—I *love* him. There's nothing like a mother's care—everyone says so.'

'Vernon darling—' she broke from her husband's clasp, came back towards the bed. 'You want me, don't you? You want Mummy?'

'I want Nurse,' sobbed Vernon. 'I want Nurse . . .'

He meant his own Nurse, not Nurse Frances.

'Oh!' said Myra. She stood there quivering.

'Come, my dear,' said Vernon's father gently. 'Come away.'

She leant against him, and together they passed from the room. Faint words floated back into the room.

'My own child, to turn from me to a stranger.'

Nurse Frances smoothed the sheet and suggested a drink of water.

'Nurse is coming back very soon,' she said. 'We'll write to her today, shall we? You shall tell me what to say.'

A queer new feeling surged over Vernon—a sort of odd gratitude. Somebody had actually understood . . .

When Vernon, later, was to look back upon his childhood, this one period was to stand out quite clearly from the rest. 'The time I broke my leg' marked a distinct era.

He was to appreciate, too, various small incidents that were accepted by him at the time as a matter of course. For instance, a rather stormy interview that took place between Dr Coles and his mother. Naturally this did not take place in Vernon's sick room, but Myra's raised voice penetrated closed doors. Vernon heard indignant exclamations of 'I don't know what you mean by upsetting him . . . I consider I ought to nurse my own child . . . Naturally I was distressed—I'm not one of these people who simply have no heart—no heart at all. Look at Walter—never turned a hair!'

There were many skirmishes, too, not to say pitched battles fought between Myra and Nurse Frances. In these cases Nurse Frances always won, but at a certain cost. Myra Deyre was wildly and furiously jealous of what she called 'the paid Nurse'. She was forced to submit to Dr Cole's dictums, but she did so with a bad grace and with an overt rudeness that Nurse Frances never seemed to notice.

In after years Vernon remembered nothing of the pain and tedium that there must have been. He only remembered happy days of playing and talking as he had never played and talked before. For in Nurse Frances, he found a grown up who didn't think things 'funny' or 'quaint'. Somebody who listened sensibly and who made serious and sensible suggestions. To Nurse Frances he was able to speak of Poodle, Squirrel and Tree, and of Mr Green and the hundred children. And instead of saying 'What a *funny* game!' Nurse Frances merely inquired whether the hundred children were girls or boys—an aspect of the matter which Vernon had never thought of before. But he and Nurse Frances decided that there were fifty of each, which seemed a very fair arrangement.

If sometimes, off his guard, he played his make-believe games aloud, Nurse Frances never seemed to notice or to think it unusual. She had the same calm comfortableness of old Nurse about her, but she had something that mattered far more to Vernon, the gift of answering questions—and he knew, instinctively, that the answers were always true. Sometimes she would say: 'I don't know that myself,' or 'You must ask someone else. I'm not clever enough to tell you that.' There was no pretence of omniscience about her.

Sometimes, after tea, she would tell Vernon stories. The stories were never the same two days running—one day they would be about naughty little boys and girls, and the next day they would be about enchanted princesses. Vernon liked the latter kind best. There was one in particular that he loved, about a princess in a tower with golden hair and a vagabond prince in a ragged green hat. The story ended up in a forest and it was possibly for that reason that Vernon liked it so much.

Sometimes there would be an extra listener. Myra used to come in and be with Vernon during the early afternoon when Nurse Frances had her time off, but Vernon's father used sometimes to come in after tea when the stories were going on. Little by little it became a habit. Walter Deyre would sit in the shadows just behind Nurse Frances' chair, and from there he would watch, not his child, but the storyteller. One day Vernon saw his father's hand steal out and close gently over Nurse Frances' wrist.

And then something happened which surprised him very much. Nurse Frances got up from her chair.

46

'I'm afraid we must turn you out for this evening, Mr Deyre,' she said quietly. 'Vernon and I have things to do.'

This astonished Vernon very much, because he couldn't think what those things were. He was still more puzzled when his father got up also and said in a low voice:

'I beg your pardon.'

Nurse Frances bent her head a little, but remained standing. Her eyes met Walter Deyre's steadily. He said quietly:

'Will you believe that I am really sorry, and let me come tomorrow?'

After that, in some way that Vernon could not have defined, his father's manner was different. He no longer sat so near Nurse Frances. He talked more to Vernon and occasionally they all three played a game—usually Old Maid for which Vernon had a wild passion. They were happy evenings enjoyed by all three.

One day when Nurse Frances was out of the room, Walter Deyre said abruptly:

'Do you like that Nurse of yours, Vernon?'

'Nurse Frances? I like her lots. Don't you, Father?'

'Yes,' said Walter Deyre, 'I do.'

There was a sadness in his voice which Vernon felt.

'Is anything the matter, Father?'

'Nothing that can be put right. The horse that gets left at the post never has much chance of making good—and the fact that it's the horse's own fault doesn't make matters any better. But that's double Dutch to you, old man. Anyway, enjoy your Nurse Frances while you've got her. There aren't many of her sort knocking about.'

And then Nurse Frances came back and they played Animal Grab.

But Walter Deyre's words had set Vernon's mind to work. He tackled Nurse Frances next morning.

'Aren't you going to be here always?'

'No. Only till you get well—or nearly well.'

'Won't you stay always? I'd like you to.'

'But you see, that's not my work. My work is to look after people who are ill.'

'Do you like doing that?'

'Yes, very much.'

'Why?'

'Well, you see, everyone has some particular kind of work that they like doing and that suits them.'

'Mummy hasn't.'

'Oh, yes, she has. Her work is to look after this big house and see that everything goes right, and to take care of you and your father.'

'Father was a soldier once. He told me that if ever there was a war, he'd go and be a soldier again.'

'Are you very fond of your father, Vernon?'

'I love Mummy best, of course. Mummy says little boys always love their mothers best. I like *being* with Father, of course, but that's different. I expect it's because he's a man. What shall I be when I grow up, do you think? I want to be a sailor.'

'Perhaps you'll write books.'

'What about?'

Nurse Frances smiled a little.

'Perhaps about Mr Green, and Poodle and Squirrel and Tree.'

'But everyone would say that that was silly.'

'Little boys wouldn't think so. And besides, when you grow up, you will have different people in your head—like Mr Green and the children, only grown up people. And then you could write about them.'

Vernon thought for a long time, then he shook his head.

'I think I'll be a soldier like Father. Most of the Deyres have been soldiers, Mummy says. Of course you have to be very brave to be a soldier, but I think I would be brave enough.'

Nurse Frances was silent a moment. She was thinking of what Walter Deyre had said of his small son.

'He's a plucky little chap—absolutely fearless. Doesn't know what fear is! You should see him on his pony.'

Yes, Vernon was fearless enough in one sense. He had the power of endurance, too. He had borne the pain and discomfort of his broken leg unusually well for so young a child.

But there was another kind of fear. She said slowly after a minute or two:

'Tell me again how you fell off the wall that day.'

She knew all about The Beast, and had been careful to display no ridicule. She listened now to Vernon and as he finished she said gently:

'But you've known for quite a long time, haven't you, that it isn't a real Beast? That it's only a thing made of wood and wires.'

'I do *know*,' said Vernon. 'But I don't dream it like that. And when I saw it in the garden coming at me—'

'You ran away—which was rather a pity, wasn't it? It would have been much better to have stayed and *looked*.

49

Then you'd have seen the men, and would have known just what it was. It's always a good thing to *look*. Then you can run away afterwards if you still want to—but you usually don't. And Vernon, I'll tell you something else.'

'Yes?'

'Things are never so frightening in front of you as they are behind you. Remember that. Anything seems frightening when it's behind your back and you can't see it. That's why it's always better to turn and face things— and then very often you find they are nothing at all.'

Vernon said thoughtfully: 'If I'd turned round I wouldn't have broken my leg, would I?'

'No.'

Vernon sighed.

'I don't mind having broken my leg very much. It has been very nice having you to play with.'

He thought Nurse Frances murmured 'Poor child' under her breath, but that, of course, was absurd. She said smiling:

'I've enjoyed it too. Some of my ill people don't like to play.'

'You really do like playing, don't you?' said Vernon. 'So does Mr Green.'

He added rather stiffly, for he felt shy:

'Please don't go away very soon, will you?'

But as it happened, Nurse Frances went away much sooner than she might have done. It all happened very suddenly, as things in Vernon's experience always did.

It started very simply—something that Myra offered

to do for Vernon and that he said he would rather have done by Nurse Frances.

He was on crutches now for a short and painful time every day, enjoying the novelty of it very much. He soon got tired, however, and was ready to go back to bed. Today, his mother had suggested his doing so, saying she would help him. But Vernon had been helped by her before. Those big white hands of hers were strangely clumsy. They hurt where they meant to help. He shrank from her well-meant efforts. He said he would wait for Nurse Frances who never hurt.

The words came out with the tactless honesty of children, and in a minute Myra Deyre was at white heat.

Nurse Frances came in two or three minutes later to be received with a flood of reproach.

Turning the boy against his own mother—cruel—wicked—They were all alike—everyone was against her—She had nothing in the world but Vernon and now he was being turned against her too.

So it went on—a ceaseless stream. Nurse Frances bore it patiently enough without surprise or rancour. Mrs Deyre, she knew, was that kind of woman. Scenes were a relief to her. And hard words, Nurse Frances reflected with grim humour, can only harm if the utterer is dear to you. She was sorry for Myra Deyre for she realized how much real unhappiness and misery lay behind these hysterical outbursts.

It was an unfortunate moment for Walter Deyre to choose to enter the nursery. For a moment or two he stood surprised, then he flushed angrily.

'Really, Myra, I'm ashamed of you. You don't know what you're saying.'

She turned on him furiously.

'I know what I'm saying well enough. And I know what you've been doing. Slinking in here every day—I've seen you. Always making love to some woman or other. Nursemaids, hospital nurses—it's all one to you.'

'Myra—be quiet!'

He was really angry now. Myra Deyre felt a throb of fear. But she hurled her last piece of invective.

'You're all alike, you hospital nurses. Flirting with other women's husbands. You ought to be ashamed of yourself— before the innocent child too—putting all sorts of things into his head. But you'll go out of my house. Yes, you'll go right out—and I shall tell Dr Coles what I think of you.'

'Would you mind continuing this edifying scene elsewhere?' Her husband's voice was as she hated it most—cold and sneering. 'Hardly judicious in front of your innocent child, is it? I apologize, Nurse, for what my wife has been saying. Come, Myra.'

She went—beginning to cry—weakly frightened at what she had done. As usual, she had said more than she meant.

'You're cruel,' she sobbed. 'Cruel. You'd like me to be dead. You hate me.'

She followed him out of the room. Nurse Frances put Vernon to bed. He wanted to ask questions but she talked of a dog, a big St Bernard, that she had had when she was a little girl and he was so much interested that he forgot everything else.

Much later that evening, Vernon's father came to the nursery. He looked white and ill. Nurse Frances rose and came to where he stood in the doorway.

'I don't know what to say—how can I apologize—the things my wife said—'

Nurse Frances replied in a quiet matter-of-fact voice.

'Oh, it's quite all right. I understand. I think, though, that I had better go as soon as it can be arranged. My being here makes Mrs Deyre unhappy, and then she works herself up.'

'If she knew how wide of the mark her wild accusations are. That she should insult *you*—'

Nurse Frances laughed—not perhaps very convincingly.

'I always think it's absurd when people complain about being insulted,' she said cheerfully. 'Such a pompous word, isn't it? Please don't worry or think I mind. You know, Mr Deyre, your wife is—'

'Yes?'

Her voice changed. It was grave and sad.

'A very unhappy and lonely woman.'

'Do you think that is entirely my fault?'

There was a pause. She lifted her eyes—those steady green eyes.

'Yes,' she said, 'I do.'

He drew a long breath.

'No one else but you would have said that to me. You—I suppose it's courage in you that I admire so much—your absolute fearless honesty. I'm sorry for Vernon that he should lose you before he need.'

She said gravely:

'Don't blame yourself for things you needn't. This has not been your fault.'

'Nurse Frances.' It was Vernon, eagerly from bed. 'I don't want you to go away. Don't go away, please—not tonight.'

'Of course not,' said Nurse Frances. 'We've got to talk to Dr Coles about it.'

Nurse Frances left three days later. Vernon wept bitterly. He had lost the first real friend he had ever had.

CHAPTER 5

The years from five to nine remained somewhat dim in Vernon's memory. Things changed—but so gradually as not to matter. Nurse did not return to her reign over the nursery. Her mother had had a stroke and was quite helpless and she was obliged to remain and look after her.

Instead, a Miss Robbins was installed as Nursery Governess. A creature so extraordinarily colourless that Vernon could never afterwards even recall what she looked like. He must have become somewhat out of hand under her regime for he was sent to school just after his eighth birthday. On his first holidays he found his cousin Josephine installed.

On her few visits to Abbots Puissants, Nina had never brought her small daughter with her. Indeed her visits had become rarer and rarer. Vernon, knowing things without thinking about them as children do, was perfectly well aware of two facts. One, that his father did not like Uncle Sydney but was always exceedingly polite to him. Two, that his mother did not like Aunt Nina and did not mind showing it.

Sometimes, when Nina was sitting talking to Walter in the garden, Myra would join them and in the momentary pause that nearly always followed, she would say:

'I suppose I'd better go away again. I see I'm in the way. No, thank you, Walter' (this in answer to a protest, gently murmured). 'I can see plainly enough when I'm not wanted.'

She would move away, biting her lip, nervously clasping and unclasping her hands, tears in her brown eyes. And, very quietly, Walter Deyre would raise his eyebrows.

One day, Nina broke out:

'She's impossible! I can't speak to you for ten minutes without an absurd scene. Walter, why did you do it? Why *did* you do it?'

Vernon remembered how his father had looked round, gazing up at the house, then letting his eyes sweep far afield to where the ruins of the old Abbey just showed.

'I cared for the place,' he said slowly. 'In the blood, I suppose. I didn't want to let it go.'

There had been a brief silence and then Nina had laughed—a queer short laugh.

'We're not a very satisfactory family,' she said. 'We've made a pretty good mess of things, you and I.'

There was another pause and then his father had said:

'Is it as bad as that?'

Nina had drawn in her breath with a sharp hiss, she nodded.

'Pretty well. I don't think, Walter, that I can go on much longer. Fred hates the sight of me. Oh! we behave very prettily in public—no one would guess—but, my God, when we're alone!'

'Yes, but, my dear girl—'

And then, for a while, Vernon heard no more. Their voices were lowered, his father seemed to be arguing with his aunt. Finally his voice rose again.

'You can't take a mad step like that. It's not even as though you cared for Anstey. You don't.'

'I suppose not—but he's crazy about me.'

His father said something that sounded like 'Social Ostriches'. Nina laughed again.

'That? We'd neither of us care.'

'Anstey would in the end.'

'Fred would divorce me—only too glad of the chance. Then we could marry.'

'Even then—'

'Walter on the social conventions! It has its humorous side!'

'Women and men are very different,' said Vernon's father drily.

'Oh! I know—I know. But anything's better than this everlasting misery. Of course at the bottom of it all is that I still care for Fred—I always did. And he never cared for me.'

'There's the kid,' said Walter Deyre. 'You can't go off and leave her.'

'Can't I? I'm not much of a mother, you know. As a matter of fact I'd take her with me. Fred wouldn't care. He hates her as much as he hates me.'

There was another pause, a long one this time. Then Nina said slowly:

'What a ghastly tangle human beings can get themselves

57

into. And in your case and mine, Walter, it's all our own fault. We're a nice family! We bring bad luck to ourselves and to anyone we have anything to do with.'

Walter Deyre got up. He filled a pipe abstractedly, then moved slowly away. For the first time Nina noticed Vernon.

'Hallo, child,' she said. 'I didn't see you were there. How much did you understand of all that, I wonder?'

'I don't know,' said Vernon vaguely, shifting from foot to foot.

Nina opened a chain bag, took out a tortoiseshell case and extracted a cigarette which she proceeded to light. Vernon watched her, fascinated. He had never seen a woman smoke.

'What's the matter?' said Nina.

'Mummy says,' said Vernon, 'that no nice woman would ever smoke. She said so to Miss Robbins.'

'Oh, well!' said Nina. She puffed out a cloud of smoke. 'I expect she was quite right. I'm not a nice woman, you see, Vernon.'

Vernon looked at her, vaguely distressed.

'I think you're very pretty,' he said rather shyly.

'That's not the same thing,' Nina's smile widened. 'Come here, Vernon.'

He came obediently. Nina put her hands on his shoulders and looked him over quizzically. He submitted patiently. He never minded being touched by Aunt Nina. Her hands were light—not clutching like his mother's.

'Yes,' said Nina. 'You're a Deyre—very much so. Rough luck on Myra, but there it is.'

'What does that mean?' said Vernon.

58

'It means that you're like your father's family and not like your mother's—worse luck for you.'

'Why worse luck for me?'

'Because the Deyres, Vernon, are neither happy nor successful. And they can't make good.'

What funny things Aunt Nina said! She said them half laughingly, so perhaps she didn't mean them. And yet somehow—there was something in them that, though he didn't understand, made him afraid.

'Would it be better,' he said suddenly, 'to be like Uncle Sydney?'

'Much better. Much better.'

Vernon considered.

'But then,' he said slowly, 'if I was like Uncle Sydney—'

He stopped, trying to get his thoughts into words.

'Yes, well?'

'If I was Uncle Sydney, I should have to live at Larch Hurst—and not here.'

Larch Hurst was a stoutly built red brick villa near Birmingham where Vernon had once been taken to stay with Uncle Sydney and Aunt Carrie. It had three acres of superb pleasure grounds, a rose garden, a pergola, a goldfish tank, and two excellently fitted bathrooms.

'And wouldn't you like that?' asked Nina, still watching him.

'No!' said Vernon. A great sigh broke from him, heaving his small chest. 'I want to live *here*—always, always, always!'

Soon after this, something queer happened about Aunt Nina. His mother began to speak of her and his father

Agatha Christie

managed to hush her down with a sideways glance at himself. He only carried away a couple of phrases: 'It's that poor child I'm so sorry for. You've only got to look at Nina to see she's a bad lot and always will be.'

The poor child, Vernon knew, was his cousin Josephine whom he had never seen, but to whom he sent presents at Christmas and duly received them in return. He wondered why Josephine was 'poor' and why his mother was sorry for her, and also why Aunt Nina was a bad lot—whatever that meant. He asked Miss Robbins, who got very pink and told him he mustn't talk about 'things like that'. Things like what? Vernon wondered.

However, he didn't think much more about it, till four months later, when the matter was mentioned once more. This time no one noticed Vernon's presence—feelings were running too high for that. His mother and father were in the middle of a vehement discussion. His mother, as usual, was vociferous, excited. His father was very quiet.

'Disgraceful!' Myra was saying. 'Within three months of running away with one man to go off with another. It shows her up in her true light. I always knew what she was like. Men, men, men, nothing but men!'

'You're welcome to any opinion you choose, Myra. That's not the point. I knew perfectly how it would strike you.'

'And anyone else too, I should think! I can't understand you, Walter. You call yourself an old family and all that—'

'We are an old family,' he put in quietly.

'I should have thought you'd have minded a bit about the honour of your name. She's disgraced it—and if you were a real man you'd cast her off utterly as she deserves.'

'Traditional scene from the melodrama, in fact.'

'You always sneer and laugh! Morals mean nothing to you—absolutely nothing.'

'At the minute, as I've been trying to make you understand, it's not a question of morals. It's a question of my sister being destitute. I must go out to Monte Carlo and see what can be done. I should have thought anyone in their senses would see that.'

'Thank you. You're not very polite, are you? And whose fault is it she's destitute, I should like to know? She had a good husband—'

'No—not that.'

'At any rate, he married her.'

It was his father who flushed this time. He said, in a very low voice:

'I can't understand you, Myra. You're a good woman—a kind, honourable, upright woman—and yet you can demean yourself to make a nasty mean taunt like that.'

'That's right! Abuse me! I'm used to it. You don't mind what you say to me.'

'That's not true. I try to be as courteous as I can.'

'Yes. And that's partly why I hate you—you never do say right out. Always polite and sneering—your tongue in your cheek. All this keeping up appearances—why should one, I should like to know? Why should I care if everyone in the house knows what I feel?'

'I've no doubt they do—thanks to the carrying power of your voice.'

'There you are—sneering again. At any rate I've enjoyed telling you what I think of your precious sister. Running

61

away with one man, going off with a second—and why can't the second man keep her, I should like to know? Or is he tired of her already?'

'I've already told you, but you didn't listen. He's threatened with galloping consumption—has had to throw up his job. He's no private means.'

'Ah! Nina brought her pigs to a bad market that time.'

'There's one thing about Nina—she's never been actuated by motives of gain. She's a fool—a damned fool or she wouldn't have got herself into this mess. But it's always her affections that run away with her common sense. It's the deuce of a tangle. She won't touch a penny from Fred. Anstey wants to make her an allowance—she won't hear of it. And mind you, I agree with her. There are things one can't do. But I've certainly got to go and see to things. I'm sorry if it annoys you, but there it is.'

'You never do anything I want! You hate me! You do this on purpose to make me miserable. But there's one thing. You don't bring this precious sister of yours under this roof while I'm here. I'm not accustomed to meeting that kind of woman. You understand?'

'You make your meaning almost offensively clear.'

'If you bring her here, I go back to Birmingham.'

There was a faint flicker in Walter Deyre's eyes, and suddenly Vernon realized something that his mother did not. He had understood very little of the actual words of the conversation though he had grasped the essentials. Aunt Nina was ill or unhappy somewhere and Mummy was angry about it. She had said that if Aunt Nina came to Abbots Puissants, she would go back to Uncle Sydney at Birmingham. She had meant that as a threat—but Vernon knew that his father would be very pleased if she did go back to Birmingham. He knew it quite certainly and uncomprehendingly. It was like some of Miss Robbins' punishments like not speaking for half an hour. She thought you minded that as much as not having jam for tea, and fortunately she had never discovered that you didn't really mind it at all—in fact rather enjoyed it.

Walter Deyre walked up and down the room. Vernon watched him, puzzled. That his father was fighting out a battle in his own mind, he knew. But he couldn't understand what it was all about.

'Well?' said Myra.

She was rather beautiful just at that moment—a great big woman, magnificently proportioned, her head thrown back and the sunlight streaming in on her golden red hair. A fit mate for some Viking seafarer.

'I made you the mistress of this house, Myra,' said Walter Deyre. 'If you object to my sister coming to it, naturally she will not come.'

He moved towards the door. There he paused and looked back at her. 'If Llewellyn dies—which seems almost certain, Nina must try to get some kind of a job. Then there will be the child to think of. Do your objections apply to her?'

'Do you think I want a girl in my home who will turn out like her mother?'

His father said quietly: 'Yes or no would have been quite sufficient answer.'

He went out. Myra stood staring after him. Tears

63

Christie

stood in her eyes and began to fall. Vernon did not like tears. He edged towards the door—but not in time.

'Darling—come to me.'

He had to come. He was enfolded—hugged. Fragments of phrases reiterated in his ears.

'You'll make up to me—you, my own boy—you shan't be like them—horrid, sneering. You won't fail me—you'll never fail me—will you? Swear it—my boy, my own boy.'

He knew it all so well. He said what was wanted of him—yes and no in the right places. How he hated the whole business. It always happened so close to your ears.

That evening after tea, Myra was in quite another mood. She was writing a letter at her writing table and looked up gaily as Vernon entered.

'I'm writing to Daddy. Perhaps, very soon, your Aunt Nina and your cousin Josephine will come to stay. Won't that be lovely?'

But they didn't come. Myra said to herself that really Walter was incomprehensible. Just because she'd said a few things she really didn't mean . . .

Vernon was not very surprised, somehow. He hadn't thought they would come.

Aunt Nina had said she wasn't a nice woman—but she was very pretty . . .

64

CHAPTER 6

If Vernon had been capable of summing up the events of the next few years, he could best have done it in one word—Scenes! Everlasting and ever recurring scenes.

And he began to notice a curious phenomenon. After each scene his mother looked larger and his father looked smaller. Emotional storms of reproach and invective exhilarated Myra mentally and physically. She emerged from them refreshed, soothed—full of good will towards all the world.

With Walter Deyre it was the opposite. He shrank into himself, every sensitive fibre in his nature shrinking from the onslaught. The faint polite sarcasm that was his weapon of defence never failed to goad his wife to the utmost fury. His quiet weary self-control exasperated her as nothing else could have done.

Not that she was lacking for very real grounds of complaint. Walter Deyre spent less and less time at Abbots Puissants. When he did return his eyes had baggy pouches under them and his hand shook. He took little notice of Vernon, and yet the child was always conscious of an underlying sympathy. It was tacitly understood that Walter should not 'interfere' with the child. A mother was the person who should have the say. Apart from supervising the boy's riding, Walter stood aside. Not to do so would have roused fresh matter for discussion and reproach. He was ready to admit that Myra had all the virtues and was a most careful and attentive mother.

And yet he sometimes had the feeling that he could give the boy something that she could not. The trouble was that they were both shy of each other. To neither of them was it easy to express their feelings—a thing Myra would have found incomprehensible. They remained gravely polite to each other.

But when a 'scene' was in progress, Vernon was full of silent sympathy. He knew exactly how his father was feeling—knew how that loud angry voice hurt the ears and the head. He knew, of course, that Mummy must be right—Mummy was always right, that was an article of belief not to be questioned—but all the same, he was unconsciously on his father's side.

Things went from bad to worse—came to a crisis. Mummy remained locked in her room for two days—servants whispered delightedly in corners—and Uncle Sydney arrived on the scene to see what he could do.

Uncle Sydney undoubtedly had a soothing influence over Myra. He walked up and down the room, jingling his money as of old, and looking stouter and more rubicund than ever.

Myra poured out her woes.

'Yes, yes, I know,' said Uncle Sydney, jingling hard. 'I

know, my dear girl. I'm not saying you haven't had a lot to put up with. You have. Nobody knows that better than I do. But there's give and take, you know. Give and take. That's married life in a nutshell—give and take.'

There was a fresh outburst from Myra.

'I'm not sticking up for Deyre,' said Uncle Sydney. 'Not at all. I'm just looking at the whole thing as a man of the world. Women lead sheltered lives and they don't look at these things as men do—quite right that they shouldn't. You're a good woman, Myra, and it's always hard for a good woman to understand these things. Carrie's just the same.'

'What has Carrie got to put up with, I should like to know?' cried Myra. '*You* don't go off racketing round with disgusting women. *You* don't make love to the servants.'

'N-no,' said her brother. 'No, of course not. It's the principle of the thing I'm talking about. And mind you, Carrie and I don't see eye to eye over everything. We have our tiffs—why sometimes we don't speak to each other for two days on end. But bless you, we make it up again, and things go on better than before. A good row clears the air—that's what I say. But there must be give and take. And no nagging afterwards. The best man in the world won't stand nagging.'

'I never nag,' said Myra tearfully, and believed it. 'How can you say such a thing?'

'Now don't get the wind up, old girl. I'm not saying you do. I'm just laying down general principles. And remember, Deyre's not our sort. He's kittle cattle—the touchy sensitive kind. A mere trifle sets them off.'

'Don't I know it,' said Myra bitterly. 'He's impossible. Why did I ever marry him?'

'Well, you know, Sis, you can't have it both ways. It was a good match. I'm bound to admit it was a good match. Here you are, living in a swell place, knowing all the County, as good as anybody short of Royalty. My word, if poor old Dad had lived, how proud he'd have been! And what I'm getting at is this—everything's got its seamy side. You can't have the halfpence without one or two of the kicks as well. They're decadent, these old families, that's what they are—decadent, and you've just got to face the fact. You've just got to sum up the situation in a business-like way—advantages, so and so. Disadvantages ditto. It's the only way. Take my word for it, it's the only way.'

'I didn't marry him for the sake of "advantages" as you call it,' said Myra. 'I hate this place. I always have. It's because of Abbots Puissants he married me—not for myself.'

'Nonsense, Sis, you were a jolly pretty girl—and still are,' he added gallantly.

'Walter married me for the sake of Abbots Puissants,' said Myra obstinately. 'I tell you I know it.'

'Well, well,' said her brother. 'Let's leave the past alone.'

'You wouldn't be so calm and cold-blooded about it if you were me,' said Myra bitterly. 'Not if you had to live with him. I do everything I can think of to please him—and he only sneers and treats me like this.'

'You nag him,' said Sydney. 'Oh, yes, you do. You can't help it.'

'If only he'd answer back! If he'd say something—instead of just sitting there.'

'Yes, but that's the kind of fellow he is. You can't alter people in this world to suit your fancy. I can't say I care for the chap myself—too la-di-da for me. Why, if you put him in to run a concern it would be bankrupt in a fort-night! But I'm bound to say he's always been very polite and decent to me. Quite the gentleman. When I've run across him in London he's taken me to lunch at that swell club of his and if I didn't feel too comfortable there that wasn't his fault. He's got his good points.'

'You're so like a man,' said Myra. 'Carrie would under-stand! He's been unfaithful to me, I tell you. Unfaithful!'

'Well, well,' said Uncle Sydney with a great deal of jingling and his eyes on the ceiling. 'Men will be men.'

'But Syd, you never—'

'Of course not,' said Uncle Sydney hastily. 'Of course not—of course not. I'm speaking generally, Myra—generally, you understand.'

'It's all finished,' said Myra. 'No woman could stand more than I've stood. And now it's the end. I never want to see him again.'

'Ah!' said Uncle Sydney. He drew a chair to the table and sat down with the air of one prepared to talk busi-ness. 'Then let's get down to brass tacks. You've made up your mind? What is it you do want to do?'

'I tell you I never want to see Walter again!'

'Yes, yes,' said Uncle Sydney patiently. 'We're taking that for granted. Now what do you want? A divorce?'

'Oh!' Myra was taken aback. 'I hadn't thought—'

'Well, we must get the thing put on a business-like footing. I doubt if you'd get a divorce. You've got to

Agatha Christie

prove cruelty, you know, as well, and I doubt if you could do that.'

'If you knew the suffering he's caused me—'

'I daresay. I'm not denying it. But you want something more than that to satisfy the law. And there's no desertion. If you wrote to him to come back, he'd come, I suppose?'

'Haven't I just told you I never want to see him again?'

'Yes, yes, yes. You women do harp on a thing so. We're looking at the thing from a business point of view now. I don't think a divorce will wash.'

'I don't want a divorce.'

'Well, what do you want, a separation?'

'So that he could go and live with that abandoned creature in London? Live with her altogether? And what would happen to me, I should like to know?'

'Plenty of nice houses near me and Carrie. You'd have the boy with you most of the time, I expect.'

'And let Walter bring disgusting women into this very house, perhaps? No, indeed, I don't intend to play into his hands like that!'

'Well, dash it all Myra, what do you want?'

Myra began to cry again.

'I'm so miserable, Syd, I'm so miserable. If only Walter were different.'

'Well, he isn't—and he never will be. You must just make up your mind to it, Myra. You've married a fellow who's a bit of a Don Jooan—and you've got to try and take a broadminded view of it. You're fond of the chap. Kiss and make friends—that's what I say. We're none of

70

us perfect. Give and take—that's the thing to remember—give and take.'

His sister continued to weep quietly.

'Marriage is a ticklish business,' went on Uncle Sydney in a ruminative voice. 'Women are too good for us, not a doubt of it.'

'I suppose,' said Myra in a tearful voice. 'One ought to forgive and forgive—again and again.'

'That's the spirit,' said Uncle Sydney. 'Women are angels and men aren't, and women have got to make allowances. Always have had to and always will.'

Myra's sobs grew less. She was seeing herself now in the role of the forgiving angel.

'It isn't as if I didn't do everything I could,' she sobbed. 'I run the house and I'm sure nobody could be a more devoted mother.'

'Of course you are,' said Uncle Sydney. 'And that's a fine youngster of yours. I wish Carrie and I had a boy. Four girls—it's a bit thick. Still as I always say to her: "Better luck next time, old girl." We both feel sure it's going to be a boy this time.'

Myra was diverted.

'I didn't know. When is it?'

'June.'

'How is Carrie?'

'Suffering a bit with her legs—swelled, you know. But she manages to get about a fair amount. Why, hallo, here's that young shaver. How long have you been here, my boy?'

'Oh, a long time,' said Vernon. 'I was here when you came in.'

'You're so quiet,' complained his uncle. 'Not like your cousins. I'm sure the racket they make is almost too much to bear sometimes. What's that you've got there?'

'It's an engine,' said Vernon.

'No, it isn't,' said Uncle Sydney. 'It's a milk cart!'

Vernon was silent.

'Hey,' said Uncle Sydney. 'Isn't it a milk cart?'

'No,' said Vernon. 'It's an engine.'

'Not a bit of it. It's a milk cart. That's funny, isn't it? You say it's an engine and I say it's a milk cart. I wonder which of us is right?'

Since Vernon knew that he was, it seemed hardly necessary to reply.

'He's a solemn child,' said Uncle Sydney turning to his sister. 'Never sees a joke. You know, my boy, you'll have to get used to being teased at school.'

'Shall I?' said Vernon, who couldn't see what that had to do with it.

'A boy who can take teasing with a laugh, that's the sort of boy who gets on in the world,' said Uncle Sydney and jingled his money again, stimulated by a natural association of ideas.

Vernon stared at him thoughtfully.

'What are you thinking about?'

'Nothing,' said Vernon.

'Take your engine on the terrace, dear,' said Myra.

Vernon obeyed.

'Now I wonder how much that little chap took in of what we were talking about?' said Sydney to his sister.

'Oh, he wouldn't understand. He's too little.'

'H'm,' said Sydney. 'I don't know. Some children take in a lot—my Ethel does. But then she's a very wide awake child.'

'I don't think Vernon ever notices anything,' said Myra. 'It's rather a blessing in some ways.'

'Mummy?' said Vernon later. 'What's going to happen in June?'

'In June, darling?'

'Yes—what you and Uncle Sydney were talking about.'

'Oh! that—' Myra was momentarily discomposed. 'Well, you see—it's a great secret—'

'Yes?' said Vernon eagerly.

'Uncle Sydney and Aunt Carrie hope that in June they will have a dear little baby boy. A boy cousin for you.'

'Oh,' said Vernon, disappointed. 'Is that all?'

After a minute or two, he said:

'Why are Aunt Carrie's legs swelled?'

'Oh, well—you see—she has been rather over-tired lately.'

Myra dreaded more questions. She tried to remember what she and Sydney had actually said.

'Mummy?'

'Yes, dear.'

'Do Uncle Sydney and Aunt Carrie want to have a baby boy?'

'Yes, of course.'

'Then why do they wait till June? Why don't they have it now?'

'Because, Vernon, God knows best. And God wants them to have it in June.'

'That's a long time to wait,' said Vernon. 'If I were God I'd send people things at once, as soon as they wanted them.'

'You mustn't be blasphemous, dear,' said Myra gently.

Vernon was silent. But he was puzzled. What was blasphemous? He rather thought that it was the same word Cook had used speaking of her brother. She had said he was a most—something—man and hardly ever touched a drop! She had spoken as though such an attitude was highly commendable. But evidently Mummy didn't seem to think the same about it.

Vernon added an extra prayer that evening to his usual petition of 'God bless Mummy and Daddy and make-meagooboy armen.'

'Dear God,' he prayed. 'Will you send me a puppy in June—or July would do if you are very busy.'

'Now why in June?' said Miss Robbins. 'You *are* a funny little boy. I should have thought you would have wanted the puppy now.'

'That would be blamafous,' said Vernon and eyed her reproachfully.

Suddenly the world became very exciting. There was a war—in South Africa—and Father was going to it!

Everyone was excited and upset. For the first time, Vernon heard of some people called the Boers. They were the people that Father was going to fight.

His father came home for a few days. He looked younger and more alive and a great deal more cheerful. He and

Mummy were quite nice to each other and there weren't any scenes or quarrels.

Once or twice, Vernon thought, his father squirmed uneasily at some of the things his mother said. Once he said irritably:

'For God's sake, Myra, don't keep talking of brave heroes laying down their lives for their country. I can't stand that sort of cant.'

But his mother had not got angry. She only said:

'I know you don't like me saying it. But it's *true*.'

On the last evening before he left, Vernon's father called to his small son to go for a walk with him. They strolled all round the place, silently at first, and then Vernon was emboldened to ask questions.

'Are you glad you're going to the war, Father?'

'Very glad.'

'Is it fun?'

'Not what you'd call fun, I expect. But it is in a way. It's excitement, and then, too, it takes you away from things—right away.'

'I suppose,' said Vernon thoughtfully, 'there aren't any ladies at the war?'

Walter Deyre looked sharply at his son, a slight smile hovering on his lips. Uncanny, the way the boy sometimes hit the nail on the head quite unconsciously.

'That makes for peace, certainly,' he said gravely.

'Will you kill a good many people, do you think?' inquired Vernon interestedly.

His father replied that it was impossible to tell accurately beforehand.

'I hope you will,' said Vernon, anxious that his father should shine. 'I hope you'll kill a hundred.'

'Thank you, old man.'

'I suppose,' began Vernon and then stopped.

'Yes?' said Walter Deyre encouragingly.

'I suppose—sometimes—people do get killed in war.'

Walter Deyre understood the ambiguous phrase.

'Sometimes,' he said.

'You don't think you will, do you?'

'I might. It's all in the day's work, you know.'

Vernon considered the phrase thoughtfully. The feeling that underlay it came dimly to him.

'Would you mind if you were, Father?'

'It might be the best thing,' said Walter Deyre, more to himself than to the child.

'I hope you won't,' said Vernon.

'Thank you.'

His father smiled a little. Vernon's wish had sounded so politely conventional. But he did not make the mistake Myra would have done, of thinking the child unfeeling.

They had reached the ruins of the Abbey. The sun was just setting. Father and son looked round and Walter Deyre drew in his breath with a little intake of pain. Perhaps he might never stand here again.

'I've made a mess of things,' he thought to himself.

'Vernon?'

'Yes, Father?'

'If I am killed, Abbots Puissants will belong to you. You know that, don't you?'

'Yes, Father.'

Silence again. So much that he would have liked to say—but he wasn't used to saying things. These were the things that one didn't put into words. Odd, how strangely at home he felt with that small person, his son. Perhaps it had been a mistake not to have got to know the boy better. They might have had some good times together. He was shy of the boy—and the boy was shy of him. And yet somehow, they were curiously in harmony. They both of them disliked saying things—

'I'm fond of the old place,' said Walter Deyre. 'I expect you will be too.'

'Yes, Father.'

'Queer to think of the old monks—catching their fish—fat fellows—that's how I always think of them—comfortable chaps.'

They lingered a few minutes longer.

'Well,' said Walter Deyre, 'we must be getting home. It's late.'

They turned. Walter Deyre squared his shoulders. There was a leave taking to be got through—an emotional one if he knew Myra—and he rather dreaded it. Well, it would soon be over. Goodbyes were painful things—better if one made no fuss about them, but then of course Myra would never see it that way.

Poor Myra. She'd had a rotten deal on the whole. A fine-looking creature, but he'd married her really for the sake of Abbots Puissants—and she had married him for love. That was the root of the whole trouble.

'Look after your mother, Vernon,' he said suddenly. 'She's been very good to you, you know.'

He rather hoped, in a way, that he wouldn't come back. It would be best so. Vernon had his mother.

And yet, at that thought, he had a queer traitorous feeling. As though he were deserting the boy . . .

'Walter,' cried Myra, 'you haven't said goodbye to Vernon.'

Walter looked across at his son, standing there wide-eyed.

'Goodbye, old chap. Have a good time.'

'Goodbye, Father.'

That was all. Myra was scandalized—had he no love for the boy? He hadn't even kissed him. How queer they were—the Deyres. So casual. Strange, the way they had nodded to each other, across the width of the room. So alike . . .

'But Vernon,' said Myra to herself, 'shall not grow up like his father.'

On the walls around her Deyres looked down and smiled sardonically . . .

CHAPTER 7

Two months after his father sailed for South Africa, Vernon went to school. It had been Walter Deyre's wish and arrangement, and Myra, at the moment, was disposed to regard any wish of his as law. He was her soldier and her hero, and everything else was forgotten. She was thoroughly happy at this time. Knitting socks for the soldiers, urging on energetic campaigns of 'white feather', sympathizing and talking with other women whose husbands had also gone to fight the wicked, ungrateful Boers.

She felt exquisite pangs parting with Vernon. Her darling—her baby—to go so far away from her. What sacrifices mothers had to make! But it had been his father's wish.

Poor darling, he was sure to be most terribly homesick! She couldn't bear to think of it.

But Vernon was not homesick. He had no real passionate attachment to his mother. All his life he was to be fondest of her when away from her. His escape from her emotional atmosphere was felt by him as a relief.

He had a good temperament for school life. He had an

aptitude for games, a quiet manner and an unusual amount of physical courage. After the dull monotony of life under the reign of Miss Robbins, school was a delightful novelty. Like all the Deyres, he had the knack of getting on with people. He made friends easily.

But the reticence of the child who so often answered 'Nothing' clung to him. Except with one or two people, that reticence was to go through life with him. His school friends were people with whom he shared 'doing things'. His thoughts he was to keep to himself and share with only one person. That person came into his life very soon.

On his very first holidays, he found Josephine.

Vernon was welcomed by his mother with an outburst of demonstrative affection. Already rather self-conscious about such things, he bore it manfully. Myra's first raptures over, she said:

'There's a lovely surprise for you, darling. Who do you think is here? Your cousin Josephine, Aunt Nina's little girl. She has come to live with us. Now isn't that nice?'

Vernon wasn't quite sure. It needed thinking over. To gain time, he said:

'Why has she come to live with us?'

'Because her mother has died. It's terribly sad for her and we must be very, very kind to her to make up.'

'Is Aunt Nina dead?'

He was sorry Aunt Nina was dead. Pretty Aunt Nina with her curling cigarette smoke.

'Yes. You can't remember her, of course, darling.'

He didn't say that he remembered her perfectly. Why should one say things?

'She's in the schoolroom, darling. Go and find her and make friends.'

Vernon went slowly. He didn't know whether he was pleased or not. A girl! He was at the age to despise girls. Rather a nuisance having a girl about. On the other hand, it would be jolly having *someone*. It depended what the kid was like. One would have to be decent to her if she'd just lost her mother.

He opened the schoolroom door and went in. Josephine was sitting on the window-sill swinging her legs. She stared at him and Vernon's attitude of kindly condescension fell from him.

She was a squarely built child of about his own age. She had dead black hair cut very straight across her forehead. Her jaw stuck out a little in a determined way. She had a very white skin and enormous eyelashes. Although she was two months younger than Vernon, she had the sophistication of twice his years—a kind of mixture of weariness and defiance.

'Hallo,' she said.

'Hallo,' said Vernon rather feebly.

They went on looking at each other, suspiciously, as is the manner of children and dogs.

'I suppose you're my cousin Josephine,' said Vernon.

'Yes, but you'd better call me Joe. Everyone does.'

'All right—Joe.'

There was a pause. To bridge it, Vernon whistled.

'Rather jolly, coming home,' he observed at last.

Agatha Christie

'It's an awfully jolly place,' said Joe.

'Oh! do you like it?' said Vernon, warming to her.

'I like it awfully. Better than any of the places I've lived.'

'Have you lived in a lot of places?'

'Oh, yes. At Coombes first—when we were with Father. And then at Monte Carlo with Colonel Anstey. And then at Toulon with Arthur—and then a lot of Swiss places because of Arthur's lungs. And then I went to a convent for a bit after Arthur died. Mother couldn't be bothered with me just then. I didn't like it much—the nuns were so silly. They made me have a bath in my chemise. And then after Mother died, Aunt Myra came and fetched me here.'

'I'm awfully sorry—about your mother, I mean,' said Vernon awkwardly.

'Yes,' said Joe, 'it's rotten in a way—though much the best thing for her.'

'Oh!' said Vernon, rather taken aback.

'Don't tell Aunt Myra,' said Joe. 'Because I think she's rather easily shocked by things—rather like the nuns. You have to be careful what you say to her. Mother didn't care for me an awful lot, you know. She was frightfully kind and all that—but she was always soppy about some man or other. I heard some people say so in the hotel, and it was quite true. She couldn't help it, of course. But it's a very bad plan. I shan't have anything to do with men when I grow up.'

'Oh!' said Vernon. He was still feeling very young and awkward beside this amazing person.

82

'I liked Colonel Anstey best,' said Joe reminiscently. 'But of course Mother only ran away with him to get away from Father. We stayed at much better hotels with Colonel Anstey, Arthur was very poor. If I ever do get soppy about a man when I grow up, I shall take care that he's rich. It makes things so much easier.'

'Wasn't your father nice?'

'Oh! Father was a devil—Mother said so. He hated us both.'

'But why?'

Joe wrinkled her straight black brows in perplexity.

'I don't quite know. I think—I think it was something to do with *me* coming. I think he had to marry Mother because she was going to have me—something like that—and it made him angry.'

They looked at each other—solemn and perplexed.

'Uncle Walter's in South Africa, isn't he?' went on Joe.

'Yes. I've had three letters from him at school. Awfully jolly letters.'

'Uncle Walter's a dear. I loved him. He came out to Monte Carlo, you know.'

Some memory stirred in Vernon. Of course, he remembered now. His father had wanted Joe to come to Abbots Puissants then.

'He arranged for me to go to the convent,' said Joe. 'Reverend Mother thought he was lovely—a true type of high-born English gentleman—such a funny way of putting it.'

They both laughed a little.

'Let's go out in the garden. Shall we?' said Vernon.

'Yes, let's. I say, I know where there are four different nests—but the birds have all flown away.'

They went out together amicably discussing birds' eggs.

To Myra, Joe was a perplexing child. She had nice manners, answered promptly and politely when spoken to, and submitted to caresses without returning them. She was very independent and gave the maid told off to attend to her little or nothing to do. She could mend her own clothes and keep herself neat and tidy without any outside urging. She was, in fact, the sophisticated hotel child whom Myra had never happened to come across. The depths of her knowledge would have horrified and shocked her aunt.

But Joe was shrewd and quick-witted, well used to summing up the people with whom she came in contact. She refrained carefully from 'shocking Aunt Myra'. She had for her something closely akin to a kindly contempt.

'Your mother,' she said to Vernon, 'is very good—but she's a little stupid too, isn't she?'

'She's very beautiful,' said Vernon hotly.

'Yes, she is,' agreed Joe. 'All but her hands. Her hair's lovely. I wish I had red gold hair.'

'It comes right down below her waist,' said Vernon.

He found Joe a wonderful companion, quite unlike his previous conception of 'girls'. She hated dolls, never cried, was as strong if not stronger than he was, and was always ready and willing for any dangerous sport. Together they climbed trees, rode bicycles, fell and cut and bumped themselves, and in the summer holidays took a wasps' nest together, with a success due more to luck than skill.

To Joe, Vernon could talk and did. She opened up to him a strange new world, a world where people ran away with other people's husbands and wives, a world of dancing and gambling and cynicism. She had loved her mother with a fierce protective tenderness that almost reversed the roles.

'She was too soft,' said Joe. 'I'm not going to be soft. People are mean to you if you are. Men are beasts anyway, but if you're a beast to them first, they're all right. All men are beasts.'

'That's a silly thing to say, and I don't think it's true.'

'That's because you're going to be a man yourself.'

'No, it isn't. And anyway I'm not a beast.'

'No, but I daresay you will be when you're grown up.'

'But, look here, Joe, you'll have to marry someone some day, and you won't think your husband a beast.'

'Why should I marry anyone?'

'Well—girls do. You don't want to be an old maid like Miss Crabtree.'

Joe wavered. Miss Crabtree was an elderly spinster who was very active in the village and who was very fond of 'the dear children'.

'I shouldn't be the kind of old maid Miss Crabtree is,' she said weakly. 'I should—oh! I should do things. Play the violin, or write books, or paint some marvellous pictures.'

'I hope you won't play the violin,' said Vernon.

'That's really what I should like to do best. Why do you hate music so, Vernon?'

'I don't know. I just do. It makes me feel all horrible inside.'

'How queer. It gives me a nice feeling. What are you going to do when you grow up?'

'Oh, I don't know. I'd like to marry someone very beautiful and live at Abbots Puissants and have lots of horses and dogs.'

'How dull,' said Joe. 'I don't think that would be exciting a bit.'

'I don't know that I want things to be very exciting,' said Vernon.

'I do,' said Joe. 'I want things to be exciting the whole time without ever stopping.'

Joe and Vernon had few other children to play with. The Vicar, whose children Vernon had played with when he was younger, had gone to another living, and his successor was unmarried. Most of the children of families in the same position as the Deyres lived too far away for more than a very occasional visit.

The only exception was Nell Vereker. Her father, Captain Vereker, was agent to Lord Coomberleigh. He was a tall stooping man, with very pale blue eyes and a hesitating manner. He had good connections but was inefficient generally. His wife made up in efficiency for what he lacked. She was a tall commanding woman, still handsome. Her hair was very golden and her eyes were very blue. She had pushed her husband into the position he held, and in the same way she pushed herself into the best houses of the neighbourhood. She had birth, but like her husband, no money. Yet she was determined to make a success of life.

Giant's Bread

Both Vernon and Joe were bored to death by Nell Vereker. She was a thin pale child with fair straggly hair. Her eyelids and the tip of her nose were faintly tinged with pink. She was no good at anything. She couldn't run and she couldn't climb. She was always dressed in starched white muslin and her favourite games were dolls' tea-parties.

Myra was very fond of Nell. 'Such a thorough little lady,' she used to say. Vernon and Joe were kindly and polite when Mrs Vereker brought Nell to tea. They tried to think of games she would like, and they used to give whoops of delight when at last she departed, sitting up very straight beside her mother in the hired carriage.

It was in Vernon's second holidays, just after the famous episode of the wasps' nest that the first rumours came about Deerfields.

Deerfields was the property adjoining Abbots Puissants. It belonged to old Sir Charles Alington. Some friends of Mrs Deyre's came to lunch and the subject came up for discussion.

'It's quite true. I had it from an absolutely authentic source. It's been sold to these people. Yes—*Jews*. Oh, of course—enormously wealthy. Yes, a fancy price, I believe. Levinne, the name is. No, Russian Jews, so I heard. Oh, of course *quite* impossible. Too bad of Sir Charles, I say. Yes, of course, there's the Yorkshire property as well and I hear he's lost a lot of money lately. No, no one will call. Naturally.'

Joe and Vernon were pleasurably excited. All titbits about Deerfields were carefully stored up. At last the strangers arrived and moved in. There was more talk of the same kind.

'Oh, absolutely impossible, Mrs Deyre . . . Just as we thought . . . One wonders what they think they are doing . . . What do they expect? . . . I daresay they'll sell the place and move away. Yes, there is a family. A boy. About your Vernon's age, I believe . . .'

'I wonder what Jews are like,' said Vernon to Joe. 'Why does everyone dislike them? We thought one boy at school was a Jew, but he eats bacon for breakfast, so he can't be.'

The Levinnes proved to be a very Christian brand of Jew. They appeared in church on Sunday, having taken a whole pew. The interest of the congregation was breath-less. First came Mr Levinne—very round and stout, tightly frock-coated—an enormous nose and a shining face. Then Mrs—an amazing sight. Colossal sleeves! Hour glass figure! Chains of diamonds! An immense hat decorated with feathers and black tightly curling ringlets underneath it. With them was a boy rather taller than Vernon with a long yellow face, and protruding ears.

A carriage and pair was waiting for them when service was over. They got into it and drove away.

'Well!' said Miss Crabtree.

Little groups formed, talking busily.

'I think it's rotten,' said Joe.

She and Vernon were in the garden together.

'What's rotten?'

'Those people.'

'Do you mean the Levinnes?'

88

'Yes. Why should everyone be so horrid about them?'

'Well,' said Vernon, trying to be strictly impartial, 'they did look queer, you know.'

'Well, I think people are beasts.'

Vernon was silent. Joe, a rebel by force of circumstances, was always putting a new point of view before him.

'That boy,' continued Joe. 'I daresay he's awfully jolly, even though his ears do stick out.'

'I wonder,' said Vernon. 'It would be jolly to have someone else. Kate says they're making a swimming pool at Deerfields.'

'They must be frightfully, frightfully rich,' said Joe.

Riches meant little to Vernon. He had never thought about them.

The Levinnes were the great topic of conversation for some time. The improvements they were making at Deerfields! The workmen they had had down from London!

Mrs Vereker brought Nell to tea one day. As soon as she was in the garden with the children, she imparted news of fascinating importance.

'They've got a motor car.'

'A motor car?'

Motor cars were almost unheard of then. One had never been seen in the Forest. Storms of envy shook Vernon. A motor car!

'A motor car *and* a swimming pool,' he murmured.

It was too much.

'It's not a swimming pool,' said Nell. 'It's a sunk garden.'

'Kate says it's a swimming pool.'

'Our gardener says it's a sunk garden.'

'What is a sunk garden?'

'I don't know,' confessed Nell. 'But it is one.'

'I don't believe it,' said Joe. 'Who'd want a silly sort of thing like that when they could have a swimming pool?'

'Well, that's what our gardener says.'

'I know,' said Joe. A wicked look came into her eyes. 'Let's go and see.'

'What?'

'Let's go and see for ourselves.'

'Oh, but we couldn't,' said Nell.

'Why not? We can creep up through the woods.'

'Jolly good idea,' said Vernon. 'Let's.'

'I don't want to,' said Nell. 'Mother wouldn't like it, I know.'

'Oh, don't be a spoilsport, Nell. Come on.'

'Mother wouldn't like it,' repeated Nell.

'All right. Wait here, then. We won't be long.'

Tears gathered slowly in Nell's eyes. She hated being left. She stood there sullenly, twisting her frock between her fingers.

'We won't be long,' Vernon repeated.

He and Joe ran off. Nell felt she couldn't bear it.

'Vernon!'

'Yes?'

'Wait for me. I'm coming too.'

She felt heroic as she made the announcement. Joe and Vernon did not seem particularly impressed by it. They waited with obvious impatience for her to come up with them.

'Now then,' said Vernon, 'I'm leader. Everyone to do as I say.'

They climbed over the Park palings and reached the shelter of the trees. Speaking in whispers under their breath they flitted through the undergrowth, drawing nearer and nearer towards the house. Now it rose before them, some way ahead to the right.

'We'll have to get farther still and keep a bit more uphill.'

They followed him obediently. And then suddenly a voice broke on their ears, speaking from a little behind them to the left.

'You're trethpassing,' it said.

They turned—startled. The yellow-faced boy with the large ears stood there. He had his hands in his pockets, and was surveying them superciliously.

'You're trethpassing,' he said again.

There was something in his manner that awoke immediate antagonism. Instead of saying, as he had meant to say, 'I'm sorry,' Vernon said, 'Oh!'

He and the other boy looked at each other—the cool measuring glance of two adversaries in a duel.

'We come from next door,' said Joe.

'Do you?' said the boy. 'Well, you'd better go back there. My father and mother don't want you in here.'

He managed to be unbearably offensive as he said this. Vernon, unpleasantly conscious of being in the wrong, flushed angrily.

'You might manage to speak politely,' he said.

'Why should I?' said the boy.

91

He turned as a footstep sounded coming through the undergrowth.

'Is that you, Sam?' he said. 'Just turn these trespassing kids off the place, will you?'

The keeper who had stepped out beside him grinned and touched his forehead. The boy strolled away, as though he had lost all interest. The keeper turned to the children and put on a ferocious scowl.

'Out of it, you young varmints! I'll turn the dogs loose on you unless you're out of here in double quick time.'

'We're not afraid of dogs,' said Vernon haughtily, as he turned to depart.

'Ho, you're not, h'aren't you? Well, then, I've got a rhinoHoceras here and I'm-a going to loose that this minute.'

He stalked off. Nell gave a terrified pull at Vernon's arm.

'He's gone to get it,' she cried. 'Oh! hurry—hurry—'

Her alarm was contagious. So much had been retailed about the Levinnes that the keeper's threat seemed a perfectly likely one to the children. With one accord they ran for home. They plunged in a bee-line, pushing their way through the undergrowth. Vernon and Joe led. A piteous cry arose from Nell.

'Vernon—Vernon—Oh! do wait. I've got stuck—'

What a nuisance Nell was! She couldn't run or do anything. He turned back—gave her frock a vigorous pull to free it from the brambles with which it was entangled (a good deal to the frock's detriment) and hauled her to her feet.

'Come on, do.'

'I'm so out of breath. I can't run any more. Oh! Vernon, I'm so frightened.'

'Come *on*.'

Hand in hand he pulled her along. They reached the Park palings, scrambled over . . .

'We-ell,' said Joe, fanning herself with a very dirty linen hat. 'That *was* an adventure.'

'My frock's all torn,' said Nell. 'What shall I do?'

'I hate that boy,' said Vernon. 'He's a beast.'

'He's a beastly beast,' agreed Joe. 'We'll declare war on him. Shall we?'

'Rather!'

'What shall I do about my frock?'

'It's very awkward their having a rhinoceros,' said Joe thoughtfully. 'Do you think Tom Boy would go for it if we trained him to?'

'I shouldn't like Tom Boy to be hurt,' said Vernon.

Tom Boy was the stable dog—a great favourite of his. His mother had always vetoed a dog in the house, so Tom Boy was the nearest Vernon had got to having a dog of his own.

'I don't know what Mother will say about my frock.'

'Oh, bother your frock, Nell. It's not the sort of frock for playing in the garden, anyway.'

'I'll tell your mother it's my fault,' said Vernon impatiently. 'Don't be so like a girl.'

'I am a girl,' said Nell.

'Well, so is Joe a girl. But she doesn't go on like you do. She's as good as a boy any day.'

Nell looked ready to cry, but at that minute they were called from the house.

'I'm sorry, Mrs Vereker,' said Vernon. 'I'm afraid I've torn Nell's frock.'

There were reproaches from Myra, civil disclaimers from Mrs Vereker. When Nell and her mother had gone, Myra said:

'You must not be so rough, Vernon, darling. When a little girl friend comes to tea, you must take great care of her.'

'Why have we got to have her to tea? We don't like her. She spoils everything.'

'Vernon! Nell is such a dear little girl.'

'She isn't, Mother. She's awful.'

'Vernon!'

'Well, she is. I don't like her mother either.'

'I don't like Mrs Vereker much,' said Myra. 'I always think she's a very hard woman. But I can't think why you children don't like Nell. Mrs Vereker tells me she's absolutely devoted to you, Vernon.'

'Well, I don't want her to be.'

He escaped with Joe.

'War,' he said. 'That's what it is—war! I daresay that Levinne boy is really a Boer in disguise. We must plan out our campaign. Why should he come and live next door to us, and spoil everything?'

The kind of guerilla warfare that followed occupied Vernon and Joe in a most pleasurable fashion. They invented all kinds of methods of harassing the enemy. Concealed in trees, they pelted him with chestnuts. They stalked him with pea-shooters. They outlined a hand in red paint and crept secretly up to the house one night after dark, and left it on the doorstep with the word 'Revenge' printed at the bottom of the sheet of paper.

Sometimes their enemy retaliated in kind. He, too, had a pea-shooter and it was he who laid in wait for them one day with a garden hose.

Hostilities had been going on for nearly ten days when Vernon came upon Joe sitting on a tree stump looking unusually despondent.

'Hallo, what's up? I thought you were going to stalk the enemy with those squashy tomatoes Cook gave us.'

'I was. I mean I did.'

'What's the matter, Joe?'

'I was up a tree and he came right by underneath. I could have got him beautifully.'

'Do you mean to say you didn't?'

'No.'

'Why ever not?'

Joe's face became very red, and she began to speak very fast.

'I couldn't. You see, he didn't know I was there, and he looked—oh, Vernon! he looked so awfully *lonely*—as though he were simply hating things. You know, it must be pretty beastly having no one to do things with.'

'Yes, but—'

Vernon paused to adjust his ideas.

'Don't you remember how we said it was all rotten?' went on Joe. 'People being so beastly about the Levinnes, and now we're being as beastly as anyone.'

'Yes, but he was beastly to *us*!'

'Perhaps he didn't mean to be.'

'That's nonsense.'

'No, it isn't. Look at the way dogs bite you if they're afraid or suspicious. I expect he just expected us to be beastly to him, and wanted to start first. Let's be friends.'

'You can't be in the middle of a war.'

'Yes, you can. We'll make a white flag, and then you march with it and demand a parley, and see if you can't agree upon honourable terms of peace.'

'Well,' said Vernon, 'I don't mind if we do. It would be a change, anyway. What shall we use for a flag of truce— my handkerchief or your pinafore?'

Marching with the flag of truce was rather exciting. It was not long before they encountered the enemy. He stared in complete surprise.

'What's up?' he said.

'We want a parley,' said Vernon.

'Well, I'm agreeable,' said the other boy, after a moment's pause.

'What we want to say is this,' said Joe. 'If you'll agree, we'd like to be friends.'

They looked from one to the other.

'Why do you want to be friends?' he asked suspiciously.

'It seems a bit silly,' said Vernon. 'Living next door and not being friends, doesn't it?'

'Which of you thought of that first?'

'I did,' said Joe.

She felt those small jet black eyes boring into her. What a queer boy he was. His ears seemed to stick out more than ever.

'All right,' said the boy. 'I'd like to.'

There was a minute's embarrassed pause.

'What's your name?' said Joe.

'Sebastian.'

There was just the faintest lisp, so little as hardly to be noticed.

'What a funny name. Mine's Joe and this is Vernon. He's at school. Do you go to school?'

'Yes. I'm going to Eton later.'

'So am I,' said Vernon.

Again a faint tide of hostility rose between them. Then it ebbed away—never to return.

'Come and see our swimming pool,' said Sebastian. 'It's rather jolly.'

CHAPTER 8

The friendship with Sebastian Levinne prospered and throve apace. Half the zest of it lay in the secrecy that had to be adopted. Vernon's mother would have been horrified if she had guessed at anything of the kind. The Levinnes would certainly not have been horrified—but their gratification might have led to equally dire results.

School time passed on leaden wings for poor Joe, cooped up with a daily governess, who arrived every morning, and who subtly disapproved of her outspoken and rebellious pupil. Joe only lived for the holidays. As soon as they came, she and Vernon would set off to a secret meeting-place where there was a convenient gap in a hedge. They had invented a code of whistles and many unnecessary signals. Sometimes Sebastian would be there before time—lying on the bracken—his yellow face and jutting out ears looking strangely at variance with his knickerbocker suit.

They played games, but they also talked—how they talked! Sebastian told them stories of Russia—they learnt of the persecution of Jews—of Pogroms! Sebastian himself had never been in Russia, but he had lived for years amongst other Russian Jews and his own father had narrowly escaped with his life in a Pogrom. Sometimes he would say sentences in Russian to please Vernon and Joe. It was all entrancing.

'Everybody hates us down here,' said Sebastian. 'But it doesn't matter. They won't be able to do without us because my father is so rich. You can buy everything with money.'

He had a certain queer arrogance about him.

'You can't buy everything,' objected Vernon. 'Old Nicoll's son has come home from the war without a leg. Money couldn't make his leg grow again.'

'No,' admitted Sebastian. 'I didn't mean things like that. But money would get you a very good wooden leg, and the best kind of crutches.'

'I had crutches once,' said Vernon. 'It was rather fun. And I had an awfully nice nurse to look after me.'

'You see, you couldn't have had that if you hadn't been rich.'

Was he rich? He supposed he was. He'd never thought about it.

'I wish I was rich,' said Joe.

'You can marry me when you grow up,' said Sebastian, 'and then you will be.'

'It wouldn't be nice for Joe if nobody came to see her,' objected Vernon.

'I wouldn't mind that a bit,' said Joe. 'I wouldn't care what Aunt Myra or anybody said. I'd marry Sebastian if I wanted to.'

'People will come and see her then,' said Sebastian. 'You don't realize. Jews are frightfully powerful. My father says people can't do without them. That's why Sir Charles Alington had to sell us Deerfields.'

A sudden chill came over Vernon. He felt without putting the thought into words that he was talking to a member of an enemy race. But he felt no antagonism towards Sebastian. That was over long ago. He and Sebastian were friends—somehow he was sure they always would be.

'Money,' said Sebastian, 'isn't just buying things. It's ever so much more than that. And it isn't only having power over people. It's—it's being able to get together lots of beauty.'

He made a queer un-English gesture with his hands.

'What do you mean,' said Vernon, 'by get together?'

Sebastian didn't know what he meant. The words had just come.

'Anyway,' said Vernon, 'things aren't beauty.'

'Yes, they are. Deerfields is beautiful—but not nearly so beautiful as Abbots Puissants.'

'When Abbots Puissants belongs to me,' said Vernon, 'you can come and stay there as much as ever you like. We're always going to be friends, aren't we? No matter what anyone says?'

'We're always going to be friends,' said Sebastian.

Little by little the Levinnes made headway. The church needed a new organ—Mr Levinne presented it with one. Deerfields was thrown open on the occasion of the choir boys' outing, and strawberries and cream provided. A large donation was given to the Primrose League. Turn where you would, you came up against the opulence and the kindness of the Levinnes.

People began to say: 'Of course they're impossible—but Mrs Levinne is wonderfully *kind*.'

And they said other things.

'Oh, of course—*Jews*! But perhaps it is absurd of one to be prejudiced. Some very good people have been Jews.'

It was rumoured that the Vicar had said: 'Including Jesus Christ,' in answer. But nobody really believed that. The Vicar was unmarried which was very unusual—and had odd ideas about Holy Communion—and sometimes preached very incomprehensible sermons; but nobody believed that he would have said anything really sacrilegious.

It was the Vicar who introduced Mrs Levinne to the Sewing Circle which met twice a week to provide comforts for our brave soldiers in South Africa. And meeting her twice a week there certainly made it awkward.

In the end, Lady Coomberleigh, softened by the immense donation to the Primrose League, took the plunge and called. And where Lady Coomberleigh led, everybody followed.

Not that the Levinnes were ever admitted to intimacy. But they were officially accepted, and people were heard saying:

'She's a very *kind* woman—even if she does wear impossible clothes for the country.'

But that, too, followed. Mrs Levinne was adaptable. A very short time elapsed before she appeared in even tweedier tweeds than her neighbour's.

Joe and Vernon were solemnly bidden to tea with Sebastian Levinne.

'We must go this once, I suppose,' said Myra, sighing. 'But we need never get really intimate. What a queer-looking boy he is. You won't be rude to him, will you, Vernon, darling?'

The children solemnly made the official acquaintance of Sebastian. It amused them very much.

But the sharp-witted Joe fancied that Mrs Levinne knew more about their friendship than Aunt Myra did. Mrs Levinne wasn't a fool. She was like Sebastian.

Walter Deyre was killed a few weeks before the war ended. His end was a gallant one. He was shot when going back to rescue a wounded comrade under heavy fire. He was awarded a posthumous VC, and the letter his colonel wrote to Myra was treasured by her as her dearest possession.

'Never,' wrote the colonel, 'have I known anyone so fearless of danger. His men adored him and would have followed him anywhere. He has risked his life again and again in the gallantest way. You can indeed be proud of him.'

Myra read that letter again and again. She read it to all her friends. It wiped away the faint sting that her husband had left no last word or letter for her.

'But being a Deyre, he wouldn't,' she said to herself.

Yet Walter Deyre had left a letter 'in case I should be killed'. But it was not to Myra, and she never knew of it. She was grief-stricken, but happy. Her husband was hers in death as he had never been in life, and with her easy power of making things as she wished them to be, she began to weave a convincing romance of her wonderfully happy married life.

It is difficult to say how Vernon was affected by his father's death. He felt no actual grief—was rendered even more stolid by his mother's obvious wish for him to display emotion. He was proud of his father—so proud that it almost hurt—yet he understood what Joe had meant when she said that it was better for her mother to be dead. He remembered very clearly that last evening walk with his father—the things he had said—the feeling there had been between them.

His father, he knew, hadn't really wanted to come back. He was sorry for his father—he always had been. He didn't know why.

It was not grief he felt for his father—it was more a kind of heart-gripping loneliness. Father was dead—Aunt Nina was dead. There was Mother, of course, but that was different.

He couldn't satisfy his mother—he never had been able to. She was always hugging him, crying over him—telling him they must be all in all to each other now. And he couldn't, he just couldn't, say the things she wanted him to say. He couldn't even put his arms round her neck and hug her back.

He longed for the holidays to be over. His mother, with her red eyes, and her widow's weeds—of the heaviest crape. Somehow she overpowered things.

Mr Flemming, the lawyer from London, came down to

Agatha Christie

stay, and Uncle Sydney came from Birmingham. He stayed two days. At the end of them, Vernon was summoned to the library.

The two men were sitting at the long table. Myra was sitting in a low chair by the fire, her handkerchief to her eyes.

'Well, my boy,' said Uncle Sydney, 'we've got something to talk to you about. How would you like to come and live near your Aunt Carrie and me at Birmingham?'

'Thank you,' said Vernon, 'but I'd rather live here.'

'A bit gloomy, don't you think?' said his uncle. 'Now I've got my eye on a jolly house—not too big, thoroughly comfortable. There'll be your cousins near for you to play with in the holidays. It's a very good idea, I think.'

'I'm sure it is,' said Vernon politely. 'But I'd really like being here best, thank you.'

'Ah! H'm,' said Uncle Sydney. He blew his nose and looked questioningly at the lawyer, who assented to the look with a slight nod.

'It's not quite so simple as that, old chap,' said Uncle Sydney. 'I think you're quite old enough to understand if I explain things to you. Now that your father's dead—er—passed from us, Abbots Puissants belongs to you.'

'I know,' said Vernon.

'Eh? How do you know? Servants been talking?'

'Father told me before he went away.'

'Oh!' said Uncle Sydney rather taken aback. 'Oh, I see. Well, as I say, Abbots Puissants belongs to you, but a place like this takes a lot of money to run—paying wages and things like that—you understand? And then there are some

104

things called Death Duties. When anyone dies, you have to pay out a lot of money to the Government.

'Now, your father wasn't a rich man. When his father died, and he came into this place, he had so little money that he thought he'd have to sell it.'

'Sell it?' burst out Vernon incredulously.

'Yes, it's not entailed.'

'What's entailed?'

Mr Flemming explained carefully and clearly.

'But—but—you aren't going to sell it now?'

Vernon gazed at him with agonizing, imploring eyes.

'Certainly not,' said Mr Flemming. 'The estate is left to you, and nothing can be done until you are of age—that means twenty-one, you know.'

Vernon breathed a sigh of relief.

'But, you see,' continued Uncle Sydney, 'there isn't enough money to go on living here. As I say, your father would have had to sell it. But he met your mother and married her, and fortunately she had enough money to—to keep things going. But your father's death has made a lot of difference—for one thing he has left certain—er—debts which your mother insists on paying.'

There was a sniff from Myra. Uncle Sydney's tone was embarrassed and he hurried on.

'The common-sense thing to do is to let Abbots Puissants for a term of years—till you are twenty-one, in fact. By then, who knows? Things may—er—change for the better. Naturally your mother will be happier living near her own relations. You must think of your mother, you know, my boy.'

105

'Yes,' said Vernon. 'Father told me to.'

'So that's settled—eh?'

How cruel they were, thought Vernon. Asking him—when he could see that there was nothing to ask him about. They could do as they liked. They meant to. Why call him in here and *pretend*!

Strangers would come and live in Abbots Puissants.

Never mind! Some day he would be twenty-one.

'Darling,' said Myra, 'I'm doing it all for you. It would be so sad here without Daddy, wouldn't it?'

She held out her arms, but Vernon pretended not to notice. He walked out of the room, saying, with difficulty:

'Thank you, Uncle Sydney, so much, for telling me . . .'

He went out into the garden and wandered on till he came to the old Abbey. He sat down with his chin in his hands.

'Mother *could*!' he said to himself. 'If she liked, she *could*! She wants to go and live in a horrid red brick house with pipes on it like Uncle Sydney's. She doesn't like Abbots Puissants—she never has. But she needn't pretend it's all for me. That's not true. She says things that aren't true. She always has—'

He sat there smouldering with indignation.

'Vernon—Vernon—I've been looking for you everywhere. I couldn't think what had become of you. What's the matter?'

It was Joe. He told her. Here was someone who would understand and sympathize. But Joe startled him.

'Well, why not? Why shouldn't Aunt Myra go and live in Birmingham if she wants to? I think you're beastly. Why should she go on living here just so that you should be here in the holidays? It's *her* money. Why shouldn't she spend it on doing as *she* likes?'

'But Joe, Abbots Puissants—'

'Well, what's Abbots Puissants to Aunt Myra? In her heart of hearts she feels about it just like you feel about Uncle Sydney's house in Birmingham. Why should she pinch and scrape to live here if she doesn't want to? If your father had made her happier here, perhaps she would want to— but he didn't. Mother said so once. I don't like Aunt Myra terribly—I know she's good and all that, but I don't love her—but I *can* be fair. It's *her* money. You can't get away from that!'

Vernon looked at her. They were antagonists. Each had their point of view and neither could see the other's. They were both ablaze with indignation.

'I think women have a rotten time,' said Joe. 'And I'm on Aunt Myra's side.'

'All right,' said Vernon, 'be on her side! I don't care.'

Joe went away. He stayed there, sitting on the ruined wall of the old Abbey.

For the first time he questioned life . . . Things weren't *sure*. How could you tell what was going to happen?

When he was twenty-one.

Yes, but you couldn't be *sure*! You couldn't be *safe*!

Look at the time when he was a baby. Nurse, God, Mr Green! How absolutely fixed they had seemed. And now they had all gone.

At least, God was still there, he supposed. But it wasn't the same God—not the same God at all.

What would have happened to everything by the time he was twenty-one? *What, strangest thought of all, would have happened to himself?*

He felt terribly alone. Father, Aunt Nina—both dead. Only Uncle Sydney and Mummy—and they weren't— didn't—belong. He paused, confused. There was Joe! Joe understood. But Joe was queer about some things.

He clenched his hands. No, everything would be all right. *When he was twenty-one . . .*

BOOK II

Nell

CHAPTER 1

The room was full of cigarette smoke. It eddied and drifted about, forming a thin blue haze. Through it came the sound of three voices occupied with the betterment of the human race and the encouragement of art—especially art that defied all known conventions.

Sebastian Levinne, leaning back against the ornate marble mantelpiece of his mother's town house, spoke didactically, gesticulating with the long yellow hand that held his cigarette. The tendency to lisp was still there, but very faint. His yellow Mongolian face, his surprised looking ears, were much the same as they had been at eleven years old. At twenty-two he was the same Sebastian, sure of himself, perceptive, with the same love of beauty and the same unemotional and unerring sense of values.

In front of him, reclining in two immense leather covered arm-chairs, were Vernon and Joe. Very much alike these two, cast in the same sharply accentuated black and white mould. But, as of old, Joe's was the more aggressive personality, energetic, rebellious, vehement. Vernon, an immense length, lay back slothfully in his chair. His long legs rested on the back of another chair. He was blowing smoke rings and smiling thoughtfully to himself. He occasionally contributed grunts to the conversation, or a short lazy sentence.

'That wouldn't pay,' Sebastian had just said decisively.

As he had half expected, Joe was roused at once to the point of virulence.

'Who wants a thing to *pay*? It's so—so *rotten*—that point of view! Treating everything from a commercial standpoint. I hate it.'

Sebastian said calmly: 'That's because you've got such an incurably romantic view of life. You like poets to starve in garrets, and artists to toil unrecognized, and sculptors to be applauded after they are dead.'

'Well—that's what happens. Always!'

'No, not *always*. Very often, perhaps. But it needn't be as often as it is. That's my point. The world never likes anything new—but I say it could be made to. Taken the right way, it could be made to. But you've got to know just what will go down and what won't.'

'That's compromise,' murmured Vernon indistinctly.

'It's common sense! Why should I lose money by backing my judgment?'

'Oh, Sebastian,' cried Joe. 'You—you—'

'Jew!' said Sebastian calmly. 'That's what you mean. Well, we Jews have got taste—we know when a thing is fine and when it isn't. We don't go by the fashion—we back our own judgment, and we're *right*! People always see the money side of it, but the other's there too.'

Vernon grunted. Sebastian went on.

'There are two sides to what we're talking about—there are people who are thinking of new things, new ways of doing old things, new thoughts altogether—and who can't get their chance because people are afraid of anything new. And there are the other people—the people who know what the public have always wanted, and who go on giving it to them, because it's safe and there's a sure profit. But there's a third way—to find things that are new and beautiful, and take a chance on them. That's what I'm going to do. I'm going to run a picture gallery in Bond Street—I signed the deeds yesterday—and a couple of theatres—and later I want to run a weekly of some kind on entirely different lines from anything that has been done before. And what's more, I'm going to make the whole thing *pay*. There are all sorts of things that I admire, that a cultivated few would admire—but I'm not going out for those. Anything I run's going to be a popular success. Dash it all, Joe, don't you see that half the fun of the thing is *making* it pay? It's justifying yourself by success.'

Joe shook her head, unconvinced.

'Are you really going to have all those things?' said Vernon.

Both the cousins looked at Sebastian with a tinge of envy. Queer, and rather wonderful, to be in old Sebastian's position. His father had died some years before. Sebastian, at twenty-two, was master of so many millions that it took one's breath away to think about them.

The friendship with Sebastian, begun all those years ago at Abbots Puissants, had endured and strengthened. He and Vernon had been friends at Eton, they were at the same college at Cambridge. In the holidays, the three had always managed to spend a good deal of time together.

'What about sculpture?' asked Joe suddenly. 'Is that included?'

'Of course. Are you still keen about taking up modelling?'

'Rather. It's the only thing I really care about.'

A derisive hoot of laughter came from Vernon.

'Yes, and what will it be this time next year? You'll be a frenzied poet or something.'

'It takes one some time to find one's true vocation,' said Joe with dignity. 'But I'm really in earnest this time.'

'You always are,' said Vernon. 'However, thank heaven you've given up that damned violin.'

'Why do you hate music so, Vernon?'

'Dunno—I always have.'

Joe turned back to Sebastian. Unconsciously her voice took on a different note. It sounded ever so faintly constrained.

'What do you think of Paul La Marre's work? Vernon and I went to his studio last Sunday.'

'No guts,' said Sebastian succinctly.

A slight flush rose in Joe's cheek.

'That's simply because you don't understand what he's aiming at. I think he's wonderful.'

'Anaemic,' said Sebastian, unperturbed.

'Sebastian, I think you're perfectly hateful sometimes. Just because La Marre has the courage to break away from tradition—'

'That's not it at all,' said Sebastian. 'A man can break

114

away from tradition by modelling a Stilton cheese and calling it his idea of a nymph bathing. But if he can't convince you and impress you by doing so, he's failed. Just doing things differently to anyone else isn't genius. Nine times out of ten it's aiming at getting cheap notoriety.'

The door opened and Mrs Levinne looked in.

'Teath ready, dearths,' she said, and beamed on them.

Jet dangled and twinkled on her immense bust. A large black hat with feathers sat on top of her elaborately arranged coiffure. She looked the complete symbol of material prosperity. Her eyes dwelt with adoration on Sebastian.

They got up, and prepared to follow her. Sebastian said in a low voice to Joe:

'Joe—you're not angry, are you?'

There was suddenly something young and pathetic about his voice—a pleading in it that exposed him as immature and vulnerable. A moment ago he had been the master spirit laying down the law in complete self-confidence.

'Why should I be angry?' said Joe coldly.

She moved towards the door without looking at him. Sebastian's eyes rested on her wistfully. She had that dark magnetic beauty that matures early. Her skin was dead white, and her eyelashes so thick and dark that they looked like jet against the even colour of her cheeks. There was magic in her way of moving, something languorous and passionate that was wholly unconscious as yet of its own appeal. Although she was the youngest of the three, just past her twentieth birthday, she was at the same time the oldest. To her Vernon and Sebastian were boys, and she despised boys. That queer dog-like

115

devotion of Sebastian's irritated her. She liked men of experience, men who could say exciting, half understood things. She lowered her white eyelids for a moment, remembering Paul La Marre.

Mrs Levinne's drawing-room was a curious mixture of sheer blatant opulence, and an almost austere good taste. The opulence was due to her—she liked velvet hangings and rich cushions and marble, and gilding—the taste was Sebastian's. It was he who had torn down a medley of pictures from the wall and substituted two of his own choosing. His mother was reconciled to their plainness (as she called it) by the immense price that had been paid for them. The old Spanish leather screen was one of her son's presents to her—so was the exquisite cloisonne vase.

Seated behind an unusually massive silver tea-tray, Mrs Levinne raised the teapot with two hands, and made conversational inquiries, lisping slightly.

'And how's your dear mother? She never comes to town nowadays. You tell her from me she'll be getting rusty.'

She laughed, a good-natured fat wheezy chuckle.

'I've never regretted having this town house as well as a country one. Deerfields is all very well, but one wants a bit of life. And of course Sebastian will be home soon for good—and that full of schemes as he is! Well, well, his father was much the same. Went into deals against everybody's advice, and instead of losing his money he doubled and trebled it every time. A smart fellow, my poor Yakob.'

Sebastian thought to himself:

'I wish she wouldn't. That's just the sort of remark Joe always hates. Joe's always against me nowadays.'

Mrs Levinne went on.

'I've got a box for *Kings in Arcady* on Wednesday night. What about it, my dears? Will you come?'

'I'm awfully sorry, Mrs Levinne,' said Vernon. 'I wish we could. But we're going down to Birmingham tomorrow.'

'Oh! you're going home.'

'Yes.'

Why hadn't he said 'going home'? Why did it sound so fantastic in his ears? There was only one home, of course, Abbots Puissants. Home! A queer word, so many meanings to it. It reminded him of the ridiculous words of a song that one of Joe's young men used to bray out (what a damnable thing music was!) while he fingered his collar and looked at her sentimentally. 'Home, love, is where the heart is, where'er the heart may be . . .'

But in that case his home ought to be in Birmingham where his mother was.

He experienced that faint feeling of disquietude that always came over him when he thought of his mother. He was very fond of her, naturally. Mothers, of course, were hopeless people to explain things to, they never understood. But he *was* very fond of her—it would be unnatural if he wasn't. As she so often said, he was all she had.

Suddenly a little imp seemed to jump in Vernon's brain. The imp said suddenly and unexpectedly: 'What rot you are talking! She's got the house, and the servants to talk to and bully, and friends to gossip with, and her own people all round her. She'd miss all that far more than she'd miss you. She loves you, but she's relieved when you go back to Cambridge—and even then she's not as relieved as you are!'

'Vernon!' It was Joe's voice, sharp with annoyance. 'What are you thinking of? Mrs Levinne was asking about Abbots Puissants—if it's still let?'

How fortunate that when people said, 'What *are* you thinking about?' they didn't in the least mean that they wanted to know! Still, you could always say 'Nothing much', just as when you were small you had said 'Nothing'.

He answered Mrs Levinne's questions, promised to deliver her various messages to his mother.

Sebastian saw them to the door, they said a final goodbye and walked out into the London streets. Joe sniffed the air ecstatically.

'How I love London! You know, Vernon, my mind's made up. I'm coming up to London to study. I'm going to tackle Aunt Myra about it this time. And I won't live with Aunt Ethel, either, I'm going to be on my own.'

'You can't do that, Joe. Girls don't.'

'They *do*. I could share rooms with another girl or girls. But to live with Aunt Ethel, always asking me where I'm going, and who with—I just can't stand it. And anyway she hates me being a suffragette.'

The Aunt Ethel they referred to was Aunt Carrie's sister, an aunt by courtesy only. They were staying with her at the present moment.

'Oh, and that reminds me,' went on Joe. 'You've got to do something for me, Vernon.'

'What?'

'Tomorrow afternoon Mrs Cartwright's taking me to that Titanic Concert as a special treat.'

'Well?'

'Well, I don't want to go—that's all.'

'You can make some excuse or other, I suppose.'

'It's not so easy as that. You see, Aunt Ethel's got to think I've gone to the concert. I don't want her ferreting out where I am going.'

Vernon gave a whistle.

'Oh! so that's it? What are you really up to, Joe? Who is it this time?'

'It's La Marre, if you really want to know.'

'That bounder.'

'He's not a bounder. He's wonderful—you don't know how wonderful he is.'

Vernon grinned.

'No, indeed I don't. I don't like Frenchmen.'

'You're so horribly insular. But it doesn't matter whether you like him or not. He's going to motor me down to the country to a friend's house where his *chef d'œuvre* is. I do so want to go, and you know perfectly that Aunt Ethel would never let me.'

'You oughtn't to go racketing about the country with a fellow like that.'

'Don't be an ass, Vernon. Don't you know that I can look after myself?'

'Oh, I suppose so.'

'I'm not one of those silly girls who know nothing about anything.'

'I don't see, though, where *I* come in.'

119

'Well, you see,' Joe displayed a trace of anxiety. 'You're to go to the concert.'

'No, I won't do anything of the kind. You know I hate music.'

'Oh, you must, Vernon. It's the only way. If I say I can't go, she'll ring up Aunt Ethel and suggest one of the girls coming instead, and then the fat will be in the fire. But if you just turn up instead of me—I'm to meet her at the Albert Hall—and give some weak excuse, everything will be all right. She's very fond of you—she likes you heaps better than me.'

'But I loathe music.'

'I know, but you can just bear it for one afternoon. An hour and a half. That's all it will be.'

'Oh, damn it all, Joe, I don't want to.'

His hand shook with irritation. Joe stared at him.

'You are *funny* about music, Vernon! I've never known anyone who sort of—well, hates it like you. Most people just don't care for it. But I do think you might go—you know *I* always do things for *you*.'

'All right,' said Vernon abruptly.

It was no good. It had got to be. Joe and he always stood together. After all, as she had said, it would only be an hour and a half. Why should he feel that he had taken a momentous decision? His heart felt like lead—right down in his boots. He didn't want to go—oh! he didn't want to go . . .

Like a visit to the dentist—best not to think about it. He forced his mind away to other things. Joe looked up sharply as she heard him give vent to a chuckle.

'What is it?'

'I was thinking of you as a kid—so grand about saying you were never going to have anything to do with men. And now it's always men with you, one after the other. You fall in and out of love about once a month.'

'Don't be so horrid, Vernon. Those were just silly girls' fancies. La Marre says if you have any temperament, that always happens—but the real grand passion is quite different when it comes.'

'Well, don't go and have a grand passion for La Marre.'

Joe did not answer. Presently she said:

'I'm not like Mother. Mother was—was so *soft* about men. She gave in to them—would do anything for anyone she was fond of. I'm not like that.'

'No,' said Vernon, after thinking for a moment. 'No, I don't think you are. You won't make a mess of your life in the same way she did. But you might make a mess of it in a different way.'

'What sort of a way?'

'I don't quite know. Going and marrying someone you thought you had a grand passion for, just because everyone else disliked him, and then spending your life fighting him. Or deciding to go and live with someone just because you thought Free Love was a fine idea.'

'So it is.'

'Oh, I am not saying it isn't—though as a matter of fact, I really think it is anti-social myself. But you're always the same. If anyone forbids you anything you always want to do it—quite irrespective of whether you really want to. I haven't put that well, but you know what I mean.'

'What I really want is to *do* something! To be a great sculptor—'

'That's because you've got a pash for La Marre—'

'It isn't. Oh! Vernon, why will you be so trying? I've *always* wanted to do something—always—always! I used to say so at Abbots Puissants.'

'It's odd,' said Vernon thoughtfully. 'Old Sebastian used to say then very much what he says now. Perhaps one doesn't change as much as one thinks.'

'You were going to marry someone very beautiful and live at Abbots Puissants always,' said Joe with slight scorn. 'You don't still feel that to be your life's ambition, do you?'

'One might do worse,' said Vernon.

'Lazy—downright lazy!'

Joe looked at him in unconcealed impatience. She and Vernon were so alike in some ways, and so different in others!

Vernon was thinking, '*Abbots Puissants. In a year I shall be twenty-one.*'

They were passing a Salvation Army meeting. Joe stopped. A thin, white-faced man was standing on a box. His voice, high and raucous, came echoing across to them.

'Why won't you be saved? Why won't you? Jesus wants you! Jesus wants *you*!' Tremendous emphasis on the you. 'Yes, brothers and sisters, and I'll tell you something more. *You want Jesus.* You won't admit it to yourselves, you turn your back on him, you're afraid—that's what it is, you're afraid, because you want him so badly—you want him and you don't know!' His arms waved, his white face shone with ecstasy. 'But you will know—you *will* know—there are things that you can't run away from for ever.' He spoke slowly, almost menacingly. '*I say unto you, this very night shall thy soul be required of thee—*'

Vernon turned away with a slight shiver. A woman on the outskirts of the crowd gave a hysterical sob.

'Disgusting,' said Joe, her nose very much in the air. 'Indecent and hysterical! For my part, I can't see how any rational being can be anything but an atheist.'

Vernon smiled to himself, though he said nothing. He was remembering the time, a year ago, when Joe had risen every day to attend early service and had insisted on eating a boiled egg with some ostentation on Fridays, and had sat spellbound listening to the somewhat uninteresting but strictly dogmatical sermons of handsome Father Cuthbert at the Church of St Bartholomew's, which was reputed to be so 'high' that Rome itself could do no more.

'I wonder,' he said aloud, 'what it would feel like to be "saved"?'

It was half-past six on the following afternoon when Joe returned from her stolen day's pleasure. Her Aunt Ethel met her in the hall.

'Where's Vernon?' inquired Joe, in case she might be asked how she had liked the concert.

'He came in about half an hour ago. He said there was nothing the matter, but somehow I don't think he's very well.'

'Oh!' Joe stared. 'Where is he? In his room? I'll go up and see.'

'I wish you would, dear. Really he didn't look well at all.'

Joe ran quickly up the stairs, gave a perfunctory rap on Vernon's door and walked in. Vernon was sitting on his bed, and something in his appearance gave Joe a shock. She had never seen Vernon look quite like this.

He didn't answer. He had the dazed look of someone who has undergone a terrible shock. It was as though he were too far away to be reached by mere words.

'Vernon.' She shook him by the shoulder. 'What *is* the matter with you?'

He heard her this time.

'Nothing.'

'There must be something. You're looking—you're looking—'

Words failed her to express how he was looking. She left it at that.

'Nothing,' he repeated dully.

She sat down on the bed beside him.

'Tell me,' she said gently but authoritatively.

A long shuddering sigh broke from Vernon.

'Joe, do you remember that man yesterday?'

'Which man?'

'That Salvation Army chap—those cant phrases he used. And that one—a fine one—from the Bible: "*This night shall thy soul be required of thee.*" I said afterwards I wondered what it would be like to be saved. Just idly. Well, I *know*!'

Joe stared at him. *Vernon.* Oh, but such a thing was impossible.

'Do you mean—do you mean—' Difficult somehow to

get the words. 'Do you mean you've "got religion"—suddenly—like people do?'

She felt it was ridiculous as she said it. She was relieved when he gave a sudden spurt of laughter.

'*Religion?* Good God, no! Or is it that for some people? I wonder . . . No, I mean—' He hesitated, brought the word out at last very softly, almost as though he dared not speak it. 'Music—'

'Music?' She was still utterly at sea.

'Yes. Joe, do you remember Nurse Frances?'

'Nurse Frances? No, I don't think I do. Who was she?'

'Of course you wouldn't. It was before you came—the time I broke my leg. I've always remembered something she said to me. About not being in a hurry to run away from things before you've had a good look. Well, that's what happened to me today. I couldn't run away any longer—I just had to look. Joe, music's the most wonderful thing in the world—'

'But—but—you've always said—'

'I know. That's why it's been such an awful shock. Not that I mean music is so wonderful *now*—but it *could* be—if you had it as it was meant to be! Little bits of it are ugly—it's like going up to a picture and seeing a nasty grey smear of paint—but go to a distance and it falls into its place as the most wonderful shadow. It's got to be a *whole*. I still think one violin's ugly, and a piano's beastly—but useful in a way, I suppose. But—oh! Joe, music could be so wonderful—I know it could.'

Joe was silent, bewildered. She understood now what Vernon had meant by his opening words. His face had the queer dreamy exaltation that one associated with religious fervour. And yet she was a little frightened. His face had always expressed so little. Now, she thought, it expressed too much. It was a worse face or a better face—just as you chose to look on it.

He went on talking, hardly to her, more to himself.

'There were nine orchestras, you know. All massed. Sound can be glorious if you get enough of it—I don't mean just loudness—it shows more when it's soft. But there must be enough. I don't know what they played—nothing, I think, that was real. But it showed one—it showed one . . .'

He turned queer bright excited eyes upon her.

'There's so much to know—to learn. I don't want to play things—never that. But I want to know about every instrument there is. What it can do—what are its limitations, what are its possibilities. And the notes, too. There are notes they don't use—notes that they ought to use. I know there are. Do you know what music's like now, Joe? It's like the little sturdy Norman pillars in the crypt of Gloucester Cathedral. It's at its beginnings, that's all.'

He sat silent, leaning forward dreamily.

'Well, I think you've gone quite mad,' said Joe.

She tried on purpose to make her voice sound practical and matter-of-fact. But, in spite of herself, she was impressed. That white hot conviction. And she had always thought Vernon rather a slow coach—reactionary, prejudiced, unimaginative.

'I've got to begin to learn. As soon as ever I can. Oh, it's awful—to have wasted twenty years!'

'Nonsense,' said Joe. 'You couldn't have studied music when you were an infant in a cot.'

He smiled at that. He was coming out of his trance by degrees.

'You think I'm mad? I suppose it must sound like that. But I'm not. And—oh! Joe, it's the most awful *relief*. As though you had been pretending for years, and now you needn't pretend any more. I've been horribly afraid of music—always. Now—'

He sat up, squared his shoulders.

'I'm going to work – work like a dog. I'm going to know the ins and outs of every instrument. By the way, there must be more instruments in the world—many more. There ought to be a kind of waily thing—I've heard it somewhere. You'd want ten—fifteen of those. And about fifty harps—'

He sat there, planning composedly details that to Joe sounded sheer nonsense. Yet it was evident that to his inner vision some event was perfectly clear.

'It'll be supper time in ten minutes,' Joe reminded him timidly.

'Oh! Will it? What a nuisance. I want to stay here and think and hear things in my head. Tell Aunt Ethel I've got a headache or that I've been frightfully sick. As a matter of fact, I think I *am* going to be sick.'

And somehow that impressed Joe more than anything else. It was a homely familiar happening. When anything upset you very much, either pleasurably or otherwise, you always wanted to be sick! She had felt that herself, often.

She stood in the door hesitating. Vernon had relapsed

into abstraction again. How queer he looked—quite different. As though—as though—Joe sought for the words she wanted—as though he had suddenly come alive.

She was a little frightened.

CHAPTER 2

Carey Lodge was the name of Myra's house. It was about eight miles from Birmingham.

A subtle depression always weighed down Vernon's spirits as he got near Carey Lodge. He hated the house, hated its solid comfort, its thick bright red carpets, its lounge hall, the carefully selected sporting prints that hung in the dining-room, the superabundance of knick-knacks that filled the drawing-room. And yet, was it so much those things he hated, as the facts that stood behind them?

He questioned himself, trying for the first time to be honest with himself. Wasn't it the truth that he hated his mother being so at home there, so placidly content? He liked to think of her in terms of Abbots Puissants—liked to think of her as being, like himself, an exile.

And she wasn't! Abbots Puissants had been to her what a foreign kingdom might be to a Queen Consort. She had felt important there, and pleased with herself. It had been new and exciting. But it hadn't been home.

Myra greeted her son with extravagant affection as always. He wished she wouldn't. In some way it made it harder than ever for him to respond. When he was away from her, he pictured himself being affectionate to his mother. When he was with her, all that illusion faded away.

Myra Deyre had altered a good deal since leaving Abbots Puissants. She had grown much stouter. Her beautiful golden red hair was flecked with grey. The expression of her face was different, it was at once more satisfied and more placid. There was now a strong resemblance between her and her brother, Sydney.

'You've had a good time in London? I'm so glad. It's so exciting to have my fine big son back with me—I've been telling everybody how excited I am. Mothers are foolish creatures, aren't they?'

Vernon thought they were rather—then was ashamed of himself.

'Very jolly to see you, Mother,' he mumbled.

Joe said:

'You're looking splendidly fit, Aunt Myra.'

'I've not really been very well, dear. I don't think Dr Grey quite understands my case. I hear there's a new doctor—Dr Littleworth—just bought Dr Armstrong's practice. They say he is wonderfully clever. I'm sure it's my heart—and it's all nonsense Dr Grey saying it's indigestion.'

She was quite animated. Her health was always an absorbing topic to Myra.

'Mary's gone—the housemaid, you know. I was really very disappointed in that girl. After all I did for her.'

It went on and on. Joe and Vernon listened perfunctorily. Their minds were full of conscious superiority. Thank Heaven they belonged to a new and enlightened generation, far above this insistence on domestic details. For them, a new and splendid world opened out. They were deeply, poignantly sorry for the contented creature who sat there chattering to them.

Joe thought:

'Poor—poor Aunt Myra. So terribly female! Of course Uncle Walter got bored with her. Not her fault! A rotten education, and brought up to believe that domesticity was all that mattered. And here she is, still young really—at least not too terribly old—and all she's got to do is to sit in the house and gossip, and think about servants, and fuss about her health. If she'd only been born twenty years later, she could have been happy and free, and independent all her life.'

And out of her intense pity for her unconscious aunt, she answered gently and pretended an interest that she certainly did not feel.

Vernon thought:

'Was Mother always like this? Somehow she didn't seem so at Abbots Puissants. Or was I too much of a kid to notice? It's rotten of me to criticize her when she's been so good to me always. Only I wish she wouldn't treat me still as though I were about six years old. Oh, well, I suppose she can't help it. I don't think I shall ever marry—'

And suddenly he jerked out abruptly, urged thereto by intense nervousness.

'I say, Mother. I'm thinking of taking Music at Cambridge.'

There, it was out! He had said it.

Myra, distracted from her account of the Armstrongs' cook, said vaguely:

'But, darling, you always were so unmusical. You used to be quite unreasonable about it.'

'I know,' said Vernon gruffly. 'But one changes one's mind about things sometimes.'

'Well, I'm very glad, dear. I used to play quite brilliant pieces myself when I was a young girl. But one never keeps up anything when one marries.'

'I know. It's a wicked shame,' said Joe hotly. 'I don't mean to marry—but if I did, I'd never give up my own career. And that reminds me, Aunt Myra, I've just got to go to London to study if I'm ever going to be any good at modelling.'

'I'm sure Mr Bradford—'

'Oh, damn Mr Bradford! I'm sorry, Aunt Myra, but you don't understand. I've got to study—*hard*. And I must be on my own. I could share diggings with another girl—'

'Joe, darling, don't be so absurd.' Myra laughed. 'I need my little Joe here. I always look on you as my daughter, you know, Joe, dear.'

Joe wriggled.

'I really am in earnest, Aunt Myra. It's my whole life.'

This tragic utterance only made her aunt laugh more.

'Girls often think like that. Now, don't let's spoil this happy evening by quarrelling.'

'But will you really seriously consider it?'

'We must see what Uncle Sydney says.'

'It's nothing to do with him. He's not *my* uncle. Surely, if I like, I can take my own money—'

'It isn't exactly your own money, Joe. Your father sends it to me as an allowance for you—though I'm sure I would be willing to have you without any allowance at all—and knows you are well and safely looked after with me.'

'Then I suppose I'd better write to Father.'

She said it valiantly, but her heart sank. She had seen her father twice in ten years, and the old antagonism held between them. The present plan doubtless commended itself to Major Waite. At the cost of a few hundreds a year, the problem of his daughter was lifted off his hands. But Joe had no money of her own. She doubted very much if her father would make her any allowance at all if she broke away from Aunt Myra and insisted on leading her own life.

Vernon murmured to her:

'Don't be so damned impatient, Joe. Wait till I'm twenty-one.'

That cheered her a little. One could always depend on Vernon.

Myra asked Vernon about the Levinnes. Was Mrs Levinne's asthma any better? Was it true that they spent almost all of their time in London nowadays?

'No, I don't think so. Of course, they don't go down to Deerfields much in the winter, but they were there all the autumn. It'll be jolly to have them next door when we go back to Abbots Puissants, won't it?'

His mother started, and said in a flustered sort of voice:

'Oh, yes—very nice.'

She added almost immediately:

'Your Uncle Sydney is coming round to tea. He's bringing Enid. By the way, I don't have late dinner any more. I really think it suits me better to have a good sit down meal at six.'

'Oh!' said Vernon, rather taken aback.

He had an unreasoning prejudice against those meals. He disliked the juxtaposition of tea and scrambled eggs, and rich plum cake. Why couldn't his mother have proper meals like other people? Of course, Uncle Sydney and Aunt Carrie always had high tea. Bother Uncle Sydney! All this was his fault.

His thought stopped—checked. All what? He couldn't answer—didn't quite know. But, anyway, when he and his mother went back to Abbots Puissants, everything would be different.

Uncle Sydney arrived very soon—very bluff and hearty, a little stouter than of old. With him came Enid, his third daughter. The two eldest were married, and the two youngest were in the schoolroom.

Uncle Sydney was full of jokes and fun. Myra looked at her brother admiringly. Really, there was nobody like Syd! He made things go.

Vernon laughed politely at his uncle's jokes which he privately thought both stupid and boring.

'I wonder where you buy your tobacco in Cambridge,' said Uncle Sydney. 'From a pretty girl, I'll be bound. Ha! Ha! Myra, the boy's blushing—actually blushing.'

'Stupid old fool,' thought Vernon disdainfully.

'And where do *you* buy your tobacco, Uncle Sydney?' said Joe, valiantly entering the lists.

'Ha! Ha!' trumpeted Uncle Sydney. 'That's a good one! You're a smart girl, Joe. We won't tell your Aunt Carrie the answer to that, eh?'

Enid said very little but giggled a good deal.

'You ought to write to your cousin,' said Uncle Sydney. 'He'd like a letter, wouldn't you, Vernon?'

'Rather,' said Vernon.

'There you are,' said Uncle Sydney. 'What did I tell you, miss? The child wanted to, but was shy. She's always thought a lot of you, Vernon. But I mustn't tell tales out of school, hey, Enid?'

Later, after the heavy composite meal was ended, he talked to Vernon at some length of the prosperity of Bent's.

'Booming, my boy, booming.'

He went into long financial explanations, profits had doubled, he was extending the premises—and so on, and so on.

Vernon much preferred this style of conversation. Not being the least interested, he could abstract his attention. An encouraging monosyllable was all that was needed from time to time.

Uncle Sydney talked on, developing the fascinating theme of the Power and Glory of Bent's, World without End, Amen.

Vernon thought about the book on musical instruments which he had bought that morning and read coming down in the train. There was a terrible lot to know. Oboes—he felt he was going to have ideas about oboes. And violas—yes, certainly, violas.

Uncle Sydney's talk made a pleasant accompaniment like a remote double bass.

Presently Uncle Sydney said he must be getting along. There was more facetiousness—should or should not Vernon kiss Enid good night?

How idiotic people were. Thank goodness he'd soon be able to get up to his own room.

Myra heaved a happy sigh as the door closed.

'Dear me,' she murmured, 'I wish your father had been here. We've had such a happy evening. He would have enjoyed it.'

'A jolly good thing he wasn't,' said Vernon. 'I don't remember he and Uncle Sydney ever hitting it off really well.'

'You were only a little boy. They were the greatest of friends, and your father was always happy when I was. Oh, dear, how happy we were together.'

She raised a handkerchief to her eyes. Vernon stared at her. For a moment he thought: 'This is the most magnificent loyalty.' And then suddenly: 'No, it isn't. She really believes it.'

Myra went on in a soft reminiscent tone.

'You were never really fond of your father, Vernon. I think it must have grieved him sometimes. But then, you were so devoted to me. It was quite ridiculous.'

Vernon said suddenly and violently, and with a strange feeling that he was defending his father by saying so:

'Father was a brute to you.'

'Vernon, how dare you say such a thing. Your father was the best man in the world.'

She looked at him defiantly. He thought: 'She's seeing herself being heroic. "How wonderful a woman's love can be—protecting her dead,"—that sort of thing. Oh! I hate it all. I hate it all.'

He mumbled something, kissed her, and went up to bed.

*

136

Later in the evening Joe tapped at his door and was bidden to enter. Vernon was sitting, sprawled out in a chair. The book on musical instruments lay on the floor beside him.

'Hallo, Joe. God, what a beastly evening!'

'Did you mind it so much?'

'Didn't you? It's all wrong. What an ass Uncle Sydney is. Those idiotic jokes! It's all so cheap.'

'H'm,' said Joe. She sat down thoughtfully on the bed and lit a cigarette.

'Don't you agree?'

'Yes—at least I do in a way.'

'Spit it out,' said Vernon encouragingly.

'Well, what I mean is, *they're* happy enough.'

'Who?'

'Aunt Myra. Uncle Sydney. Enid. They're a united happy lot, thoroughly content with one another. It's we who are wrong, Vernon. You and I. We've lived here all these years—but we don't belong. That's why—we've got to get out of it.'

Vernon nodded thoughtfully.

'Yes, Joe, you're right. We've got to get out of it.'

He smiled happily, because the way was so clear.

Twenty-one . . . Abbots Puissants . . . Music . . .

CHAPTER 3

'Do you mind just going over that once more, Mr Flemming?'

'Willingly.'

Precise, dry, even, word after word fell from the old lawyer's lips. His meaning was clear and unmistakable! Too much so! It didn't leave a loophole for doubt.

Vernon listened. His face was very white, his hands grasped the arms of the chair in which he was sitting.

It couldn't be true—it *couldn't*! And yet, after all, hadn't Mr Flemming said very much the same, years ago? Yes, but then there had been the magic words 'twenty-one' to look forward to. 'Twenty-one' which by a blessed miracle was to make everything right. Instead of which:

'Mind you, the position is infinitely improved from what it was at the time of your father's death, but it is no good pretending we are out of the wood. The mortgage—'

Surely, surely, they had never mentioned a mortgage? Well, it wouldn't have been much use, he supposed, to a boy of nine. No good trying to get round it. The plain truth was that he couldn't afford to live at Abbots Puissants.

He waited till Mr Flemming had finished, and then said: 'But if my Mother—'

'Oh, of course. If Mrs Deyre were prepared to—' He left the sentence unfinished, paused and then added: 'But, if I may say so, every time that I have had the pleasure of seeing Mrs Deyre, she has seemed to me to be very settled— very settled indeed. I suppose you know that she bought the freehold of Carey Lodge two years ago?'

Vernon hadn't known it. He saw plainly enough what it meant. Why hadn't his mother told him? Hadn't she had the courage? He had always taken it for granted that she would come back with him to Abbots Puissants, not so much because he longed for her presence there, as because it was—quite naturally—her home.

But it wasn't her home. It never could be in the sense that Carey Lodge was her home.

He could appeal to her, of course. Beg her, for his sake, because he wanted it so much.

No, a thousand times no! You couldn't beg favours from people you didn't really love. And he didn't really love his mother. He didn't believe he ever really had. Queer and sad, and a little dreadful, but there it was.

If he never saw her again, would he mind? Not really. He would like to know that she was well and happy—cared for. But he wouldn't miss her, would never feel a longing for her presence. Because, in a queer way, he didn't really *like* her. He disliked the touch of her hands, always had to take a hold on himself before kissing her good night. He'd never been able to tell her anything—she never understood or knew what he was feeling. She had been a good loving mother—and he didn't even like her! Rather horrible, he supposed, most people would say . . .

He said quietly to Mr Flemming:

'You are quite right. I am sure my mother would not wish to leave Carey Lodge.'

'Now, there are one or two alternatives open to you, Mr Deyre. Major Salmon, who, as you know, has rented it furnished all these years, is anxious to buy—'

'No!' The word burst from Vernon like a pistol shot.

Mr Flemming smiled.

'I was sure you would say that. And I must confess I am glad. There have been—er—Deyres at Abbots Puissants for, let me see, nearly five hundred years. Nevertheless, I should be failing in my duty if I didn't point out to you that the price offered is a good one, and that if, later, you should decide to sell, it may not be easy to find a suitable purchaser.'

'It's out of the question.'

'Very good. Then the best thing, I think, is to try and let once more. Major Salmon definitely wants to buy a place, so it will mean finding a new tenant. But I dare say we shall have no great difficulty. The point is, how long do you want to let for? To let the place for another long term of years is, I should say, not very desirable. Life is very uncertain. Who knows, in a few years the state of affairs may have—er—changed very considerably, and you may be in a position to take up residence there yourself.'

'So I shall, but not the way you think, you old dunderhead,' thought Vernon. 'It'll be because I've made a name for myself in music—not because Mother is dead. I'm sure I hope she'll live to be ninety.'

He exchanged a few more words with Mr Flemming, then rose to go.

'I'm afraid this has been rather a shock to you,' said the old lawyer as he shook hands.

'Yes—just a bit. I've been building castles in the air, I suppose.'

'You're going down to spend your twenty-first birthday with your mother, I suppose?'

'Yes.'

'You might talk things over with your uncle, Mr Bent. A very shrewd man of business. He has a daughter about your age, I think?'

'Yes, Enid. The two eldest are married, and the two youngest are at school. Enid's about a year younger than I am.'

'Ah! very pleasant to have a cousin of one's own age. I dare say you will see a good deal of her.'

'Oh, I don't suppose I shall,' said Vernon vaguely.

Why should he be seeing a lot of Enid? She was a dull girl. But of course Mr Flemming didn't know that.

Funny old chap. What on earth was there to put on such a sly, knowing expression about?

'Well, Mother, I don't seem to be exactly the young heir!'

'Oh, well, dear, you mustn't worry. Things arrange themselves, you know. You must have a good talk with your Uncle Sydney.'

Silly! What good could a talk with his Uncle Sydney do him?

Fortunately the matter was not referred to again. The extraordinary surprise was that Joe had been allowed to have her way. She was actually in London—somewhat dragoned and chaperoned, it is true—but still she had got her way.

His mother seemed always to be whispering mysteriously to friends. Vernon caught her at it one day.

'Yes—quite inseparable, they were—so I thought it wiser—it would be such a pity—'

And what Vernon called the 'other tabby' said something about 'First cousins—most unwise—' And his mother with a suddenly heightened colour and raised voice had said:

'Oh! I don't think in *every* case.'

'Who were first cousins?' asked Vernon later. 'What was all the mystery about?'

'Mystery, darling? I don't know what you mean.'

'Well, you shut up when I came in. I wondered what it was all about?'

'Oh, nothing interesting. Some people you don't know.'

She looked rather red and confused.

Vernon wasn't curious. He asked no more.

He missed Joe most frightfully. Carey Lodge was pretty deadly without her. For one thing, he saw more of Enid than he had ever done before. She was always coming in to see Myra, and Vernon would find himself let in for taking her to roller skate at the new rink, or for some deadly party or other.

Myra told Vernon that it would be nice if he asked Enid

up to Cambridge for May week. She was so persistent about it that Vernon gave in. After all, it didn't matter. Sebastian would have Joe and he himself didn't much care. Dancing was rather rot—everything was rot that interfered with music . . .

The evening before his departure Uncle Sydney came to Carey Lodge and Myra pushed Vernon into the study with him and said:

'Your Uncle Sydney's come to have a little talk with you, Vernon.'

Mr Bent hemmed and hawed for a minute or two and then, rather surprisingly, came straight to the point. Vernon had never liked his uncle as much. His facetious manner had been entirely laid aside.

'I'm coming straight out with what I want to say, my boy—but I don't want you interrupting till I've finished. See?'

'Yes, Uncle Sydney.'

'The long and short of it is just this. *I want you to come into Bent's.* Now remember what I said—no interruptions! I know you've never thought of such a thing, and I dare say the idea isn't very congenial to you now. I'm a plain man, and I can face facts as well as anyone. If you'd got a good income and could live at Abbots Puissants like a gentleman, there wouldn't be any question of the thing. Well, I accept that. You're like your father's people. But for all that, you've got good Bent blood in your veins, my boy, and blood's bound to tell.

'I've got no son of my own. I'm willing—if you're willing—to look upon you as a son. The girls are provided for, and handsomely provided for at that. And mind you, it won't be a case of toiling for life. I'm not unreasonable—and I realize just as much as you do what that place of yours stands for. You're a young fellow. You go into the business when you come down from Cambridge—mind you, you go into it from the bottom. You'll start at a moderate salary and work up. If you want to retire before you're forty—well, you can do so. Please yourself. You'll be a rich man by then, and you'll be able to run Abbots Puissants as it should be run.

'You'll marry young, I hope. Excellent thing, young marriages. Your eldest boy succeeds to the place, the younger sons find a first-class business to step into where they can show what they're made of. I'm proud of Bent's—as proud of Bent's as you are of Abbots Puissants—that's why I understand your feeling about the old place. I don't want you to have to sell it. Let it go out of the family after all these years. That would be a shame. Well, there's the offer.'

'It's most awfully good of you, Uncle Sydney—' began Vernon.

His uncle threw up a large square hand and stopped him.

'We'll leave it at that, if you please. I don't want an answer now. In fact I won't have one. When you come down from Cambridge—that's time enough.'

He rose.

'Kind of you to ask Enid up for May week. Very excited about it, she is. If you knew what that girl thought of you, Vernon, you'd be quite conceited. Ah, well, girls will be girls.'

144

Laughing boisterously, he slammed the front door.

Vernon remained in the hall frowning. It was really jolly decent of Uncle Sydney—*jolly* decent. Not that he was going to accept. All the money in the world wouldn't tear him from music . . .

And somehow, he would have Abbots Puissants as well.

May week!

Joe and Enid were at Cambridge. Vernon had been let in for Ethel, too, as chaperon. The world seemed largely composed of Bents just at present.

Joe had burst out at once with: 'Why on earth did you ask Enid?'

He had answered: 'Oh, Mother went on about it—it doesn't really matter.'

Nothing mattered to Vernon just then except one thing. Joe talked privately to Sebastian about that.

'Is Vernon really in earnest about this music business? Will he ever be any good? I suppose it's just a passing craze?'

But Sebastian was unexpectedly serious.

'It's extraordinarily interesting, you know,' he said. 'As far as I can make out, what Vernon is aiming at is something entirely revolutionary. He's mastering now what you might call the main facts, and mastering them at an extraordinary rate. Old Coddington admits that, though, of course, he snorts at Vernon's ideas—or would if Vernon ever let out about them. The person who's interested is old Jeffries—mathematics! He says Vernon's ideas of music are fourth dimensional.

'I don't know if Vernon will ever pull it off—or whether he'll be considered as a harmless lunatic. The border-line is very narrow, I imagine. Old Jeffries is very enthusiastic. But not in the least encouraging. He points out, quite rightly, that to attempt to discover something new and force it on the world is always a thankless task, and that in all probability the truths that Vernon is discovering won't be accepted for at least another two hundred years. He's a queer old codger. Sits about thinking of imaginary curves in space—that sort of thing.

'But I see his point. Vernon isn't creating something new. He's discovering something that's already there. Rather like a scientist. Jeffries says that Vernon's dislike of music as a child is perfectly understandable—to his ear music's incomplete—it's like a picture out of drawing. The whole perspective is wrong. It sounds to Vernon like—I suppose—a primitive savage's music would sound to us— mostly unendurable discord.

'Jeffries is full of queer ideas. Start him off on squares and cubes, and geometrical figures and the speed of light, and he goes quite mad. He writes to a German fellow called Einstein. The queer thing is that he isn't a bit musical, and yet he can see—or says he can—exactly what Vernon is driving at.'

Joe cogitated deeply.

'Well,' she said at last, 'I don't understand a word of all this. But it looks as though Vernon might make a success of it all.'

Sebastian was discouraging.

'I wouldn't say that. Vernon may be a genius—and that's

146

quite a different thing. Nobody welcomes genius. On the other hand he may be just slightly mad. He sounds mad enough sometimes when he gets going—and yet, somehow, I've always got a kind of feeling that he's right—that in some odd way, he knows what he's talking about.'

'You've heard about Uncle Sydney's offer?'

'Yes. Vernon seems to be turning it down very light-heartedly, and yet, you know, it's a good thing.'

'You wouldn't have him accept it?' flamed out Joe.

Sebastian remained provokingly cool.

'I don't know. It needs thinking about. Vernon may have wonderful theories about this music business—there's nothing to show that he's ever going to be able to put them into practice.'

'You're maddening,' said Joe, turning away.

Sebastian annoyed her nowadays. All his cool analytical faculties seemed to be uppermost. If he had enthusiasms, he hid them carefully.

And to Joe, just now, enthusiasm seemed the most necessary thing in the world. She had a passion for lost causes, for minorities. She was a passionate champion of the weak and oppressed.

Sebastian, she felt, was only interested in successes. She accused him in her own mind of judging everyone and everything from a monetary standard. Most of the time they were together, they fought and bickered incessantly.

Vernon, too, seemed separated from her. Music was the only thing he wanted to talk about, and even then on lines that were not familiar to her.

His preoccupation was entirely with instruments—their scope and power, and the violin which Joe herself played seemed the instrument in which he was least interested. Joe was quite unfitted to talk about clarinets, trombones and bassoons. Vernon's ambition in life seemed to be to form friendships with players of these instruments so as to be able to acquire some practical as opposed to theoretical knowledge.

'Don't you know any bassoon players?'

Joe said she didn't.

Vernon said that she might as well make herself useful, and try to pick up some musical friends. 'Even a French horn would do,' he said kindly.

He drew an experimental finger round the edge of his finger-bowl. Joe shuddered and clapped both hands to her ears. The sound increased in volume. Vernon smiled dreamily and ecstatically.

'One ought to be able to catch that and harness it. I wonder how it could be done. It's a lovely round sound, isn't it? Like a circle.'

Sebastian took the finger-bowl forcibly away from him, and he wandered round the room and rang various goblets experimentally.

'Nice lot of glasses in this room,' he said appreciatively.

'You're drowning sailors,' said Joe.

'Can't you be satisfied with bells and a triangle?' asked Sebastian. 'And a little gong to beat—'

'No,' said Vernon. 'I want glass . . . Let's have the Venetian and the Waterford together . . . I'm glad you have these aesthetic tastes, Sebastian. Have you got a common glass that I can smash—all the tinkling fragments. Wonderful stuff—glass!'

'Symphony of goblets,' said Joe scathingly.

'Well, why not? I suppose somebody once pulled a bit of catgut tight and found it made a squawky noise, and somebody once blew through a reed and liked it. I wonder when they first thought of making things of brass and metal—I dare say some book tells you—'

'Columbus and the egg. You and Sebastian's glass goblets. Why not a slate and a slate pencil.'

'If you've got one—'

'Isn't he too funny?' giggled Enid. And that stopped the conversation—for the time, at any rate.

Not that Vernon really minded her presence. He was far too wrapped up in his ideas to be sensitive about them. Enid and Ethel were welcome to laugh as much as they chose.

But he was slightly disturbed by the lack of harmony between Joe and Sebastian. The three of them had always been such a united trio.

'I don't think this "living your own life" stunt agrees with Joe,' said Vernon to his friend. 'She's like an angry cat most of the time. I can't think why Mother agreed. She was dead against it about six months ago. I can't imagine what made her change her mind, can you?'

A smile creased Sebastian's long yellow face.

'I could make a guess,' he said.

'What?'

'I shan't say. In the first place, I may be wrong, and in the second place I should hate to interfere with the (possibly) normal course of events.'

'That's your tortuous Russian mind.'

'I dare say.'

Vernon didn't insist. He was much too lazy to probe for reasons that weren't given him.

Day succeeded day. They danced, breakfasted, drove at incredibly fast speeds through the countryside, sat and smoked and talked in Vernon's rooms, danced again. It was a point of honour not to sleep. At five in the morning they went on the river.

Vernon's right arm ached. Enid fell to his share and she was a heavy partner. Well, it didn't matter. Uncle Sydney had seemed pleased, and he was a decent old boy. Jolly good of him to make that offer. What a pity it was that he—Vernon—was not more of a Bent and less of a Deyre.

A vague memory stirred in his mind—somebody saying, 'The Deyres, Vernon, are neither happy nor successful. They can't make good—' Who was it who had said that? A woman's voice, it had been, in a garden—and there had been curling cigarette smoke.

Sebastian's voice said: 'He's going to sleep. Wake up, you blighter! Chuck a chocolate at him, Enid.'

A chocolate whizzed past his head. Enid's voice said with a giggle:

'I can't throw straight for nuts.'

She giggled again as though she thought it very funny. Tiresome girl—always giggling. Besides, her teeth stuck out.

He heaved himself over on his side. Not usually very appreciative of the beauties of Nature, this morning he was struck by the beauty of the world. The pale gleaming river, here and there on the banks a flowering tree.

The boat drifted slowly downstream—a queer silent enchanted world. Because, he supposed, there were no human beings about. It was, when you came to think of it, an excess of human beings who spoilt the world. Always chattering and talking and giggling—and asking you what you were thinking of when all you wanted was to be let alone.

He always remembered feeling that as a kid. If they'd only let him alone. He smiled to himself as he remembered the ridiculous games he had been in the habit of inventing. Mr Green! He remembered Mr Green perfectly. And those three playmates—what were their names, now?

A funny child's world—a world of dragons and princesses and strangely concrete realities mixed up with them. There had been a story someone had told him—a ragged prince with a little green hat and a princess in a tower whose hair when she combed it was so golden that it could be seen in four kingdoms.

He raised his head a little, looked along the river bank. There was a punt tied up under some trees. Four people in it—but Vernon only saw one.

A girl in a pink evening-frock with hair like spun gold standing under a tree laden with pink blossom.

He looked and he looked.

'Vernon—' Joe kicked him correctively. 'You're not asleep, because your eyes are open. You've been spoken to four times.'

'Sorry. I was looking at that lot over there. That's rather a pretty girl, don't you think so?'

He tried to make his tone light-casual. Inside him a riotous voice was saying:

'Pretty? She's lovely. She's the most lovely girl in the world. I'm going to get to know her. I've got to know her. I'm going to marry her—'

Joe heaved herself up on her elbows, looked, uttered an exclamation.

'Why,' she exclaimed, 'I do believe—yes, I'm sure it is. It's Nell Vereker—'

Impossible! It couldn't be. Nell Vereker? Pale scraggy Nell, with her pink nose and her inappropriate starched dresses. Surely it couldn't be. Was Time capable of that kind of practical joke? If so, one couldn't be sure of anything. That long-ago Nell—and this Nell—they were two different people.

The whole world felt dream-like. Joe was saying:

'If that's Nell, I really must speak to her. Let's go across.'

And then the greetings, exclamations, surprise.

'Why, of course, Joe Waite. And Vernon! It's years ago, isn't it?'

Very soft her voice was. Her eyes smiled into his—a trifle shyly. Lovely—lovely—lovelier even than he had thought. Tongue-tied fool, why couldn't he say anything? Something brilliant, witty, arresting. How blue her eyes were with their long soft golden-brown lashes. She was like the blossom above her head—untouched— Spring-like.

A great wave of despondency swept over him. She would never marry him. Was it likely? A great clumsy tongue-tied creature such as he was. She was talking to him—Heavens, he must try and listen to what she said—answer intelligently.

'We left very soon after you did. Father gave up his job.'

An echo came into his head of past gossip.

'*Vereker got the sack. Hopelessly incompetent—it was bound to come.*'

Her voice went on—such a lovely voice. You wanted to listen to it instead of to the words.

'We live in London now. Father died five years ago.'

He said, feeling idiotic, 'Oh, I say, I'm sorry, awfully sorry!'

'I'll give you our address. You must come and see us.'

He blundered out hopes of meeting her that evening—what dance was she going to? She told him. No good there. The night after—thank goodness, they'd be at the same. He said hurriedly:

'Look here. You've got to save me a dance or two—you must—we've not seen each other for years.'

'Oh! but can I?' Her voice was doubtful.

'I'll fix it somehow. Leave it to me.'

It was over all too soon. Goodbyes were said. They were going upstream again.

Joe said in an incredibly matter-of-fact tone:

'Well, isn't that strange? Who would ever have thought that Nell Vereker would have turned out so good-looking? I wonder if she's as much of an ass as ever.'

Sacrilege! He felt oceans removed from Joe. Joe couldn't see anything at all.

Would Nell ever marry him? *Would* she? Probably she'd never look at him. All sorts of fellows must be in love with her.

He felt terribly despondent. Black misery swept over him.

He was dancing with her. Never had he imagined that he could be so happy. She was like a feather, a rose leaf in his arms. She was wearing a pink dress again—a different one. It floated out all round her.

If life could only go on like this for ever—for ever.

But, of course, life never did. In what seemed to Vernon like one second the music stopped. They were sitting together on two chairs.

He wanted to say a thousand things to her—but he didn't know how to begin. He heard himself saying foolish things about the floor and the music.

Fool—unutterable fool! In a few minutes another dance would begin. She would be swept away from him. He must make some plan—some arrangement to meet her again.

She was talking—desultory in-between-dance talk. London—the season. Horrible to think of—she was going to dances night after night—three dances a night sometimes. And here was he tied by the leg. She would marry someone—some rich, clever, amusing fellow would snap her up.

He mumbled something about being in town—she gave him their address. Mother would be so pleased to see him again. He wrote it down.

The music struck up. He said desperately:

'Nell, I say, I do call you Nell, don't I?'

154

'Why, of course.' She laughed. 'Do you remember hauling me over the palings that day we thought the rhinoceros was after us?'

And he had thought her a nuisance, he remembered. Nell! A nuisance!

She went on: 'I used to think you were wonderful then, Vernon.'

She had, had she? But she couldn't think him wonderful now. His mood drooped to despondency once more.

'I—I was an awful little rotter, I expect,' he mumbled.

Why couldn't he be intelligent and clever, and say witty things?

'Oh, you were a dear. Sebastian hasn't changed much, has he?'

Sebastian. She called him Sebastian. Well, after all, he supposed she would—since she called him Vernon. What a lucky thing it was that Sebastian cared for nobody but Joe. Sebastian with his money and his brains. Did Nell like Sebastian, he wondered?

'One would know his ears anywhere!' said Nell with a laugh.

Vernon felt comforted. He had forgotten Sebastian's ears. No girl who had noticed Sebastian's ears could go falling in love with him. Poor old Sebastian—rather rough luck to be handicapped with those ears.

He saw Nell's partner arriving. He blurted out quickly and hurriedly:

'I say, it's wonderful to have seen you again, Nell. Don't forget me, will you? I shall be turning up in town. It's—it's been awfully jolly seeing you again.' (Oh! damn, I said that before!) 'I mean—it's been simply ripping. You don't know. But you won't forget, will you?'

She had gone from him. He saw her whirling round in Barnard's arms. She couldn't like Barnard surely, could she? Barnard was such an absolute ass.

Her eyes met his over Barnard's shoulder. She smiled.

He was in heaven again. She liked him—he knew she liked him. She had smiled . . .

May week was over. Vernon was sitting at a table writing.

'Dear Uncle Sydney,—I've thought over your offer, and I'd like to come into Bent's if you still want me. I'm afraid I shall be rather useless, but I will try all I know how. I still think it's most awfully good of you.'

He paused. Sebastian was walking up and down restlessly. His pacing disturbed Vernon.

'For goodness' sake, sit down,' he said irritably. 'What's the matter with you?'

'Nothing.'

Sebastian sat down with unusual mildness. He filled and lighted a pipe. From behind a sheltering haze of smoke, he spoke.

'I say, Vernon. I asked Joe to marry me that last night. She turned me down.'

'Oh! rough luck!' said Vernon, trying to bring his mind back and be sympathetic. 'Perhaps she'll change her mind,' he said vaguely. 'They say girls do.'

'It's this damned money,' said Sebastian angrily.

'What damned money?'

'Mine. Joe always said she would marry me when we were kids together. She likes me—I'm sure she does. And now—everything I say or do always seems to be wrong. If I were only persecuted, or looked down on, or socially undesirable, I believe she'd marry me like a shot. But she's always got to be on the losing side. It's a ripping quality in a way; but you can carry it to a pitch where it's damned illogical. Joe is illogical.'

'H'm,' said Vernon vaguely.

He was selfishly intent on his own affairs. It seemed to him curious that Sebastian should be so keen on marrying Joe. There were lots of other girls who would suit him just as well. He re-read his letter and added another sentence.

'*I will work like a dog.*'

CHAPTER 4

'We want another man,' said Mrs Vereker.

Her eyebrows, slightly enhanced by art, drew together in a straight line as she frowned.

'It's too annoying young Wetherill failing us,' she added.

Nell nodded apathetically. She was sitting on the arm of a chair, not yet dressed. Her golden hair hung in a stream over the pale-pink kimono she was wearing. She looked very lovely and very young and defenceless.

Mrs Vereker, sitting at her inlaid desk, frowned still more and bit the end of her penholder thoughtfully. The hardness that had always been noticeable was now accentuated and, as it were, crystallized. This was a woman who had battled steadily and unceasingly through life and was now engaged in a supreme struggle. She lived in a house the rent of which she could not afford to pay, and she dressed her daughter in clothes she could not afford to buy. She got things on credit, not, like some others, by cajolery but by sheer driving power. She never appealed to her creditors, she browbeat them.

And the result was that Nell went everywhere and did

everything that other girls did, and was better dressed while doing so.

'Mademoiselle is lovely,' said the dressmakers, and their eyes would meet Mrs Vereker's in a glance of understanding.

A girl so beautiful, so well turned out, would marry probably in her first season, certainly in her second—and then—a rich harvest would be reaped. They were used to taking risks of this kind. Mademoiselle was lovely, Madame, her mother, was a woman of the world and a woman, they could see, who was accustomed to success in her undertakings. She would assuredly see to it that her daughter made a good match and did not marry a nobody.

Nobody but Mrs Vereker herself knew the difficulties, the setbacks, the galling defeats of the campaign she had undertaken.

'There is young Earnescliff,' she said thoughtfully. 'But he is really too much of an outsider, and not even money to recommend him.'

Nell looked at her pink polished nails.

'What about Vernon Deyre?' she suggested. 'He wrote he was coming up to town this weekend.'

'He would do,' said Mrs Vereker. She looked sharply at her daughter. 'Nell—you're not—you're not allowing yourself to become foolish about that young man, are you? We seem to have seen a great deal of him lately.'

'He dances well,' said Nell. 'And he's frightfully useful.'

'Yes,' said Mrs Vereker. 'Yes. It's a pity.'

'What's a pity?'

'That he hasn't got a few more of this world's goods. He'll have to marry money if he's ever going to be able to keep up Abbots Puissants. It's mortgaged, you know. I found that out. Of course, when his mother dies . . . But she's one of those large healthy women who go on living till they're eighty or ninety. And besides, she may marry again. No, Vernon Deyre is hopeless considered as a *parti*. He's very much in love with you, too, poor boy.'

'Do you think so?' said Nell in a low voice.

'Anyone can see it. It sticks out all over him—it always does with boys of that age. Well, they've got to go through calf love, I suppose. But no foolishness on your part, Nell.'

'Oh, Mother, he's only a boy—a very nice boy, but a boy.'

'He's a good-looking boy,' said her mother drily. 'I'm only warning you. Being in love is a painful process when you can't have the man you want. And worse—'

She stopped. Nell knew well enough how her thoughts ran on. Captain Vereker had once been a handsome, blue-eyed, impecunious young subaltern. Her mother had been guilty of the folly of marrying him for love. She had lived to rue the day bitterly. A weak man, a failure, a drunkard. Disillusionment enough there in all conscience.

'Someone devoted is always useful,' said Mrs Vereker, reverting to her utilitarian standpoint. 'He mustn't, of course, spoil your chances with other men. But you're too wise to let him monopolize you to that extent. Yes, write and ask him to drive down to Ranelagh and dine with us there on Sunday next.'

Nell nodded. She got up and went to her own room, flung off the trailing kimono and started dressing. With a stiff brush, she brushed out the long golden hair, before coiling it round her small lovely head.

The window was open. A sooty London sparrow chirped and sang with the arrogance of his kind.

Something caught at Nell's heart. Oh, why was everything so—so—

So what? She didn't know—couldn't put into words, the feeling that surged over her. Why couldn't things be nice instead of nasty? It would be just as easy for God.

Nell never thought much about God, but she knew, of course, that he was there. Perhaps, somehow or other, God would make everything come right for her.

There was something child-like about Nell Vereker on that summer's morning in London.

Vernon was in the seventh heaven. He had had the luck to meet Nell in the park that morning, and now there was a whole glorious rapturous evening! So happy was he that he almost felt affectionate towards Mrs Vereker.

Instead of saying to himself: 'That woman is a gorgon!' as he usually did, he found himself thinking, 'She may not be so bad after all. Anyhow, she's very fond of Nell.'

At dinner he studied the other members of the party. There was an inferior girl dressed in green, a being not to be mentioned in the same breath with Nell, and there was a tall, dark man, a Major Somebody whose evening dress was very faultless, and who talked about India a lot. An insufferably conceited being. Vernon hated him. Boasting and swaggering, and showing off! A cold hand closed round his heart. Nell would marry this blighter and go away to India. He knew it, he simply knew it. He refused a course that was handed to him and gave the girl in green a hard time, so monosyllabic were his responses to her efforts.

The other man was older—very old to Vernon. A rather wooden figure, very upright. Grey hair, blue eyes, a square determined face. It turned out that he was an American though no one would have known it, for he had no trace of accent.

He spoke stiffly and a little punctiliously. He sounded rich. A very suitable companion for Mrs Vereker, Vernon thought him. She might even marry him, and then, perhaps, she would cease worrying Nell and making her lead this insane life.

Mr Chetwynd seemed to admire Nell a good deal, which was only natural, and he paid her one or two rather old-fashioned compliments. He sat between her and her mother.

'You must bring Miss Nell to Dinard this summer, Mrs Vereker,' he said. 'You really must. Quite a party of us going. Wonderful place.'

'It sounds delightful, Mr Chetwynd, but I don't know whether we can manage it. We seem to have promised so many people for visits and one thing and another—'

'I know you're always so much in request that it's hard to get hold of you. I hope your daughter's not listening when I congratulate you on being the mother of the beauty of the season.'

'And I said to the syce—'

This from Major Dacre.

All the Deyres had been soldiers. Why wasn't he a soldier,

thought Vernon, instead of being in business in Birmingham? Then he laughed to himself. Absurd to be so jealous. What could be worse than to be a penniless subaltern—there would be no hope of Nell then.

Americans were rather long-winded—he was getting tired of the sound of Chetwynd's voice. If only dinner could come to an end! If he and Nell could wander together under the trees.

Wandering with Nell wasn't easy. He was foiled by Mrs Vereker. She asked him questions about his mother and Joe, kept him by her side. He was no match for her in tactics. He had to stay there, answer, pretend he liked it.

There was only one crumb of comfort. Nell was walking with the old boy—not with Dacre.

Suddenly they encountered friends. Everyone stood talking. It was his chance. He found his way to Nell's side.

'Come with me—do. Quickly—now.'

He had done it! He had got her away from the others. He was hurrying so that she had almost to run to keep up with him, but she didn't say anything—didn't protest or make a joke about it.

The voices sounded from farther and farther away. He could hear other sounds now—the hurried unevenness of Nell's breathing. Was that because they had walked so fast—he didn't somehow think it was.

He slowed up. They were alone now—alone in the world. They couldn't have been more alone, he felt, on a desert island.

He must say something—something ordinary and commonplace. Otherwise she might think of going back to the others—and he couldn't bear that. Lucky she didn't know how his heart was beating—in great throbs, right up in his throat somewhere.

He said abruptly:

'I've gone into my uncle's business, you know.'

'Yes, I know. Do you like it?'

A cool, sweet voice. No trace of agitation in it now.

'I don't like it much. I expect I shall get to, though.'

'I suppose it will be more interesting when you understand it more.'

'I don't see how it ever could be. It's making the shanks of buttons, you know.'

'Oh, I see—no, that doesn't sound very thrilling.'

There was a pause, and then she said, very softly:

'Do you hate it very much, Vernon?'

'I'm afraid I do.'

'I'm awfully sorry. I—I understand just how you feel.'

If someone understood, it made the whole world different. Adorable Nell! He said unsteadily:

'I say, that's—that's most awfully sweet of you.'

Another pause—one of those pauses that are heavy with the weight of latent emotion. Nell seemed to take fright. She said rather hurriedly:

'Weren't you—I mean, I thought you were taking up music?'

'I was. I—I gave that up.'

'But why? Isn't that the most awful pity?'

'It's the thing I wanted to do most in the world. But it's no good. I've got to make some money somehow—' Should he tell her? Was this the moment? No, he daren't—he simply daren't. He blundered on quickly. 'You see, Abbots Puissants—you remember Abbots Puissants?'

'Of course. Why, Vernon, we were talking about it the other day.'

'Sorry. I'm stupid tonight. Well, you see I want awfully to live there again some day.'

'I think you're wonderful.'

'Wonderful?'

'Yes. To give up everything you cared about and set to like you are doing. It's splendid!'

'It's ripping of you to say that. It makes—oh! you don't know what a difference it makes.'

'Does it?' said Nell in a very low voice. 'I'm glad.'

She thought to herself: 'I ought to go back. Oh! I ought to go back. Mother will be very angry about this. What am I doing? I ought to go back and listen to George Chetwynd, but he's so *dull*. Oh, God, don't let Mother be very cross.'

And she walked on by Vernon's side. She felt out of breath—strange—what was the matter with her? If only Vernon would say something. What was he thinking about?

She said in a would-be detached voice:

'How's Joe?'

'Very artistic at present. I thought perhaps you might have been seeing something of each other as you were both in town?'

'I've seen her once, I think. That's all.' She paused and then added, rather diffidently: 'I don't think Joe likes me.'

'Nonsense. Of course she does.'

'No, she thinks I'm frivolous, that I only care for social things—dances and parties.'

'Nobody who really knew you could think that.'

'I don't know. I feel awfully—well, stupid sometimes.'

'You? Stupid?'

That warm incredulous voice. Darling Vernon. He did think her nice, then. Her mother had been right.

They came to a little bridge across some water. They walked on to it, stood there, side by side, leaning over, looking down on the water below.

Vernon said in a choked kind of voice:

'It's jolly here.'

'Yes.'

It was coming—it was coming. She couldn't have defined what she meant, but that was the feeling. The world standing still, gathering itself for a leap and a spring.

'Nell—'

Why did her knees feel so shaky? Why did her voice sound so far away?

'Yes.'

Was that queer little 'Yes' hers?

'Oh, Nell—'

He had got to tell her. He must.

'I love you so—I do love you so—'

'Do you?'

It couldn't be her speaking? What an idiotic thing to say! 'Do you?' Her voice sounded stiff and unnatural.

His hand found hers. His hand was hot—hers was cold—they both shook.

'Could you—do you—do you think you could ever manage to love me?'

She answered, hardly knowing what she was saying. 'I don't know.'

They continued to stand there like dazed children, hand in hand, lost in a kind of rapture that was almost fear.

Something must happen soon. They didn't know what.

Out of the darkness two figures appeared—a hoarse laugh, a girl's giggle.

'So here you are! What a romantic spot!'

The green girl and that ass Dacre. Nell said something, a saucy something—said it with the utmost self-possession—women were wonderful. She moved out into the moonlight—calm, detached, at ease. They all walked together, talking, chaffing each other. They found George Chetwynd with Mrs Vereker on the lawn. He looked very glum, Vernon thought.

Mrs Vereker was distinctly nasty to him. Her manner when bidding him goodbye was quite offensive.

He didn't care. All he wanted was to get away and lose himself in an orgy of remembrance.

He'd told her—he'd told her. He'd asked her whether she loved him—yes, he had dared to do that, and instead of laughing at him, she had said, '*I don't know.*'

But that meant—that meant—Oh! it was incredible! Nell, fairy-like Nell, so wonderful, so inaccessible. She loved him, or at least, she was willing to love him.

He wanted to walk on and on through the night. Instead he had to catch the midnight train to Birmingham. Damn! If he could only have walked—walked till morning.

With a little green hat and a magic flute, like the prince in that tale!

Suddenly he saw the whole thing in music—the high tower and the princess's cascade of golden hair—and the eerie haunting tune of the prince's pipe which called the princess out from her tower.

Insensibly, this music was more in accordance with recognized canons than Vernon's original conception had been. It was adapted to the limits of known dimensions, though at the same time, the inner vision remained unaltered.

He heard the music of the tower—the round globular music of the princess's jewels—and the gay, wild, lawless strain of the vagabond prince, 'Come out, my love, come out—'

He walked through the bare drab streets of London as through an enchanted world. The black mass of Paddington station loomed up before him.

In the train he didn't sleep. Instead, on the back of an envelope, he wrote microscopic notes. 'Trumpets', 'French Horns', 'Cor Anglais', and alongside them lines and curves that to his understanding represented what he heard.

He was happy . . .

'I'm ashamed of you. What can you be thinking of?'

Mrs Vereker was very angry. Nell stood before her, dumb and lovely.

Her mother uttered a few more virulent and incisive words, then turned and left the room without saying good night.

Ten minutes later, as Mrs Vereker completed her preparations for the night, she suddenly laughed to herself—a grim chuckle.

'I needn't have been so angry with the child. As a matter of fact, it will do George Chetwynd good. Wake him up. He needed prodding.'

She turned out her light and slept, satisfied.

Nell lay awake. Again and again she went over the evening, trying to recapture each feeling, each word that had been spoken.

What had Vernon said? What had she answered? Queer that she couldn't remember.

He had asked her whether she loved him—what had she said to that? She couldn't tell. But in the darkness the scene rose up before her eyes—she felt her hand in Vernon's, heard his voice, husky and ill-assured. She shut her eyes, lost in a hazy delicious dream.

Life was so lovely—so lovely . . .

CHAPTER 5

'Then you can't love me!'

'Oh, but, Vernon, I do. If you'd only try and understand.'

They faced each other desperately, bewildered by this sudden rift between them—by the queer unexpected vagaries of life. One minute they had been so near that each thought even had seemed to be shared by the other—now they were poles apart, angry and hurt by the other's lack of comprehension.

Nell turned away with a little gesture of despair and sank down on a chair.

Why was it all like this? Why couldn't things stay as they ought to be, as you had felt they were going to be for ever? That evening at Ranelagh—and the night afterwards when she had lain awake, wrapped in a happy dream. Enough that night just to know that she was loved. Why, even her mother's scathing words had failed to upset her. They had come from so far away. They couldn't penetrate that shining web of misty dream.

She had woken up happy the next morning. Her mother had been pleasant, had said nothing more. Wrapped in her secret thoughts Nell had gone through the day doing all the usual things, chattering with friends, walking in the park, lunching, teaing, dancing. Nobody, she was sure, could have noticed anything different, and yet all the time she herself was conscious of that one deep strand underneath everything else. Just for a minute, sometimes, she would lose the thread of what she was saying, she would remember, 'Oh, Nell, I do love you so—' The moonlight on the dark water. His hand in hers . . . A little shiver and she would recall herself hastily, chatter, laugh. Oh, how happy one could be—how happy she had been.

Then she had wondered if, perhaps, he would write. She watched for the post, her heart giving little throbs whenever the postman knocked. It came the second day. She hid it beneath a pile of others, kept it till she went up to bed, then opened it with a beating heart.

'Oh, Nell!—oh, darling Nell! Did you really mean it? I've written three letters to you and torn them up. I'm so afraid of saying something that might make you angry. Because perhaps you didn't mean it after all. But you did, didn't you? You are so lovely, Nell, and I do love you so dreadfully. I'm always thinking about you, the whole time. I make awful mistakes at the office just because I'm thinking about you. But—oh, Nell, I will work so hard. I want so dreadfully to see you. When can I come up to town? I must see you. Darling, darling Nell, I want to say such lots and lots of things, and I can't in a letter, and, anyway, perhaps I'm boring you.

Write and tell me when I can see you. Very soon, please.
I shall go mad if I can't see you very soon.

 'Yours ever,
  'Vernon.'

She read it again and again, put it under her pillow when she slept, read it again the next morning. She was so happy, so dreadfully happy. It was not till the day after that she wrote to him. When the pen was in her hand she felt stiff and awkward. She didn't know what to say.

Dear Vernon—
Was that silly? Ought she to say Dearest Vernon? Oh, no, she couldn't—she couldn't.

'Dear Vernon,—Thank you for your letter.'

A long pause. She bit the stem of her penholder and gazed in an agonized way at the wall in front of her.

'A party of us are going to the Howards' dance on
Friday. Will you dine here first and come with us? Eight o'clock.'

A longer pause. She'd got to say something—she wanted to say something. She bent over, and wrote hastily.

'I want to see you too—very much. Yours, Nell.'

He wrote back:

'Dear Nell,—I'd love to come on Friday. Thanks ever so much. Yours,—Vernon.'

A little panic swept over her when she read it. Had she offended him? Did he think she ought to have said more in her letter? Happiness fled. She lay awake, miserable, uncertain, hating herself in case it had been her fault.

Then had come Friday night. The moment she saw him she knew it was all right. Their eyes met across the room. The world changed back to radiant happiness again.

They did not sit near each other at dinner. It was not till the third dance at the Howards' that they were able really to speak to each other. They moved round the crowded room, gyrating in a deep-toned, sentimental waltz. He whispered:

'I haven't asked for too many dances, have I?'

'No.'

Queer how absolutely tongue-tied it made her feel being with Vernon. He held her just a minute longer when the music stopped. His fingers tightened over hers. She looked at him and smiled. They were both deliriously happy. In a few minutes he was dancing with another girl, talking airily in her ear, Nell was dancing with George Chetwynd. Once or twice her eyes met Vernon's and they both smiled very faintly. Their secret was so wonderful.

At his next dance with her, his mood had changed.

'Nell, darling, isn't there anywhere where I can talk to you? I've got such heaps of things I want to say. What a ridiculous house this is—nowhere to go.'

They tried the stairs, mounting higher and higher as you

173

do in London houses. Still, it seemed impossible to get away from people. Then they saw a tiny iron ladder that led to the roof.

'Nell, let's get up there? Could you? Would it ruin your dress?'

'I don't care about my dress.'

Vernon went up first, unbolted the trap-door, climbed out and knelt down to help Nell. She climbed through safely.

They were alone, looking down on London. Insensibly they drew nearer to each other. Her hand found its way into his.

'Nell—darling . . .'

'Vernon . . .'

Her voice could only whisper.

'It *is* true? You do love me?'

'I do love you.'

'It's too wonderful to be true. Oh, Nell, I do so want to kiss you.'

She turned her face to his. They kissed, rather shakily and timidly.

'Your face is so soft and lovely,' murmured Vernon.

Oblivious of dirt and smuts they sat down on a little ledge. His arms went round her, held her. She turned her face to his kisses.

'I do love you so, Nell—I love you so much that I'm almost afraid to touch you.'

She didn't understand that—it seemed queer. She drew a little closer to him. The magic of the night was made complete by their kisses.

*

They woke from a happy dream. 'Oh, Vernon, I believe we've been here *ages*!'

Conscience-stricken they hurried to the trap-door. On the landing below, Vernon surveyed Nell anxiously.

'I'm afraid you've been sitting on an awful lot of smuts, Nell.'

'Oh, have I? How awful.'

'It's my fault, darling. But, oh, Nell! it was worth it, wasn't it?'

She smiled up at him, gently, happily.

'It was worth it,' she said softly.

As they went down the stairs she said with a little laugh:

'What about all the things you wanted to say? Lots and lots of them.'

They both laughed in perfect understanding. They re-entered the dancing room rather sheepishly. They had missed six dances.

A lovely evening. Nell had gone to sleep and dreamed of more kisses.

And then, this morning, Saturday, Vernon had rung up.

'I want to talk to you. Can I come round?'

'Oh, Vernon, dear, you can't. I'm going out now to meet people. I can't get out of it.'

'Why not?'

'I mean I wouldn't know what to say to Mother.'

'You haven't told her anything?'

'Oh, *no*!'

The vehemence of that 'Oh, *no*!' had checked Vernon. He thought: 'Poor little darling. Of course she hasn't.' He said: 'Hadn't I better do that? I'll come round now.'

'Oh, no, Vernon, not until we've talked.'

'Well, when can we talk?'

'I don't know. I'm lunching with people and going to a matinée, and theatreing again tonight. If you'd only told me you were going to be up this weekend I'd have arranged something.'

'What about tomorrow?'

'Well, there's church—'

'That'll do! Don't go to church. Say you've got a head-ache or something. I'll come round. We can talk then, and when your mother comes back from church I can have it out with her.'

'Oh, Vernon, I don't think I can—'

'Yes, you can. I'm going to ring off now before you can make any more excuses. At eleven tomorrow.'

He rang off. He hadn't even told Nell where he was staying. She admired him for this masculine decision even while it caused her anxiety. She was afraid he was going to spoil everything.

And now, here they were, in the middle of a heated discussion. Nell had begged him to say nothing to her mother.

'It will spoil everything. We shan't be allowed to.'

'Shan't be allowed to what?'

'See each other or anything.'

'But, Nell, darling, I want to marry you. And you want to marry me, don't you? I want to marry you awfully soon.'

She had her first feeling of exasperation then. Couldn't he see things as they were? He was talking like a mere boy.

176

'But, Vernon, we haven't any money.'

'I know. But I'm going to work awfully hard. You won't mind being poor, will you, Nell?'

She said no since it was expected of her, but she was conscious that she did not say it whole-heartedly. It was dreadful being poor. Vernon didn't know how dreadful it was. She suddenly felt years and years older and more experienced than he. He was talking like a romantic boy—he didn't know what things were really like.

'Oh, Vernon, can't we just go on as we are? We're so happy now.'

'Of course we're happy; but we could be happier still. I want to be really engaged to you—I want everyone to know that you belong to me.'

'I don't see that that makes any difference.'

'I suppose it doesn't. But I want to have a right to see you, instead of being miserable about you going round with chaps like that ass, Dacre.'

'Oh, Vernon, you're not jealous?'

'I know I oughtn't to be. But you don't really know how lovely you are, Nell! Everyone must be in love with you. I believe even that solemn old American fellow is.'

Nell changed colour slightly.

'Well, I think you'll spoil everything,' she murmured.

'You think your mother will be horrid to you about it? I'm awfully sorry. I'll tell her it's all my fault. And after all, she's got to know. I expect she'll be disappointed because she probably wanted you to marry someone rich. That's quite natural. But it doesn't really make you happy being rich, does it?'

Nell said suddenly in a hard, desperate little voice:

'You talk like that, but what do you know about being poor?'

Vernon was astonished.

'But I am poor.'

'No, you're not. You've been to schools and universities and in the holidays you've lived with your mother who's rich. You don't know anything at all about it. You don't know—'

She stopped in despair. She wasn't clever with words. How could she paint the picture she knew so well? The shifts, the struggles, the evasions, the desperate fight to keep up appearances. The ease with which friends dropped you if you 'couldn't keep up with things', the slights, the snubs—worse—the galling patronage! In Captain Vereker's lifetime, and since his death, it had always been the same. You could, of course, live in a cottage in the country and never see anyone, never go to dances like other girls, never have pretty clothes, live within your income and rot away slowly! Either way was pretty beastly. It was so unfair—one ought to have money. And always marriage lay ahead of you clearly designated as the way of escape. No more striving and snubs, and subterfuges.

You didn't think of it as marrying for money. Nell, with the boundless optimism of youth, had always pictured herself falling in love with a nice, rich man. And now she had fallen in love with Vernon Deyre. Her thoughts hadn't gone as far as marriage. She was just happy—wonderfully happy.

She almost hated Vernon for dragging her down from

the clouds. And she resented his easy taking for granted of her readiness to face poverty for his sake. If he'd put it differently. If he'd said: 'I oughtn't to ask you; but do you think you *could* for my sake?' Something like that.

So that she could feel that her sacrifice was being appreciated. For after all, it *was* a sacrifice! She didn't want to be poor—she hated the idea of being poor. She was afraid of it. Vernon's contemptuous unworldly attitude infuriated her. It was so easy not to care about money when you'd never felt the lack of it. And Vernon hadn't— he wasn't aware of the fact but, there it was. He'd lived softly and comfortably, and well.

He said now in an astonished kind of way:

'Oh, Nell, surely you wouldn't mind being poor?'

'I've been poor, I tell you. I know what it's like.'

She felt years and years older than Vernon. He was a child—a baby! What did he know of the difficulties of getting credit? Of the money that she and her mother already owed? She felt suddenly terribly lonely and miserable. What was the good of men? They said wonderful things to you, they loved you, but did they ever try to understand? Vernon wasn't trying now. He was just saying condemnatory things, showing her how she had fallen in his estimation.

'If you say that you can't love me.'

She replied helplessly:

'You don't understand—'

They gazed at each other hopelessly. What had happened? Why were things like this between them?

'You don't love me,' repeated Vernon angrily.

'Oh, Vernon, I do, I do—'

Suddenly, like an enchantment, their love swept over them again. They clung together, kissing. They felt that age-long lovers' delusion that everything *must* come right because they loved. It was Vernon's victory. He still insisted on telling Mrs Vereker. Nell opposed him no longer. His arms round her, his lips on hers. She couldn't go on arguing. Better to give oneself up to the joy of being loved, to say: 'Yes—yes, darling, if you like—anything you like—'

Yet, almost unknown to herself, under her love was a faint resentment . . .

Mrs Vereker was a clever woman. She was taken by surprise but she did not show it, and she adopted a different line from any that Vernon had pictured her taking. She was faintly derisively amused.

'So you children think you are in love with one another? Well, well!'

She listened to Vernon with such an expression of kindly irony that despite himself his tongue flustered and tripped.

She gave a faint sigh as he subsided into silence.

'What it is to be young! I feel quite envious. Now, my dear boy, just listen to me. I'm not going to forbid the banns or do anything melodramatic. If Nell really wants to marry you she shall. I don't say I won't be very disappointed if she does. She's my only child. I naturally hope that she will marry someone who can give her the best of everything, and surround her with every luxury and comfort. That, I think, is only natural.'

Vernon was forced to agree. Mrs Vereker's reasonableness was extremely disconcerting, being so unexpected.

'But as I say, I'm not going to forbid the banns. What I do stipulate is that Nell should be thoroughly sure that she really knows her own mind. You agree to that, I'm sure?'

Vernon agreed to that with an uneasy feeling of being entangled in a mesh from which he was presently not going to be able to escape.

'Nell is very young. This is her first season. I want her to have every chance of being sure that she does like you better than any other man. If you agree between yourselves that you are engaged that is one thing—a public announcement of your engagement is another. I could not agree to that. Any understanding between yourselves must be kept quite secret. I think you will see that that is only fair. Nell must be given every chance to change her mind if she wants to.'

'She doesn't want to!'

'Then there is certainly no reason for objecting. As a gentleman you can hardly act otherwise. If you agree to these stipulations, I will put no obstacle in the way of your seeing Nell.'

'But, Mrs Vereker, I want to marry Nell quite soon.'

'And what exactly do you propose to marry on?'

Vernon told her the salary he was getting from his uncle and explained the position in regard to Abbots Puissants.

When he had finished she spoke. She gave a brief and succinct résumé of house rent, servants' wages, the cost of clothes, alluded delicately to possible perambulators, and then contrasted the picture with Nell's present position.

Vernon was like the Queen of Sheba—no spirit was left in him. He was beaten by the relentless logic of facts. A terrible woman, Nell's mother—implacable. But he saw her point. He and Nell would have to wait. He must, as Mrs Vereker said, give her every chance of changing her mind. Not that she would, bless her lovely heart.

He essayed one last venture.

'My uncle might increase my salary. He has spoken to me several times on the advantages of early marriages. He seems very keen on the subject.'

'Oh!' Mrs Vereker was thoughtful for a minute or two. 'Has he any daughters of his own?'

'Yes, five, and the two eldest are married already.'

Mrs Vereker smiled. A simple boy. He had quite misunderstood the point of her question. Still, she had found out what she wanted to know.

'We'll leave it like that, then,' she said.

A clever woman!

Vernon left the house in a restless mood. He wanted badly to talk to someone sympathetic. He thought of Joe, then shook his head. He and Joe had almost quarrelled about Nell. Joe despised Nell as what she called a 'regular empty-headed society girl'. She was unfair and prejudiced. As a passport to Joe's favour, you had to have short hair, wear art smocks and live in Chelsea.

Sebastian, on the whole, was the best person. Sebastian was always willing to see your point of view, and he was occasionally unusually useful with his matter-of-fact common-sense point of view. A very sound fellow, Sebastian.

Rich, too. How queer things were! If only he had Sebastian's money, he could probably marry Nell tomorrow. Yet, with all that money, Sebastian couldn't get hold of the girl he wanted. Rather a pity. He wished Joe would marry Sebastian instead of some rotter or other who called himself artistic.

Sebastian, alas, was not at home. Vernon was entertained by Mrs Levinne. Strangely enough, he found a kind of comfort in her bulky presence. Funny, fat, old Mrs Levinne with her jet and her diamonds and her greasy black hair, managed to be more understanding than his own mother.

'You mustn't be unhappy, my dear,' she said. 'I can see you are. It's some girl, I suppose? Ah well, well, Sebastian is just the same about Joe. I tell him he must be patient. Joe's just kicking up her heels at present. She'll settle down soon and begin to find out what it is she really does want.'

'It would be awfully jolly if she married Sebastian. I wish she would. It would keep us all together.'

'Yes—I'm very fond of Joe myself. Not that I think she's really the wife for Sebastian—they'd be too far away to understand each other. I'm old-fashioned, my dear. I'd like my boy to marry one of our own people. It always works out best. The same interests, and the same instincts, and Jewish women are good mothers. Well, well, it may come, if Joe is really in earnest about not marrying him. And the same thing with you, Vernon. There are worse things than marrying a cousin.'

'Me? Marry Joe?'

Vernon stared at her in utter astonishment. Mrs Levinne laughed, a fat, good-natured chuckle that shook her various chins.

'Joe? No, indeed. It's your cousin Enid I'm talking about. That's the idea at Birmingham, isn't it?'

'Oh, no—at least—I'm sure it isn't.'

Mrs Levinne laughed again.

'I can see that you at any rate have never thought of it till this minute. But it would be a wise plan, you know— that is, if the other girl won't have you. Keeps the money in the family.'

Vernon went away with his brain tingling. All sorts of things fell into line. Uncle Sydney's chaff and hints. The way Enid was always being thrust at him. That, of course, was what Mrs Vereker had been hinting at. They wanted him to marry Enid! Enid!

Another memory came back to him. His mother and some old friend of hers whispering together. Something about first cousins. A sudden idea occurred to him. That was why Joe had been allowed to go to London. His mother had thought that he and Joe might—

He gave a sudden shout of laughter. He and Joe! It showed how little his mother had ever understood. He could never, under any circumstances, imagine himself falling in love with Joe. They were exactly like brother and sister and always would be. They had the same sympathies, the same sharp divergences and differences of opinion. They were cast in the same mould, devoid of any glamour and romance for each other.

Enid! So this was what Uncle Sydney was after. Poor old Uncle Sydney, doomed to disappointment—but he shouldn't have been such an ass.

Perhaps, though, he was jumping to conclusions. Perhaps it wasn't Uncle Sydney—only his mother. Women were always marrying you to someone in their minds. Anyway, Uncle Sydney would soon know the truth.

The interview between Vernon and his uncle wasn't very satisfactory. Uncle Sydney was both annoyed and upset though he tried to conceal the fact from Vernon. He was uncertain at first which line to take, and made one or two vague sallies in different directions.

'Nonsense, all nonsense, much too young to marry. Packet of nonsense.'

Vernon reminded his uncle of his own words.

'Pooh—I didn't mean this kind of marriage. Society girl—I know what they are.'

Vernon broke out hotly.

'Sorry, my boy, I didn't mean to hurt your feelings. But that kind of girl wants to marry money. You'll be no use to her for many years to come.'

'I thought perhaps—'

Vernon paused. He felt ashamed, uncomfortable.

'That I'd set you up with a large income, hey? Is that what the young lady suggested? Now, I put it to you, my boy, would that be business? No, I see that you know it isn't.'

'I don't feel that I'm even worth what you give me, Uncle Sydney.'

'Pooh, pooh, I wasn't saying that. You're doing very well for a start. I'm sorry about this affair—it will upset you. My advice to you is, give the whole thing up. Much the best thing to do.'

'I can't do that, Uncle Sydney.'

'Well, it's not my business. By the way, have you talked it over with your mother? No? Well, you have a good talk with her. See if she doesn't say the same as I do. I bet she will. And remember the old saying, a boy's best friend is his mother—hey?'

Why did Uncle Sydney say such idiotic things? He always had as far back as Vernon could remember. And yet he was a shrewd and clever business man.

Well, there was nothing for it. He must buckle to— and wait. The first misty enchantment of love was wearing off. It could be hell as well as heaven. He wanted Nell so badly—so badly.

He wrote to her:–

'Darling,—There is nothing for it. We must be patient and wait. At any rate we'll see each other often. Your mother was really very decent about it—much more so than I thought she'd be. I do quite see the force of all she said. It's only fair that you should be free to see if you like anyone better than me. But you won't, will you, darling? I know you won't. We're going to love each other for ever and ever. And it won't matter how poor we are . . . the tiniest place with you . . .'

CHAPTER 6

Nell was relieved by her mother's attitude. She had feared recriminations, reproaches. Insensibly she always shrank from harsh words or any kind of scene. Sometimes she thought to herself bitterly, 'I'm a coward. I can't stand up to things.'

She was definitely afraid of her mother. She had been dominated by her always from the first moment she could remember. Mrs Vereker had the hard, imperious character which can rule most weaker natures with whom it comes in contact. And Nell was the more easily subdued because she understood well enough that her mother loved her and that it was because of that love that she was so determined that Nell should have the happiness out of life that she herself had failed to get.

So Nell was immeasurably relieved when her mother uttered no reproaches, merely observed:

'If you're determined to be foolish, well, there it is. Most girls have some little love affair or other which comes to nothing in the end. I haven't much patience with this sentimental nonsense myself. The boy can't possibly afford

Agatha Christie

to marry for years to come and you'll only make yourself very unhappy. But you must please yourself.'

In spite of herself, Nell was influenced by this contemptuous attitude. She hoped against hope that Vernon's uncle might perhaps do something. Vernon's letter dashed her hopes.

They must wait—and perhaps wait a very long time.

In the meantime Mrs Vereker had her own methods. One day she asked Nell to go and see an old friend—a girl who had married some few years ago. Amelie King had been a brilliant dashing creature whom Nell, as a schoolgirl, had admired enviously. She might have made a very good marriage, but to everyone's surprise she had married a struggling young man and had disappeared from her own particular gay world.

'It seems unkind to drop old friends,' said Mrs Vereker. 'I'm sure Amelie would be pleased if you went to see her, and you're not doing anything this afternoon.'

So Nell went off obediently to call on Mrs Horton at 35 Glenster Gardens, Ealing.

It was a hot day. Nell took the District Railway and inquired her way from Ealing Broadway station when she got there.

Glenster Gardens proved to be about a mile from the station—a long depressing road of little houses, all exactly alike. The door of No. 35 was opened by a frowsy-looking maid with a dirty apron and Nell was shown into a small

188

drawing-room. There were one or two nice old pieces of furniture in it and the cretonnes and curtains were of an attractive pattern though very faded, but the place was very untidy and littered with children's toys and odd bits of mending. A child's fretful wail rose from somewhere in the house as the door opened and Amelie came in.

'Nell, why how nice of you! I haven't seen you for years.'

Nell had quite a shock on seeing her. Could this be the well turned out attractive Amelie? Her figure had got sloppy, her blouse was shapeless and evidently home-made, and her face was tired and worried with all the old dash and sparkle gone out of it.

She sat down and they talked. Presently Nell was taken to see the two children, a boy and a girl, the younger a baby in a cot.

'I ought to take them out now,' said Amelie, 'but really I'm too tired this afternoon. You don't know how tired one can get pushing a perambulator all the way up from the shops as I did this morning.'

The boy was an attractive child, the baby girl looked sickly and peevish.

'It's partly her teeth,' said Amelie. 'And then her digestion is weak, the doctor says. I do wish she wouldn't cry so at night. It's annoying for Jack, who needs his sleep after working all day.'

'You don't have a nurse?'

'Can't afford it, my dear. We have the half-wit—that's what we call the girl who opened the door to you. She's a complete idiot, but she comes cheap and she really will set to and do some work which is more than most of them will do. A general servant hates coming anywhere where there are children.'

She called out: 'Mary, bring some tea,' and led the way back to the drawing-room.

'Oh, dear Nell, do you know I almost wish you hadn't come to see me. You look so smart and cool—you remind me of all the fun one used to have in the old days. Tennis and dancing and golf and parties.'

Nell said timidly: 'But you're happy . . .'

'Oh, of course. I'm only enjoying a grumble. Jack's a dear, and then there are the children, only sometimes—well, one is really too tired to care for anyone or anything. I feel I'd sell my nearest and dearest for a tiled bathroom and bath salts and a maid to brush my hair and lovely silken garments to slip into. And then you hear some rich idiot holding forth on how money doesn't bring happiness. Fools!'

She laughed.

'Tell me some news, Nell. I'm so out of things nowadays. You can't keep up if you have no money. I never see any of the old crowd.'

They gossiped a little, so-and-so was married, so-and-so had had a row with her husband, so-and-so had got a new baby, and about so-and-so there was the most terrible scandal.

Tea was brought, rather untidily, with smeary silver and thick bread and butter. As they were finishing, the front door was opened with a key and a man's voice sounded from the hall fretful and irritable.

'Amelie—I say, it is too bad. I only ask you to do one thing and you go and forget it. This parcel has never been taken down to Jones's. You said you would.'

Amelie ran out to him in the hall. There was a quick interchange of whispers. She brought him into the drawing-room where he greeted Nell. The child in the nursery began to wail again.

'I must go to her,' said Amelie, and hurried away.

'What a life!' said Jack Horton. He was still very good-looking, though his clothes were distinctly shabby and there were bad-tempered lines coming round his mouth. He laughed as though it were a great joke. 'You've found us at sixes and sevens, Miss Vereker. We always are. Travelling to and fro in trains this weather is very trying and no peace in the home when you get there!'

He laughed again, and Nell laughed too, politely. Amelie came back holding the child in her arms. Nell rose to go. They came with her to the door, Amelie sent messages to Mrs Vereker, and waved her hand.

At the gate Nell looked back and caught the expression on Amelie's face. A hungry, envious look.

In spite of herself Nell's heart sank. Was this the inevitable end? Did poverty kill love?

She reached the main road and was walking along it in the direction of the station when an unexpected voice made her start.

'Miss Nell, by all that's wonderful!'

A big Rolls-Royce had drawn up to the kerb, George Chetwynd sat behind the wheel smiling at her.

'If this isn't too good to be true! I thought I saw a girl

who was mighty like you—from the back view anyhow—so
I slowed down to have a look at her face, and it was your very
self. Are you going back to town? Because, if so, step in.'

Nell stepped in obediently and settled herself contentedly beside the driver. The car glided forward smoothly,
gathering power. A heavenly sensation, Nell thought—
effortless, delightful.

'And what are you doing in Ealing?'

'I've been to see some friends.'

Moved by some obscure prompting, she described her
visit. Chetwynd listened sympathetically, nodding his head
from side to side, all the while driving the car with the
perfection of a master.

'If that isn't too bad,' he said sympathetically. 'You
know, I hate to think of that poor girl. Women ought to
be taken care of—to have their lives made easy for them.
They ought to be surrounded with everything they want.'

He looked at Nell and said kindly:

'It's upset you, I can see. You must have a very soft
heart, Miss Nell.'

Nell looked at him with a sudden warming of her heart.
She did like George Chetwynd. There was something so
kind and reliable and strong about him. She liked his
rather wooden face, and the way his greying hair grew
back from his temples. She liked the square, upright way
he sat, and the firm precision of his hands on the wheel.
He looked the kind of man who could deal with any
emergency, a man on whom you could *depend*. The brunt
of things would always be on his shoulders, not on yours.

Oh, yes, she liked George. He was a nice person to meet when you were tired at the end of a bothering day.

'Is my tie crooked?' he asked suddenly, without looking round.

Nell laughed.

'Was I staring? I'm afraid I was.'

'I felt the glance. What were you doing—sizing me up?'

'I believe I was.'

'And I suppose I've been found utterly wanting.'

'No, very much the other way about.'

'Don't say these nice things—which I'm sure you don't mean. You excited me so much that I nearly collided with a tram then.'

'I never say things I don't mean.'

'Don't you? I wonder now.' His voice altered. 'There's something I've wanted to say to you for a long time. This is a funny place to say it, but I'm going to take the plunge here and now. Will you marry me, Nell? I want you very badly.'

'Oh!' Nell was startled. 'Oh, no, I couldn't.'

He shot a quick glance at her before returning to his task of steering through the traffic. He slowed down a little.

'Do you mean that, I wonder? I know I'm too old for you—'

'No—you're not—I mean it's not that—'

A little smile twisted his mouth.

'I must be twenty years older than you, Nell, at least. It's a lot, I know. But I do honestly believe that I could make you happy. Queerly enough, I'm sure of it.'

Agatha Christie

Nell didn't answer for a minute or two. Then she said rather weakly:

'Oh, but really, I couldn't . . .'

'Splendid. You said it much less decidedly that time.'

'But indeed—'

'I'm not going to bother you any more just now. We'll take it that you've said no this time. But you aren't always going to say no, Nell. I can afford to wait quite a long time for what I want to have. Some day you'll find yourself saying "yes".'

'No, I shan't.'

'Yes, you will, dear. There's no one else, is there? Ah! but I know there isn't.'

Nell didn't answer. She told herself that she didn't know what to say. She had tacitly promised her mother that nothing should be said about her engagement.

And yet, somewhere, deep down, she felt ashamed . . .

George Chetwynd began cheerfully to talk of various outside topics.

CHAPTER 7

August was a difficult month for Vernon. Nell and her mother were in Dinard. He wrote to her and she to him, but her letters told him little or nothing of what he wanted to know. She was having a gay time, he gathered, and enjoying herself though longing for Vernon to be there.

Vernon's work was of the purely routine order. It required little intelligence. You needed to be careful and methodical, that was all. His mind, free from other distractions, swung back to its secret love, music.

He had formed the idea of writing an opera and had taken for his theme the half-forgotten fairy story of his youth. It was now bound up in his mind with Nell—the whole strength of his love for her flowed into this new channel.

He worked feverishly. Nell's words about his living comfortably with his mother had rankled, and he had insisted on having rooms of his own. The ones he had found were very cheap, but they gave him an unexpected sense of freedom. At Carey Lodge he would never have been able to concentrate. His mother would have been, he knew, for ever fussing after him, urging him to get to bed. Here, in Arthur Street, he could and often did, sit up till five in the morning if he liked.

He got very thin and haggard looking. Myra worried about his health and urged patent restoratives upon him. He assured her curtly that he was all right. He told her nothing of what he was doing. Sometimes he would be full of despair over his work, at others a sudden sense of power would rush over him as he knew that some small infinitesimal fragment was good.

Occasionally he went to town and spent a weekend with Sebastian, and on two occasions Sebastian came down to Birmingham. Sebastian was Vernon's most valued stand-by at this time. His sympathy was real, not assumed, and it had a two-fold character. He was interested as a friend and also from his own professional standpoint. Vernon had an enormous respect for Sebastian's judgment in all things artistic. He would play excerpts on the piano he had hired, explaining as he did so the proper orchestration. Sebastian listened, nodding very quietly, speaking little. At the end he would say:

'It's going to be good, Vernon. Get on with it.'

He never uttered a word of destructive criticism, for in his belief, such a word might be fatal. Vernon needed encouragement and nothing but encouragement.

He said one day: 'Is this what you meant to do at Cambridge?'

Vernon considered for a minute.

'No,' he said at last. 'At least it's not what I meant originally. After that concert, you know. It's gone again—the thing I saw then. Perhaps it'll come back again some time. This is, I suppose, the usual sort of thing, conventional—and all that. But here and there I've got what I mean into it.'

'I see.'

To Joe, Sebastian said plainly what he thought.

'Vernon calls this the "usual sort of thing", but, as a matter of fact, it isn't. It's entirely unusual. The whole orchestration is conducted on an unusual plan. What it is, though, is immature. Brilliant but immature.'

'Have you told him so?'

'Good lord, no. One disparaging word and he'd shrivel up and consign the whole thing to the waste-paper basket. I know these people. I'm spoon-feeding him with praise at present. We'll have the pruning knife and the garden syringe later. I've mixed my metaphors, but you know what I mean.'

In early September Sebastian gave a party to meet Herr Radmaager, the famous composer. Vernon and Joe were bidden to attend.

'Only about a dozen of us,' said Sebastian. 'Anita Quarll, whose dancing I'm interested in—she's a rotten little devil, though; Jane Harding—you'll like her. She's singing in this English Opera business. Wrong vocation, she's an actress, not a singer. You and Vernon—Radmaager—two or three others. Radmaager will be interested in Vernon—he's well disposed towards the younger generation.'

Both Joe and Vernon were elated.

'Do you think I'll ever do anything, Joe? Really do anything, I mean.'

Vernon sounded dispirited.

'Why not?' said Joe valiantly.

'I don't know. Everything I've done just lately is rotten. I started all right. But now I'm stale as stale. I'm tired before I start.'

'I suppose that's because you work all day.'

'I suppose it is.'

He was silent for a minute or two and then said:

'It'll be wonderful meeting Radmaager. He's one of the only men who write what I call music. I wish I could talk to him about what I really think—but it would be such awful cheek.'

The party was of an informal character. Sebastian had a large studio, empty save for a dais, a grand piano and a large quantity of cushions thrown down at random about the floor. At one end was a hastily put trestle table and on this were piled viands of all descriptions.

You collected what you wanted and then pitched your cushion. When Joe and Vernon arrived a girl was dancing— a small red-haired girl with a lithe, sinewy body. Her dancing was ugly but alluring.

She finished to loud applause and leapt down from the dais.

'Bravo, Anita,' said Sebastian. 'Now then, Vernon and Joe, have you got what you want? That's right. You'd better sink down gracefully by Jane. This is Jane.'

They sank down as bidden. Jane was a tall creature with a beautiful body and a mass of very dark brown hair coiled low on her neck. Her face was too broad for beauty and her chin too sharp. Her eyes were deep set and green. She was about thirty, Vernon thought. He found her disconcerting, but attractive.

Joe began to talk to her eagerly. Her enthusiasm for sculpture had been waning of late. She had always had a high soprano voice and she was now coquetting with the idea of becoming an opera singer.

Jane Harding listened sympathetically enough, emitting a faintly amused monosyllable from time to time. Finally she said:

'If you like to come round to my flat, I'll try your voice, and I can tell you in two minutes just what your voice is good for.'

'Would you really? That's awfully kind of you.'

'Oh, not at all. You can trust me. You can't trust someone who makes their living by teaching to tell you the truth.'

Sebastian came up and said:

'What about it, Jane?'

She got up from the floor—rather a beautiful movement. Then, looking round, she said in the curt voice of command one would use to a dog:

'Mr Hill.'

A small man, rather like a white worm, bustled forward with an ingratiating twist of the body. He followed her up to the dais.

She sang a French song Vernon had never heard before.

'J'ai perdu mon amie—elle est morte
Tout s'en va cette fois pour jamais
Pour jamais, pour toujours elle emporte
Le dernier des amours que j'aimais.

'*Pauvre nous! Rien ne m'a crie l'heure*
Ou la bas se nouait son linceuil
On m'a dit "Elle est morte!" Et tout seul
Je répète "Elle est morte!" Et je pleure . . .'

Like most people who heard Jane Harding sing, Vernon was quite unable to criticize the voice. She created an emotional atmosphere—the voice was only an instrument. The sense of overwhelming loss, of dazed grief, the final relief of tears.

There was applause. Sebastian murmured:

'Enormous emotional power—that's it.'

She sang again. This time it was a Norwegian song about falling snow. There was no emotion in her voice whatsoever—it was like the white flakes of the snow—monotonous, exquisitely clear, finally dying away to silence on the last line.

In response to applause, she sang yet a third song. Vernon sat up, suddenly alert.

'*I saw a fairy lady there*
With long white hands and drowning hair,
And oh! her face was wild and sweet,
Was sweet and wild and wild and strange and fair . . .'

It was like a spell laid on the room—the sense of magic—of terrified enchantment. Jane's face was thrust forward. Her eyes looked out, past beyond—seeing—frightened yet fascinated.

There was a sigh as she finished. A stout burly man with white hair *en brosse* pushed his way to Sebastian.

'Ah! my good Sebastian, I have arrived. I will talk to that young lady—at once, immediately.'

Sebastian went with him across the room to Jane. Herr Radmaager took her by both hands. He looked at her earnestly.

'Yes,' he said at last. 'Your physique is good. I should say that both the digestion and the circulation were excellent. You will give me your address and I will come and see you. Is it not so?'

Vernon thought: 'These people are mad.'

But he noticed that Jane Harding seemed to take it as a matter of course. She wrote down her address, talked to Radmaager for a few minutes longer, then came and rejoined Joe and Vernon.

'Sebastian is a good friend,' she remarked. 'He knows that Herr Radmaager is looking for a Solveig for his new opera, *Peer Gynt*. That is why he asked me here tonight.'

Joe got up and went to talk to Sebastian. Vernon and Jane Harding were left alone.

'Tell me,' said Vernon stammering a little. 'That song you sang—'

'Frosted snow?'

'No, the last one. I—I heard it years ago—when I was a kid.'

'How curious. I thought it was a family secret.'

'A hospital nurse sang it to me when I broke my leg. I always loved it—but never thought I should hear it again.'

Jane Harding said thoughtfully:

'I wonder now. Could that have been my Aunt Frances?'

Agatha Christie

'Yes, that was her name. Nurse Frances. Was she your aunt? What's happened to her?'

'She died a good many years ago. Diphtheria, caught from a patient.'

'Oh! I'm sorry.' He paused, hesitated, then blundered on. 'I've always remembered her. She was—she was a wonderful friend to me as a kid.'

He caught Jane's green eyes looking at him, a steady, kindly glance, and he knew at once of whom she had reminded him the first moment he saw her. She was like Nurse Frances.

She said quietly:

'You write music, don't you? Sebastian told me about you.'

'Yes—at least I try to.'

He stopped, hesitated again. He thought: 'She's terribly attractive. Do I like her? Why am I afraid of her?'

He felt suddenly excited and exalted. He could do things—he *knew* he could do things . . .

'Vernon!'

Sebastian was calling him. He got up. Sebastian presented him to Radmaager. The great man was kindly and sympathetic.

'I am interested,' he said, 'in what I hear about your work from my young friend here.' He laid his hand on Sebastian's shoulder. 'He is very astute, my young friend. In spite of his youth, he is seldom wrong. We will arrange a meeting, and you shall show me your work.'

He moved on. Vernon was left quivering with excitement. Did he really mean it? He went back to Jane. She

202

was smiling. Vernon sat down by her. A sudden wave of depression succeeded the exhilaration. What was the good of it all? He was tied, hand and foot, to Uncle Sydney and Birmingham. You couldn't write music unless you gave your whole time, your whole thoughts, your whole soul to it.

He felt injured—miserable—yearning for sympathy. If only Nell were here. Darling Nell who always understood.

He looked up and found Jane Harding watching him.

'What's the matter?' she said.

'I wish I were dead,' said Vernon bitterly.

Jane raised her eyebrows slightly.

'Well,' she said, 'if you walk up to the top of this building and jump off, you can be.'

It was hardly the answer that Vernon had expected. He looked up resentfully, but her cool, kindly glance disarmed him.

'There's only one thing I care about in the whole world,' he said passionately. 'I want to write music. I *could* write music. And instead of that I'm stuck in a beastly business that I hate. Grinding away day after day! It's too sickening.'

'Why do you do it if you don't like it?'

'Because I have to.'

'I expect you want to really—otherwise you wouldn't,' said Jane indifferently.

'Haven't I told you that I want to write music more than anything else in the world?'

'Then why don't you do it?'

'Because I can't, I tell you.'

He felt exasperated with her. She didn't seem to under-stand at all. Her view on life seemed to be that if you wanted to do anything, you just went and did it.

He began pouring out things. Abbots Puissants, the concert, his uncle's offer, and then—Nell . . .

When he had finished, she said:

'You do expect life to be rather a fairy story, don't you?'

'What do you mean?'

'Just that. You want to be able to live in the house of your forefathers, and to marry the girl you love, and to grow immensely rich, and to be a great composer. I daresay you might manage to do one of those four things if you give your whole mind to it. But it's not likely that you'll have everything, you know. Life isn't like a penny novelette.'

He hated her for the moment. And yet, even while he hated, he was attracted. He felt again the curious emotional atmosphere that she had created when singing. He thought to himself: 'A magnetic field, that's what it is.' And then again: 'I don't like her. I'm afraid of her.'

A long-haired young man came up and joined them. He was a Swede, but he spoke excellent English.

'Sebastian tells me that you will write the music of the future,' he said to Vernon. 'I have theories about the future. Time is only another dimension of space. You can move to and fro in time just as you can move to and fro in space. Half your dreams are only confused memories of the future. And as you can be separated from your dear ones in space, so you can be separated from them in time, and that is the greatest tragedy there is or can be.'

Since he was clearly mad, Vernon paid no attention. He was not interested in theories of space and time. But Jane Harding leaned forward.

'To be separated in time,' she said. 'I never thought of that.'

Encouraged, the Swede went on. He talked of time, and of ultimate space, and of time one, and of time two. Whether Jane was interested or not, Vernon did not know. She looked straight in front of her and did not appear to be listening. The Swede went on to time three, and Vernon escaped.

He joined Joe and Sebastian. Joe was being enthusiastic on the subject of Jane Harding.

'I think she's wonderful. Don't you, Vernon? She's asked me to go and see her. I wish I could sing like that.'

'She's an actress, not a singer,' said Sebastian. 'A good sort, Jane. She's had rather a tragic life. For five years she lived with Boris Androv, the sculptor.'

Joe glanced over in Jane's direction with enhanced interest. Vernon felt suddenly young and crude. He could still see those enigmatical slightly mocking green eyes. He heard that amused ironical voice. '*You do expect life to be a fairy story, don't you?*' Hang it all, that hurt!

And yet he had an immense desire to see her again.

Should he ask her if he might . . .

No, he couldn't . . .

Besides, he was so seldom in town . . .

He heard her voice behind him—a singer's voice, slightly husky.

'Good night, Sebastian. Thank you.'

She moved towards the door, looked over her shoulder at Vernon.

'Come and see me some time,' she said carelessly. 'Your cousin has got my address.'

BOOK III

Jane

CHAPTER 1

Jane Harding had a flat at the top of a block of mansions overlooking the river in Chelsea.

Here, on the evening following the party, came Sebastian Levinne.

'I've fixed it up, Jane,' he said. 'Radmaager is coming here to see you some time tomorrow. He prefers to do that, it seems.'

'"*Come, tell me how you live, he cried,*"' quoted Jane. 'Well, I'm living very nicely and respectably, entirely alone! Do you want something to eat, Sebastian?'

'If there is anything?'

'There are scrambled eggs and mushrooms, anchovy toast and black coffee if you'll sit here peaceably while I get them.'

She put the cigarette box and the matches beside him and left the room. In a quarter of an hour, the meal was ready.

'I like coming to see you, Jane,' said Sebastian. 'You never treat me as a bloated young Jew to whom only the flesh pots of the Savoy would make appeal.'

Jane smiled without speaking.

Presently she said: 'I like your girl, Sebastian.'

'Joe?'

'Yes, Joe.'

Sebastian said gruffly: 'What—what do you really think of her?'

Again Jane paused before answering.

'So young,' she said at last. 'So terribly young.'

Sebastian chuckled.

'She'd be very angry if she heard you.'

'Probably.' After a minute she said: 'You care for her very much, don't you, Sebastian?'

'Yes. It's odd, isn't it, Jane, how little all the things you've got matter? I've got practically all the things I want, except Joe, and Joe is all that matters. I can see what a fool I am, but it doesn't make a bit of difference! What's the difference between Joe and a hundred other girls? Very little. And yet she's the only thing in the world that matters to me just now.'

'Partly because you can't get her.'

'Perhaps. But I don't think that's so entirely.'

'Neither do I.'

'What do you think of Vernon?' asked Sebastian, after a pause.

Jane changed her position, shading her face from the fire.

'He's interesting,' she said slowly, 'partly, I think, because he is so completely unambitious.'

'Unambitious, do you think?'

'Yes. He wants things made easy.'

210

'If so, he'll never do anything in music. You want driving power for that.'

'Yes, you want driving power. But music will be the power that drives *him*!'

Sebastian looked up, his face alight and appreciative.

'Do you know, Jane?' he said. 'I believe you're right!'

She smiled but made no answer.

'I wish I knew what to make of the girl he's engaged to,' said Sebastian.

'What is she like?'

'Pretty. Some people might call it lovely—but I'd call it pretty. She does the things that other people do, and does them very sweetly. She's not a cat. I'm afraid—yes, I am afraid now, that she definitely cares for Vernon.'

'You needn't be afraid. Your pet genius won't be turned aside or held down. That doesn't happen. I'm more than ever sure, every day I live, that that doesn't happen.'

'Nothing would turn *you* aside, Jane, but then you have got driving power.'

'And yet, do you know, Sebastian, I believe I should be more easily "turned aside" as you call it, than your Vernon? I know what I want and go for it—he doesn't know what he wants, or rather doesn't want it, but *it* goes for *him* . . . And that *It* whatever It is, *will* be served—no matter at what cost.'

'Cost to whom?'

'Ah! I wonder . . .'

Sebastian rose.

'I must go. Thanks for feeding me, Jane.'

'Thank you for what you've done for me with Radmaager.

211

You're a very good friend, Sebastian. And I don't think success will ever spoil you.'

'Oh! success—' He held out his hand.

She laid both hands on his shoulders and kissed him.

'My dear, I hope you will get your Joe. But if not I am quite sure you will get everything else!'

Herr Radmaager did not come to see Jane Harding for nearly a fortnight. He arrived without warning of any kind at half-past ten in the morning. He stumped into the flat without a word of apology and looked round the walls of the sitting-room.

'It is you who have furnished and papered this? Yes?'

'Yes.'

'You live here alone?'

'Yes.'

'But you have not always lived alone?'

'No.'

Radmaager said unexpectedly:

'That is good.'

Then he said commandingly:

'Come here.'

He took her by both arms, and drew her towards the window. There he looked her over from head to foot. He pinched the flesh of her arm between finger and thumb, opened her mouth and looked down her throat, and finally put a large hand on each side of her waist.

'Breathe in—good! Now out—sharply.'

He took a tape measure out of his pocket, made her

repeat the two movements, passing the tape measure round her each time. Finally he pocketed it and put it away. Neither he nor Jane seemed to see anything curious in the proceedings.

'It is well,' said Radmaager. 'Your chest is excellent, your throat is strong. You are intelligent—since you have not interrupted me. I can find many singers with a better voice than yours—your voice is very true, very beautiful—very clear, a silver thread. But if you force it, it will go—and where will you be then, I ask you? The music you sing now is absurd—if you were not pig-headed as the devil you would not sing those roles. Yet I respect you because you are an artist.'

He paused, then went on:

'Now listen to me. My music is beautiful and it will not hurt your voice. When Ibsen created Solveig, he created the most wonderful woman character that has ever been created. My opera will stand and fall by its Solveig—and it is not sufficient to have a singer. There are Cavarossi—Mary Wontner—Jeanne Dorta—all hope to sing Solveig. But I will not have it. What are they? Unintelligent animals with marvellous vocal cords. For my Solveig I must have a perfect instrument, an instrument with intelligence. You are a young singer—as yet unknown. You shall sing at Covent Garden next year in my *Peer Gynt* if you satisfy me. Now listen . . .'

He sat down at Jane's piano and began to play—queer rhythmic monotonous notes . . .

'It is the snow, you comprehend—the northern snow. That is what your voice must be like—the snow. It is white

213

like damask—and the pattern runs through it. But the pattern is in the music, not in your voice.'

He went on playing. Endless monotony—endless repetition—and yet suddenly the something that was woven through it caught your ear—what he had called the pattern.

He stopped.

'Well?'

'It will be very difficult to sing.'

'Quite right. But you have an excellent ear. You wish to sing Solveig—yes?'

'Naturally. It's the chance of a lifetime. If I can satisfy you—'

'I think you can.' He got up again, laid his hands on her shoulders. 'How old are you?'

'Thirty-three.'

'And you have been very unhappy—that is so?'

'Yes.'

'How many men have you lived with?'

'One.'

'And he was not a good man?'

Jane answered evenly:

'He was a very bad one.'

'I see. Yes, it is that which is written in your face. Now listen to me, all that you have suffered, all that you have enjoyed, you will put it into my music not with abandon, not with unrestraint, but with controlled and disciplined force. You have intelligence and you have courage. Without courage nothing can ever be accomplished. Those without courage turn their backs on life. You will never turn your back on life. Whatever comes you will stand

214

there facing it with your chin up and your eyes very steady . . . But I hope, my child, that you will not be too much hurt . . .'

He turned away.

'I will send on the score,' he said over his shoulder. 'And you will study it.'

He stumped out of the room and the flat door banged.

Jane sat down by the table. She stared at the wall in front of her with unseeing eyes. Her chance had come.

She murmured very softly to herself:

'I'm afraid.'

For a whole week Vernon debated the question of whether he should or should not take Jane at her word. He could get up to town at the weekend—but then perhaps Jane would be away. He felt miserably self-conscious and shy. Perhaps by now she had forgotten that she had asked him.

He let the weekend go by. He felt that certainly by now she would have forgotten him. Then he got a letter from Joe in which she mentioned having seen Jane twice. That decided Vernon. At six o'clock on the following Saturday, he rang the bell of Jane's flat.

Jane herself opened it. Her eyes opened a little wider when she saw who it was. Otherwise she displayed no surprise.

'Come in,' she said. 'I'm finishing my practising. But you won't mind.'

He followed her into a long room whose windows overlooked the river. It was very empty. A grand piano, a divan,

Agatha Christie

a couple of chairs and walls that were papered with a wild riot of bluebells and daffodils. One wall alone was papered in sober dark green and on it hung a single picture—a queer study of bare tree trunks. Something about it reminded Vernon of his early adventures in the Forest.

On the music stool was the little man like a white worm.

Jane pushed a cigarette box towards Vernon, said in her brutal commanding voice, 'Now, Mr Hill,' and began to walk up and down the room.

Mr Hill flung himself upon the piano. His hands twinkled up and down it with marvellous speed and dexterity. Jane sang. Most of the time *sotto voce*, almost under her breath. Occasionally she would take a phrase full pitch. Once or twice she stopped with an exclamation of what sounded like furious impatience, and Mr Hill was made to repeat from several bars back.

She broke off quite suddenly by clapping her hands. She crossed to the fireplace, pushed the bell, and turning her head addressed Mr Hill for the first time as a human being.

'You'll stay and have some tea, won't you, Mr Hill?'

Mr Hill was afraid he couldn't. He twisted his body apologetically several times and sidled out of the room. A maid brought in black coffee and hot buttered toast which appeared to be Jane's conception of afternoon tea.

'What was that you were singing?'

'*Electra*—Richard Strauss.'

'Oh! I liked it. It was like dogs fighting.'

'Strauss would be flattered. All the same, I know what you mean. It is combative.'

She pushed the toast towards him and added:

216

'Your cousin's been here twice.'

'I know. She wrote and told me.'

He felt tongue-tied and uncomfortable. He had wanted so much to come, and now that he was here he didn't know what to say. Something about Jane made him uncomfortable. He blurted out at last:

'Tell me truthfully—would you advise me to chuck work altogether and stick to music?'

'How can I possibly tell? I don't know what you want to do.'

'You spoke like that the other night. As though everyone can do just what they like.'

'So they can. Not always, of course—but very nearly always. If you want to murder someone, there is really nothing to stop you. But you will be hanged afterwards—naturally.'

'I don't want to murder anyone.'

'No, you want your fairy story to end happily. Uncle dies and leaves you all his money. You marry your lady love and live at Abbots—whatever it's called—happily ever afterwards.'

Vernon said angrily:

'I wish you wouldn't laugh at me.'

Jane was silent a minute, then she said in a different voice:

'I wasn't laughing at you. I was doing something I'd no business to do—trying to interfere.'

'What do you mean, trying to interfere?'

'Trying to make you face reality, and forgetting that you are—what—about eight years younger than I am?—and that your time for that hasn't yet come.'

217

He thought suddenly: 'I could say anything to her—anything at all. She wouldn't always answer the way I wanted her to, though.'

Aloud he said: 'Please go on—I'm afraid it's very egotistical my talking about myself like this, but I'm so worried and unhappy. I want to know what you meant when you said the other evening that of the four things I wanted, I could get any one of them but not all together.'

Jane considered a minute.

'What did I mean exactly? Why, just this. To get what you want, you must usually pay a price or take a risk—sometimes both. For instance, I love music—a certain kind of music. My voice is suitable for a totally different kind of music. It's an unusually good concert voice—not an operatic one—except for very light opera. But I've sung in Wagner, in Strauss—in all the things I like. I haven't exactly paid a price—but I take an enormous risk. My voice may give out any minute. I know that. I've looked the fact in the face and I've decided that the game is worth the candle.

'Now in your case, you mentioned four things. For the first, I suppose that if you remain in your uncle's business for a sufficient number of years, you will grow rich without any further trouble. That's not very interesting. Secondly, you want to live at Abbots Puissants—you could do that tomorrow if you married a girl with money. Then the girl you're fond of, the girl you want to marry—'

'Can I get her tomorrow?' asked Vernon. He spoke with a kind of angry irony.

'I should say so—quite easily.'

'How?'

'By selling Abbots Puissants. It is yours to sell, isn't it?'

'Yes, but I couldn't do that—I couldn't—I couldn't . . .'

Jane leaned back in her chair and smiled.

'You prefer to go on believing that life is a fairy story?'

'There must be some other way.'

'Yes, of course there is another. Probably the simplest. There's nothing to stop you both going out to the nearest Registry Office. You've both got the use of your limbs.'

'You don't understand. There are hundreds of difficulties in the way. I couldn't ask Nell to face a life of poverty. She doesn't want to be poor.'

'Perhaps she can't.'

'What do you mean by can't?'

'Just that. Can't. Some people can't be poor, you know.'

Vernon got up, walked twice up and down the room. Then he came back, dropped on the hearth-rug beside Jane's chair, and looked up at her.

'What about the fourth thing? Music? Do you think I could ever do that?'

'That I can't say. Wanting mayn't be any use there. But if it does happen—I expect it will swallow up all the rest. They'll all go—Abbots Puissants—money—the girl. My dear, I don't feel life's going to be easy for you. Ugh! a goose is walking over my grave. Now tell me something about this opera Sebastian Levinne says you are writing.'

When he had finished telling her, it was nine o'clock. They both exclaimed and went out to a little restaurant together. As he said goodbye afterwards, his first diffidence returned.

'I think you are one of the—the nicest people I ever met.

Agatha Christie

You will let me come again and talk, won't you? If I haven't
bored you too frightfully.'

'Any time you like. Good night.'

Myra wrote to Joe:

'Dearest Josephine,—I am so worried about Vernon and
this woman he is always going up to town to see—
some opera singer or other. Years older than he is. It's
so dreadful the way women like that get hold of boys. I
am terribly worried and don't know what to do about
it. I have spoken to your Uncle Sydney, but he was not
very helpful about it and just said that boys will be
boys. But I don't want *my* boy to be like that. I was
wondering, dear Joe, if it would be any good my seeing
this woman and begging her to leave my boy alone.
Even a *bad* woman would listen to a mother, I think.
Vernon is too young to have his life ruined. I really
don't know what to do. I seem to have no influence
over Vernon nowadays.

'With much love, Your affectionate
'Aunt Myra.'

Joe showed this letter to Sebastian.

'I suppose she means Jane,' said Sebastian. 'I'd rather
like to see an interview between them. Frankly, I think Jane
would be amused.'

'It's too silly,' said Joe hotly. 'I wish to goodness Vernon
would fall in love with Jane. It would be a hundred times

220

better for him than being in love with that silly stick of a Nell.'

'You don't like Nell, do you, Joe?'

'You don't like her either.'

'Oh, yes, I do, in a way. She doesn't interest me very much, but I can quite see the attraction. In her own way, she's quite lovely.'

'Yes, in a chocolate box way.'

'She doesn't attract me, because to my mind there's nothing there to attract as yet. The real Nell hasn't happened. Perhaps she never will. I suppose to some people that is very attractive because it opens out all sorts of possibilities.'

'Well, I think Jane is worth ten of Nell! The sooner Vernon gets over his silly calf love for Nell and falls in love with Jane instead, the better it will be.'

Sebastian lit a cigarette and said slowly:

'I'm not sure that I agree with you.'

'Why?'

'Well, it's not very easy to explain. But, you see, Jane is a real person—very much so. To be in love with Jane might be a whole-time job. We're agreed, aren't we, that Vernon is very possibly a genius? Well, I don't think a genius wants to be married to a real person. He wants to be married to someone rather negligible—someone whose personality won't interfere. Now it may sound cynical, but that's what will probably happen if Vernon marries Nell. At the moment she represents—I don't quite know what to call it—what's that line? "The apple tree, the singing and the gold . . ." Something like that. Once he's married to her, that will go.

221

She'll just be a nice pretty sweet-tempered girl whom, naturally, he loves very much. But she won't *interfere*—she'll never get between him and his work—she hasn't got sufficient personality. Now Jane might—she wouldn't mean to, but she might. It isn't Jane's beauty that attracts you— it's herself. She might be absolutely fatal to Vernon . . .'

'Well,' said Joe, 'I don't agree with you. I think Nell's a silly little ass, and I should hate to see Vernon married to her . . . I hope it will all come to nothing . . .'

'Which is much the likeliest thing to happen,' said Sebastian.

CHAPTER 2

Nell was back in London. Vernon came up to see her the day after her return. She noticed the change in him at once. He looked haggard, excited. He said abruptly:

'Nell, I'm going to chuck Birmingham.'

'*What?*'

'Listen while I tell you . . .'

He talked eagerly, excitedly. His music—he'd got to give himself up to it. He told her of the opera.

'Listen, Nell. This is you—in your tower—with your golden hair hanging down and shining . . . shining in the sun.'

He went to the piano, began to play, explaining as he did so . . . 'Violins—you see—and this is all for harps . . . and these are the round jewels . . .'

He played what seemed to Nell to be a series of rather ugly discords. She privately thought it all hideous. Perhaps it would sound different played by an orchestra.

But she loved him—and because she loved him, everything he did must be right. She smiled and said:

'It's lovely, Vernon.'

'Do you really like it, Nell? Oh, sweetheart—you are so wonderful. You always understand. You're so sweet about everything.'

He came across to her, knelt down and buried his face on her lap.

'I love you so . . . I love you so . . .'

She stroked his dark head.

'Tell me the story of it.'

'Shall I? Well, you see, there's a princess in a tower with golden hair and kings and knights come from all over the world to try and get her to marry them. But she's too haughty to look at any of them—the real good old fairy story touch. And at last one comes—a kind of gipsy fellow—very ragged, with a little green hat on his head and a kind of pipe he plays on. And he sings and says that he has the biggest kingdom of anyone because his kingdom is the whole world—and that there are no jewels like his jewels which are dewdrops. And they say he's mad and throw him out. But that night when the princess is lying in bed, she hears him playing his song in the castle garden and she listens.

'Then there's an old Jew pedlar man in the town, and he offers the fellow gold and riches with which to win the princess, but the gipsy laughs and says what could he give in exchange? And the old man says his green hat and the pipe he plays on, but the gipsy says he will never part with those.

'He plays in the palace garden every night—*Come out, my love, come out!* and every night the princess lies awake and listens. There's an old bard in the palace, and he tells a tale of how a hundred years ago a prince of the Royal house was bewitched by a gipsy maid and wandered forth and was never seen again. And the princess listens to it, and at last one night she gets up and comes to the window. And he tells her to leave all her robes and jewels behind and to come out in a simple white gown. But she thinks in her heart that it's as well to be on the safe side, so she puts a pearl in the hem of her skirt, and she comes out, and they go off in the moonlight while he sings . . . But the pearl in her dress weighs her down and she can't keep up. And he goes on not realizing that she's left behind . . .

'I've told this very badly—like a story, but that's the end of the first act—his going off in the moonlight and her left behind weeping. There are three scenes. The Castle hall—the market-place, and the palace garden outside her window.'

'Won't that be very expensive—in the way of scenery, I mean?' suggested Nell.

'I don't know—I hadn't thought—oh! it can be managed, I expect.' Vernon was irritated by these prosaic details.

'Now the second act is near the market-place. There is a girl there mending dolls—with black hair hanging down round her face. The gipsy comes along, and asks her what she's doing, and she says she's mending the children's toys— she's got the most wonderful needle and thread in the world. He tells her all about the princess and how he's lost her again, and he says he's going to the old Jew pedlar to sell his hat and his pipe, and she warns him not to—but he says he must.

'I wish I could tell things better—I'm just giving you the

225

Agatha Christie

story now—not the way I've divided it up, because I'm not exactly sure myself yet about that. I've got the music—that's the great thing—the heavy empty palace music—and the noisy clattering market-place music—and the princess—like that line of poetry "a singing stream in a silent vale", and the doll mender, all trees and dark woods like the Forest used to sound at Abbots Puissants; you know, enchanted and mysterious and a little frightening . . . I think you'll have to have some instruments specially tuned for it . . . Well, I won't go into that, it wouldn't interest you—it's too technical.

'Where was I? Oh, yes, he turns up at the palace—as a great king this time—all clanking swords and horse trappings and blazing jewels, and the princess is overjoyed and they're going to be married and everything's all right. But he begins to get pale and weary, worse every day, and when anyone asks him what is the matter, he says "Nothing."'

'Like you when you were a little boy at Abbots Puissants,' said Nell, smiling.

'Did I say that? I don't remember. Well, then the night before the wedding he can't bear it any more, and he steals away from the palace and down to the market and wakes up the old Jew and says he must have back his hat and his pipe. He'll give back everything he got in exchange. The old Jew laughs, and throws down the hat, torn across, and the pipe, broken, at the prince's feet.

'He's broken-hearted—the bottom knocked out of his world, and he wanders away with them in his hand, till he comes to where the doll mender is sitting with her feet tucked up under her, and he tells her what has

226

happened and she tells him to lie down and sleep. And when he wakes in the morning there are his green hat and his pipe, mended so beautifully that no one could tell they had been mended.

'And then he laughs for joy, and she goes to a cupboard and pulls out a similar little green hat and a pipe, and they go out together through the forest, and just as the sun rises on the edge of the forest, he looks at her and remembers. He says, "Why, a hundred years ago, I left my palace and my throne for love of you." And she says, "Yes. But because you were afraid you hid a piece of gold in the lining of your doublet, and the gleam of it enchanted your eyes and we lost each other. But now the whole world is ours and we will wander through it together for ever and ever."'

Vernon stopped. He turned an enthusiastic face upon Nell. 'It ought to be lovely, the end . . . so lovely. If I can get into the music what I see and hear . . . the two of them in their little green hats . . . playing their pipes . . . and the forest and the sun rising . . .'

His face grew dreamy and ecstatic. He seemed to have forgotten Nell.

Nell herself felt indescribable sensations sweep over her. She was afraid of this queer, rapt Vernon. He had talked of music before to her, but never with this strange exalted passion. She knew that Sebastian Levinne thought Vernon might do wonderful things some day, but she remembered lives she had read of musical geniuses and suddenly she wished with all her heart that Vernon might not have this marvellous gift. She wanted him as he had been heretofore, her eager boyish lover, the two of them wrapped in their common dream.

The wives of musicians were always unhappy, she had read that somewhere. She didn't want Vernon to be a great musician. She wanted him to make some money quickly and live with her at Abbots Puissants. She wanted a sweet, sane, normal, everyday life. Love—and Vernon . . .

This thing—this kind of possession—was *dangerous*. She was sure it was dangerous.

But she couldn't damp Vernon's ardour. She loved him far too much for that. She said, trying to make her voice sound sympathetic and interested:

'What an unusual fairy story! Do you mean to say you've remembered it from ever since you were a child?'

'More or less. I thought of it again that morning on the river at Cambridge—just before I saw you standing under that tree. Darling, you were so lovely—so lovely . . . You always will be lovely, won't you? I couldn't bear it if you weren't. What idiotic things I am saying! And then, after that night at Ranelagh, that wonderful night when I told you that I loved you, all the music came pouring into my mind. Only I couldn't remember the story clearly—only really the bit about the tower.

'But, I've had marvellous luck. I've met a girl who is actually the niece of the hospital nurse who told me the story. And she remembered it perfectly and helped me to get it quite clearly again. Isn't it extraordinary the way things happen?'

'Who is she, this woman?'

'She's really rather a wonderful person, I think. Awfully

nice and frightfully clever. She's a singer—Jane Harding. She sings *Electra* and *Brunhilde* and *Isolde* with the new English Opera Company; and she may sing at Covent Garden next year. I met her at a party of Sebastian's. I want you to meet her. I'm sure you'd like her awfully.'

'How old is she? Young?'

'Youngish—about thirty, I should think. She has an awfully queer effect on one. In a way you almost dislike her, and yet she makes you feel you can do things. She's been very good to me.'

'I dare say.'

Why did she say that? Why should she feel an unreasoning prejudice against this woman—this Jane Harding?

Vernon was staring at her with rather a puzzled expression.

'What's the matter, darling? You said that so queerly.'

'I don't know.' She tried to laugh. 'A goose walking over my grave, perhaps.'

'Funny,' said Vernon, frowning. 'Somebody else said that just lately.'

'Lots of people say it,' said Nell, laughing. She paused and then said: 'I'd—I'd like to meet this friend of yours very much, Vernon.'

'I know. I want her to meet you. I've talked a lot about you to her.'

'I wish you wouldn't. Talk about me, I mean. After all, we promised Mother no one should know.'

'Nobody outside—but Sebastian knows and Joe.'

'That's different. You've known them all your life.'

'Yes, of course. I'm sorry. I didn't think. I didn't say we

were engaged, or tell your name or anything. You're not cross, are you, Nell darling?'

'Of course not.'

Even in her own ears her voice sounded hard. Why was life so horribly difficult? She was afraid of this music. Already it had made Vernon chuck up a good job. *Was* it the music? Or was it Jane Harding?

She thought to herself desperately:

'I wish I'd never met Vernon. I wish I'd never loved him. I wish—oh! I wish I didn't love him so much. I'm afraid. I'm afraid . . .'

It was over! The plunge was taken! There was unpleasantness of course. Uncle Sydney was furious, not, Vernon was forced to confess, without reason. There were scenes with his mother—tears—recriminations. A dozen times, he was on the point of giving way, and yet somehow or other, he didn't.

He had a curious sense of desolation all the time. He was alone in this thing. Nell, because she loved him, agreed to all he said, but he was uncomfortably conscious that his decision had grieved and disturbed her, and might even shake her faith in the future. Sebastian thought the move premature. For the time being, he would have advised making the best of two worlds. Not that he said so. Sebastian never gave advice to anybody. Even the staunch Joe was doubtful. She realized that for Vernon to sever his connection with the Bents was serious, and she had not got the real faith in Vernon's musical future which would have made her heartily applaud the step.

So far, in his life, Vernon had never had the courage to set himself definitely in opposition to everybody. When it was all over, and he was settled in the very cheap rooms which were all he could afford in London, he felt as one might who had overcome invincible odds. Then, and not till then, he went a second time to see Jane Harding.

He had held boyish imaginary conversations with her in his mind.

'I have done what you told me.'

'Splendid! I knew you had the courage really.'

He was modest, she applauded. He was sustained and uplifted by her praise.

The reality, as always, fell out quite differently. His intercourse with Jane always did. He was always holding imaginary conversations with Jane in his mind, and the reality was always totally different.

In this case, when he announced, with due modesty, what he had done, she seemed to take it as a matter of course, with nothing particularly heroic about it. She said:

'Well, you must have wanted to do it or you wouldn't have done it.'

He felt baffled, almost angry. A curious sense of constraint always came over him in Jane's presence. He could never be wholly natural with her. He had so much he wanted to say—but he found it difficult to say it. He was tongue-tied—embarrassed. And then suddenly, for no reason, it seemed, the cloud would lift and he would be talking happily and easily, saying the things that came into his head.

He thought: 'Why am I so embarrassed with her? *She's* natural enough.'

Agatha Christie

It worried him . . . From the first moment he had met her, he had felt disturbed . . . afraid. He resented the effect she had on him and yet he was unwilling to admit how strong that effect was.

An attempt to bring about a friendship between her and Nell failed. Vernon could feel that behind the outward cordiality that politeness dictates, there was very little real feeling.

When he asked Nell what she thought of Jane, she answered:

'I like her very much. I think she's most interesting.'

He was more awkward approaching Jane, but she helped him.

'You want to know what I think of your Nell? She is lovely—and very sweet.'

He said, 'And you really think you'll be friends?'

'No, of course not. Why should we?'

'Well, but—'

He stammered, taken aback.

'Friendship is not a kind of equilateral triangle. If A likes B and loves C, then C and B, etcetera, etcetera . . . We've nothing in common, your Nell and I. She, too, expects life to be a fairy story, and is just beginning to be afraid, poor child, that it mayn't be, after all. She's a Sleeping Beauty waking in the forest. Love, to her, is something very wonderful and very beautiful.'

'Isn't it that to you?'

He had to ask. He wanted to know so badly. So often, so often, he'd wondered about Boris Androv, about those five years.

She looked at him with a face from which all expression had died out.

'Some day—I'll tell you . . .'

He wanted to say—'Tell me now,' but he didn't. He said instead:

'Tell me, Jane, what is life to you?'

She paused a minute and then said:

'A difficult, dangerous, but endlessly interesting adventure.'

At last, he was able to work. He began to appreciate to the full the joys of freedom. There was nothing to fray his nerves, nothing to dissipate his energy. It could flow, all in one steady stream, into his work. There were few distractions. At the moment, he had only just enough money to keep body and soul together. Abbots Puissants was still unlet . . .

The autumn passed and most of the winter. He saw Nell once or twice a week, stolen unsatisfactory meetings. They were both conscious of the loss of the first fine rapture. She questioned him closely about the progress of the opera. How was it going? When did he expect it would be finished? What chances were there of its being produced?

Vernon was vague to all these practical aspects. He was concerned at the moment only with the creative side. The opera was getting itself born, slowly, with innumerable pangs and difficulties, with a hundred setbacks owing to Vernon's own lack of experience and technique. His conversation was mostly of instrumental difficulties or possibilities. He went out with odd musicians who played in orchestras. Nell went to many concerts and was fond of music, but it is doubtful if she could have told an oboe from a clarinet. She'd always imagined a horn and a French horn to be much the same thing.

The technical knowledge needed in score writing appalled her, and Vernon's indifference to how and when the opera would be produced made her uneasy.

He hardly realized himself how much his uncertain answers depressed and alienated Nell. He was startled one day when she said to him—indeed not so much said as wailed:

'Oh, Vernon, don't try me too hard. It's so difficult—so difficult . . . I must have some hope. You don't understand.'

He looked at her astonished.

'But, Nell, it's all right, *really*. It's only a question of being patient.'

'I know, Vernon. I shouldn't have said that, but you see—'
She paused.

'It makes it so much more difficult for me, darling,' said Vernon, 'if I feel that you're unhappy.'

'Oh, I'm not—I won't be . . .'

But underneath, choked down, that old feeling of resentment lifted its head again. Vernon didn't understand or care how difficult things were for her. He never had the faintest conception of her difficulties. He would, perhaps, have called them silly or trivial—they were, in one sense, but in another they weren't—since the sum total of them went to make up her life. Vernon didn't see or realize that she was fighting a battle—fighting it all the time. She could never relax. If he could only realize that, give her a word of cheer, show her that he understood the difficult position in which she was placed. But he never would see.

A devastating sense of loneliness swept over Nell. Men were like that—they never understood or cared. Love, that seemed to solve everything. But really it didn't solve anything at all. She almost hated Vernon. Selfishly absorbed in his work, disliking her to be unhappy because it upset *him* . . .

She thought: 'Any *woman* would understand.'

And moved by some obscure impulse, she went of her own accord to see Jane Harding.

Jane was in, and if she was surprised to see Nell, she did not show it. They talked for some time on desultory things. Yet Nell had a feeling that Jane was waiting and watching, biding her time.

Why had she come? She didn't know. She feared and distrusted Jane—perhaps that was why! Jane was her enemy. Yes, but she had a fear that her enemy had a wisdom denied to her. Jane (she put it to herself) was clever. She was, very possibly, bad—yes, she was sure Jane was bad, but somehow or other one might learn from her.

She began rather blunderingly. Did Jane think that Vernon's music was likely to be successful—that is to say successful *soon*? She tried in vain to keep a quaver out of her voice.

She felt Jane's cool green eyes upon her.

'Things getting difficult?'

'Yes, you see—'

It tumbled out, a great deal of it, the shifts, the difficulties, the unspoken force of her mother's silent pressure, a dimly veiled reference to Someone, name not given, Someone who understood and was kind and was rich.

How easy to say these things to a woman—even a woman like Jane who couldn't know anything about them. Women understood—they didn't pooh-pooh trifles and make everything out to be unimportant.

When she had finished, Jane said:

'It's a little hard on you. When you first met Vernon, you had no idea of this music business.'

'I didn't think it would be like this,' said Nell bitterly.

'Well, it's no good going back to what you didn't think, is it?'

'I suppose not.' Nell felt vaguely annoyed at Jane's tone. 'Oh!' she broke out. 'You feel, of course, that everything ought to give way to his music—that he's a genius—that I ought to be glad to make any sacrifice—'

'No, I don't,' said Jane. 'I don't think any of those things. I don't know what good geniuses are, or works of art either. Some people are born with a feeling that they matter more than anything else, and some people aren't. It's impossible to say who's right. The best thing for you would be to persuade Vernon to give up music, sell Abbots Puissants, and settle down with you on the proceeds. But I do know this, that you haven't an earthly chance of getting him to give up music. These things, genius, art, whatever you like to call it, are much stronger than you are. You might just as well be King Canute on the sea shore. You can't turn back Vernon from music.'

'What can I do?' said Nell hopelessly.

'Well, you can either marry this other man you were talking of and be reasonably happy, or you can marry Vernon and be actively unhappy with periods of bliss.'

Nell looked at her.

'What would you do?' she whispered.

'Oh! I should marry Vernon and be unhappy, but then some of us like taking our pleasures sadly.'

Nell got up. She stood in the doorway looking back at Jane who had not moved. She was lying back against the wall, smoking a cigarette, her eyes half closed. She looked a little like a cat, or a Chinese idol. A sudden wave of fury came over Nell.

'I hate you,' she cried. 'You're taking Vernon away from me. Yes—*you*. You're bad—evil—I know it, I can feel it. You're a bad woman.'

'You're jealous,' said Jane quietly.

'You admit then, there's something to be jealous of? Not that Vernon loves you. He doesn't. He never would. It's you who want to get hold of him.'

There was silence—a pulsating silence. Then, without moving, Jane laughed. Nell hurried out of the flat, hardly knowing what she was doing.

Sebastian came very often to see Jane. He usually came after dinner, ringing up first to find if she would be at home. They both found a curious pleasure in each other's company. To Sebastian Jane recounted her struggles with the role of Solveig, the difficulties of the music, the difficulty of pleasing Radmaager, the still greater difficulty of pleasing herself. To Jane, Sebastian imparted his ambitions, his present plans, his future vague ideas.

One evening, after they had both been silent after a long spell of talking, he said:

'I can talk to you better than anyone I know, Jane. I don't quite know why, either.'

'Well, in a way, we're both the same kind of person, aren't we?'

'Are we?'

'I think so. Not superficially, perhaps, but fundamentally. We both like truth. I think, as far as one can say that of oneself we both see things as they are.'

'And you think most people don't?'

'Of course they don't. Nell Vereker, for instance. She sees things as they've been shown her, as she hopes they are.'

'A slave of convention, you mean?'

'Yes, but it works both ways. Joe, for instance, prides herself on being unconventional, but that makes just as much for narrowness and prejudice.'

'Yes, if you're "agin" everything irrespective of what it is. Joe is like that. She *must* be a rebel. She never really examines a thing on its merits. And that's what damns me so hopelessly in her eyes. I'm successful—and she admires failures. I'm rich, so she'd gain instead of lose if she married me. And being a Jew doesn't count against you much nowadays.'

'It's even fashionable,' said Jane laughing.

'And yet, do you know, Jane, I always have a queer feeling that Joe really likes me?'

'Perhaps she does. She's the wrong age for you, Sebastian. That Swede at your party said something wonderfully true—about being separated in time being worse than being separated in space. If you're the wrong age for a person, nothing keeps you apart so hopelessly. You may be made for one another, but be born at the wrong time for each other. Does that sound nonsense? I believe when she's about thirty-five, Joe could love you—the real essential you—madly. It'll take a woman to love you, Sebastian, not a girl.'

Sebastian was looking into the fire. It was a cold February day, and there were logs piled up on the coals. Jane hated gas fires.

'Have you ever wondered, Jane, why we don't fall in love with each other, you and I? Platonic friendship doesn't usually work. And you're very attractive. There's a lot of the siren about you—quite unconscious, but it's there.'

'Perhaps we should under normal conditions.'

'Aren't we under normal conditions? Oh! wait a minute— I know what you mean. You mean "the line's already engaged."'

'Yes. If you didn't love Joe—'

'And if you—'

He stopped.

'Well?' said Jane. 'You knew, didn't you?'

'Yes, I suppose so. You don't mind talking about it?'

'Not in the least. If a thing's there, what does it matter if you talk of it or not?'

'Are you one of the people, Jane, who believe that if you want a thing enough you can make it happen?'

Jane considered.

'No—I don't think I am. So many things happen to you naturally that it keeps you busy without—well—looking for things as well. When a thing's offered you, you've got to choose whether you'll accept it or refuse it. That's destiny. And when you've made your choice you must abide by it without looking back.'

'That's the spirit of Greek tragedy. You've got Electra into your bones, Jane.' He picked up a book from the table. '*Peer Gynt*? You're steeping yourself in Solveig, I see.'

'Yes. It's more her opera than Peer's. You know, Sebastian, Solveig is a wonderfully fascinating character—so impassive, so calm, and yet so utterly certain that her love for Peer is the only thing in Heaven or earth. She knows that he wants and needs her though he never tells her so, she is abandoned and deserted by him, and manages to turn that desertion into a crowning proof of his love. By the way, that Whitsuntide music of Radmaager's is perfectly glorious. You know—"Blessed is he who has made my life blessed!" To show that the love of a man can turn you into a kind of impassioned nun is difficult but rather wonderful.'

'Is Radmaager pleased with you?'

'Sometimes he is. Yesterday, on the other hand, he consigned my soul to Hell and shook me till my teeth rattled. He was perfectly right, too. I sang it all wrong—like a melodramatic stage-struck girl. It's got to be sheer force of will—restraint—Solveig must be so soft and gentle, but really so terribly strong. It's like Radmaager said the first day. Snow—smooth snow—with a wonderful clear design running through it.'

She went on to talk of Vernon's work.

'It's almost finished, you know. I want him to show it to Radmaager.'

'Will he?'

'I think so. Have you seen it?'

'Parts of it only.'

'What do you think of it?'

'I'll hear what you think of it first, Jane. Your judgment's as good as mine any day where music is concerned.'

'It's crude. There's too much in it—too much good stuff. He hasn't learnt how to handle his material—but the material is there—masses and masses of it. Do you agree?'

Sebastian nodded.

'Absolutely. I'm more sure than ever that Vernon is going to—well, revolutionize things. But there's a nasty time coming. He'll have to face the fact that what he's written isn't, when all's said and done, a commercial proposition.'

'You mean, it couldn't be produced?'

'That's what I mean.'

'*You* could produce it.'

'You mean—out of friendship?'

'That's what I meant.'

Sebastian got up and began to pace up and down.

'To my way of thinking, that's unethical,' he said at last.

'And also you don't like losing money.'

'Quite true.'

'But you could afford to lose a certain amount without—well, noticing it?'

'I always notice losing money. It affects—well, my pride.'

Jane nodded.

'I understand that. But I don't think, Sebastian, that you need lose money.'

'My dear Jane—'

'Don't argue with me till you know what I'm arguing about. You're going to produce a certain amount of what the world calls "Highbrow" stuff at the little Holborn theatre, aren't you? Well, this summer—say the beginning of July, produce the *Princess in the Tower* for—say, two weeks. Don't produce it from the point of view of an opera (don't tell Vernon this, by the way—but there, you wouldn't. You're not an idiot), but from the point of view of a musical spectacular play. Unusual scenery and weird lighting effects—you're keen on lighting, I know. The Russian ballet—that's what you've got to aim at—that's the—the *tone* of it. Have good singers—but attractive ones to look at as well. And now, putting modesty in the background, I'll tell you this. I'll make a success of it for you.'

'You—as the Princess?'

'No, my dear child, as the doll mender. It's a weird character—a character that will attract and arrest. The music of the doll mender is the best thing Vernon has done. Sebastian, you've always said I could act. They're going to let me sing at Covent Garden this season because I can act. I shall make a hit. I know I can act—and acting counts for a lot in opera. I can—I can *sway* people—I can make them *feel*. Vernon's opera will need licking into shape from the dramatic point of view. Leave that to me. From the musical side, you and Radmaager may be able to make suggestions—if he'll take them. Musicians are the devil to deal with as we all know. The thing can be done, Sebastian.'

She leaned forward, her face vivid and impressive. Sebastian's face grew more impassive as it always did when he was thinking hard. He looked appraisingly at Jane, weighing her, not from the personal standpoint, but from the impersonal. He believed in Jane, in her dynamic force, in her magnetism, in her wonderful power of communicating emotion over the footlights.

'I'll think it over,' he said quietly. 'There's something in what you say.'

Jane laughed suddenly.

'And you'll be able to get me very cheap, Sebastian,' she said.

'I shall expect to,' said Sebastian gravely. 'My Jewish instincts must be appeased somehow. You're putting this thing over on me, Jane—don't imagine that I don't know it!'

CHAPTER 3

At last the *Princess in the Tower* was finished. Vernon suffered from a tremendous wave of reaction. The whole thing was rotten—hopeless. Best to chuck it into the fire.

Nell's sweetness and encouragement were like manna to him at this time. She had that wonderful instinct for always saying the words he longed to hear. But for her, as he constantly told her, he would have given way to despair long ago.

He had seen less of Jane during the winter. She had been on tour with the British Opera Company part of the time. When she sang in *Electra* in Birmingham, he went down for it. He was tremendously impressed—loved both the music and Jane's impersonation of Electra. That ruthless will, that determined: 'Say naught but dance on!' She gave the impression of being more spirit than flesh. He was conscious that her voice was really too weak for the part, but somehow it didn't seem to matter. She *was* Electra—that fanatical fiery spirit of relentless doom.

He stayed a few days with his mother—days which he found trying and difficult. He went to see his Uncle Sydney

244

and was received coldly. Enid was engaged to be married to a solicitor, and Uncle Sydney was not too pleased about it.

Nell and her mother were away for Easter. On their return Vernon rang up and said he must see her immediately. He arrived with a white face and burning eyes.

'Nell, do you know what I've heard? Everyone has been saying that you are going to marry George Chetwynd. *George Chetwynd!*'

'Who said so?'

'Lots of people. They say you go round with him everywhere.'

Nell looked frightened and unhappy.

'I wish you wouldn't believe things. And Vernon, don't look so—so accusing. It's perfectly true that he has asked me to marry him—twice, as a matter of fact.'

'That old man?'

'Oh, Vernon, don't be ridiculous. He's only about forty-one or two.'

'Nearly double your age. Why, I thought he wanted to marry your mother, perhaps.'

Nell laughed in spite of herself.

'Oh, dear, I wish he would. Mother's really awfully handsome still.'

'That's what I thought that night at Ranelagh. I never guessed—I never dreamed—that it was *you*! Or hadn't it begun then?'

'Oh, yes, it had begun—as you call it. That was why Mother was so angry that night—at my going off alone with you.'

'And I never guessed! Nell, you might have told me!'

'Told you what? There wasn't anything to tell—then!'

'No, I suppose not. I'm being an idiot. But I do know he's awfully rich. I get frightened sometimes. Oh, darling Nell, it was beastly of me to doubt you—even for a minute. As though you'd ever care how rich anyone were.'

Nell said irritably:

'Rich, rich, rich! You harp on that. He's awfully kind and awfully nice, too.'

'Oh, I dare say.'

'He is, Vernon. Really he is.'

'It's nice of you to stick up for him, darling, but he must be an insensitive sort of brute to hang round after you've refused him twice.'

Nell did not answer. She looked at him in a way he did not understand—something piteous and appealing and yet defiant in that strange limpid gaze. It was as though she looked at him from a world so far removed from his that they might be on different spheres.

He said:

'I feel ashamed of myself, Nell. But you're so lovely—everyone must want you . . .'

She broke down suddenly—began to cry. He was startled. She cried on, sobbed on his shoulder.

'I don't know what to do—I don't know what to do. I'm so unhappy. If I could only talk to you.'

'But you can talk to me, darling. I'm here listening.'

'No, no, no . . . I can never talk to you. You don't understand. It's all no use . . .'

She cried on. He kissed her, soothed her, poured out all his love . . .

246

When he had gone, her mother came into the room, an open letter in her hand.

She did not appear to notice Nell's tear-stained face.

'George Chetwynd sails for America on the 30th of May,' she remarked, as she went across to her desk.

'I don't care when he sails,' said Nell rebelliously.

Mrs Vereker did not answer.

That night Nell knelt longer than usual by her narrow white bed.

'Oh, God, please let me marry Vernon. I want to so much. I do love him so. Please let things come right and let us be married. Make something happen . . . Please God . . .'

At the end of April Abbots Puissants was let. Vernon came to Nell in some excitement.

'Nell, will you marry me now? We could just manage. It's a bad let—an awfully bad one, but I simply had to take it. You see, there's been the mortgage interest to pay and all the expenses of the upkeep while it's been unlet. I've had to borrow for all that and now, of course, it's got to be paid back. We'll be pretty short for a year or two, but then it won't be so bad . . .'

He talked on, explaining the financial details.

'I've been into it all, Nell. I have really. Sensibly, I mean. We could afford a tiny flat and one maid and have a little left over to play with. Oh, Nell, you wouldn't mind being poor with me, would you? You said once I didn't know what it was to be poor, but you can't say that now. I've lived on frightfully little since I came to London, and I haven't minded a bit.'

No, Nell knew he hadn't. The fact was in some way a vague reproach to her. And yet, though she couldn't quite express it to herself, she felt that the two cases were not on a par. It made much more difference to women—to be gay and pretty and admired and have a good time—none of those things affected men. They hadn't that everlasting problem of clothes—nobody minded if they were shabby.

But how explain these things to Vernon? One couldn't. He wasn't like George Chetwynd. George understood things like that.

'Nell.'

She sat there, irresolute, his arm round her. She had got to decide. Visions floated before her eyes. Amelie . . . the hot little house, the wailing children . . . George Chetwynd and his car . . . a stuffy little flat—a dirty incompetent maid . . . dances . . . clothes . . . the money they owed dressmakers . . . the rent of the London house—unpaid . . . Herself at Ascot, smiling, chattering in a lovely model gown . . . then, with a sudden revulsion she was back at Ranelagh on the bridge over the water with Vernon . . .

In almost the same voice as she had used that evening she said:

'I don't know. Oh, Vernon, I don't know.'

'Oh, Nell, darling, do . . . do . . .'

She disengaged herself from him, got up.

'Please, Vernon—I must think . . . yes, think. I—I can't when I'm with you.'

She wrote to him later that night:

'Dearest Vernon,—Let us wait a little longer—say six months. I don't feel I want to be married now. Besides, something might have happened about your opera then. You think I'm afraid of being poor, but it's not quite that. I've seen people—people who loved each other, and they didn't any more because of all the bothers and worries. I feel that if we wait and are patient everything will come right. Oh! Vernon, I know it will—and then everything will be so lovely. If only we wait and have patience . . .'

Vernon was angry when he got this letter. He did not show the letter to Jane, but he broke out into sufficiently unguarded speech to let her see how the land lay. She said at once in her disconcerting fashion:

'You do think you're sufficient prize for any girl, don't you, Vernon?'

'What do you mean?'

'Well, do you think it will be awfully jolly for a girl who has danced and been to parties and had lots of fun and people admiring her to be stuck down in a poky hole with no more fun?'

'We'd have each other.'

'You can't make love to her for twenty-four hours on end. Whilst you're working what is she to do?'

'Don't you think a woman can be poor and happy?'

'Certainly, given the necessary qualifications.'

'Which are—what? Love and trust?'

'No, you idiotic child. A sense of humour, a tough hide and the valuable quality of being sufficient unto oneself.

Agatha Christie

You will insist on love in a cottage being a sentimental problem dependent on the amount of love concerned. It's far more a problem of mental outlook. You'd be all right stuck down anywhere—Buckingham Palace or the Sahara—because you've got your mental preoccupation—music. But Nell's dependent on extraneous circumstances. Marrying you will cut her off from all her friends.'

'Why should it?'

'Because it's the hardest thing in the world for people with different incomes to continue friends. They're not all doing the same thing naturally.'

'You always put me in the wrong,' said Vernon savagely. 'Or at any rate you try to.'

'Well, it annoys me to see you put yourself on a pedestal and stand admiring yourself for nothing at all,' said Jane calmly. 'You expect Nell to sacrifice her friends and life to you, but you wouldn't make your sacrifice for her.'

'What sacrifice? I'd do anything.'

'Except sell Abbots Puissants!'

'You don't understand . . .'

Jane looked at him gently.

'Perhaps I do. Oh, yes, my dear, I do very well. But don't be noble. It always annoys me to see people being noble! Let's talk about the *Princess in the Tower*. I want you to show it to Radmaager.'

'Oh, it's so rotten. I couldn't. You know, I didn't realize myself, Jane, how rotten it was until I had finished it.'

'No,' said Jane. 'Nobody ever does. Fortunately—or nothing ever would be finished. Show it to Radmaager. What he says will be interesting at all events.'

250

Vernon yielded rather grudgingly.

'He'll think it such awful cheek.'

'No, he won't. He's a very high opinion of what Sebastian says, and Sebastian has always believed in you. Radmaager says that for so young a man, Sebastian's judgment is amazing.'

'Good old Sebastian. He's wonderful,' said Vernon warmly. 'Nearly everything he's done has been a success. Shekels are rolling in. God, how I envy him sometimes.'

'You needn't. He's not such a very happy person really.'

'You mean Joe? Oh! that will all come right.'

'I wonder. Vernon, do you see much of Joe?'

'A fair amount. Not as much as I used to. I can't stand that queer artistic set she's drifted into—their hair's all wrong and they look unwashed and they talk what seems to me the most arrant drivel. They're not a bit like your crowd—the people who really do things.'

'We're what Sebastian would call the successful commercial propositions. All the same, I'm worried about Joe. I'm afraid she's going to do something foolish.'

'That bounder La Marre, you mean?'

'Yes, I mean that bounder, La Marre. He's clever with women, you know, Vernon. Some men are.'

'You think she'd go off with him or something? Of course Joe is a damned fool in some ways.' He looked curiously at Jane: 'But I should have thought you—'

He stopped, suddenly crimson. Jane looked very faintly amused.

'You really needn't be embarrassed by my morals.'

'I wasn't. I mean—I've always wondered . . . Oh! I've wondered such an awful lot . . .'

His voice died away. There was silence. Jane sat very upright. She did not look at Vernon. She looked straight ahead of her. Presently in a quiet even voice, she began to speak. She spoke quite unemotionally and evenly, as though recounting something that had happened to someone else. It was a cold, concise recital of horror, and to Vernon the most dreadful thing about it was her own detached calm. She spoke as a scientist might speak, impersonally.

He buried his face in his hands.

Jane brought her recital to an end. Her quiet voice ceased.

Vernon said in a low shuddering voice:

'And you lived through *that*? I—didn't know that such things were.'

Jane said calmly:

'He was a Russian and a degenerate. It's hard for an Anglo-Saxon to understand that peculiar refined lust of cruelty. You understand brutality. You don't understand anything else.'

Vernon said, feeling childish and awkward as he put the question:

'You—you loved him very much?'

She shook her head slowly—began to speak, and then stopped.

'Why dissect the past?' she said, after a minute or two. 'He did some fine work. There's a thing of his in the South Kensington. It's macabre, but it's good.'

Then she began once more to talk of the *Princess in the Tower*.

Vernon went to the South Kensington two days later. He found the solitary representation of Boris Androv's work easily enough. A drowned woman—the face was horrible, puffed, bloated, decomposed, but the body was beautiful . . . a lovely body. Vernon knew instinctively that it was Jane's body.

He stood looking down on the bronze nude figure, with arms spread wide and long lank hair reaching out mournfully . . .

Such a beautiful body . . . Jane's body. Androv had modelled that nude body from her.

For the first time for years a queer remembrance of The Beast came over him. He felt afraid.

He turned quickly away from the beautiful bronze figure and left the building hurriedly, almost running.

It was the first night of Radmaager's new opera, *Peer Gynt*. Vernon was going to it and had been asked by Radmaager to attend a supper party afterwards. He was dining first with Nell at her mother's house. She was not coming to the opera.

Much to Nell's surprise, Vernon did not turn up to dinner. They waited some time, and then began without him. He arrived just as dessert was being put on the table.

'I'm most awfully sorry, Mrs Vereker. I can't tell you how sorry I am. Something very—very unexpected occurred. I'll tell you later.'

His face was so white and he was so obviously upset that Mrs Vereker forgot her annoyance. She was always a tactful woman of the world and she treated the present situation with her usual discretion.

'Well,' she said, rising, 'now you are here, Vernon, you can talk to Nell. If you're going to the opera you won't have much time.'

She left the room. Nell looked inquiringly at Vernon. He answered her look.

'Joe's gone off with La Marre.'

'Oh, Vernon, she hasn't!'

'She has.'

'Do you mean that she has eloped? That she's married him? That they've run away to get married?'

Vernon said grimly:

'He can't marry her. He's got a wife already.'

'Oh, Vernon, how awful! How could she?'

'Joe was always wrong-headed. She'll regret this—I know she will. I don't believe she really cares for him.'

'What about Sebastian? Won't he feel this terribly?'

'Yes, poor devil. I've been with him now. He's absolutely broken up over it. I'd no idea how much he cared for Joe.'

'I know he did.'

'You see, there were the three of us—always. Joe and I and Sebastian. We belonged together.'

A faint pang of jealousy shot through Nell. Vernon repeated:

'The three of us. It's—oh! I don't know—I feel as though I'd been to blame in some way. I've let myself get out of touch with Joe. Dear old Joe, she was so staunch always— better than any sister could be. It hurts me to think of the things she used to say when she was a kid—how she'd never have anything to do with men. And now she's come a mucker like this.'

Nell said in a shocked voice:

'A married man. That's what makes it so awful. Had he any children?'

'How should I know anything about his beastly children?'

'Vernon—don't be so cross.'

'Sorry, Nell. I'm upset, that's all.'

'How could she do such a thing,' said Nell. She had always rather resented Joe's unspoken contempt of which she had been subconsciously aware. She would not have been human had she not felt a faint sense of superiority. 'To run away with anyone married! It's dreadful!'

'Well, she had courage, anyway,' said Vernon.

He felt a sudden passionate desire to defend Joe—Joe who belonged to Abbots Puissants and the old days.

'Courage?' said Nell.

'Yes, courage!' said Vernon. 'At any rate she wasn't prudent. She didn't count the cost. She's chucked away everything in the world for love. That's more than some people will do.'

'Vernon!'

She got up, breathing hard.

'Well, it's true.' All his smouldering resentment came bursting out. 'You won't even face a little discomfort for me, Nell. You're always saying "Wait" and "Let's be careful." You aren't capable of chucking everything to the winds for love of anyone.'

'Oh, Vernon, how cruel you are . . . how cruel . . .'

He saw the tears come into her eyes and was immediately all compunction.

'Oh, Nell, I didn't mean it—I didn't mean it, sweetheart.'

His arms went round her, held her to him. Her sobs lessened. He glanced at his watch.

'Damn, I must go. Good night, Nell darling. You do love me, don't you?'

'Yes, of course—of course I do.'

He kissed her once more, hurried off. She sat down again by the disordered dinner table. Sat there—lost in thought . . .

He got to Covent Garden late. *Peer Gynt* had begun. The scene was Ingrid's wedding and Vernon arrived just at the moment of the first brief meeting of Peer and Solveig. He wondered if Jane were nervous. She managed to look marvellously young with her fair plaits and her innocent calm bearing. She looked nineteen. The act ended with the carrying off of Ingrid by Peer.

Vernon found himself interested less in the music than in Jane. Tonight was Jane's ordeal. She had to make good or go under. Vernon knew how anxious she was, above everything else, to justify Radmaager's trust in her.

Presently he knew that all was well. Jane was the perfect Solveig. Her voice, clear and true—the crystal thread as Radmaager had called it—sang unfalteringly and her acting was wonderful. The calm steadfast personality of Solveig dominated the opera.

Vernon found himself for the first time interested in the story of the weak, storm-torn Peer, the coward who ran from reality at every opportunity. The music of Peer's conflict with the great Boyg stirred him, reminding him of his childish terror of The Beast. It was the same formless bogey fear of childhood. Unseen, Solveig's clear voice delivered him from it. The scene in the forest where Solveig comes to Peer was infinitely beautiful, ending with Peer bidding Solveig remain while he went out to take up his burden. Her reply, 'If it is so heavy it is best two should share it.' And then Peer's departure, his final evasion, 'Bring sorrow on her? No. Go roundabout, Peer, go roundabout.'

The Whitsuntide music was the most beautiful—but in atmosphere very Radmaagian, Vernon thought. It led up to and prepared for the effect of the final scene. The weary Peer asleep with his head on Solveig's lap, and Solveig, her hair silvered, a Madonna blue cloak round her in the middle of the stage, her head silhouetted against the rising sun, singing valiantly against the Buttons Moulder.

It was a wonderful duet—Chavaranov, the famous Russian bass, his voice deepening and deepening, and Jane, with her silver thread singing steadily upward and ever upward, higher and higher—till the last note was left to her—high and incredibly pure . . . And the sun rose . . .

Vernon, feeling boyishly important, went behind afterwards. The opera had been a terrific success. The applause had been long and enthusiastic. He found Radmaager holding Jane by the hand and kissing her with artistic fervour and thoroughness.

'You are an angel—you are magnificent—yes, magnificent! You are an artist—Ah!' he burst into a torrent of words in his native language, then reverted to English. 'I will reward you—yes, little one, I will reward you. I know very well how to do it. I will persuade the long Sebastian. Together we will—'

'Hush,' said Jane.

Vernon came forward awkwardly, said shyly, 'It was splendid!'

He squeezed Jane's hand, and she gave him a brief affectionate smile.

'Where's Sebastian? Wasn't he here just now?'

Sebastian was no longer to be seen. Vernon volunteered to go in search of him and bring him along to supper. He said vaguely that he thought he knew where he was. Jane knew nothing of the news about Joe, and he didn't see how he could tell her at the moment.

He got a taxi and drove to Sebastian's house, but did not find him. Vernon wondered if perhaps Sebastian might be at his own rooms where he had left him earlier in the evening. He drove there straight away. He was feeling suddenly elated and triumphant. Even Joe did not seem to matter for the moment. He felt suddenly convinced that his own work was good—or rather that it would be some day. And somehow or other he also felt that things were coming right with Nell. She had clung to him differently tonight—more closely—more as though she could not bear to let him go . . . Yes, he was sure of it. Everything was coming right.

He ran up the stairs to his room. It was in darkness. Sebastian was not here then. He switched on the light— looked round. A note lay on the table, sent by hand. He picked it up. It was addressed to him in Nell's handwriting. He tore it open . . .

He stood there a long time. Then, carefully and methodically he drew up a chair to the table, setting it very exactly straight as though that were important, and sat down holding the note in his hand. He read it again for the tenth or eleventh time:

'Dearest Vernon,—Forgive me—please forgive me. I am going to marry George Chetwynd. I don't love him like I love you, but I shall be safe with him. Again—do forgive me—please.

'Your always loving

'Nell.'

He said aloud: '*Safe with him.* What does she mean by that? She'd have been safe with me. *Safe with him?* That hurts . . .'

He sat there. Minutes passed . . . Hours passed . . . He sat there, motionless, almost unable to think . . . Once the thought rose dully in his brain, 'Was this how Sebastian felt? I didn't understand . . .'

When he heard a rustle in the doorway he didn't look up. His first sight of Jane was when she came round the table, dropped on her knees beside him.

'Vernon—my dear—what is it? I knew there was something when you didn't come to the supper. I came to see . . .'

Dully, mechanically, he held out the note to her. She took it and read it. She laid it down again on the table.

He said in a dull bewildered voice: 'She needn't have said that—about not being safe with me. She would have been safe with me . . .'

'Oh, Vernon—my dear . . .'

Her arms went round him. He clutched at her suddenly—a frightened clutch such as a child might give at its mother. A sob burst from his throat. He laid his face down on the gleaming white skin of her neck.

'Oh! Jane . . . Jane . . .'

She held him closer. She stroked his hair. He murmured:

'Stay with me . . . Stay with me . . . Don't leave me . . .'

She answered:

'I won't leave you. It's all right . . .'

Her voice was tender—motherly. Something broke in him like the breaking of a dam. Ideas swirled and rushed through his head. His father kissing Winnie at Abbots Puissants . . . the statue in the South Kensington . . . Jane's body . . . her beautiful body.

He said hoarsely: 'Stay with me . . .'

Her arms round him, her lips on his forehead, she murmured back:

'I'll stay with you, dear.'

Like a mother to a child.

He wrenched himself suddenly free.

'Not like that. Not like that. Like this.'

His lips fastened on hers—fiercely, hungrily, his hand clutched at the roundness of her breast. He'd always wanted her—always—he knew it now. It was her body he wanted, that beautiful gracious body that Boris Androv had known so well.

He said again:

'Stay with me . . .'

There was a long pause—it seemed to him as though minutes, hours, years passed before she answered:

She said: '*I'll stay . . .*'

CHAPTER 4

On a day in July Sebastian Levinne walked along the Embankment in the direction of Jane's flat. It was a day more suggestive of early spring than of summer. A cold wind blew the dust in his face and made him blink.

There was a change visible in Sebastian. He had grown perceptibly older. There was very little of the boy about him now—there never had been much. He had always had that curious maturity of outlook which is the Semitic inheritance. As he walked along now, frowning to himself and pondering, he would easily have been taken for a man over thirty.

Jane herself opened the door of the flat to him. She spoke in a low, unusually husky voice.

'Vernon's out. He couldn't wait for you. You said three, you know, and it's past four now.'

'I was kept. Just as well, perhaps. I'm never quite sure of the best way of dealing with Vernon's nerves.'

'Don't tell me any fresh crises have arisen? I couldn't bear it.'

'Oh you'll get used to them. I've had to. What's the matter with your voice, Jane?'

'A cold. A throat, rather. It's all right. I'm nursing it.'

'My God! And the *Princess in the Tower* tomorrow night. Suppose you can't sing.'

'Oh! I shall sing. Don't be afraid. Only don't mind my whispering. I want to save it every bit I can.'

'Of course. You've seen someone, I suppose?'

'My usual man in Harley Street.'

'What did he say?'

'The usual things.'

'He didn't forbid you to sing tomorrow?'

'Oh, no.'

'You're an awfully good liar, aren't you, Jane?'

'I thought it would save trouble. But I might have known it would be no good with you. I'll be honest. He warned me that I'd been persistently over-straining my voice for years. He said it was madness to sing tomorrow night. But I don't care.'

'My dear Jane, I'm not going to risk your losing your voice.'

'Mind your own business, Sebastian. My voice is my affair. I don't interfere in your concerns, don't interfere in mine.'

Sebastian grinned.

'The tiger cat at home,' he remarked. 'But you mustn't, Jane, all the same. Does Vernon know?'

'Of course not. What do you think? And you're not to tell him, Sebastian.'

'I don't interfere really,' said Sebastian. 'I never have. But Jane dear, it will be ten thousand pities. The opera's not worth it. And Vernon's not worth it either. Be angry with me if you like for saying so.'

263

'Why should I be angry with you? It's the truth, and I know it. All the same, I'm going through with it. Call me any kind of a conceited egoist you like, but the *Princess in the Tower* won't be a success without me. I've been a success as Isolde and a furore in Solveig. It's my moment. And it's going to be Vernon's moment too. I can at least do that for him.'

He heard the undercurrent of feeling—the unconscious betrayal of that 'at least', but not by a muscle of his face did he show that he had realized its significance. He only said again very gently: 'He's not worth it, Jane. Paddle your own canoe. It's the only way. You've arrived. Vernon hasn't, and never may.'

'I know. I know. No one's what you call "worth it"—except perhaps one person.'

'Who?'

'*You*, Sebastian. *You're* worth it—and yet it's not for you I'm doing it!'

Sebastian was surprised and touched. A sudden mist came over his eyes. He stretched out his hand and took Jane's. They sat for a minute or two in silence.

'That was nice of you, Jane,' he said at last.

'Well, it's true. You're worth a dozen of Vernon. You've got brains, initiative, strength of character . . .'

Her husky voice died away. After another minute or two, he said very gently:

'How are things? Much as usual?'

'Yes, I think so. You know Mrs Deyre came to see me?'

'No, I didn't. What did she want?'

'She came to beg me to give up her boy. Pointed out

264

how I was ruining his life. Only a really bad woman would do what I was doing. And so on. You can guess the kind of thing.'

'And what did you say to her?' asked Sebastian curiously.

Jane shrugged her shoulders.

'What could I say? That to Vernon one harlot was as good as another?'

'Oh, my dear,' said Sebastian gently. 'Is it as bad as that?'

Jane got up, lighted a cigarette and walked restlessly about the room. Sebastian noticed how haggard her face had become.

'Is he—more or less all right?' he ventured.

'He drinks too much,' said Jane curtly.

'Can't you prevent it?'

'No, I can't.'

'It's queer. I should have thought you would always have great influence over Vernon.'

'Well, I haven't. Not now.' She was silent for a moment and then said: 'Nell's being married in the autumn, isn't she?'

'Yes. Do you think things will be—better then?'

'I haven't the least idea.'

'I wish to God he'd pull up,' said Sebastian. 'If you can't keep him straight, Jane, nobody can. Of course—it's in the blood.'

She came and sat down again.

'Tell me—tell me everything you know. About his people—his father, his mother.'

Sebastian gave a succinct account of the Deyres. Jane listened.

'His mother you've seen,' he concluded. 'Queer, isn't it, that Vernon doesn't seem to have inherited one single thing from her? He's a Deyre through and through. They are all artistic—musical—weak-willed, self-indulgent and attractive to women. Heredity's an odd thing.'

'I don't quite agree with you,' said Jane. 'Vernon's not like his mother, but he *has* inherited something from her.'

'What?'

'Vitality. She's an extraordinarily fine animal—have you ever thought of her that way? Well, Vernon's inherited some of that. Without it he'd never have been a composer. If he was a Deyre pure and simple, he'd only have *dallied* with music. It's the Bent force that gives him the power to create. You say his grandfather built up their business single-handed. Well, there's the same thing in Vernon.'

'I wonder if you're right.'

'I'm sure I am.'

Sebastian considered silently for some minutes.

'Is it only drink?' he said at last. 'Or is it—well, I mean, are there—other people?'

'Oh! there are others.'

'And you don't mind?'

'Mind? Mind? Of course I mind. What do you think I'm made of, Sebastian? I'm nearly killed with minding . . . But what can I do? Make scenes? Rant and rave and drive Vernon away from me altogether?'

Her beautiful husky voice rose from its whisper. Sebastian made a quick gesture and she stopped.

'You're right. I must be careful.'

'I can't understand it,' grumbled Sebastian. 'Even his music doesn't seem to mean anything to Vernon now. He's taken every suggestion from Radmaager and been like a lamb. It's unnatural!'

'We must wait. It will come back. It's reaction—reaction and Nell together. I can't help feeling that if the *Princess in the Tower* is a success, Vernon will pull himself together. He must feel a certain pride—a sense of achievement.'

'I hope so,' said Sebastian heavily. 'But I'm a bit worried about the future.'

'In what way? What are you afraid of?'

'War.'

Jane looked at him in astonishment. She could hardly believe her ears. She thought she must have mistaken the word.

'*War?*'

'Yes. The outcome of this Sarajevo business.'

It still seemed to Jane a little absurd and ridiculous.

'War with whom?'

'Germany—principally.'

'Oh, surely, Sebastian. Such a—a—far-away thing.'

'What does the pretext matter?' said Sebastian impatiently. 'It's the way money has been going. Money talks. I handle money—our relations in Russia handle money. We know. From the way money has been behaving for some time, we can guess what is in the wind. War's coming, Jane.'

Jane looked at him and changed her mind. Sebastian was in earnest and Sebastian usually knew what he was talking about. If he said war was coming, then, fantastic as it seemed, war would come.

Sebastian sat still, lost in thought. Money, investments, various loans, financial responsibilities he had undertaken, the future of his theatres, the policy to be adopted by the weekly paper he owned. Then, of course, there would be fighting. He was the son of a naturalized Englishman. He didn't wish in the least to go and fight, but he supposed it would be necessary. Everyone below a certain age would do so as a matter of course. It was not the danger that worried him, it was the annoyance of leaving his pet schemes to be looked after by someone else. 'They'll make a mess of it, sure to,' thought Sebastian bitterly. He put the war down as being a long job—two years—perhaps more. In the end, he shouldn't wonder if America was dragged into it.

The Government would issue loans—War Loan would be a good investment. No highbrow stuff for the theatres—soldiers on leave would want light comedy—pretty girls—legs—dancing. He thought it all out carefully. It was a good thing to get a chance to think uninterruptedly. Being with Jane was like being alone. She always knew when you didn't want to be spoken to.

He looked across at her. She, too, was thinking. He wondered what she was thinking about—you never quite knew with Jane. She and Vernon were alike there—didn't tell her thoughts. She was probably thinking about Vernon. If Vernon should go to the war and be killed! But no—that mustn't be. Sebastian's artistic soul rebelled. Vernon mustn't be killed.

*

The production of the *Princess in the Tower* has been forgotten by now. It came at an unfortunate time, since war broke out only about three weeks later.

At the time it was what is called 'well received'. Certain critics waxed a little sarcastic over this 'new school of young musicians' who thought they could revolutionize all existing ideas. Others praised it with sincerity as a work of great promise, though immature. But one and all spoke enthusiastically of the perfect beauty and artistry of the whole performance. Everyone 'went to Holborn', 'such miles out of the way, dear, but really worth it' to see the attractive fantastic drama, and 'that wonderful new singer, Jane Harding. Her *face*, dear, is simply wonderful—quite medieval. It wouldn't be the same without her!' It was a triumph for Jane, though a triumph that was short lived. On the fifth day she was forced to retire from the cast.

Sebastian was summoned by telephone at an hour when Vernon would not be there. Jane met him with such a radiant smile that he thought at first that his fears were not going to be realized.

'It's no good, Sebastian. Mary Lloyd must go on with it. She's not too bad, considering. As a matter of fact, she's got a better voice than I have and she's quite nice-looking.'

'H'm, I was afraid Hershall would say that. I'd like to see him myself.'

'Yes, he wants to see you. Not that there's anything to be done, I'm afraid.'

'What do you mean? Nothing to be done?'

'It's gone, my child. Gone for good. Hershall's too honest to hold out any real hope. He says of course you

Agatha Christie

never can be absolutely sure. It might come back with rest, etcetera, etcetera. He said it very well, and then I looked at him and laughed—and then he had to look shamefaced and own up. He was relieved, I think, at the way I took it.'

'But Jane, darling Jane . . .'

'Oh, don't mind so much, Sebastian. Please don't. It's so much easier if you don't. It's been a gamble, you know, all along—my voice was never really strong enough. I gambled with it—so far I won—now—I've lost. Well, there it is! One must be a good gambler and not let the hands twitch. Isn't that what they say at Monte Carlo?'

'Does Vernon know?'

'Yes, he's most awfully upset. He loved my voice. He's really quite broken-hearted about it.'

'But he doesn't know that—'

'That if I had waited two days, and not sung on the opening night of his opera, it would have been all right? No, he doesn't know that. And if you are loyal to me, Sebastian, he never will.'

'I shan't make promises. I think he ought to know.'

'No, because really it's unwarrantable what I've done! I've laid him under an obligation to me without his knowledge. That's a thing one shouldn't do. It isn't fair. If I had gone to Vernon and told him what Hershall said, do you suppose he would ever have consented to let me sing? He'd have prevented me by main force. It would be the meanest and cruellest thing in the world to go to Vernon now and say: "See what I have done for you!" Snivelling and asking for sympathy and gratitude ladled out in a soup plate.'

Sebastian was silent.

'Come now, my dear, agree.'

'Yes,' said Sebastian at last. 'You're right. What you did was unethical. You did it without Vernon's knowledge, and it's got to be kept from him now. But oh! Jane darling, why did you? Is Vernon's music worth it?'

'It will be—some day.'

'Is that why you did it?'

Jane shook her head.

'I thought not.'

There was a pause. Sebastian said:

'What will you do now, Jane?'

'Possibly teach. Possibly go on the stage. I don't know. If the worst comes to the worst, I can always cook.'

They both laughed, but Jane was very near tears.

She looked across the table at Sebastian and then suddenly rose and came and knelt down beside him. She laid her head down on his shoulder and he put his arm round her.

'Oh, Sebastian—Sebastian . . .'

'Poor old Jane.'

'I pretend I don't mind—but I do . . . I do . . . I loved singing. I loved it, loved it, loved it . . . That lovely Whitsuntide music of Solveig. I shall never sing it again.'

'I know. Why were you such a fool, Jane?'

'I don't know. Sheer idiocy.'

'If you had the choice again—'

'I'd do the same thing again.'

A silence. Then Jane lifted her head and said:

'Do you remember saying, Sebastian, that I had great

"driving power"? That nothing would turn me aside? And I said that I might be more easily turned aside than you thought. That between Vernon and me, I should go to the wall.'

Sebastian said:

'Things are queer.'

Jane slipped down on the floor beside him, her hand still in his.

'You can be clever,' said Sebastian, breaking the silence. 'You can have the brains to foresee things, and the wits to plan things and the force to succeed, but with all the cleverness in the world you can't avoid suffering some way or another. That's what's so odd. I know I've got brains, I know I'll get to the top of anything I undertake. I'm not like Vernon. Vernon will either be a Heaven-sent genius, or else he'll be an idle dissipated young man. He's got a gift if he's got anything, I've got ability. And yet with all the ability in the world, I can't prevent myself getting hurt.'

'No one can.'

'One might, perhaps, if one gave up one's whole life to it. If you pursued safety and nothing but safety, you'd get your wings singed, perhaps, but that would be all. You'd build a nice smooth wall and hide yourself inside it.'

'You're thinking of somebody in particular? Who?'

'Just a fancy. The future Mrs George Chetwynd if you want to be exact.'

'Nell? Do you think Nell has the strength of character to shut herself out from life?'

'Oh, Nell has got an enormous power of developing

272

protective colouring. Some species have.' He paused, then went on. 'Jane—have you ever heard from—Joe?'

'Yes, my dear, twice.'

'What did she say?'

'Very little. Just what fun everything was, and how she was enjoying herself, and how splendid one felt when one had had the courage to defy convention.' She paused and then added, 'She's not happy, Sebastian.'

'You think not?'

'I'm sure of it.'

There was a long silence. Two unhappy faces looked into the empty fireplace. Outside taxis hooted as they sped rapidly down the Embankment. Life went on . . .

It was the ninth of August. Nell Vereker turned out of Paddington station and walked slowly down towards the park. Four-wheelers passed her with old ladies in them laden with many hams. Staring placards were flaunted at every street corner. In every shop was a queue of people anxious to buy commodities.

Nell had said to herself many times:

'We're at war—actually at war,' and had not been able to believe it. Today, for the first time, it seemed to come home to her. A train journey where the ticket office refused to change a five pound note had proved the turning point. Ridiculous, but there it was.

A taxi passed and Nell hailed it. She got in, giving the address of Jane's flat in Chelsea. She glanced at her watch. It was just half-past ten. No fear that Jane would be out so early.

Agatha Christie

Nell went up in the lift and stood outside the door, having rung the bell. Her heart was beating nervously. In another minute the door would open. Her small face grew white and strained. Ah! now the door was opening. She and Jane were face to face.

She thought Jane started a little—that was all.

'Oh!' she said. 'It's you.'

'Yes,' said Nell. 'May I come in, please?'

It seemed to her that Jane hesitated a minute before drawing back to let her enter. She retreated into the hall, shut a door at the far end and then drew open the sitting-room door for Nell to pass in. She followed her, closing the door behind her.

'Well?'

'Jane, I've come to ask you if you know where Vernon is?'

'Vernon?'

'Yes. I went to his rooms—yesterday. He's left. The woman there didn't know where he'd gone. She said his letters were forwarded to you. I went home and wrote to you asking for his address. Then I was afraid you wouldn't tell me, wouldn't even answer, perhaps, and I thought I'd come instead.'

'I see.'

The tone was non-committal, unhelpful. Nell hurried on.

'I was sure you'd know where he was. You do, don't you?'

'Yes, I know.'

A slow answer, unnecessarily slow, Nell thought. Either Jane knew or she didn't.

'Well, then?'

Again a pause. Then Jane said:

'Why do you want to see Vernon, Nell?'

Nell raised a white face.

'Because I've been such a beast—such a beast! I see it now—now that this awful war has come. I was such a miserable coward—I hate myself—simply hate myself. Just because George was kind and good—and—yes, rich! Oh, Jane, how you must despise me. I know you do. You're quite right to despise me. Somehow this war has made everything clear—don't you find that?'

'Not particularly. There have been wars before and there will be wars again. They don't really alter anything underneath, you know.'

Nell was not paying attention.

'It's wicked to do anything except marry the man you love. I do love Vernon. I always knew I loved him, but I just hadn't the courage . . . Oh, Jane, do you think it's too late? Perhaps it is. Perhaps he won't want me now. But I *must* see him. Even if he doesn't want me, I must tell him . . .'

She stood there looking piteously up at Jane. Would Jane help her? If not, she must try Sebastian—but she was afraid of Sebastian. He might refuse flatly to do anything.

'I could get hold of him for you,' said Jane slowly, after a minute or two.

'Oh, thank you, Jane. And Jane—tell me—the war?'

'He's applied to join up—if that's what you mean.'

'Yes. Oh, it's dreadful—if he should be killed. But it can't last long—it'll be over by Christmas—everybody says so.'

'Sebastian says it will last two years.'

'Oh, but Sebastian can't know. He's not really English. He's Russian.'

Jane shook her head. Then she said:

'I'll go and—' she paused—'telephone. Wait here.'

She went out, closing the door behind her. She went to the end of the passage and into the bedroom. Vernon raised a dark rumpled head from the pillow.

'Get up,' said Jane curtly. 'Wash yourself and shave yourself and try and make yourself reasonably decent. Nell's here and wants to see you.'

'Nell. But—'

'She thinks I'm telephoning to you. When you're ready, you can go outside the front door and ring the bell—and may God have mercy on both our souls.'

'But Jane. Nell . . . what does she want?'

'If you still want to marry her, Vernon, now is your chance.'

'But I'll have to tell her—'

'What? That you've been leading a "gay life", that you've been "wild"? All the usual euphemisms! That's all she'll expect—and she'll be grateful to you for laying as little stress on that as possible. But tell her about you and me— and you bring it from the general to the particular—and take the child through Hell. Muzzle that noble conscience of yours and think of her.'

Vernon rose slowly from the bed.

'I don't understand you, Jane.'

'No, probably you never will.'

He said, 'Has Nell thrown over George Chetwynd?'

'I haven't asked for details. I'm going back to her now. Hurry up.'

She left the room. Vernon thought, 'I've never understood Jane, I never shall. She's so damned disconcerting. Well, I suppose I've been a sort of passing amusement to her. No, that's ungrateful. She's been damned decent to me. Nobody could have been more decent than Jane has been. But I couldn't make Nell understand that. She'd think Jane was dreadful . . .'

As he shaved and washed rapidly, he said to himself:

'All the same, it's out of the question. Nell and I could never come together again—Oh! I don't suppose there's any question of that. She's probably only come to ask me to forgive her, to make her feel comfortable in case I get killed in this bloody war. The sort of thing a girl would do. Anyway, I don't believe I care any more.'

Another voice, deep down, said ironically, 'Oh, no, not at all. Then why is your heart beating and your hand shaking? You bloody ass, of course you care!'

He was ready. He went outside—rang the bell. A mean subterfuge—unworthy—he felt ashamed. Jane opened the door. She said, rather like a parlour-maid, 'In here,' and waved him towards the sitting-room. He went in, closing the door behind him.

Nell had risen at his entrance. She stood with her hands clasped in front of her.

Her voice came faint and weak, like a guilty child.

'Oh, Vernon . . .'

Time swept backwards. He was in the boat at Cambridge . . . on the bridge at Ranelagh. He forgot Jane, he forgot everything. He and Nell were the only people in the world.

'Nell.'

They were clinging together, breathless as though they had been running. Words tumbled from Nell's lips.

'Vernon—if you want—I do love you—Oh! I do . . . I'll marry you any time—at once—today. I don't mind about being poor or *anything*!'

He lifted her off her feet, kissed her eyes, her hair, her lips.

'Darling—oh! darling. Don't let's waste a minute—not a minute. I don't know how you get married. I've never thought about it. But let's go out and see. We'll go to the Archbishop of Canterbury—isn't that what you do—and get a special licence? How the devil *do* you get married?'

'We might ask a clergyman?'

'Or there's a Registry Office. That's the thing.'

'I don't think I want to be married at a Registry Office. I'd feel rather like a cook or a house parlourmaid being engaged.'

'I don't think it's that kind, darling. But if you'd rather be married in a church, let's be married in a church. There are thousands of churches in London, all with nothing to do. I'm sure one of them will love to marry us.'

They went out together, laughing happily. Vernon had forgotten everything—remorse—conscience—Jane . . .

At half-past two that afternoon Vernon Deyre and Eleanor Vereker were married in the church of St Ethelred's, Chelsea.

BOOK IV

War

CHAPTER 1

It was six months later that Sebastian Levinne had a letter from Joe.

> 'St George's Hotel, Soho.
> Dear Sebastian,—I'm over in England for a few days. I should love to see you.—Yours, Joe.'

Sebastian read and re-read the brief note. He was at his mother's house on a few days' leave, so it had reached him with no delay. Across the breakfast table he was conscious of his mother's eyes watching him, and he marvelled, as he had often done before, at the quickness of her maternal apprehension. She read his face, which most people found so inscrutable, as easily as he read the note in his hand.

When she spoke it was in ordinary commonplace tones.

'Thome more marmalade, dear?' she said.

'No, thanks, Mother.' He answered the spoken question first, then went on to the unspoken one of which he was so keenly conscious. 'It's from Joe.'

'Joe,' said Mrs Levinne. Her voice expressed nothing.

'She's in London.'

There was a pause.

'I see,' said Mrs Levinne.

Still her voice expressed nothing. But Sebastian was aware of a whole tumult of feeling. It was the same to him as though his mother had burst out, 'My son, my son! And you were just beginning to forget her! Why does she come back like this? Why can't she leave you alone? This girl who has nothing to do with us or our race? This girl who was never the right wife for you and never will be.'

Sebastian rose.

'I think I must go round and see her.'

His mother answered in the same voice, 'I suppose so.'

They said no more. They understood each other. Each respected the other's point of view.

As he swung along the street, it suddenly occurred to Sebastian that Joe had given him no clue as to what name she was staying under at the hotel. Did she call herself Miss Waite or Madame La Marre? Unimportant, of course, but one of those silly conventional absurdities that made one feel awkward. He must ask for her under one or the other. How like Joe it was to have completely over-looked the point!

But as it happened there was no awkwardness, for the first person he saw as he passed through the swing doors was Joe herself. She greeted him with a glad cry of surprise.

'Sebastian! I'd no idea you could possibly have got my letter so soon!'

She led the way to a retired corner of the lounge and he followed her.

His first feeling was that she had changed—she had gone so far away that she was almost a stranger. It was partly, he thought, her clothes. They were ultra French clothes. Very quiet and dark and discreet, but utterly un-English. Her face, too, was very much made up. Its creamy pallor was enhanced by art, her lips were impossibly red and she had done something to the corners of her eyes.

He thought, 'She's a stranger—and yet she's Joe! She's the same Joe but she's gone a long way away—so far away that one can only just get in touch with her.'

But they talked together easily enough, each, as it were, putting out little feelers, as though sounding the distance that separated them. And suddenly the distance itself lessened, and the elegant Parisian stranger melted into Joe.

They talked of Vernon. Where was he? He never wrote or told one anything.

'He's on Salisbury Plain—near Wiltsbury. He may be going out to France any minute.'

'And Nell married him after all! Sebastian, I feel I was rather a beast about Nell. I didn't think she had it in her. I don't think she *would* have had it in her if it hadn't been for the war. Sebastian, isn't the war wonderful? What it's doing for people, I mean.'

Sebastian said drily that he supposed it was very much like any other war. Joe flew out at him vehemently.

'It isn't. It isn't. That's just where you're wrong. There's going to be a new world after it. People are beginning to see things—things they never saw before. All the cruelty and the wickedness and the waste of war. And they'll stand together so that such a thing shall never happen again.'

Her face was flushed and exalted. Sebastian perceived that the war had, as he phrased it, 'got' Joe. The war did get people. He had discussed it and deplored it with Jane. It made him sick to read the things that were printed and said about the war. 'A world fit for heroes', 'The war to end war', 'The fight for democracy'. And really all the time, it was the same old bloody business it always had been. Why couldn't people speak the truth about it?

Jane had disagreed with him. She maintained that the clap-trap (for she agreed it *was* clap-trap) which was written about war was inevitable, a kind of accompanying phenomenon inseparable from it. It was Nature's way of providing a way of escape—you had to have that wall of illusion and lies to help you to endure the solid facts. It was, to her, pitiable and almost beautiful—these things that we wanted to believe and told ourselves so speciously.

Sebastian had said, 'I dare say, but it's going to play Hell with the nation afterwards.'

He was saddened and a little depressed by Joe's fiery enthusiasm. And yet, after all, it was typical of Joe. Her enthusiasm always was red hot. It was a toss up which camp he found her in, that was all. She might just as easily have been a white hot pacifist, embracing martyrdom with fervour.

She said now accusingly to Sebastian:

'You don't agree! You think everything's going to be just the same.'

'There have always been wars, and they have never made any great difference.'

'Yes, but this is a different kind of war altogether.'

He smiled. He could not help it.

'My dear Joe, the things that happen to us personally are always different.'

'Oh! I've no patience with you. It's people like you—'
She stopped.

'Yes,' said Sebastian encouragingly. 'People like me—'

'You usen't to be like that. You used to have ideas. Now—'

'Now,' said Sebastian gravely, 'I am sunk in money. I'm a capitalist. Everyone knows what a hoggish creature the capitalist is.'

'Don't be absurd. But I do think that money is rather—well, stifling.'

'Yes,' said Sebastian, 'that's true enough. But that's a question of effect on an individual. I will quite agree with you that poverty is a blessed state. Talking in terms of art, it's probably as valuable as manure in a garden. But it's nonsense to say that because I've got money, I'm unfit to make prognostications as to the future, and especially as to the state obtaining after the war. Just because I've got money I'm all the more likely to be a good judge. Money has got a lot to do with war.'

'Yes, but because you think of everything in terms of money, you say that there always will be wars.'

'I didn't say anything of the kind. I think war will eventually be abolished—I'd give it roughly another two hundred years.'

'Ah! you do admit that by then we may have purer ideals.'

'I don't think it's got anything to do with ideals. It's probably a question of transport. Once you get flying going

285

on a commercial scale and you fuse countries together. Air charabancs to the Sahara, Wednesdays and Saturdays. That kind of thing. Countries getting mixed up and matey. Trade revolutionized. For all practical purposes, you make the world smaller. You reduce it in time to the level of a nation with counties in it. I don't think what's always alluded to as the Brotherhood of Man will ever develop from fine ideas—it will be a simple matter of common sense.'

'Oh, Sebastian!'

'I'm annoying you. I'm sorry, Joe dear.'

'You don't believe in anything.'

'Well, it's you who are the atheist, you know. Though, as a matter of fact, that word has gone out of fashion. We say nowadays that we believe in *Something*! Personally I'm quite satisfied with Jehovah. But I know what you meant when you said that, and you're wrong. I believe in beauty, in creation, in things like Vernon's music. I can't see any real defence for them economically, and yet I'm perfectly sure that they matter more than anything else in the world. I'm even prepared (sometimes) to drop money over them. That's a lot for a Jew!'

Joe laughed in spite of herself. Then she asked:

'What was the *Princess in the Tower* really like? Honestly, Sebastian?'

'Oh, rather like a giant toddling—an unconvincing performance and yet a performance on a different scale from anything else.'

'You think that some day—'

'I'm sure of it. There's nothing I'm so sure of as that. If only he isn't killed in this bloody war.'

286

Joe shivered.

'It's so awful,' she murmured. 'I've been working in the hospitals in Paris. Some of the things one sees!'

'I know. If he's only maimed it doesn't matter—not like a violinist who is finished if he loses his right hand. No, they can mess up his body any way they like—so long as his brain is left untouched. That sounds brutal, but you know what I mean—'

'I know. But sometimes—even then—' She broke off and then went on, speaking in a new tone of voice. 'Sebastian, I'm married.'

If something in him winced he didn't show it.

'Are you, my dear? Did La Marre get a divorce?'

'No. I left him. He was a beast—a beast, Sebastian.'

'I can imagine he might be.'

'Not that I regret anything. One has to live one's life—to gain experience. Anything is better than shrinking from life. That's just what people like Aunt Myra can't understand. I'm not going near them at Birmingham. I'm not ashamed or repentant of anything I've done.'

She gazed at him defiantly and his mind went back to Joe in the woods at Abbots Puissants. He thought, 'She's just the same. Wrong-headed, rebellious, adorable. One might have known then that she'd do these sort of things.'

He said gently, 'I'm only sorry that you've been unhappy. Because you have been unhappy, haven't you?'

'Horribly. But I've found my real life now. There was a boy in hospital—terribly badly wounded. They gave him morphia. He's been discharged now—cured, though of course he isn't fit for service. But the morphia—it's got hold

287

of him. That's why—we were married. A fortnight ago. We're going to fight it together.'

Sebastian did not trust himself to speak. Joe all over. But why, in the name of fortune, couldn't she have been content with physical disabilities? Morphia. A ghastly business.

And suddenly a pang shot through him. It was as though he resigned his last hope of her. Their ways led in opposite directions—Joe amongst her lost causes and her lame dogs, and he on an upward route. He might, of course, be killed in the war, but somehow he didn't think he would be. He was almost certain that he wouldn't even be picturesquely wounded. He felt a kind of certitude that he would come through safely, probably with moderate distinction, that he would come back to his enterprises, reorganizing and revitalizing them, that he would be successful—notably successful—in a world that did not tolerate failures. And the higher he climbed the further he would be separated from Joe.

He thought bitterly, 'There's always some woman to pull you out of a pit, but nobody will come and keep you company on a mountain peak, and yet you may be damned lonely there.'

He didn't quite know what to say to Joe. No good depressing her, poor child. He said rather weakly:

'What's your name now?'

'Valnière. You must meet François some time. I've just come over to settle up some legal bothers. Father died about a month ago, you know.'

Sebastian nodded. He remembered hearing of Colonel Waite's death.

Joe went on.

'I want to see Jane. And I want to see Vernon and Nell.'

It was settled that he should motor her down to Wiltsbury on the following day.

Nell and Vernon had rooms in a small prim house about a mile out of Wiltsbury. Vernon, looking well and brown, fell upon Joe and hugged her with enthusiasm.

They all went into a room full of antimacassars and lunched off boiled mutton and caper sauce.

'Vernon, you look splendid—and almost good-looking, doesn't he, Nell?'

'That's the uniform,' said Nell demurely.

She had changed, Sebastian thought, looking at her. He had not seen her since her marriage, four months previously. To him she had always fallen into a class—a certain type of charming young girl. Now he saw her as an individual—the real Nell bursting out of her chrysalis.

There was a subdued radiance about her. She was quieter than she used to be—and yet she was more alive. They were happy together—no one who looked at them could doubt it. They seldom looked at each other, but when they did you felt it . . . something passed between them— delicate, evanescent, but unmistakable.

It was a happy meal. They talked of old days—of Abbots Puissants.

'And here we are, all four of us together again,' said Joe.

A warm feeling fastened round Nell's heart. Joe had included her. All *four* of us, she had said. Nell remembered how once Vernon had said 'We three—' and the words had hurt her. But that was over now. She was one of them. That was her reward—one of her rewards. Life seemed full of rewards at the moment.

She was happy—so terribly happy, and she might so easily not have been happy. She might have been actually married to George when the war broke out. How could she ever have been so incredibly foolish as to think that anything mattered except marrying Vernon? How extraordinarily happy they were and how right he had been to say poverty didn't matter.

It wasn't as though she were the only one. Lots of girls were doing it—flinging up everything—marrying the man they cared for no matter how poor he was. After the war, something would turn up. That was the attitude. And behind it lay that awful secret fear that you never took out and looked at properly. The nearest you ever got to it was saying defiantly, 'And no matter *what* happens, we'll have had *something*.'

She thought, '*The world's changing. Everything's different now. It always will be. We'll never go back . . .*'

She looked across the table at Joe. Joe looked different somehow—very *queer*. What you would have called before the war—well, '*not quite*'. What had Joe been doing with herself? That nasty man, La Marre . . . Oh, well, better not think about it. Nothing mattered nowadays.

Joe was so nice to her—so different to what she used to be in the old days when Nell had always felt uncomfortably that Joe despised her. Perhaps she had cause. She *had* been a little coward.

The war was awful, of course, but it had simplified things. Her mother, for instance, had come round almost at once. She was disappointed naturally about George Chetwynd (poor George, he really *was* a dear and she'd been a beast to him) but Mrs Vereker proceeded to make the best of things with admirable common sense.

'These war marriages!' She used that phrase with a tiny shrug of the shoulders. 'Poor children—you can't blame them. Not wise, perhaps—but what is wisdom at a time like this?' Mrs Vereker needed all her skill and all her wit to deal with her creditors and she had come off pretty well. Some of them even felt sympathy for her.

If she and Vernon didn't really like each other, they concealed the fact quite creditably, and as a matter of fact, had only met once since the marriage. It had all been so easy.

Perhaps, if you had courage, things were always easy. Perhaps that was the great secret of life.

Nell pondered, then waking from her reverie plunged once more into the conversation.

Sebastian was speaking.

'We're going to look Jane up when we get back to town. I've not so much as heard of her for ages. Have you, Vernon?'

Vernon shook his head.

'No,' he said, 'I haven't.'

He tried to speak naturally but didn't quite succeed.

'She's very nice,' said Nell. 'But—well—rather difficult, isn't she? I mean you never quite know what she's thinking about.'

291

'She might be occasionally disconcerting,' Sebastian allowed.

'She's an angel,' said Joe with vehemence.

Nell was watching Vernon. She thought, 'I wish he'd say something . . . anything . . . I'm afraid of Jane. I always have been. She's a devil . . .'

'Probably,' said Sebastian, 'she's gone to Russia or Timbuctoo or Mozambique. One would never be surprised with Jane.'

'How long is it since you've seen her?' asked Joe.

'Exactly? Oh! about three weeks.'

'Is that all? I thought you meant really ages.'

'It seems like it,' said Sebastian.

They began to talk of Joe's hospital in Paris. Then they talked of Myra and Uncle Sydney. Myra was very well and making an incredible quantity of swabs and also did duty twice a week at a canteen. Uncle Sydney was well on the way to making a second fortune having started the manufacture of explosives.

'He's got off the mark early,' said Sebastian appreciatively. 'This war's not going to be over for three years at least.'

They argued the point. The days of an 'optimistic six months' were over, but three years were regarded as too gloomy a view. Sebastian talked about explosives, the state of Russia, the food question, and submarines. He was a little dictatorial, since he was perfectly sure that he was right.

At five o'clock Sebastian and Joe got into the car and drove back to London. Vernon and Nell stood in the road waving.

'Well,' said Nell, 'that's that.' She slipped her arm through Vernon's. 'I'm glad you were able to get off today. Joe would have been awfully disappointed not to see you.'

'Do you think she's changed?'

'A little. Don't you?'

They were strolling along the road and they turned off where a track led over the downs.

'Yes,' said Vernon, with a sigh, 'I suppose it was inevitable.'

'I'm glad she's married. I think it's very fine of her. Don't you?'

'Oh, yes. Joe was always warm-hearted, bless her.'

He spoke abstractedly. Nell glanced up at him. She realized now that he had been rather silent all day. The others had done most of the talking.

'I'm glad they came,' she said again.

Vernon didn't answer. She pressed her arm against his and felt him press it against his side. But his silence persisted.

It was getting dark and the air came sharp and cold, but they did not turn back, walked on and on without speaking. So they had often walked before—silent and happy. But this silence was different. There was weight in it and menace.

Suddenly Nell knew . . .

'Vernon! It's come! You've got to go . . .'

He pressed her hand closer still but did not speak.

'Vernon . . . when?'

'Next Thursday.'

'Oh!' She stood still. Agony shot through her. It had

come. She had known it was bound to come, but she hadn't known—quite—what it was going to feel like.

'Nell. Nell . . . Don't mind so much. Please don't mind so much.' The words came tumbling out now. 'It'll be all right. I *know* it'll be all right. I'm not going to get killed. I couldn't now that you love me—now that we're so happy. Some fellows feel their number's up when they go out—but I don't. I've a kind of certainty that I'm going to come through. I want you to feel that too.'

She stood there frozen. This was what war was really. It took the heart out of your body, the blood out of your veins. She clung to him with a sob. He held her to him.

'It's all right, Nell. We knew it was coming soon. And I'm really frightfully keen to go—at least I would be if it wasn't for leaving you. You wouldn't like me to have spent the whole war guarding a bridge in England, would you? And there will be the leaves to look forward to—we'll have the most frightfully jolly leaves. There will be lots of money, and we'll simply blue it. Oh, Nell darling, I just know that nothing can happen to me now that you care for me.'

She agreed with him.

'It can't—it can't—God couldn't be so cruel . . .'

But the thought came to her that God was letting a lot of cruel things happen.

She said valiantly, forcing back her tears:

'It'll be all right, darling. I know it too.'

'And even—even if it isn't—you must remember—how perfect this has been . . . Darling, you have been happy, haven't you?'

She lifted her lips to his. They clung together, dumb,

agonizing . . . the shadow of their first parting hanging over them.

How long they stood there they hardly knew.

When they went back to the antimacassars, they talked cheerfully of ordinary things. Vernon only touched once on the future.

'Nell, when I'm gone, will you go to your mother or what?'

'No. I'd rather stay down here. There are lots of things to do in Wiltsbury—hospital, canteen.'

'Yes, but I don't want you to do anything. I think you'd be better distracted in London, there will still be theatres and things like that.'

'No, Vernon, I must do something—work, I mean.'

'Well, if you want to work, you can knit me socks. I hate all this nursing business. I suppose it's necessary but I don't like it. You wouldn't care to go to Birmingham?'

Nell said very decidedly that she would *not* like to go to Birmingham.

The actual parting when it came was less strenuous. Vernon kissed her almost off-handedly.

'Well, so long. Cheer up. Everything's going to be all right. I'll write as much as I can, though I expect we're not allowed to say much that's interesting. Take care of yourself, Nell darling.'

One almost involuntary tightening of his arms round her, and then he almost pushed her from him.

He was gone.

She thought, 'I shall never sleep tonight—never . . .'

But she did. A deep heavy sleep. She went down into it as into an abyss. A haunted sleep—full of terror and apprehension that gradually faded into the unconsciousness of exhaustion.

She woke with a keen sword of pain piercing her heart.

She thought, 'Vernon's gone to the war. I must get something to do.'

CHAPTER 2

Nell went to see Mrs Curtis, the Red Cross Commandant. Mrs Curtis was benign and affable. She was enjoying her importance and was convinced that she was a born organizer. Actually, she was a very bad one. But everyone said she had a wonderful manner. She condescended graciously to Nell.

'Let me see, Mrs—ah! Deyre. You've got your VAD and Nursing Certificates?'

'Yes.'

'But you don't belong to any of the local detachments?'

Nell's exact standing was discussed at some length.

'Well, we must see what we can do for you,' said Mrs Curtis. 'The hospital is fully staffed at present, but of course they are always falling out. Two days after the first convoy came in, we had seventeen resignations. All women of a certain age. They didn't like the way the sisters spoke to them. I myself think the sisters were perhaps a little unnecessarily brutal, but of course there's a great deal of jealousy of the Red Cross. And these were all well-to-do women

297

Agatha Christie

who didn't like being "spoken to". You are not sensitive in that way, Mrs Deyre?'

Nell said that she didn't mind anything.

'That is the spirit,' said Mrs Curtis approvingly. 'I myself,' she continued, 'consider it in the light of good discipline. And where should we all be without discipline?'

It shot through Nell's mind that Mrs Curtis had not had to endure any discipline, which robbed her pronouncement of some of its impressiveness. But she continued to stand there looking attentive and impressed.

'I have a list of girls on the reserve,' continued Mrs Curtis. 'I will add your name. Two days a week you will attend at the Out Patient ward at the Town Hospital, and thereby gain a little experience. They are short-handed there and are willing to accept our help. Then you and Miss—' she consulted a list—'I think Miss Cardner—yes, Miss Cardner—will go with the District Nurse on her rounds on Tuesdays and Fridays. You've got your uniform, of course. Then that is all right.'

Mary Cardner was a pleasant plump girl whose father was a retired butcher. She was very friendly to Nell, explained that the days were Wednesday and Saturday and not Tuesday and Friday—'But old Curtis always gets something wrong'—that the District Nurse was a dear, and never jumped on you and that Sister Margaret at the hospital was a holy terror.

On the following Wednesday, Nell did her first round with the District Nurse, a little bustling woman very much overworked. At the end of the day, she patted Nell kindly on the shoulder.

'I'm glad to see you have a head on your shoulders, my dear. Really some of the girls who come seem to me half-witted—they do indeed. And such fine ladies—you wouldn't believe! Not by birth—I don't mean that. But half-educated girls who think nursing is all smoothing a pillow and feeding the patient with grapes. You'll know your way about in no time.'

Heartened by this, Nell presented herself at the Out Patient Department at the given time without too much trepidation. She was received by a tall gaunt Sister with a malevolent eye.

'Another raw beginner,' she grumbled. 'Mrs Curtis sent you, I suppose? I'm sick of that woman. Takes me more time and trouble teaching silly girls who think they know everything than it would to do everything myself.'

'I'm sorry,' said Nell meekly.

'Get a couple of certificates, attend a dozen lectures and think you know everything,' said Sister Margaret bitterly. 'Here they come. Don't get in my way more than you can help.'

A typical batch of patients were assembled. A young boy with legs riddled with ulcers, a child with scalded legs from an overturned kettle, a girl with a needle in her finger, various sufferers with 'bad ears', 'bad legs', 'bad arms'.

Sister Margaret said sharply to Nell:

'Know how to syringe an ear? I thought not. Watch me.'

Nell watched.

'You can do it next time,' said Sister Margaret. 'Get the bandage off that boy's finger, and let him soak it in hot boracic and water till I'm ready for him.'

Nell felt nervous and clumsy. Sister Margaret was paralysing her. Almost immediately, it seemed, Sister was by her side.

'We haven't got all day here to do things in,' she remarked. 'There, leave it to me. You seem to be all thumbs. Soak the bandages off that kid's legs. Tepid water.'

Nell got a basin of tepid water and knelt down before the child, a mere mite of three. She was badly burnt, and the bandages had stuck to the tiny legs. Nell sponged and soaked very gently, but the baby screamed. It was a loud long-drawn yell of terror and agony, and it defeated Nell utterly.

She felt suddenly sick and faint. She couldn't do this work—she simply couldn't do it. She drew back, and as she did so she glanced up to find Sister Margaret watching her, a gleam of malicious pleasure showing in her eye.

'I thought you couldn't stick it,' that eye said.

It rallied Nell as nothing else would have done. She bent her head, and setting her teeth, went on with her job, trying to avert her mind from the child's shrieks. It was done at last, and Nell stood up, white and trembling and feeling deathly sick.

Sister Margaret came along. She seemed disappointed.

'Oh, you've done it,' she said. She spoke to the child's mother. 'I'd be a bit more careful how you let the child get at the kettle in future, Mrs Somers,' she said.

Mrs Somers complained that you couldn't be everywhere at once.

Nell was ordered off to foment a poisoned finger. Next, she assisted Sister to syringe the ulcerated leg, and after

that stood by while a young doctor extracted the needle
from the girl's finger. As he probed and cut, the girl winced
and shrank and he spoke to her sharply.

'Keep quiet, can't you?'

Nell thought: 'One never sees this side of things. One is
only used to a doctor with a bedside manner. "*I'm afraid
this will hurt a little. Be as still as you can.*"'

The young doctor proceeded to extract a couple of teeth,
flinging them carelessly on the floor, then he treated a
smashed hand that had just come in from an accident.

It was not, Nell reflected, that he was unskilful. It was
the absence of manner that was so disturbing to one's
preconceived ideas. Whatever he did, Sister Margaret
accompanied him, tittering in a sycophantic manner at any
jokes he was pleased to make. Of Nell he took no notice.

At last the hour was over. Nell was thankful. She said
goodbye timidly to Sister Margaret.

'Like it?' asked Sister with a demoniac grin.

'I'm afraid I'm very stupid,' said Nell.

'How can you be anything else?' said Sister Margaret.
'A lot of amateurs like you Red Cross people. And thinking
you know everything on earth. Well, perhaps, you'll be a
little less clumsy next time!'

Such was Nell's encouraging début at the hospital.

It grew less terrible as time went on, however. Sister
Margaret softened, and relaxed her attitude of fierce defen-
siveness. She even permitted herself to answer questions.

'You're not so stuck up as most,' she allowed graciously.

Nell, in her turn, was impressed by the enormous amount
of competent work Sister Margaret managed to put in in

a very short time. And she understood a little her soreness on the subject of amateurs.

What struck Nell most was the enormous number of 'bad legs' and their prototypes, most of them evidently old friends. She asked Sister Margaret timidly about them.

'Nothing much to be done about it,' Sister Margaret replied. 'Hereditary, most of them. Bad blood. You can't cure it.'

Another thing that impressed Nell was the uncomplaining heroism of the poor. They came and were treated, suffered great pain, and went off to walk several miles home without a thought.

She saw it too in their homes. She and Mary Cardner had taken over a certain amount of the District Nurse's round. They washed bedridden old women, tended 'bad legs', occasionally washed and tended babies whose mothers were too ill to do anything. The cottages were small, the windows usually hermetically sealed, and the place littered with treasures dear to the hearts of the owners. The stuffiness was often unbearable.

The worst shock was about two weeks after beginning work, when they found a bedridden old man dead in his bed and had to lay him out. But for Mary Cardner's matter-of-fact cheerfulness, Nell felt she could not have done it.

The District Nurse praised them.

'You're good girls. And you're being a real help.' They went home glowing with satisfaction. Never in her life had Nell so appreciated a hot bath and a lavish allowance of bath salts.

She had had two postcards from Vernon. Mere scrawls saying he was all right and everything was splendid. She wrote to him every day describing her adventures, trying to make them sound as amusing as possible. He wrote back: 'Somewhere in France.

'Darling Nell,

'I'm all right. Feeling splendidly fit. It's all a great adventure, but I do long to see you. I do wish you wouldn't go into these beastly cottages and places and mess about with diseased people. I'm sure you'll catch something. Why you want to, I can't think. I'm sure it isn't necessary. Do give it up.

'We think mostly about our food out here, and the Tommies think of nothing but their tea. They'll risk being blown to bits any time for a cup of hot tea. I have to censor their letters. One man always ends "Yours till Hell freezes," so I'll say the same.

'Yours Vernon.'

One morning Nell received a telephone call from Mrs Curtis.

'There is a vacancy for a ward maid, Mrs Deyre. Afternoon duty. Be at the hospital at two-thirty.'

The Town Hall of Wiltsbury had been turned into a hospital. It was a big new building standing in the cathedral square and overshadowed by the tall spire of the cathedral. A handsome being in uniform with a game leg and medals received her kindly at the front entrance.

'You've come to the wrong door, Missie. Staff through the quartermaster's stores. Here, the scout will show you the way.'

A diminutive scout conducted her down steps, through a kind of gloomy crypt where an elderly lady in Red Cross uniform sat surrounded with bales of hospital shirts, wearing several shawls and shivering a good deal, then along stoneflagged passages, and finally into a gloomy underground chamber where she was received by Miss Curtain, the chief of the ward maids, a tall thin lady with a face like a dreaming duchess and charming gentle manners.

Nell was instructed in her duties which were simple enough to understand. They entailed hard work, but no difficulty. A certain area of stone passages and steps to scrub. Then the nurses' tea to lay, wait on, and finally clear away. Then the ward maids had their own tea. Then the same routine for supper.

Nell soon got the hang of things. The salient points of the new life were, one, war with the kitchen, two, the difficulty of providing the sisters with the right kind of tea.

There was a long table where the VAD nurses sat, pouring down in a stream, frantically hungry, and always the food seemed to fail before the last three were seated. You then applied to the kitchen through a tube and got a biting rejoinder. The right amount of bread and butter had been sent up, three pieces for each. Somebody must have eaten more than their share. Loud disclaimers from the VADs. They chatted to each other amiably and freely, addressing each other by their surnames.

'I didn't eat your slice of bread, Jones. I wouldn't do such a mean thing!' 'They always send it up wrong.' 'Look here, Catford's got to have something to eat. She's got an

op. in half an hour.' 'Hurry up, Bulgy (an affectionate
nickname, this) we've got all those mackintoshes to scrub.'

Very different the behaviour at the sisters' table at the
other side of the room. Conversation there went on genteelly
in frosty whispers. Before each sister was a small brown
pot of tea. It was Nell's business to know exactly how
strong each sister liked it. It was never a question of
how weak! To bring 'washy' tea to a sister was to fall from
grace for ever.

The whispers went on incessantly.

'I said to her: "Naturally the surgical cases receive the
first attention."' 'I only passed the remark, so to speak.'
'Pushing herself forward. Always the same thing.' 'Would
you believe it, she forgot to hold the towel for the doctor's
hands.' 'I said to Doctor this morning . . .' 'I passed the
remark to Nurse . . .'

Again and again that one phrase recurred. 'I passed the
remark.' Nell grew to listen for it. When she approached
the table, the whispers became lower and the sisters
looked at her suspiciously. Their conversation was secretive
and shrouded in dignity. With enormous formality, they
offered each other tea.

'Some of mine, Sister Westhaven? There's plenty in the
pot.' 'Would you oblige me with the sugar, Sister Carr?'
'Pardon me.'

Nell had just begun to realize the hospital atmosphere,
the feuds, the jealousies, the cabals, and the hundred
and one undercurrents, when she was promoted to the
ward, one of the nurses having gone sick.

She had a row of twelve beds to attend to, mostly

surgical cases. Her companion was Gladys Potts, a small giggling creature, intelligent but lazy. The ward was under the charge of Sister Westhaven, a tall thin acid woman with a look of permanent disapproval. Nell's heart sank when she saw her, but later she congratulated herself. Sister Westhaven was far the pleasantest nurse in the hospital to work under.

There were five sisters in all. Sister Carr, round and good-tempered looking. The men liked her and she giggled and joked with them a good deal, and was then late over her dressings and hurried over them. She called the VADs 'dear', and patted them affectionately but her temper was uncertain. She herself was so unpunctual that everything went wrong and the 'dear' was blamed for it. She was maddening to work under.

Sister Barnes was impossible. Everyone said so. She ranted and scolded from morning to night. She hated VADs and let them know it. 'I'll teach them to come here thinking they know everything,' was her constant declaration. Apart from her biting sarcasm, she was a good nurse, and some of the girls liked working under her in spite of her lashing tongue.

Sister Dunlop was a dug-out. She was kindly and placid, but thoroughly lazy. She drank a great deal of tea and did as little work as possible.

Sister Norris was theatre sister. She was competent at her job, rouged her lips and was cattish to her underlings.

Sister Westhaven was by far the best nurse in the hospital. She was enthusiastic over work and was a good judge of those under her. If they showed promise she was reasonably amiable to them. If she judged them fools they led a miserable life.

On the fourth day, she said to Nell:

'I thought you weren't worth much at first, Nurse. But you've got a good lot of work in you.'

So much imbued by now was Nell by the hospital spirit that she went home in the seventh heaven.

Little by little she sank into the hospital rut. At first she had suffered a heartrending pang at the sight of the wounded. The first dressing of wounds at which she assisted was almost more than she could bear. Those who 'Longed to nurse' usually brought a certain amount of emotionalism to the task. But they were soon purged of it. Blood, wounds, suffering were everyday matters.

Nell was popular with the men. In the slack hour after tea, she wrote letters for them, fetched books she thought they would like from the shelves at the end of the ward, heard stories of their families and sweethearts. She became in common with the other nurses zealous to defend them from the cruelties and stupidities of the would-be kind.

On visitors' days streams of elderly ladies arrived. They sat down by beds and did their best to 'cheer our brave soldier'.

Certain things were conventions. 'You're longing to get back, I suppose?' And 'Yes, M'am,' was always the answer given. Descriptions were sought of the Angels at Mons.

There were also concerts. Some were well organized and were thoroughly enjoyed. Others—! They were summed up by the nurse on the next row to Nell, Phillis Deacon.

'Anybody who thinks they can sing, but has never been allowed to by their families, has got their chance now!'

There were also clergymen. Never, Nell thought, had she seen so many clergymen. One or two were appreciated. They were fine men, with sympathy and understanding, and they knew the right things to say and did not stress the religious side of their duties unduly. But there were many others.

'Nurse.'

Nell paused in a hurried progress along the ward, having just been told sharply by Sister: 'Nurse, your beds are crooked. No. 7's sticking out.'

'Yes.'

'Couldn't you wash me now, Nurse?'

Nell stared at the unusual request.

'It's not nearly half-past seven.'

'It's the parson. He's at me to be confirmed. He's coming in now.'

Nell took pity on him. The Reverend Canon Edgerton found his prospective convert barred from him by screens and basins of water.

'Thank yer, Nurse,' said the patient hoarsely. 'It seems a bit hard to go on nagging at a feller when he can't get away from yer, doesn't it?'

Washing—interminable washing. The patients were washed, the ward was washed, and at every hour of the day there were mackintoshes to scrub.

And eternal tidiness.

'Nurse—your beds. The bedclothes are hanging down on No. 9. No. 2 has pushed his bed sideways. What will Doctor think?'

Doctor—Doctor—Doctor. Morning, noon and night, Doctor! Doctor was a god. For a mere VAD to speak to Doctor was *lese-majesty* and brought down the vials of wrath on your head from Sister. Some of the VADs offended innocently. They were Wiltsbury girls and they knew the doctors—knew them as ordinary human beings. They said good morning blithely. Soon they knew better—knew they had been guilty of that awful sin 'pushing yourself forward'. Mary Cardner 'pushed herself forward'. Doctor asked for some scissors and unthinkingly, she handed him the pair she wore. Sister explained her crime to her at length. She ended thus:

'I don't say you mightn't have done this. Seeing you had the exact thing that was wanted, you might have said to me—in a whisper, that is—"Is this what is needed, Sister?" And I would have taken them from you and handed them to Doctor. No one could have objected to that.'

You got tired of the word 'Doctor'. Every remark Sister made was punctuated with it, even when speaking to him.

'Yes, Doctor.' '102 this morning, Doctor.' 'I don't think so, Doctor.' 'Pardon, Doctor? I didn't quite catch.' 'Nurse, hold the towel for Doctor's hands.'

And you held the towel meekly, standing like a glorified towel horse. And Doctor, having wiped his sacred hands, flung the towel on the floor where you meekly picked it up. You poured water for Doctor, you handed soap to Doctor, and finally you received the command:

'Nurse, open the door for Doctor.'

'And what I'm afraid is, we shan't be able to grow out of it afterwards,' said Phillis Deacon wrathfully. 'I shall never feel the same about doctors again. Even the scrubbiest little doctors I shall be subservient to, and when they come to dine, I shall find myself rushing to open the door for them. I know I shall.'

There was a great freemasonry in the hospital. Class distinctions were a thing of the past. The dean's daughter, the butcher's daughter, Mrs Manfred, who was the wife of a draper's assistant, Phillis Deacon who was the daughter of a baronet, they all called each other by their surnames and shared the common interest of 'What would there be for supper, and would it go round?' Undoubtedly there was cheating. Gladys Potts, the giggler, was discovered to go down early and surreptitiously to filch an extra piece of bread and butter or an unfair helping of rice.

'You know,' said Phillis Deacon. 'I do sympathize with servants now. One always thinks they mind so much about their food—and here are we getting just the same. It's having nothing else to look forward to. I could have cried when the scrambled eggs didn't go round last night.'

'They oughtn't to have scrambled eggs,' said Mary Cardner angrily. 'The eggs ought to be separate, poached or boiled. Scrambled gives too much opportunity to unscrupulous people.'

And she looked with significance at Gladys Potts, who giggled nervously and moved away.

'That girl's a slacker,' said Phillis Deacon. 'She's always got something else to do when it's screens. And she sucks up to Sister. It doesn't matter with Westhaven. Westhaven's fair. But she flattered little Carr till she got all the soft jobs.'

Little Potts was unpopular. Strenuous efforts were made

to force her to do the more disagreeable work sometimes, but Potts was wily. Only the resourceful Deacon was a match for her.

There were also the jealousies amongst the doctors themselves. Naturally they all wanted the more interesting surgical cases. The allotting of cases to different wards gave rise to feeling.

Nell soon knew all the doctors and their various attributes. There was Doctor Lang, tall, untidy, slouching, with long nervous fingers. He was the cleverest surgeon of the lot. He had a sarcastic tongue, and was ruthless in his treatments, but he was clever. All the sisters adored him.

Then there was Doctor Wilbraham who had the fashionable practice of Wiltsbury. A big florid man, genial in temper when things went well, and the manners of a spoilt child when he was put out. If he was tired and cross he was unnecessarily rough and Nell hated him.

There was Doctor Meadows, a quiet efficient GP. He was content not to do operations and he gave every case unfailing attention. He always spoke politely to the VADs and omitted to throw towels on the floor.

Then there was Doctor Bury who was not supposed to be much good and who was himself convinced that he knew everything. He was always wishing to try extraordinary new methods, and he never continued one treatment for more than a couple of days. If one of his patients died, it was the fashion to say: 'Do you wonder with Doctor Bury?'

Then there was young Doctor Keen, who had been invalided home from the front. He was little more than a

311

medical student, but he was full of importance. He even demeaned himself to chat with the VADs, explaining the importance of an operation that had just taken place. Nell said to Sister Westhaven: 'I didn't know Doctor Keen was operating. I thought it was Doctor Lang.' Sister replied grimly: 'Doctor Keen held the leg. That's all.'

Operations had been a nightmare to Nell at first. At the first one she attended, the floor rose at her, and a nurse led her out. She hardly dared to face Sister, but Sister was unexpectedly kind.

'It's partly the lack of air and the smell of the ether, Nurse,' she said kindly. 'Go into a short one next. You'll get used to it.'

Next time Nell felt faint, but did not have to go out, the time after she felt sick only, and the time after that she didn't feel sick at all.

Once or twice she was lent to help the theatre nurse clear up the operating theatre after an unusually big op. The place was like a shambles, blood everywhere. The theatre nurse was only eighteen, a determined slip of a thing. She owned to Nell that she had hated it at first.

'The very first op. was a leg,' she said. 'Amputation. And Sister went off afterwards and left me to clear up, and I had to take the leg down to the furnace myself. It was awful.'

On her days out Nell went to tea with friends. Some of them were kindly old ladies and sentimentalized over her and told her she was splendid.

'You don't work on Sundays, do you, dear? Really? Oh, but that isn't right. Sunday should be a day of rest.'

Nell pointed out gently that the soldiers had to be washed and fed on Sundays just as much as any other day, and the old ladies admitted this but seemed to think that the matter should have been better organized. They were also very distressed at Nell's having to walk home alone at midnight.

Others were even more difficult.

'I hear these hospital nurses give themselves great airs, ordering everyone about. I shouldn't stand that kind of thing myself. I am willing to do anything I can to help in this dreadful war, but impertinence I will not stand. I told Mrs Curtis so, and she agreed it would be better for me not to do hospital work.'

To these ladies Nell made no reply at all.

The rumour of 'the Russians' was sweeping through England at this time. Everyone had seen them—or if not actually seen them, their cook's second cousin had, which was practically the same thing. The rumour died hard—it was so pleasing and so exciting.

A very old lady who came to the hospital took Nell aside.

'My dear,' she said, 'don't believe that story. It's true, but not in the way we think.'

Nell looked inquiringly at her.

'Eggs!' said the old lady in a poignant whisper. 'Russian eggs! Several millions of them—to keep us from starving . . .'

Nell wrote all these things to Vernon. She felt terribly cut off from him. His letters were naturally terse and constrained and he seemed to dislike the idea of her working

in hospital. He urged her again and again to go to London—
enjoy herself . . .

How queer men were, Nell thought. They didn't seem
to understand. She would hate to be one of the 'Keeping
themselves bright for the Boys' brigade. How soon you
drifted apart when you were doing different things! She
couldn't share Vernon's life and he couldn't share hers.

The first agony of parting when she had felt sure he
would be killed was over. She had fallen into the routine
of wives. Four months had passed and he hadn't been even
wounded. He wouldn't be. Everything was all right.

Five months after he had gone out he wired that he had
got leave. Nell's heart almost stopped beating. She was so
excited! She went off to Matron and was granted leave of
absence.

She travelled to London feeling strange and unusual in
ordinary clothes. Their first leave!

It was true, really true! The leave train came in and
disgorged its multitudes. She saw him. He was actually
there. They met. Neither could speak. He squeezed her
hand frantically. She knew then how afraid she had
been . . .

That five days went by in a flash. It was like some
queer delirious dream. She adored Vernon and he adored
her, but they were in some ways like strangers to each
other. He was off-hand when she spoke about France. It
was all right—everything was all right. One made jokes
about it and refused to treat it seriously. 'For goodness'

sake, Nell, don't sentimentalize. It's awful to come home
and find everyone with long faces. And don't talk slush
about our brave soldiers laying down their lives, etc. That
sort of stuff makes me sick. Let's get tickets for another
show.'

Something in his absolute callousness perturbed her—
it seemed somehow rather dreadful to treat everything so
lightly. When he asked her what she had been doing, she
could only give him hospital news, and that he didn't like.
He begged her again to give it up.

'It's a filthy job, nursing. I hate to think of your doing it.'

She felt chilled—rebuffed, then rebuked herself. They
were together again. What did anything else matter?

They had a wild delightful time. They went to a show
and danced every night. In the daytime they went shop-
ping. Vernon bought her everything that took his fancy.
They went to a Paris firm of dressmakers and sat there
whilst airy young duchesses floated past in wisps of chiffon
and Vernon chose the most expensive model. They felt
horribly wicked but dreadfully happy when Nell wore it
that night.

Then Nell told him he ought to go and see his mother.
Vernon rebelled.

'Oh, darling, I don't want to! Our little short precious
time. I can't miss a minute of it.'

Nell pleaded. Myra would be terribly hurt and
disappointed.

'Well, then, you've got to come with me.'

'No, that wouldn't do at all.'

In the end, he went down to Birmingham for a flying

visit. His mother made a tremendous fuss over him—greeted him with floods of what she called 'glad proud tears'—and trotted him round to see the Bents. Vernon came back seething with conscious virtue.

'You are a hard-hearted devil, Nell. We've missed a whole day! God, how I've been slobbered over.'

He felt ashamed as soon as he had said it. Why couldn't he love his mother better? Why did she always manage to rub him up the wrong way, no matter how good his resolutions were? He gave Nell a hug.

'I didn't mean it. I'm glad you made me go. You're so sweet, Nell. You never think of yourself. It's so wonderful being with you again. You don't know . . .'

And she put on the French model gown and they went out to dine with a ridiculous feeling of having been model children and deserving a reward.

They had nearly finished dinner when Nell saw Vernon's face change. It stiffened and grew anxious.

'What is it?'

'Nothing,' he said hastily.

But she turned and looked behind her. At a small table against the wall was Jane.

Something cold seemed for a moment to rest on Nell's heart. Then she said easily:

'Why, it's Jane. Let's go and speak to her.'

'No, I'd rather not.' She was a little surprised by the vehemence of his tone. He saw that and went on: 'I'm stupid, darling. I want to have you and nothing but you—not other people butting in. Have you finished? Let's go. I don't want to miss the beginning of the play.'

They paid the bill and went. Jane nodded to them carelessly and Nell waved her hand to her. They arrived at the theatre ten minutes early.

Later, as Nell was slipping the gown from her white shoulders, Vernon said suddenly:

'Nell, do you think I shall ever write music again?'

'Of course. Why not?'

'Oh, I don't know. I don't think I want to.'

She looked at him in surprise. He was sitting on a chair, frowning into space.

'I thought it was the only thing you cared about.'

'Cared about—cared about—that doesn't express it in the least. It isn't the things you care about that matter. It's the things you can't get rid of—the things that won't let you go—that haunt you—like a face that you can't help seeing even when you don't want to . . .'

'Darling Vernon—don't—'

She came and knelt down beside him. He clutched her to him convulsively.

'Nell—darling Nell—nothing matters but you . . . Kiss me . . .'

But he reverted presently to the topic. He said irrelevantly, 'Guns make a pattern, you know. A musical pattern, I mean. Not the sound one hears. I mean the pattern the sound makes in space. I suppose that's nonsense—but I know what I mean.'

And again a minute or two later:

'If one could only get hold of it properly.'

Ever so slightly, she moved her body away from him. It was as though she challenged her rival. She never admitted it openly, but secretly she feared Vernon's music. If only he didn't care so much.

And tonight, at any rate, she was triumphant. He drew her back holding her close, showering kisses on her.

But long after Nell was asleep Vernon lay staring into the darkness, seeing against his will, Jane's face and the outline of her body in its dull green satin sheath as he had seen it against the crimson curtain at the restaurant.

He said to himself very softly under his breath:

'Damn Jane.'

But he knew that you couldn't get rid of Jane as easily as that.

He wished he hadn't seen her.

There was something so damnably disturbing about Jane.

He forgot her the next day. It was their last, and it went terribly quickly.

All too soon, it was over.

It had been like a dream. Now the dream was over. Nell was back at the hospital. It seemed to her she had never been away. She waited desperately for the post—for Vernon's first letter. It came—more ardent and unrestrained than usual, as though even censorship had been forgotten. Nell wore it against her heart and the indelible pencil came off on her skin. She wrote and told him so.

Life went on as usual. Dr Lang went out to the front and was replaced by an elderly doctor with a beard who said 'Thank ye, thank ye, Sister,' every time he was offered a towel or was helped on with his white linen coat. They had a slack time with most of the beds empty and Nell found the enforced idleness trying.

One day, to her surprise and delight, Sebastian walked in. He was home on leave and had come down to look her up. Vernon had asked him to.

'You've seen him then?'

Sebastian said yes, his lot had taken over from Vernon.

'And he's all right?'

'Oh, yes, he's all *right*!'

Something in the way he said it caused her alarm. She pressed him. Sebastian frowned in perplexity.

'It's difficult to explain, Nell. You see, Vernon's an odd beggar—always has been. He doesn't like looking things in the face.'

He quelled the fierce retort that he saw rising to her lips.

'I don't mean in the least what you think I mean. He isn't *afraid*. Lucky devil, I don't think he knows what fear is. I wish I didn't. No, it's different from that. It's the whole life—it's pretty ghastly, you know. Dirt and blood and filth, and noise—above all, noise! Recurrent noise at fixed times. It gets on my nerves—so what must it do to Vernon's?'

'Yes, but what did you mean by not facing things?'

'Simply that he won't admit that there's anything to face. He's afraid of minding, so he says there's nothing *to* mind. If he'd only admit that it's a bloody filthy business like I do he'd be all right. But it's like that old piano business—he won't look at the thing fair and square. And it's no good saying "there ain't no such thing" when there *is*. But that's always been Vernon's way. He's in good spirits—enjoys everything—and it isn't natural. I'm afraid of his—Oh! I don't know what I'm afraid of. But I know that telling yourself fairy stories is about the worst thing you can do. Vernon's a musician, and he's got the nerves of a musician. The worst of him is that he doesn't know anything about himself. He never has.'

Nell looked troubled.

'Sebastian, what do you think will happen?'

'Oh, nothing, probably. What I should like to happen would be for Vernon to stop one—in as conveniently painless a place as possible and come back to be nursed for a bit.'

'How I wish that would happen!'

'Poor old Nell. It's rotten for all you people. I'm glad I haven't got a wife.'

'If you had—' Nell paused, then went on. 'Would you want her to work in a hospital or would you rather she did nothing?'

'Everybody will be working sooner or later. It's as well to get down to it as soon as possible, I should say.'

'Vernon doesn't like my doing this.'

'That's his ostrich act again—plus the reactionary spirit that he's inherited and will never quite outgrow. Sooner or later he'll face the fact that women are working— but he won't admit it till the last minute.'

Nell sighed.

'How worrying everything is.'

'I know. And I've made things worse for you. But I'm awfully fond of Vernon. He's the one friend I care about. And I hoped if I told you what I thought you'd encourage him to—well—give way a little—at any rate to you. But perhaps to you he does let himself go?'

Nell shook her head.

'He won't do anything but joke about the war.'

Sebastian whistled.

'Well, next time—get it out of him. Stick to it.'

Nell said suddenly and sharply: 'Do you think he'd talk better—to Jane?'

'To Jane?' Sebastian looked rather embarrassed. 'I don't know. Perhaps. It all depends.'

'You do think so! Why? Tell me why? Is she more sympathetic, or what?'

'Oh, Lord, no. Jane's not exactly sympathetic. Provocative is more the word. You get annoyed with her—and out pops the truth. She makes you aware of yourself in ways you don't want to be. There's nobody like Jane for pulling you off your high horse.'

'You think she's a lot of influence over Vernon?'

'Oh! I wouldn't say that. And anyhow, it wouldn't matter if she had. She's doing relief work in Serbia. Sailed a fortnight ago.'

'Oh!' said Nell. She drew a deep breath and smiled. Somehow she felt happier.

'Darling Nell,—Do you know I dream of you every night. Usually you're nice to me, but sometimes you're a little beast. Cold and hard and far away. You couldn't be that really, could you? Not now. Darling, will the indelible pencil ever come off?

321

'Nell, sweetheart, I never believe I'm going to be
killed, but if I were what would it matter? We've had so
much. You'd think of me always as happy and loving
you, wouldn't you, sweetheart? I know I'd go on loving
you after I was dead. That's the only bit of me that
couldn't die. I love you—love you—love you . . .'

He had never written to her quite like that before.
She put the letter in its usual place.

That day she was absent-minded at the hospital.
She forgot things. The men noticed it.

'Nurse is daydreaming.' They teased her, making little
jokes. And she laughed back.

It was so wonderful, so very wonderful to be loved.
Sister Westhaven was in a temper, Nurse Potts slacked more
than usual. But it didn't matter. Nothing mattered.

Even the monumental Sister Jenkins who came on night
duty and was always full of pessimism failed to impress
her with any kind of gloom.

'Ah!' Sister Jenkins would say, settling her cuffs and
moving three double chins round inside her collar in an
effort to alleviate their mass. 'No. 3 still alive? You surprise
me. I didn't think he'd last through the day. Well, he'll be
gone tomorrow, poor young chap. (Sister Jenkins was
always prophesying that patients would be gone tomorrow
and the failure of her prognostications to come true never
seemed to induce in her a more hopeful attitude.) I don't
like the look of No. 18—that last operation was worse
than useless. No. 8 is going to take a turn for the worse
unless I'm much mistaken. I said so to Doctor, but he didn't

322

listen to me. Now then, Nurse (with sudden acerbity) no need for you to hang about. Off duty is off duty.' Nell accepted this gracious permission to depart, well aware that if she had not lingered Sister Jenkins would have asked her, 'What she meant by hurrying away like that—not even willing to wait a minute over time?'

It took twenty minutes to walk home. The night was a clear starry one and Nell enjoyed the walk. If only Vernon could have been walking beside her.

She let herself into the house very quietly with her latch-key. Her landlady always went to bed early. On the tray in the hall was an orange-coloured envelope.

She knew then . . .

Telling herself that it wasn't—that it couldn't be—that he was only wounded—surely he was only wounded . . . yet she knew . . .

A sentence from the letter she had received that morning leapt out at her. '*Nell, sweetheart, I never believe I am going to be killed, but if I were what would it matter? We've had so much . . .*'

He had never written like that before . . . He must have felt—have known. Sensitive people did know sometimes beforehand.

She stood there, holding the telegram. Vernon—her lover, her husband . . . She stood there a long time . . .

Then at last she opened the telegram which informed her with deep regret that Lieutenant Vernon Deyre had been killed in action.

CHAPTER 3

A Memorial Service was held for Vernon in the little old church at Abbotsford under the shadows of Abbots Puissants, as it had been held for his father. The two last of the Deyres were not to lie in the family vault. One in South Africa, one in France.

In Nell's memory afterwards the proceedings seemed shadowed by the monumental bulk of Mrs Levinne—a vast matriarchal figure dwarfing everything else. She herself had to bite her lips not to laugh hysterically. The whole thing was so funny somehow—so unlike Vernon.

Her mother was there, elegant and aloof, Uncle Sydney was there, in black broadcloth, restraining himself from jingling his money with great difficulty, and with a suitable 'mourner's' face. Myra Deyre was there in heavy crape, weeping copiously and unrestrainedly. But it was Mrs Levinne who dominated the proceedings. She came back with them afterwards to the sitting-room at the inn, identifying herself with the family.

'Poor dear boy—poor dear gallant boy. I've always thought of him like another thon.'

She was genuinely distressed. Tears splashed down on her black bodice. She patted Myra on the shoulder.

'Now, now, my dear, you mustn't take on so. You mustn't indeed. It's our duty, all of us, to bear up. You gave him to his country. You couldn't do more. Here's Nell—as brave as can be.'

'Everything I had in the world,' sobbed Myra. 'First husband, then son. Nothing left.'

She stared ahead of her through blood-suffused eyes in a kind of ecstasy of bereavement.

'The very best son—we were everything to each other.' She caught Mrs Levinne's hand. 'You'll know what it feels like if Sebastian . . .'

A spasm of fear passed across Mrs Levinne's face. She clenched her hands.

'I see they've sent up some sandwiches and some port,' said Uncle Sydney, creating a diversion. 'Very thoughtful. Very thoughtful. A little drop of port, Myra dear. You've been through a great strain, you know.'

Myra waved away port with a horror-stricken hand. Uncle Sydney was made to feel that he had displayed callousness.

'We've all got to keep up,' he said. 'It's our duty.'

His hand stole to his pocket and he began to jingle.

'Syd!'

'Sorry, Myra.'

Again Nell felt that wild desire to giggle. She didn't want to cry. She wanted to laugh and laugh and laugh . . . Awful—to feel like that.

'I thought everything went off very nicely,' said Uncle

Sydney. 'Very nicely indeed. A most impressive lot of the villagers attended. You wouldn't like to stroll round Abbots Puissants? That was a very nice letter putting it at our disposal today.'

'I hate the place,' said Myra vehemently. 'I always have.'

'I suppose, Nell, you've seen the lawyers? I understand Vernon made a perfectly simple will before going out to France, leaving everything to you. In that case, Abbots Puissants is now yours. It was not entailed and in any case there are no Deyres now in existence.'

Nell said: 'Thank you, Uncle Sydney, I've seen the lawyer. He was very kind and explained everything to me.'

'That's more than any lawyer can do as a rule,' said Uncle Sydney. 'They make the simplest thing sound difficult. It's not my business to advise you, but I know there's no man in your family who can do so. Much the best thing you can do is to sell it. There's no money to keep it up, you know. You understand that?'

Nell did understand. She saw that Uncle Sydney was making it clear to her that no Bent money was coming her way. Myra would leave her money back to her own family. That, of course, was only natural. Nell would never have dreamed of anything else.

As a matter of fact, Uncle Sydney had at once tackled Myra as to whether there was a child coming. Myra said she didn't think so. Uncle Sydney said she had better make sure. 'I don't know exactly how the law stands, but as it is, if you were to pop off tomorrow having left your money to Vernon, it might go to her. No good taking any chances.'

Myra said tearfully that it was very unkind of him to suggest that she was going to die.

'Nothing of the sort. You women are all alike. Carrie sulked for a week when I insisted on her making a proper will. We don't want good money to go out of the family.'

Above all, he did not want good money to go to Nell. He disliked Nell whom he regarded as Enid's supplanter. And he loathed Mrs Vereker who always managed to make him feel hot and clumsy and uncertain about his hands.

'Nell, of course, will take legal advice,' said Mrs Vereker sweetly.

'Don't think *I* want to butt in,' said Uncle Sydney.

Nell felt a passionate pang of regret. If only she were going to have a child. Vernon had been so afraid for her. 'It would be so dreadful for you, darling, if I were to be killed and you were left with all the trouble and worry of a child and very little money. Besides—you never know— you might die. I couldn't bear to risk it.'

And really, it *had* seemed better and more prudent to wait.

But now, she was sorry. Her mother's consolations had seemed coldly brutal to her.

'You're not going to have a baby, are you, Nell? Well, I must say I'm thankful. Naturally, you'll marry again and it's so much better when there are no encumbrances.'

In answer to a passionate protest, Mrs Vereker had smiled. 'I oughtn't to have said that just now. But you are only a girl still. Vernon himself would have wanted you to be happy.'

Nell thought: 'Never! She doesn't understand!'

Agatha Christie

'Well, well, it's a sad world,' said Mr Bent, surreptitiously helping himself to a sandwich. 'The flower of our manhood being mown down. But all the same I'm proud of England. I'm proud of being an Englishman. I like to feel that I'm doing my bit in England just as much as these boys are doing it out there. We're doubling our output of explosives next month. Night and day shifts. I'm proud of Bent's, I can tell you.'

'It must be wonderfully profitable,' said Mrs Vereker.

'That's not the way I like to look at it,' said Mr Bent. 'I like to look at it that I'm serving my country.'

'Well, I hope we all try to do our bit,' said Mrs Levinne. 'I have a working party twice a week, and I'm interethting myself in all these poor girls who are having war babieth.'

'There's too much loose thinking going about,' said Mr Bent. 'We mustn't get lax. England has never been lax.'

'Well, we've got to look after the children at any rate,' said Mrs Levinne. She added: 'How is Joe? I thought I might see her here today.'

Both Uncle Sydney and Myra looked embarrassed. It was clear that Joe was what is known as a 'delicate subject'. They skated lightly over the topic. War work in Paris—very busy—unable to get leave.

Mr Bent looked at his watch.

'Myra, we've not too much time before the train. Must get back tonight. Carrie, my wife, you know, is very far from well. That's why she wasn't able to be here today.' He sighed. 'It's odd how often things turn out for the best. It was a great disappointment to us not having a son. And yet, in a way, we've been spared a good deal. Think of the anxiety we might be in today. The ways of Providence are wonderful.'

Mrs Vereker said to Nell when they had taken leave of Mrs Levinne, who motored them back to London:

'One thing I do hope, Nell, is that you won't think it your duty to see a lot of your in-laws. I dislike the way that woman wallowed in her grief more than I can tell you. She was thoroughly enjoying herself, though I dare say she'd have preferred a proper coffin.'

'Oh, Mother—she was really unhappy. She was awfully fond of Vernon. As she said, he was all she had in the world.'

'That's a phrase women like her are very fond of using. It means nothing at all. And you're not going to pretend to me that Vernon adored his mother. He merely tolerated her. They had nothing in common. He was a Deyre through and through.'

Nell couldn't deny that.

She stayed at her mother's flat in town for three weeks. Mrs Vereker was very kind within her own limits. She was not a sympathetic woman at any time, but she respected Nell's grief and did not intrude upon it. Upon practical matters her judgment was, as it always had been, excellent. There were various interviews with lawyers and Mrs Vereker was present at all of them.

Abbots Puissants was still let. The tenancy would be up the following year, and the lawyer strongly advised its sale rather than reletting it. Mrs Vereker, to Nell's surprise, did not seem to concur with this view. She suggested a further let of not too long duration.

'So much may happen in a few years,' she said.

Mr Flemming looked hard at her and seemed to catch her meaning. His glance rested just for a moment on Nell, fair and childish-looking in her mourning.

'As you say,' he remarked. 'Much may happen. At any rate nothing need be decided for a year.'

Business matters settled, Nell returned to the hospital at Wiltsbury. She felt that there, and there only, could life be at all possible. Mrs Vereker did not oppose her. She was a sensible woman and she had her own plans.

A month after Vernon's death, Nell was once more back in the ward. Nobody ever referred to her loss and she was grateful. To carry on as usual was the motto of the moment.

Nell carried on.

'There's someone asking for you, Nurse Deyre.'

'For me?' Nell was surprised.

It must be Sebastian. Only he was likely to come down here and look her up. Did she want to see him or not? She hardly knew.

But to her great surprise her visitor was George Chetwynd. He explained that he was passing through Wiltsbury, and had stopped to see if he could see her. He asked whether she couldn't come out to lunch with him.

'I thought you were on afternoon duty,' he explained.

'I was changed to the morning shift yesterday. I'll ask Matron. We're not very busy.'

Permission was accorded her, and half an hour later she was sitting opposite George Chetwynd at the County Hotel with a plate of roast beef in front of her and a waiter hovering over her with a vast dish of cabbage.

'The only vegetable the County Hotel knows,' observed Chetwynd.

He talked interestingly and made no reference to her loss. All he said was that her continuing to work here was the pluckiest thing he had ever heard of.

'I can't tell you how I admire all you women. Carrying on, tackling one job after another. No fuss—no heroics—just sticking to it as though it were the most natural thing in the world. I think Englishwomen are fine.'

'One must do something.'

'I know. I can understand that feeling. Anything's better than sitting with your hands in your lap, eh?'

'That's it.'

She was grateful. George always understood. He told her that he was off to Serbia in a day or two, organizing relief work there.

'Frankly,' he said, 'I'm ashamed of my country for not coming in. But they will. I'm convinced of that. It's only a matter of time. In the meantime we do what we can to alleviate the horrors of war.'

'You look very well.'

He looked younger than she remembered him—well set up, bronzed, the grey in his hair a mere distinction rather than a sign of age.

'I'm feeling well. Nothing like having plenty to do. Relief work's pretty strenuous.'

'When are you off?'

'Day after tomorrow.' He paused, then said in a different

voice. 'Look here—you didn't mind my looking you up like this? You don't feel I'd no business to butt in?'

'No—no. It was very kind of you. Especially after I—I—'

'You know I've never borne any rancour over that. I admire you for following your heart. You loved him and you didn't love me. But there's no reason we shouldn't be friends, is there?'

He looked so friendly, so very unsentimental, that Nell answered happily that there wasn't.

He said: 'That's fine. And you'll let me do anything for you that a friend can? Advise you in any bothers that arise, I mean?'

Nell said she'd be only too grateful.

They left it like that. He departed in his car shortly after lunch, wringing her hand and saying he hoped they'd meet again in about six months' time, and begging her again to consult him if she were in a difficulty any time.

Nell promised that she would.

The winter was a bad one for Nell. She caught a cold, neglected to take proper care of herself, and was quite ill for a week or so. She was quite unfit to resume hospital work at the end of it, and Mrs Vereker carried her off to London to her flat. There she regained strength slowly.

Endless bothers seemed to arise. Abbots Puissants appeared to need an entire new roof. New water pipes had to be installed. The fencing was in a bad state.

Nell appreciated for the first time the awful drain property can be. The rent was eaten up many times over with

332

the necessary repairs, and Mrs Vereker had to come to the rescue to tide Nell over a difficult corner and not let her get too much into debt. They were living as penuriously as possible. Vanished were the days of outward show and credit. Mrs Vereker managed to make both ends meet by a very narrow margin, and would hardly have done that but for what she won at the bridge table. She was a first-class player and added materially to her income by play. She was out most of the day at a bridge club that still survived.

It was a dull unhappy life for Nell. Worried over money, not strong enough to undertake fresh work, nothing to do but sit and brood. Poverty combined with love in a cottage was one thing. Poverty without love to soften it was another. Sometimes Nell wondered how she was ever going to get through a life that stretched drear and bleak ahead of her. She couldn't bear things. She simply couldn't.

Then Mr Flemming urged her to make a decision concerning Abbots Puissants. The tenancy would be up in a month or two. Something must be done. He could not hold out any hopes of letting it for a higher rent. Nobody wanted to rent big places without central heating or modern conveniences. He strongly advised her to sell.

He knew the feeling her husband had had about the place. But since she herself was never likely to be able to afford to live in it . . .

Nell admitted the wisdom of what he said, but still pleaded for time to decide. She was reluctant to sell it, but she could not help feeling that the worry of Abbots Puissants once off her mind she would be relieved from her heaviest burden. Then one day Mr Flemming rang up to say that he had had a very good offer for Abbots Puissants. He mentioned a sum far in excess of her—or indeed his—expectations. He very strongly advised her to close with it without delay.

Nell hesitated a minute—then said 'Yes.'

It was extraordinary how much happier she felt at once. Free of that terrible incubus! It wasn't as though Vernon had lived. Houses and estates were simply white elephants when you hadn't the necessary money to keep them up properly.

She was undisturbed even by a letter from Joe in Paris.

'How *can* you sell Abbots Puissants when you know what Vernon felt about it? I should have thought it would be the last thing you could have done.'

She thought: 'Joe doesn't understand.'

She wrote back:

'What was I to do? I don't know where to turn for money. There's been the roof and the drains and the water—it's endless. I can't go on running into debt. Everything's so tiring I wish I were dead . . .'

Three days later she got a letter from George Chetwynd, asking if he might come and see her. He had, he said, something to confess.

Mrs Vereker was out. She received him alone. He broke it rather apprehensively to her. It was he who had purchased Abbots Puissants.

Just at first she recoiled from the idea. Not George! Not

George at Abbots Puissants! Then with admirable common sense he argued the point.

Surely it was better that it should pass into his hands instead of those of a stranger? He hoped that sometimes she and her mother would come and stay there.

'I'd like you to feel that your husband's home is open to you at any time. I want to change things there as little as possible. You shall advise me. Surely you prefer my having it, to its passing into the hands of some vulgarian who will fill it with gilt and spurious old masters?'

In the end she wondered why she had felt any objection. Better George than anyone. And he was so kind and understanding about everything. She was tired and worried. She broke down suddenly, cried on his shoulder whilst he put an arm round her and told her that everything was all right, that it was only because she'd been ill.

Nobody could have been kinder or more brotherly.

When she told her mother Mrs Vereker said:

'I knew George was looking out for a place. It's lucky he's chosen Abbots Puissants. He's probably haggled less about the price simply because he was once in love with you.'

The remote way she said 'once in love with you' made Nell feel comfortable. She had imagined that her mother might have 'ideas' still about George Chetwynd.

That summer they went down and stayed at Abbots Puissants. They were the only guests. Nell had not been there since she was a child. A deep regret came upon her that she could not have lived there with Vernon. The house was truly beautiful, and so were the stately gardens and the ruined Abbey.

George was in the middle of doing up the house and he consulted her taste at every turn. Nell began to feel quite a proprietary interest. She was almost happy again, enjoying the ease and luxury and the freedom from anxiety.

True, once she received the money from Abbots Puissants and had invested it she would have a nice little income, but she dreaded the onus of deciding where to live and what to do. She was not really happy with her mother, and all her own friends seemed to have drifted out of touch. She hardly knew where to go or what to do with her life.

Abbots Puissants gave her just the peace and rest she needed. She felt sheltered there and safe. She dreaded the return to town.

It was the last evening. George had pressed them to remain longer, but Mrs Vereker had declared that they really couldn't trespass any longer on his hospitality.

Nell and George walked together on the long flagged walk. It was a still, balmy evening.

'It has been lovely here,' said Nell, with a little sigh. 'I hate going back.'

'I hate your going back too.' He paused and then said very quietly: 'I suppose there's no chance for me, is there, Nell?'

'I don't know what you mean?'

But she did know—she knew at once.

'I bought this house because I hoped some day you'd

live here. I wanted you to have the home that was rightly
yours. Are you going to spend your whole life nursing a
memory, Nell? Do you think he—Vernon—would wish it?
I never think of the dead like that—as grudging happiness
to the living. I think he would want you to be looked after
and taken care of now that he isn't here to do it.'

She said in a low voice: 'I can't . . . I can't . . .'

'You mean you can't forget him? I know that. But I'd
be very good to you, Nell. You'd be wrapped round with
love and care. I think I could make you happy—happier
at any rate than you'll be facing life by yourself. I do
honestly and truly believe that Vernon would wish it . . .'

Would he? She wondered. She thought George was right.
People might call it disloyalty, but it wasn't. That life of
hers with Vernon was something by itself—nothing could
touch it ever . . .

But oh! to be looked after, cared for, petted and understood. She always *had* been fond of George.

She answered very softly . . . 'Yes . . .'

The person who was angry about it was Myra. She wrote
long abusive letters to Nell. 'You can forget so soon. Vernon
has only one home—in my heart. You never loved him.'

Uncle Sydney twirled his thumbs and said: 'That young
woman knows which side her bread is buttered'; and wrote
her a stereotyped letter of congratulation.

An unexpected ally was Joe who was paying a flying
visit to London and came round to see Nell at her mother's
flat.

'I'm very glad,' she said, kissing her. 'And I'm sure Vernon would be. You're not the kind that can face life on your own. You never were. Don't you mind what Aunt Myra says. *I'll* talk to her. Life's a rotten business for women—I think you'll be happy with George. Vernon would want you to be happy, I know.'

Joe's support heartened Nell more than anything. Joe had always been the nearest person to Vernon. On the night before her wedding, she knelt by her bed and looked up to where Vernon's sword hung over the head of it.

She pressed her hands over her closed eyes.

'You do understand, beloved? You do? It's you I love and always shall . . . Oh, Vernon, if only I could know that you understood.'

She tried to send her very soul out questing in search of him. He must—he *must*—know and understand . . .

CHAPTER 4

In the town of A_____ in Holland—not far from the German frontier—is an inconspicuous inn. Here on a certain evening in 1917 a dark young man with a haggard face pushed open the door and in very halting Dutch asked for a lodging for the night. He breathed hard and his eyes were restless. Anna Schlieder, the fat proprietress of the inn, looked at him attentively up and down in her usual deliberate way before she replied. Then she told him that he could have a room. Her daughter Freda took him up to it. When she came back, her mother said laconically: 'English—escaped prisoner.'

Freda nodded but said nothing. Her china-blue eyes were soft and sentimental. She had reasons of her own for taking an interest in the English. Presently she again mounted the stairs and knocked on the door. She went in on top of the knock which, as a matter of fact, the young man had not heard. He was so sunk in a stupor of exhaustion that external sounds and happenings had hardly any meaning for him. For days and weeks he had been on the qui vive, escaping dangers by a hairsbreadth, never daring to be caught napping either physically or mentally. Now he was suffering the reaction. He lay where he had fallen, half sprawling across the bed. Freda stood and watched him. At last she said:

'I bring you hot water.'

'Oh!' he started up. 'I'm sorry. I didn't hear you.'

She said slowly and carefully in his own language:

'You are English—yes?'

'Yes. Yes, that is—'

He stopped suddenly in doubt. One must be careful. The danger was over—he was out of Germany. He felt slightly lightheaded. A diet of raw potatoes, dug up from the fields, was not stimulating to the brain. But he still felt he *must* be careful. It was so difficult—he felt queer—felt that he wanted to talk and talk, pour out everything now that at last that fearful long strain was over.

The Dutch girl was nodding her head at him gravely, wisely.

'I know,' she said. 'You come from over there—'

Her hand pointed in the direction of the frontier.

He looked at her, still irresolute.

'You have escaped—yes. We had before one like you.'

A wave of reassurance passed over him. She was all right, this girl. His legs suddenly felt weak under him. He dropped down on the bed again.

'You are hungry? Yes. I see. I go and bring you something.'

Was he hungry? He supposed he was. How long was it since he had eaten? One day, two days? He couldn't remember. The end had been like a nightmare—just keeping blindly on. He had a map and a compass. He knew the place where he wanted to cross the frontier, the spot that seemed to him to offer the best chance. A thousand to one chances against him being able to pass the frontier—but he had passed it. They had shot at him and missed. Or was that all a dream? He had swum down the river—that was it—No, that was all wrong, too. Well, he wouldn't think about it—he had escaped, that was the great thing.

He leaned forward supporting his aching head in his hands.

Very soon, Freda returned carrying a tray with food on it and a great tankard of beer. He ate and drank whilst she stood watching him. The effect was magical. His head cleared. He *had* been lightheaded, he realized that now. He smiled up at Freda.

'That's splendid,' he said. 'Thanks awfully.'

Encouraged by his smile, she sat down on a chair.

'You know London?'

'Yes, I know it.' He smiled a little. She had asked that so quaintly.

Freda did not smile. She was in deadly earnest.

'You know a soldier there? A what is it? Corporal Green?'

He shook his head, a little touched.

'I'm afraid not,' he said gently. 'Do you know his regiment?'

'It was a London regiment—the London Fusiliers.'

She had no further information than that. He said kindly: 'When I get back to London, I'll try to find out. If you like to give me a letter.'

She looked at him doubtfully, yet with a certain air of trusting appeal. In the end the doubt was vanquished.

'I will write—yes,' she said.

She rose to leave the room and said abruptly: 'We have an English paper here—two English papers here. My cousin brought them from the hotel. You would like to see them, yes?'

He thanked her and she returned bringing a tattered *Eve* and a *Sketch* which she handed to him with some pride.

When she left the room again, he laid down the papers by his side and lighted a cigarette—his last cigarette! What would he have done without those cigarettes—stolen at that! Perhaps Freda would bring him some—he had money to pay for them. A kind girl, Freda, in spite of her thick ankles and an unprepossessing exterior.

He took out a small notebook from his pocket. The pages were blank and he wrote in it: *Corporal Green, London Fusiliers*. He would do what he could for the girl. He wondered idly what story lay behind it. What had Corporal Green been doing in Holland in A —? Poor Freda. It was the usual thing, he supposed.

Green—it reminded him of his childhood. *Mr Green*. The omnipotent delightful Mr Green—his playfellow and protector. Funny, the things one thought of when one was a kid!

He'd never told Nell about Mr Green. Perhaps she'd had a Mr Green of her own. Perhaps all children did.

He thought: 'Nell—Oh, Nell . . .' and his heart missed a beat. Then he turned his thoughts resolutely away. Very soon now . . . Poor darling, what she must have suffered

342

knowing him to be a prisoner in Germany. But that was all over now. Very soon now they'd be together. Very soon. Oh, he mustn't think of it. The task in hand—no looking forward.

He picked up the *Sketch* and idly turned over the pages. A lot of new shows seemed to be on. What fun to go to a show again. Pictures of generals all looking very fierce and warlike. Pictures of people getting married. Not a bad-looking crowd. That one—Why—

It wasn't true—it couldn't be true . . . Another dream—a nightmare . . .

Mrs Vernon Deyre who is to marry Mr George Chetwynd. Mrs Deyre's first husband was killed in action over a year ago. Mr George Chetwynd is an American who has done very valuable relief work in Serbia.

Killed in action—yes, he supposed that might be. In spite of all conceivable precautions mistakes like that *did* arise. A man Vernon knew had been reported killed. A thousandth chance, but it happened.

Naturally, Nell would have believed—and naturally, quite naturally, she would marry again.

What nonsense he was talking! Nell—marry again! So soon. Marry George—*George* with his grey hair—A sudden sharp pang shot through him. He had visualized George too clearly. Damn George—blast and curse George.

But it wasn't true. No, it wasn't true!

He stood up, steadying himself as he swayed on his feet. To anyone who had seen him, he would have appeared a little drunk.

He was perfectly calm—yes, he was perfectly calm. The

thing was not to believe—not to think. Put it away—right away. It wasn't true—it couldn't be true—if you once admitted that it might be true, you were done.

He went out of his room, down the stairs. He passed the girl, Freda, who stared at him. He said very quietly and calmly (marvellous that he should be so calm!):

'I'm going out for a walk.'

He went out, oblivious of old Anna Schlieder's eyes that raked his back as he passed her. The girl, Freda, said to her:

'He passed me on the stairs like—like—what has happened to him?'

Anna tapped her forehead significantly. Nothing ever surprised her.

Out on the road Vernon was walking—walking very fast. He must get away—get away from the thing that was following him. If he looked round—if he thought about it—but he wouldn't think about it.

Everything was all right—*everything*.

Only he mustn't think. This queer dark thing that was following him—following him . . . If he didn't think he was all right.

Nell—Nell with her golden hair and her sweet smile. His Nell. Nell and George . . . No, no, NO! It wasn't so, he was in time.

And suddenly, lucidly, there ran through his mind the thought, 'That paper was six months old at least. They've been married five months.'

He reeled. He thought, 'I can't bear it. No, this I can't bear. Something must happen . . .'

344

He held on blindly to that: *Something must happen* . . .

Somebody would help him. Mr Green. What was this awful thing that was dogging him? Of course, The Beast. The Beast.

He could hear it coming. He gave one panic-stricken glance over his shoulder. He was out of the town now, walking on a straight road between dykes. The Beast was coming lumbering along at a great pace, rattling and bumping.

The Beast . . . Oh! if only he could go back—to The Beast and Mr Green—the old terrors, the old comforts. They didn't hurt you like the new things—like Nell and George Chetwynd. George—Nell belonging to George . . .

No—No, it wasn't true—it mustn't be true—He couldn't face any more. Not that—not that . . .

There was only one way to get out of it all—to be at peace—only one way—Vernon Deyre had made a mess of life—better to get out of it . . .

One last flaming agony shot through his brain—Nell—George—No! he thrust them out with a last effort. Mr Green—kind Mr Green.

He stepped out into the roadway right in the path of the lurching lorry that tried to avoid him too late—and struck him down and backwards . . .

A horrible searing shock—thank God, this was death . . .

BOOK V

George Green

CHAPTER 1

In the yard of the County Hotel in Wiltsbury two chauffeurs were busy with cars. George Green finished his work on the interior of the big Daimler, wiped his hands on a bit of oily rag and stood upright with a sigh of satisfaction. He was a cheerful young fellow and was smiling now because he was pleased with himself for locating the trouble and dealing with it. He strolled along to where his fellow chauffeur was completing the toilet of a Minerva.

The latter looked up.

'Hullo, George—you through?'

'Yes.'

'Your boss is a Yank, isn't he? What's he like?'

'He's all right. Fussy, though. Won't go more than forty.'

'Well, thank your stars you don't drive for a woman,' said the other. His name was Evans. 'Always changing their minds. And no idea of the proper times for meals. Picnic lunches as often as not—and you know what that means, a hard-boiled egg and a leaf of lettuce.'

Green sat down on an adjacent barrel.

'Why don't you chuck it?'

'Not so easy to get another job, these days,' said Evans.

'No, that's true,' said Green. He looked thoughtful.

'And I've got a missus and two kids,' went on the other. 'What's the rot that was talked about a country fit for heroes? No, if you've got a job—any kind of a job—it's better to freeze on to it in 1920.'

He was silent for a minute, and then went on.

'Funny business—the war. I was hit twice—shrapnel. Makes you go a bit queer afterwards. My missus says I frighten her—go quite batty sometimes. Wake up in the middle of the night hollering and not knowing where I am.'

'I know,' said Green. 'I'm the same. When my guvnor picked me up—in Holland that was—I couldn't remember a thing about myself except my name.'

'When was that? After the war?'

'Six months after the armistice. I was working in a garage there. Some chaps who were drunk ran me down one night in a lorry. Fairly scared 'em sober. They picked me up and took me along with them. I'd got a whacking great bash on the head. They looked after me and got me a job. Good chaps they were. I'd been working there two years when Mr Bleibner came along. He hired a car from our place once or twice and I drove him. He talked to me a good bit and finally he offered to take me on as chauffeur.'

'Mean to say you never thought of getting back home before that?'

'No—I didn't want to somehow. I'd no folks there as far as I could remember and I've an idea I'd had a bit of trouble there of some kind.'

'I shouldn't associate trouble with you, mate,' said Evans with a laugh.

George Green laughed too. He was indeed a most cheerful-looking young man, tall and dark with broad shoulders and an ever ready smile.

'Nothing much ever worries me,' he boasted. 'I was born the happy-go-lucky kind, I guess.'

He moved away smiling happily. A few minutes later he was reporting to his employer that the Daimler was ready for the road.

Mr Bleibner was a tall thin dyspeptic-looking American with very pure speech.

'Very good. Now, Green, I am going to Lord Datchet's for luncheon. Abingworth Friars. It's about six miles from here.'

'Yes, sir.'

'After luncheon I am going to a place called Abbots Puissants. Abbotsford is the village. Do you know it?'

'I've heard of it, I think, sir. But I don't know exactly where it is. I'll look it up on the map.'

'Yes, please do so. It cannot, I think, be more than twenty miles—in the direction of Ringwood, I fancy.'

'Very good, sir.'

Green touched his cap and withdrew.

Nell Chetwynd stepped through the french window of the drawing-room and came out upon the terrace at Abbots Puissants.

It was one of those still early autumn days when there

Agatha Christie

seems no stirring of life anywhere, as though Nature herself feigned unconsciousness. The sky was a pale, not a deep, blue and there was a very faint haze in the atmosphere.

Nell leaned against a big stone urn and gazed out over the silent prospect. Everything was very beautiful and very English. The formal gardens were exquisitely kept. The house itself had been very judiciously and carefully repaired.

Not habitually given to emotion, as Nell looked up at the rose-red brick of the walls, she felt a sudden swelling of the heart. It was all so perfect. She wished that Vernon could know—could see.

Four years of marriage had dealt kindly with Nell, but they had changed her. There was no suggestion of the nymph about her now. She was a beautiful woman instead of a lovely girl. She was poised—assured. Her beauty was a very definite kind of beauty—it never varied or altered. Her movements were more deliberate than of old, she had filled out a little—there was no suggestion of immaturity. She was the perfect full-blown rose.

A voice called her from the house.

'Nell!'

'I'm here, George, on the terrace.'

'Right. I'll be out in a minute.'

What a dear George was! A little smile creased her lips. The perfect husband! Perhaps that was because he was an American. You always heard that Americans made perfect husbands. Certainly, George had been one to her. The marriage had been a complete success. It was true that she had never felt for George what she had felt for Vernon— but almost reluctantly she had admitted that perhaps that

352

was a good thing. These tempestuous emotions that tore and rent one—they couldn't last. Every day you had evidence that they *didn't* last.

All her old revolt was quelled now. She no longer questioned passionately the reason why Vernon should have been taken from her. God knew best. One rebelled at the time, but one came at last to realize that whatever happened was really for the best.

They had known supreme happiness, she and Vernon, and nothing could ever mar or take away from it. It was there for ever—a precious secret possession—a hidden jewel. She could think of him now without regret or longing. They had loved each other and had risked everything to be together. Then had come that awful pain of separation—and then—peace.

Yes, that was the predominant factor in her life now—peace. George had given her that. He had wrapped her round with comfort, with luxury, with tenderness. She hoped that she was a good wife to him, even if she didn't care like she had cared for Vernon. But she *was* fond of him—of course she was! The quiet affectionate feeling she had for him was by far the safest emotion to go through life with.

Yes, that expressed exactly what she felt—safe and happy. She wished that Vernon knew. He would be glad, she was sure.

George Chetwynd came out and joined her. He wore English country clothes and looked very much the country squire. He had not aged at all—indeed he looked younger. In his hand he held some letters.

'I've agreed to share that shooting with Drummond. I think we'll enjoy it.'

'I'm so glad.'

'We must decide who we want to ask.'

'Yes, we'll talk about it tonight. I'm rather glad the Hays couldn't come and dine. It will be nice to have an evening to ourselves.'

'I was afraid you were overdoing it in town, Nell.'

'We *did* rush about rather. But I think it's good for one really. And anyway it's been splendidly peaceful down here.'

'It's wonderful.' George threw an appreciative glance over the landscape. 'I'd rather have Abbots Puissants than any place in England. It's got an atmosphere.'

Nell nodded.

'I know what you mean.'

'I should hate to think of it in the hands of—well, people like the Levinnes, for instance.'

'I know. One would resent it. And yet Sebastian is a dear—and his taste at any rate is perfect.'

'He knows the taste of the public all right,' said George drily. 'One success after another—with occasionally a *succès d'estime* just to show he's not a mere money maker. He's beginning to look the part though—getting not exactly fat, but sleek. Adopting all sorts of mannerisms. There's a caricature of him in *Punch* this week. Very clever.'

'Sebastian would lend himself to caricaturing,' said Nell, smiling. 'Those enormous ears, and those funny high cheek-bones. He was an extraordinary-looking boy.'

'It's odd to think of you all playing together as children.

354

By the way, I've got a surprise for you. A friend you haven't seen for some time is coming to lunch today.'

'Not Josephine?'

'No. Jane Harding.'

'Jane Harding! But how on earth—?'

'I ran into her at Wiltsbury yesterday. She's on tour, acting in some company or other.'

'Jane! Why, George, I didn't even realize you knew her?'

'I came across her when we were both doing relief work in Serbia. I saw a lot of her. I wrote to you about it.'

'Did you? I don't remember.'

Something in her tone seemed to strike him and he said anxiously:

'It's all right, isn't it, dear? I thought it would be a pleasant surprise for you. I always thought she was a great friend of yours. I can put her off in a minute if—'

'No, no. Of course, I'll be delighted to see her. I was only surprised.'

George was reassured.

'That's all right then. By the way, she told me that a man called Bleibner, a man I knew very well in New York, is also in Wiltsbury. I'd like him to see the Abbey ruins— that sort of thing is a speciality of his. Do you mind if I ask him to lunch too?'

'No, of course not. Do ask him.'

'I'll see if I can get him on the phone now. I meant to do it last night, but it slipped my memory.'

He went indoors again. Nell was left on the terrace frowning slightly.

George in this had been right. For some reason or other,

she was not pleased at the thought of Jane's coming to lunch. She felt very definitely that she didn't want to see Jane. Already, the mere mention of Jane seemed to have disturbed the serenity of the morning. She thought: 'I was so peaceful, and now—'

Annoying—yes, it was annoying. She was, had always been, afraid of Jane. Jane was the kind of person you could never be sure about. She—how could one put it?— she upset things. She was disturbing—and Nell didn't want to be disturbed.

She thought unreasonably: 'Why on earth did George have to meet her in Serbia? How trying things are.'

But it was absurd to be afraid of Jane. Jane couldn't hurt her—now. Poor Jane, she must have made rather a mess of things to have come down to acting in a touring company.

One must be loyal to one's old friends, Jane was an old friend. She should see how loyal Nell could be. And with a glow of self-approval she went upstairs and changed into a dress of dove-coloured georgette with which she wore one very beautifully matched string of pearls that George had given her on the last anniversary of their marriage. She took particular pains over her toilet, satisfying thereby some obscure female instinct.

'At any rate,' she thought, 'the Bleibner man will be there and that will make things easier.'

Though why she expected things to be difficult she could not have explained.

George came up to fetch her just as she was applying a final dusting of powder.

'Jane's arrived,' he said. 'She's in the drawing-room.'

'And Mr Bleibner?'

'He's engaged for lunch unfortunately. But he's coming along this afternoon.'

'Oh!'

She went downstairs slowly. Absurd to feel so apprehensive. Poor Jane—one simply must be nice to her. It was such terribly bad luck to have lost her voice and come down to this.

Jane, however, did not seem aware of bad luck. She was sprawling back on the sofa in an attitude of easy unconcern, looking round the room with keen appreciation.

'Hullo, Nell,' she said. 'Well, you seem to have dug yourself in pretty comfortably.'

It was an outrageous remark. Nell stiffened. She couldn't think for a moment of what to say. She met Jane's eyes which were full of a mocking maliciousness. They shook hands and Nell said at the same time, 'I don't know what you mean?'

'I meant all this. Palatial dwelling, well-proportioned footmen, highly paid cook, soft-footed servants, possibly a French maid, baths prepared for one with the latest unguents and bath salts, five or six gardeners, luxurious limousines, expensive clothes and I perceive, genuine pearls! Are you enjoying it all frightfully? I am sure you are.'

'Tell me about yourself,' said Nell, seating herself beside Jane on the sofa.

Jane's eyes narrowed.

'That's a very clever answer. And I fully deserved it.

357

Sorry, Nell. I was a beast. But you were being so queenly and so gracious. I never can stand people being gracious.'

She got up and began to stroll round the room.

'So this is Vernon's home,' she said softly. 'I've never seen it before—only heard him talk about it.'

She was silent for a minute, then asked abruptly:

'How much have you changed?'

Nell explained that everything had been left as it was as far as possible. Curtains, covers, carpets, etc., had all been renewed. The old ones were too shabby. And one or two priceless pieces of furniture had been added. Whenever George came across anything that was in keeping with the place he bought it.

Jane's eyes were fixed on her while she made this explanation and Nell felt uneasy because she couldn't read the expression in them.

George came in before she had finished talking and they went in to lunch.

The talk was at first of Serbia, of a few mutual friends out there. Then they passed on to Jane's affairs. George referred delicately to Jane's voice—the sorrow he had felt—that everyone must feel. Jane passed it off carelessly enough.

'My own fault,' she said. 'I would sing a certain kind of music and my voice wasn't made for it.'

Sebastian Levinne, she went on to say, had been a wonderful friend. He was willing now to star her in London, but she had wished to learn her trade first.

'Singing in opera is, of course, acting too. But there are all sorts of things to learn—to manage one's speaking voice, for instance. And then one's effects are all different—they must be more subtle, less broad.'

Next autumn, she explained, she was to appear in London in a dramatized version of *Tosca*.

Then dismissing her own affairs, she began to talk of Abbots Puissants. She led George on to discuss his plans, his ideas about the estate. He was made to display himself the complete country squire.

There was, apparently, no mockery in Jane's eyes or her voice, but nevertheless Nell felt acutely uncomfortable. She wished George would stop talking. It was a little ridiculous the way he spoke as though he and his forefathers before him had lived for centuries at Abbots Puissants.

After coffee, they went out on the terrace again, and here George was summoned to the telephone and left them with a word of excuse. Nell suggested a tour through the gardens and Jane acquiesced.

'I'd like to see everything,' she said.

Nell thought: 'It's Vernon's home she wants to see. That's why she's come. But Vernon never meant to her what he meant to me!'

She had a passionate desire to vindicate herself—to make Jane see—See what? She didn't quite know herself, but she felt that Jane was judging her—condemning her even.

She stopped suddenly as they were walking down a long herbaceous border, gay with Michaelmas daisies against the old rose-coloured brick wall behind it.

'Jane. I want to tell you—to explain—'

She paused, gathering herself together. Jane merely looked at her inquiringly.

'You must think it—very dreadful of me—marrying again so soon.'

'Not at all,' said Jane. 'It was very sensible.'

Nell didn't want that. That wasn't the point of view at all.

'I adored Vernon—*adored* him. When he was killed it nearly broke my heart. I mean it. But I knew so well that he himself wouldn't wish me to grieve. The dead don't want us to grieve—'

'Don't they?'

Nell stared at her.

'Oh, I know you're voicing the popular idea,' said Jane. 'The dead want us to be brave and bear up and carry on as usual. They hate us being unhappy about them. That's what everybody goes about saying—but I never have seen that they've any foundation for that cheering belief. I think they've invented it themselves to make things easier for them. The living don't all want exactly the same thing, so I don't see why the dead should either. There must be heaps of selfish dead—if they exist at all they must be very much the same as they were in life. They can't be full of beautiful and unselfish feelings all at once. It always makes me laugh when I see a bereaved widower tucking into his breakfast the day after the funeral and saying solemnly, "Mary wouldn't wish me to grieve!" How does he know? Mary may be simply weeping and gnashing her teeth (astral teeth, of course) at seeing him going on as usual just as though she had never existed. Heaps of women like a fuss being made over them. Why should they change their characters when they're dead?'

Nell was silent. She couldn't for the moment collect her thoughts.

'Not that I mean Vernon was like that,' went on Jane. 'He may really have wished you not to grieve. You'd know best about that, because you knew him better than anyone else.'

'Yes,' said Nell eagerly. 'That's just it. I know he would want me to be happy. And he wanted me to have Abbots Puissants. I know he'd love to think of my being here.'

'He wanted to live here with you. That's not quite the same thing.'

'No, but it isn't as though I were living here with George like—like it would have been with him. Oh, Jane, I want to make you understand. George is a dear, but he isn't—he can never be—what—what Vernon was to me.'

There was a long pause and then Jane said: 'You're lucky, Nell.'

'If you think I really love all this luxury! Why, for Vernon I'd give it up in a minute!'

'I wonder.'

'Jane! You—'

'You think you would—but—I wonder.'

'I did before.'

'No—you only gave up the prospect of it. That's different. It hadn't eaten into you like it has now.'

'Jane!'

Nell's eyes filled with tears. She turned away.

'My dear—I'm being a beast. There's no harm in what you've done. I dare say you're right—about Vernon wishing it. You need kindness and protection—but all the same soft

Agatha Christie

living does eat into one. You'll know what I mean some day. By the way, I didn't mean what you thought when I said just now that you were lucky. By lucky, I meant that you'd had the best of both worlds. If you'd married your George when you originally intended, you'd have gone through life with a secret regret, a longing for Vernon, a feeling that you'd been cheated out of life through your own cowardice. And if Vernon had lived you might have grown away from each other, quarrelled, come to hate each other. But as it is, you've had Vernon, made your sacrifice—you've got him where nothing can ever touch him. Love will be a thing of beauty to you for ever. And you've got all the other things as well. This!'

She swept her arm round in a sudden embracing gesture.

Nell had hardly paid any attention to the end part of the speech. Her eyes had grown soft and melting.

'I know. Everything turns out for the best. They tell you so when you're a child and later you find it out for yourself. God does know best.'

'What do you know about God, Nell Chetwynd?'

There was savagery in the question that brought Nell's eyes to Jane in astonishment. She looked menacing—fiercely accusing. The gentleness of a minute ago was gone.

'The will of God! Would you be able to say that if God's will didn't happen to coincide with Nell Chetwynd's comfort, I wonder? You don't know anything about God or you couldn't have spoken like that, gently patting God on the back for making life comfortable and easy for you. Do you know a text that used to frighten me in the Bible? *This night shall thy soul be required of thee.* When

362

God requires *your* soul of you, be sure you've got a soul to give Him!'

She paused and then said quietly:

'I'll go now. I shouldn't have come. But I wanted to see Vernon's home. I apologize for what I've said. But you're so damned smug, Nell. You don't know it, but you are. Smug—that's the word. Life to you means yourself and yourself only. What about Vernon? Was it best for him? Do you think *he* wanted to die right at the beginning of everything he cared for?'

Nell flung her head back defiantly.

'I made him happy.'

'I wasn't thinking of his happiness. I was thinking of his music. You and Abbots Puissants—what do you matter? Vernon had genius—that's the wrong way of putting it—he *belonged* to his genius. And genius is the hardest master there is—everything has got to be sacrificed to it—your trumpery happiness even would have had to go if it stood in the way. Genius has got to be served. Music wanted Vernon—and he's dead. That's the crying shame, the thing that matters, the thing you never even consider. I know why—because you were afraid of it, Nell. It doesn't make for peace and happiness and security. But I tell you, *it's got to be served . . .*'

Suddenly her face relaxed, the old mocking light that Nell hated came back to her eyes. She said:

'Don't worry, Nell. You're much the strongest of us all. Protective colouring! Sebastian told me so long ago, and he was right. You'll endure when we've all perished. Goodbye—I'm sorry I've been a devil, but I'm made that way.'

Nell stood staring after her retreating figure. She clenched her hands and said under her breath:

'I hate you. I've always hated you . . .'

The day had begun so peacefully—and now it was spoilt. Tears came into Nell's eyes. Why couldn't people let her alone? Jane and her horrid sneering. Jane was a beast—an uncanny beast. She knew where things hurt you most.

Why, even Joe had said that she, Nell, was quite right to marry George! Joe had understood perfectly. Nell felt aggrieved and hurt. Why should Jane be so horrid? And saying things like that about the dead—irreligious things— when everyone knew that the dead liked one to be brave and cheerful.

The impertinence of Jane to hurl a text at her head. A woman like Jane who had lived with people and done all kinds of immoral things. Nell felt a glow of superior virtue. In spite of everything that was said nowadays, there were two different kinds of women. She belonged to one kind and Jane to the other. Jane was attractive—that kind of woman always was attractive—that was why in the past she had felt afraid of Jane. Jane had some queer power over men—she was bad through and through.

Thinking these thoughts, Nell paced restlessly up and down. She felt disinclined to go back to the house. In any case, there was nothing particular to do this afternoon. There were some letters that must be written some time but she really couldn't settle to them at present.

She had forgotten about her husband's American friend,

and was quite surprised when George joined her with Mr Bleibner in tow. The American was a tall thin man, very precise. He paid her grave compliments on the house. They were now, he explained, going to view the ruins of the Abbey. George suggested she should come with them.

'You go on,' said Nell. 'I'll follow you presently. I must get a hat. The sun is so hot.'

'Shall I get it for you, dear?'

'No, thanks. You and Mr Bleibner go on. You'll be ages pottering about there, I know.'

'Why, I should say that is very certain to be the case, Mrs Chetwynd. I understand your husband has some idea of restoring the Abbey. That is very interesting.'

'It's one of our many projects, Mr Bleibner.'

'You are fortunate to own this place. By the way, I hope you've no objection, I told my chauffeur (with your husband's assent, naturally) that he might stroll round the grounds. He is a most intelligent young man of quite a superior class.'

'That's quite all right. And if he'd like to see the house the butler can take him over it later.'

'Now I call that very kind of you, Mrs Chetwynd. What I feel is that we want beauty appreciated by all classes. The idea that's going to weld together the League of Nations—'

Nell felt suddenly that she couldn't bear to hear Mr Bleibner's views on the League of Nations. They were sure to be ponderous and lengthy. She excused herself on the plea of the hot sun.

Some Americans could be very boring. What a mercy

George was not like that. Dear George—really he was very nearly perfect. She experienced again that warm happy feeling that had surged over her earlier in the day.

What an idiot she was to have let herself be upset by Jane. *Jane* of all people! What did it matter what Jane said or thought? It didn't, of course—but there was something about Jane—she had the power of—well—upsetting one.

But that was all over now. The old tide of reassurance and safety welled up again. Abbots Puissants, George, the tender memory of Vernon. Everything was all right.

She ran down the stairs happily, hat in hand. She paused a minute to adjust it in front of the mirror. She would go now and join them at the Abbey. She would make herself absolutely charming to Mr Bleibner.

She went down the steps of the terrace and along the garden walk. It was later than she thought. The sun was not far from setting—a beautiful sunset with a crimson sky.

By the goldfish pond a young man in chauffeur's livery was standing with his back to her. He turned at her approach and civilly raised a finger to his cap.

She stood stock still and slowly an unconscious hand crept up to her heart as she stood there staring.

George Green stared.

Then he ejaculated to himself, 'Well, that's a rum go.'

On arrival at their destination, his master had said to him:

'This is one of the oldest and most interesting places in England, Green. I shall be here at least an hour—perhaps longer. I will ask Mr Chetwynd if you may stroll about the grounds.'

A kind old buffer, Green had thought indulgently, but terribly keen on what was called 'uplift'. Couldn't let one alone. And he had that extraordinary American reverence for anything that was hallowed by antiquity.

Certainly, this was a nice old place, though. He had looked up at it appreciatively. He'd seen pictures of it somewhere, he was sure. He wouldn't mind having a stroll round as he'd been told to do.

It was well kept up, he noticed that. Who owned it? Some American chap? These Americans, they had all the money. He wondered who had owned it originally. Whoever it was must have been sick having to let it go.

He thought wistfully: 'I wish I'd been born a toff. I'd like to own a place like this.'

He had wandered some way through the gardens. In the distance he had noticed a heap of ruins and amongst them two figures, one of which he recognized as being that of his employer. Funny old josser—always poking about ruins.

The sun had been setting—there had been a wonderful lurid sky and against it Abbots Puissants stood out in all its beauty.

Funny, the way you thought of things as having happened before! Just for a minute Green could have sworn that he had once stood just where he was standing now and seen the house outlined against a red sky. Could swear too, that he had felt just that same keen pang as of something that hurt. But it wanted something else—a woman with red hair like the sunset.

Agatha Christie

There had been a step behind him and he had started and turned. For a minute he had felt a vague pang of disappointment. For standing there was a young slender woman and her hair, escaping each side from under her hat, was golden, not red.

He had touched his cap respectfully.

A queer sort of lady, he thought. She had stared at him with every bit of colour draining slowly from her face. She looked absolutely terrified.

Then, with a sudden gasp, she turned and almost ran down the path.

It was then that he ejaculated:

'Well, that's a rum go.'

She must, he decided, be a bit queer in the head.

He resumed his aimless strolling.

CHAPTER 2

Sebastian Levinne was in his office going into the details of a ticklish contract, when a telegram was brought to him. He opened it carelessly, for he received forty or fifty telegrams a day. After he had read it, he held it in his hand looking at it.

Then he crumpled it up, slipped it into his pocket and spoke to Lewis, his right-hand man.

'Get on with this thing as best you can,' he said curtly. 'I'm called out of town.'

He took no heed of the protestations that arose, but left the room. He paused to tell his secretary to see to the cancelling of various appointments and then went home, packed a bag and took a taxi to Waterloo. There he unfolded the telegram and read it.

Please come at once if you can very urgent Jane Wilts Hotel Wiltsbury.

It was a proof of his confidence and respect for Jane that he never hesitated. He trusted Jane as he trusted no one else in the world. If Jane said a thing was urgent, it was urgent. He obeyed the summons without wasting a thought of regret on the necessary complications it would cause. For no one else in the world, be it said, would he have done that.

On arriving at Wiltsbury he drove straight to the hotel and asked for her. She had engaged a private room, and there she met him with outstretched hands.

'Sebastian—my dear—you've been marvellously quick.'

'I came at once.' He slipped off his coat and threw it over the back of a chair. 'What is it, Jane?'

'It's Vernon.'

Sebastian looked puzzled. 'What about him?'

'He's not dead. I've seen him.'

Sebastian stared at her for a minute, then drew a chair to the table and sat down.

'It's not like you, Jane, but I think, for once in your life, you must have been mistaken.'

'I wasn't mistaken. It's possible, I suppose, for the War Office to have made an error?'

'Errors have been made more than once—but they've usually been contradicted fairly soon. It stands to reason that they must be. If Vernon's alive, what's he been doing all this time?'

She shook her head.

'That I can't say. But I'm as sure about its being Vernon as I am that it's you here now.'

She spoke curtly, but very confidently.

He stared at her very hard, then nodded.

'Tell me,' he said.

Jane spoke quietly and composedly.

'There's an American here, a Mr Bleibner. I met him out

in Serbia. We recognized each other in the street. He told me he was staying at the County Hotel and asked me to lunch today. I went. Afterwards it was raining. He wouldn't hear of my walking back. His car was there and would take me. His car did take me. Sebastian, the chauffeur was Vernon—*and he didn't know me.*'

Sebastian considered the matter. 'You're sure you weren't deceived by some strong resemblance?'

'Perfectly sure.'

'Then why didn't Vernon recognize you? He was pretending, I suppose.'

'No, I don't think so—in fact, I'm sure he wasn't. He would be bound to give some sign—a start—something. He couldn't have been *expecting* to see me. He couldn't have controlled his first surprise. Besides, he looked—different.'

'How different?'

Jane considered.

'It's hard to explain. Rather happy and jolly and—just faintly—like his mother.'

'Extraordinary,' said Sebastian. 'I'm glad you sent for me. If it *is* Vernon—well, it's going to be the devil of a business. Nell having married again and everything. We don't want reporters coming down like wolves on the fold. I suppose there'll have to be *some* publicity.' He got up, walked up and down. 'The first thing is to get hold of Bleibner.'

'I telephoned to him, asking him to be here at six-thirty. I didn't dare leave it, though I was afraid you wouldn't be able to get here so soon. Bleibner will be here any minute.'

Agatha Christie

'Good for you, Jane. We must hear what he's got to say.'

There was a knock at the door and Mr Bleibner was announced. Jane rose to meet him.

'It's very good of you to come, Mr Bleibner,' she began.

'Not at all,' said the American. 'Always delighted to oblige a lady. And you said that the matter you wanted to see me about was urgent.'

'It is. This is Mr Sebastian Levinne.'

'*The* Mr Sebastian Levinne? I'm very pleased to meet you, sir.'

The two men shook hands.

'And now, Mr Bleibner,' said Jane. 'I'll come straight to what I want to talk to you about. How long have you had your chauffeur, and what can you tell us about him?'

Mr Bleibner was plainly surprised and showed it.

'Green? You want to know about Green?'

'Yes.'

'Well—' The American reflected. 'I've no objections to telling you what I know. I guess you wouldn't ask without a good reason. I know you well enough for that, Miss Harding. I picked up Green in Holland not long after the armistice. He was working in a local garage. I discovered he was an Englishman and began to take an interest in him. I asked him his history and he was pretty vague about it. I thought at first he had something to conceal, but I soon convinced myself that he was genuine enough. The man was in a kind of mental fog. He knew his name and where he came from but very little else.'

'Lost memory,' said Sebastian softly. 'I see.'

'His father was killed in the South African war, he

told me. He remembered his father singing in the village choir, and he remembered a brother whom he used to call Squirrel.'

'And he was quite sure about his own name?'

'Oh, yes. As a matter of fact he'd got it written down in a small pocket book. There was an accident, you know. He was knocked down by a lorry. That's how they knew who he was. They asked him if his name was Green and he said Yes—George. He was very popular at the garage, he was so sunny and lighthearted. I don't believe I've ever seen Green out of temper.

'Well—I took a fancy to the young chap. I've seen a few shell-shocked cases, and his state wasn't any mystery to me. He showed me the entry in his pocket book, and I made a few inquiries. I soon found the reason—there always is a reason, you know—for his loss of memory. Corporal George Green, London Fusiliers, was a deserter.

'There you have it. He'd funked things—and being a decent young fellow really, he couldn't face the fact. I explained it all to him. He said—rather wonderingly: "I shouldn't have thought I could ever desert—not *desert*." I explained to him that that point of view was just the reason he couldn't remember. He couldn't remember because he didn't want to remember.

'He listened but I don't think he was very convinced. I felt, and still feel, extremely sorry for him. I didn't think there was any obligation on my part to report his existence to the military authorities. I took him into my service and offered him a chance to make good. I've never had cause to regret it. He's an excellent chauffeur—punctual, intelligent, a good mechanic, and always sunny tempered and obliging.'

Mr Bleibner paused and looked inquiringly at Jane and Sebastian. Their pale serious faces impressed him.

'It's frightening,' said Jane in her low voice. 'It's one of the most frightening things that could happen.'

Sebastian took her hand and squeezed it.

'It's all right, Jane.'

Jane roused herself with a slight shiver and spoke to the American.

'I think it's our turn to explain. You see, Mr Bleibner, in your chauffeur I recognized an old friend—and he didn't recognize me.'

'In—deed!'

'But his name wasn't Green,' said Sebastian.

'No? You mean he enlisted under another name?'

'No. There's something there that seems incomprehensible. I suppose we shall get at it some day. In the meantime, I will ask you, Mr Bleibner, not to repeat this conversation to *anyone*. There's a wife in the matter—and—oh! many other considerations.'

'My dear sir,' said Mr Bleibner. 'You can trust me to be absolutely silent. But what next? Do you want to see Green?'

Sebastian looked at Jane and she bowed her head.

'Yes,' said Sebastian slowly. 'I think perhaps that would be the best plan.'

The American rose.

'He's below now. He brought me here. I'll send him up right away.'

*

George Green mounted the stairs with his usual buoyant step. As he did so he wondered what had happened to upset the old josser—by that term meaning his employer. Very queer the old buffer had looked.

'The door at the top of the stairs,' Mr Bleibner had said.

George Green rapped on it sharply with his knuckles and waited. A voice called 'Come in' and he obeyed.

There were two people in the room—the lady he had driven home yesterday (whom he thought of in his own mind as a tip-topper) and a big rather fat man with a very yellow face and projecting ears. His face seemed vaguely familiar to the chauffeur. For a moment he stood there while they both stared at him. He thought: 'What's the matter with everybody this evening?'

He said, 'Yes, sir?' in a respectful voice to the yellow gentleman. He went on: 'Mr Bleibner told me to come up—'

The yellow gentleman seemed to recover himself.

'Yes, yes,' he said. 'That's right. Sit down—er—Green. That's your name, isn't it?'

'Yes, sir. George Green.'

He sat down, respectfully, in the chair indicated. The yellow gentleman handed him a cigarette case and said, 'Help yourself.' And all the time, his eyes, small piercing eyes, never left Green's face. That intent burning gaze made the chauffeur uneasy. What *was* up with everyone tonight?

'I wanted to ask you a few questions. To begin with, have you ever seen me before?'

Green shook his head.

'No, sir.'

'Sure?' persisted the other.

A faint trace of uncertainty crept into Green's voice.

'I—I don't think so,' he said doubtfully.

'My name is Sebastian Levinne.'

The chauffeur's face cleared.

'Of course, sir, I've seen your picture in the papers. I thought it seemed familiar somehow.'

There was a pause and then Sebastian Levinne asked casually:

'Have you ever heard the name of Vernon Deyre?'

'Vernon Deyre,' Green repeated the name thoughtfully. He frowned perplexedly. 'The name seems somehow familiar to me, sir, but I can't quite place it.' He paused, the frown deepening. 'I think I've heard it.' And then added, 'The gentleman's dead, isn't he?'

'So that's your impression, is it? That the gentleman is dead.'

'Yes, sir, and a good—'

He stopped suddenly, crimsoning.

'Go on,' said Levinne. 'What were you going to say?' He added shrewdly, perceiving where the trouble lay, 'You need not mince your words. Mr Deyre was no relation of mine.'

The chauffeur accepted the implication.

'I was going to say a good job too—but I don't know that I ought to say it, since I can't remember anything about him. But I've got a kind of impression that—well, that he was best out of the way, so to speak. Made rather a mess of things, hadn't he?'

'You knew him?'

The frown deepened in an agony of attempted recollection.

'I'm sorry, sir,' the chauffeur apologized. 'Since the war

things seemed to have got a bit mixed up. I can't always recollect things clearly. I don't know where I came across Mr Deyre, and why I disliked him, but I do know that I'm thankful to hear that he's dead. He was no good—you can take my word for that.'

There was a silence—only broken by something like a smothered sob from the other occupant of the room. Levinne turned to her.

'Telephone to the theatre, Jane,' he said. 'You can't appear tonight.'

She nodded and left the room. Levinne looked after her and then said abruptly:

'You've seen Miss Harding before?'

'Yes, sir. I drove her home today.'

Levinne sighed. Green looked at him inquiringly.

'Is—is that all, sir? I'm sorry to have been so little use. I know I've been a bit—well, queer since the war. My own fault. Perhaps Mr Bleibner told you—I—I didn't do my duty as I should have done.'

His face flushed but he brought out the words resolutely. Had the old josser told them or not? Better to say that anyway. At the same time, a pang of shame pierced him keenly. He was a deserter—a man who had run away! A rotten business.

Jane Harding came back into the room and resumed her place behind the table. She looked paler than when she had gone out, Green thought. Curious eyes she had— so deep and tragic. He wondered what she was thinking about. Perhaps she had been engaged to this Mr Deyre. No, Mr Levinne wouldn't have urged him to speak out if that had been the case. It was probably all to do with money. A will or something like that.

Mr Levinne began questioning him again. He made no reference to the last sentence.

'Your father was killed in the Boer War, I believe?'

'Yes, sir.'

'You remember him?'

'Oh, yes, sir.'

'What did he look like?'

Green smiled. The memory was pleasant to him.

'A burly sort of chap. Mutton chop whiskers. Very bright blue eyes. I remember him as well as anything singing in the choir. Baritone voice he had.'

He smiled happily.

'And he was killed in the Boer War?'

A sudden look of doubt crept into Green's face. He seemed worried—distressed. His eyes looked pathetically across the table like a dog at fault.

'It's queer,' he said. 'I never thought of that. He'd be too old. He—and yet I'd swear—I'm sure . . .'

The look of distress in his eyes was so acute that the other said, 'Never mind,' and went on: 'Are you married, Green?'

'No, sir.'

The answer came with prompt assurance.

'You seem very certain about that,' said Mr Levinne smiling.

'I am, sir. It leads to nothing but trouble—mixing yourself up with women.' He stopped abruptly and said to Jane, 'I beg your pardon.'

She smiled faintly and said: 'It doesn't matter.'

There was a pause. Levinne turned to her and said something so quickly that Green could not catch it. It sounded like:

'Extraordinary likeness to Sydney Bent. Never imagined it was there.'

Then they both stared at him again.

And suddenly he was afraid—definitely childishly afraid—in the same way that he remembered being afraid of the dark when he was a baby. There was something up—that was how he put it to himself—and these two knew it. Something about him.

He leant forward—acutely apprehensive.

'What's the matter?' he said sharply. 'There's something . . .'

They didn't deny it—just continued to look at him.

And his terror grew. Why couldn't they tell a chap? They knew something that he didn't. Something dreadful . . . He said again, and this time his voice was high and shrill:

'*What's the matter?*'

The lady got up—he noticed in the background of his mind as it were how splendidly she moved. She was like a statue he'd seen somewhere—she came round the table and laid a hand on his shoulder. She said comfortingly and reassuringly: 'It's all right. You mustn't be frightened.'

But Green's eyes continued to question Levinne. This man knew—this man was going to tell him. What was this horrible thing that they knew and he didn't?

'Very odd things have happened in this war,' began Levinne. 'People have sometimes forgotten their own names.'

He paused significantly, but the significance was lost on Green. He said with a momentary return to cheerfulness:

'I'm not as bad as that. I've never forgotten my name.'

'But you *have*.' He stopped—then went on: 'Your real name is Vernon Deyre.'

The announcement ought to have been dramatic, but it wasn't. The words seemed to Green simply silly. He looked amused.

'I'm Mr Vernon Deyre? You mean I'm his double or something?'

'I mean you *are* him.'

Green laughed frankly.

'I can't monkey about with that stuff, sir. Not even if it means a title or a fortune! Whatever the resemblance I'd be bound to be found out.'

Sebastian Levinne leant forward over the table and rapped out each word separately with emphasis:

'You—are—Vernon—Deyre . . .'

Green stared. The emphasis impressed him.

'You're kidding me?'

Levinne slowly shook his head. Green turned suddenly to the woman who stood beside him. Her eyes, very grave and absolutely assured, met his. She said very quietly:

'You are Vernon Deyre. We both know it.'

There was dead silence in the room. To Green, it seemed as though the whole world was spinning round. It was like a fairy story, fantastic and impossible. And yet something about these two compelled credence. He said uncertainly:

'But—but things don't happen like that. You couldn't forget your own name!'

'Evidently—since you have done so.'

'But—but, look here, sir—I *know* I'm George Green. I—well—I just know it!'

He looked at them triumphantly, but slowly and remorselessly Sebaștian Levinne shook his head.

'I don't know how that's come about,' he said. 'A doctor would probably be able to tell you. But I do know this— that you are my friend, Vernon Deyre. There is no possible doubt of that.'

'But—but, if that's true, I ought to know it.'

He felt bewildered, horribly uncertain. A strange sickening world where you couldn't be sure of anything. These were kindly sane people—he trusted them—what they said must be so—and yet something in him refused to be convinced. They were sorry for him—he felt that. And that frightened him. There was something more yet—something that he hadn't been told.

'Who is he?' he said sharply. 'This Vernon Deyre, I mean.'

'You come from this part of the world. You were born and spent most of your childhood at a place called Abbots Puissants—'

Green interrupted him in astonishment.

'Abbots Puissants? Why, I drove Mr Bleibner there yesterday. And you say it's my old home and I never recognized it!'

He felt suddenly buoyed up and scornful. The whole thing was a pack of lies! Of course it was! He had known it all the time. These people were honest, but they were mistaken. He felt relieved—happier.

'After that you went to live near Birmingham,' continued

Levinne. 'You went to school at Eton and from there you went on to Cambridge. After that you went to London and studied music. You composed an opera.'

Green laughed outright.

'There you're quite wrong, sir. Why, I don't know one note of music from another.'

'The war broke out. You obtained a commission in the Yeomanry. You were married—' he paused, but Green gave no sign, 'and went out to France. In the spring of the following year you were reported "Killed in Action".'

Green stared at him incredulously. What sort of a rigmarole was this? He couldn't remember a thing about any of it.

'There must be some mistake,' he said confidently. 'Mr Deyre must have been what they call my "double".'

'There is no mistake, Vernon,' said Jane Harding.

Green looked from her to Sebastian. The confident intimacy of her tone had done more to convince him than anything else. He thought: 'This is awful. A nightmare. Such things can't happen.' He began to shake all over, unable to stop.

Levinne got up, mixed him a stiff drink from materials that stood on a tray in the corner and brought it back to him.

'Swallow this,' he said. 'And you'll feel better. It's been a shock.'

Green gulped down the draught. It steadied him. The trembling ceased.

'Before God, sir,' he said. 'Is this true?'

'Before God, it is,' said Sebastian.

He brought a chair forward, sat down close by his friend.

'Vernon, dear old chap—don't you remember me at all?'

Green stared at him—an anguished stare. Something seemed to stir ever so faintly. How it hurt, this trying to remember. There was *something*—what was it? He said doubtfully:

'You—you've grown up.' He stretched out a hand and touched Sebastian's ear. 'I seem to remember—'

'He remembers your ears, Sebastian,' cried Jane and going over to the mantelpiece she laid her head down upon it and began to laugh.

'Stop it, Jane.' Sebastian rose, poured out another drink and took it to her. 'Some medicine for you.'

She drank it, handed the glass back to him, smiled faintly and said:

'I'm sorry. I won't do it again.'

Green was going on with his discoveries.

'You're—you're not a brother, are you? No, you lived next door. That's it—you lived next door . . .'

'That's right, old chap.' Sebastian patted him on the shoulder. 'Don't worry to think—it'll come back soon. Take it easy.'

Green looked at Jane. He said timidly and politely:

'Were you—are you—my sister? I seem to remember something about a sister.'

Jane shook her head, unable to speak. Green flushed.

'I'm sorry. I shouldn't have—'

Sebastian interrupted.

'You didn't have a sister. There was a cousin who lived with you. Her name was Josephine. We called her Joe.'

Green pondered.

'Josephine—Joe. Yes, I seem to remember something about that.' He paused and then reiterated pathetically, 'Are you *sure* my name isn't Green?'

'Quite sure. Do you still feel it is?'

'Yes . . . And you say I make up music—music of my own? Highbrow stuff—not ragtime?'

'Yes.'

'It all seems—well, mad. Just that—mad!'

'You mustn't worry,' said Jane gently. 'I dare say we have been wrong to tell you all this the way we have.'

Green looked from one to the other of them. He felt dazed.

'What am I to do?' he asked helplessly.

Sebastian gave an answer with decision.

'You must stay here with us. You've had a great shock, you know. I'll go and square things with old Bleibner. He's a very decent chap and he'll understand.'

'I shouldn't like to put him out in any way. He's been a thundering good boss to me.'

'He'll understand. I've already told him something.'

'What about the car? I don't like to think of another chap driving that car. She's running now as sweetly—'

He was once again the chauffeur, intent on his charge.

'I know. I know.' Sebastian was impatient. 'But the great thing, my dear fellow, is to get you right as soon as possible. We want to get a first-class doctor on to you.'

'What's a doctor got to do with it?' Green was slightly hostile. 'I'm perfectly fit.'

'Perhaps, a doctor ought to see you all the same. Not here—in London. We don't want any talk down here.'

Something in the tone of the speaker's voice attracted Green's attention. The flush came over his face.

'You mean the deserting business . . .?'

'No, no. To tell the truth, I can't get the hang of that. I mean something quite different.'

Green looked at him inquiringly.

Sebastian thought: 'Well, I suppose he's got to know some time.' Aloud he said:

'You see—thinking you were dead—your wife has—well—married again.'

He was a little afraid of the effect of those words. But Green seemed to see the matter in a humorous light.

'That *is* a bit awkward,' he said with a grin.

'It doesn't upset you in any way?'

'You can't be upset by a thing you don't remember.' He paused, as though really considering the matter for the first time. 'Was Mr Deyre—I mean, was I—fond of her?'

'Well—yes.'

But again the grin came over Green's face.

'And I to be so positive I wasn't married! All the same—' his face changed—'it's rather frightening—all this!'

He looked suddenly at Jane, as though seeking assurance.

'Dear Vernon,' she said, 'it will be all right.'

She paused, and then said in a quiet casual tone:

'You drove Mr Bleibner over to Abbots Puissants, you say. Did you—did you see anyone there? Any of the people of the house?'

'I saw Mr Chetwynd—and I saw a lady in the sunk gardens. I took her to be Mrs Chetwynd, fair-haired and good-looking.'

'Did—did she see you?'

'Yes. Seemed—well, scared. Went dead white and bolted like a rabbit.'

'Oh, God,' said Jane, and bit off the exclamation almost before it was uttered.

Green was cogitating quietly over the matter.

'Perhaps she thought she knew me,' he said. 'She must have been one of them who knew him—me—in the old days, and it gave her a turn. Yes, that must have been it.'

He was quite happy with his solution.

Suddenly he asked:

'Had my mother got red hair?'

Jane nodded.

'Then that was it . . .' He looked up apologetically. 'Sorry. I was just thinking of something.'

'I'll go and see Bleibner now,' said Sebastian. 'Jane will look after you.'

He left the room. Green leant forward in his chair, his head held between his hands. He felt acutely uncomfortable and miserable—especially with Jane. Clearly he ought to know her—and he didn't. She had said 'Dear Vernon' just now. It was terribly awkward when people knew you and you felt they were strangers. If he spoke to her he supposed he ought to call her Jane—but he couldn't. She was a stranger. Still he supposed he'd have to get used to it. They'd have to be Sebastian and George and Jane together—no, not George—Vernon. Silly sort of name, Vernon. Probably he'd been a silly sort of chap.

'I mean,' he thought, trying desperately to force the

realization upon himself, '*I* must have been a silly sort of chap.'

He felt horribly lonely—cut off from reality. He looked up to find Jane watching him, and the pity and understanding in her eyes made him feel a shade less forlorn.

'It's rather terrible just at first, isn't it?' she said.

He said politely:

'It is rather difficult. You don't—you don't know where you are with things.'

'I understand.'

She said no more—just sat there quietly beside him. His head jerked forward. He began to doze. In reality he only slept for a few minutes, but it seemed to him hours. Jane had turned all the lamps out but one. He woke with a start. She said quickly:

'It's all right.'

He stared at her, his breath coming in gasps. He was still in the nightmare then, he hadn't woken up. And there was something worse to come—something he didn't know yet. He was sure of it. That was why they all looked at him so pityingly.

Jane got up suddenly. Wildly, he cried out:

'Stay with me. Oh! please stay with me.'

He couldn't understand why her face should suddenly twist with pain. What was there in what he had said to make her look like that? He said again: 'Don't leave me. Stay with me.'

She sat down again beside him and took his hand in hers. She said very gently:

'I won't go away.'

He felt soothed—reassured. After a minute or two, he dozed again. He woke quietly this time. The room was as before and his hand was still in Jane's. He spoke diffidently:

'You—you aren't my sister? You were—you are, I mean—a friend of mine?'

'Yes.'

'A great friend?'

'A great friend.'

He paused. Yet the conviction in his mind was growing stronger and stronger. He blurted out suddenly:

'You're—you're my wife, aren't you?'

He was sure of it.

She drew her hand away. He couldn't understand the look in her face. It frightened him. She got up.

'No,' she said. 'I'm not your wife.'

'Oh! I'm sorry. I thought—'

'It's all right.'

And at that minute Sebastian came back. His eyes went to Jane. She said, with a little twisted smile:

'I'm glad you've come . . . I'm—glad you've come . . .'

Jane and Sebastian talked long into the night. What was to be done? Who was to be told?

There was Nell and Nell's position to consider. Presumably Nell should be told first of all. She was the one most vitally concerned.

Jane agreed. 'If she doesn't know already.'

'You think she knows?'

'Well, evidently she met Vernon that day face to face.'

'Yes, but she must have thought it just a very strong resemblance.'

Jane was silent.

'Don't you think so?'

'I don't know.'

'But hang it all, Jane, if she'd recognized him, she'd have done something—got hold of him or of Bleibner. It's two days ago now.'

'I know.'

'She can't have recognized him. She just saw Bleibner's chauffeur and his likeness to Vernon gave her such a shock that she couldn't stand it and rushed away.'

'I suppose so.'

'What's in your mind, Jane?'

'*We* recognized him, Sebastian.'

'You mean you did. I'd been told by you.'

'But you would have known him anywhere, wouldn't you?'

'Yes, I would . . . But then I know him so well.'

Jane said in a hard voice: 'So does Nell . . .'

Sebastian looked sharply at her and said, 'What are you getting at, Jane?'

'I don't know.'

'Yes, you do. What do you really think happened?'

Jane paused before speaking.

'I think Nell came upon him suddenly in the garden and thought it was Vernon. Afterwards she persuaded herself that it had only been a chance resemblance that had upset her so.'

'Well—that's very much what I said.'

He was a little surprised when she said meekly:

'Yes, it is.'

'What's the difference?'

'Practically none, only—'

'Yes?'

'You and I would have wanted to believe it was Vernon even if it wasn't.'

'Wouldn't Nell? Surely she hasn't come to care for George Chetwynd to such an extent—'

'Nell is very fond of George, but Vernon is the only person she's ever been in love with.'

'Then that's all right. Or is it worse that way? It's the deuce of a tangle . . . What about his people? Mrs Deyre and the Bents?'

Jane said decidedly: 'Nell must be told before they are. Mrs Deyre will broadcast it over England as soon as she knows, and that will be very unfair to both Vernon and Nell.'

'Yes, I think you're right. Now my plan is this. To take Vernon up to town tomorrow and go and see a specialist—then be guided by what he advises.'

Jane said Yes, she thought that would be the best plan. She got up to go to bed. On the stairs she paused and said to Sebastian:

'I wonder if we're right. Bringing him back, I mean. He looked so happy. Oh, Sebastian, he looked so happy . . .'

'As George Green, you mean?'

'Yes. Are you sure we're right?'

'Yes, I'm pretty sure. It can't be right for anyone to be in that unnatural sort of state.'

'I suppose it *is* unnatural. The queer thing is he looked

390

so normal and commonplace. And happy—that's what I can't get over, Sebastian—*happy* . . . We're none of us very happy, are we?'

He couldn't answer that.

CHAPTER 3

Two days later Sebastian came to Abbots Puissants. The butler was not sure that Mrs Chetwynd could see him. She was lying down.

Sebastian gave his name and said he was sure Mrs Chetwynd would see him. He was shown into the drawing-room to wait. The room seemed very empty and silent but unusually luxurious—very different from what it had looked in his childish days. He thought to himself, 'It was a *real* house then,' and wondered what exactly he meant by that. He got it presently. Now it suggested, very faintly, a museum. Everything was beautifully arranged, and harmonized perfectly, every piece that was not perfect had been replaced by one that was. All the carpets and covers and hangings were new.

'And they must have cost a pretty penny,' thought Sebastian appreciatively, and priced them with a fair degree of accuracy. He always knew the cost of things.

He was interrupted in this salutary exercise by the door opening. Nell came in, a pink colour in her cheeks and her hand outstretched.

'Sebastian! What a surprise! I thought you were too busy ever to leave London except at a weekend—and not often then!'

'I've lost just twenty thousand pounds in the last two days,' said Sebastian gruffly as he took her hand. 'Simply from gadding about and letting things go anyhow. How are you, Nell?'

'Oh, I'm feeling splendid.'

She didn't look very splendid, though, he thought, now that the flush of surprise had died away. Besides, hadn't the butler said she was lying down, not feeling well? He fancied that her face looked a little strained and haggard.

She went on:

'Sit down, Sebastian. You look as though you were on the point of going off to catch a train. George is away—in Spain. He had to go on business. He'll be away a week at least.'

'Will he?'

That was a good thing anyway. A damned awkward business. Nell had simply no idea . . .

'You're very glum, Sebastian. Is anything the matter?'

She asked the question quite lightly, but he seized upon it eagerly. It was the opening he needed.

'Yes, Nell,' he said gravely. 'As a matter of fact there is.'

He heard her draw in her breath with a sudden catch. Her eyes looked watchful.

'What is it?' she said.

Her voice sounded different—hard and suspicious.

Agatha Christie

'I'm afraid what I'm going to say will be a great shock to you. It's about Vernon.'

'What about Vernon?'

Sebastian waited a minute. Then he said:

'Vernon—is alive, Nell.'

'Alive?' she whispered. Her hand crept up to her heart.

'Yes.'

She didn't do any of the things he expected her to do—didn't faint, or cry out, or ask eager questions. She just stared straight ahead of her. And a sudden quick suspicion came into his shrewd Jewish mind.

'You knew it?'

'No, no.'

'I thought perhaps you saw him—the other day—when he came here?'

'Then it *was* Vernon?'

It broke from her like a cry. Sebastian nodded his head. It was as he had thought and said to Jane. She had not trusted her eyes.

'What did you think—that it was a very close resemblance?'

'Yes—yes, that's what I thought. How could I think it was Vernon? He looked at me and didn't know me.'

'He's lost his memory, Nell.'

'Lost his memory?'

'Yes.'

He told her the story, giving the details as carefully as possible. She listened but paid less attention than he expected. When he had finished she said: 'Yes—but what's to be done about it all? Will he get it back? What are we to do?'

394

He explained that Vernon was having treatment from a specialist. Already, under hypnosis, part of the lost memory had returned. The whole process would not be long delayed. He did not enter into the technical details, judging rightly that these would have no interest for her.

'And then he'll know—everything?'

'Yes.'

She shrank back in her chair. He felt a sudden rush of pity.

'He can't blame you, Nell. You didn't know—nobody could know. The report of his death was absolutely definite. It's an almost unique case. I've heard of one other. In most cases, of course, a report of death was contradicted almost immediately. Vernon loves you enough to understand and forgive.'

She said nothing but she put up both hands to cover her face.

'We think—if you agree—that everything had better be kept quiet for the present. You'll tell Chetwynd, of course. And you and he and Vernon can—well, thrash it out together—'

'Don't! Don't! Don't go into details. Just let's leave it for the present—till I've seen Vernon.'

'Do you want to see him at once? Will you come up to town with me?'

'No—I can't do that. Let him come here—to see me. Nobody will recognize him. The servants are all new.'

Sebastian said slowly: 'Very well . . . I'll tell him.'

Nell got up.

'I—I—you must go away now, Sebastian. I can't bear

any more. I can't indeed. It's all so dreadful. And only two days ago 'I was so happy and peaceful . . .'

'But, Nell—surely to have Vernon back again.'

'Oh, yes, I didn't mean *that*. You don't understand. That's wonderful, of course. Oh! do go, Sebastian. It's awful of me turning you out like this, but I can't bear any more. You must go.'

Sebastian went. On the way back to town he wondered a good deal.

Left alone, Nell went back to her bedroom and lay down on her bed, pulling the silk eiderdown tightly over her.

So it was true after all. It *had* been Vernon. She had told herself that it couldn't be—that she had made a ridiculous mistake. But she'd been uneasy ever since.

What was going to happen? What would George say about it all? Poor George. He'd been so good to her.

Of course there were women who'd married again, and then had found their first husbands were alive. Rather an awful position. She had never really been George's wife at all.

Oh! it couldn't be true. Such things didn't happen. God wouldn't let—

But perhaps she had better not think of God. It reminded her of those very unpleasant things that Jane had said the other day. That very same day.

She thought with a rush of self-pity: 'I was so happy . . .'

Was Vernon going to understand? Would he—perhaps—blame her? He'd want her, of course, to come back. Or wouldn't he—now that she and George—What *did* men think?

There could be a divorce, of course, and then she could marry George. But that would make a lot of talk. How difficult everything was.

She thought with a sudden shock: 'But I *love* Vernon. How can I contemplate a divorce and marrying George when I love Vernon? He's been given back to me—from the dead.'

She turned over restlessly on the bed. It was a beautiful Empire bed. George had bought it out of an old château in France. It was perfect and quite unique. She looked round the room—a charming room, everything in harmony—perfect taste, perfect unostentatious luxury.

She remembered suddenly the horsehair sofa and the antimacassars in the furnished rooms at Wiltsbury.

. . . Dreadful! But they had been happy there.

But now? She looked round the room with new eyes. Of course, Abbots Puissants belonged to George. Or didn't it, now that Vernon had come back? Anyway, Vernon would be just as poor as ever—they couldn't afford to live here . . . there were all the things that George had done to it . . . thought after thought raced confusedly through her brain.

She must write to George—beg him to come home. Just say it was urgent—nothing more. He was so clever. He might see a way.

Or perhaps she wouldn't write to him—not till she had seen Vernon. Would Vernon be very angry? How terrible it all was.

The tears came to her eyes. She sobbed: 'It's unfair—it's unfair—I've never done anything. Why should this happen to me? Vernon will blame me and I couldn't know. How could I know?'

Again the thought flitted across her mind:

'I *was* so happy!'

Vernon was listening, trying to understand what the doctor was saying to him. He looked across the table at him. A tall thin man with eyes that seemed to see right into the centre of you and to read there things that you didn't even know about yourself.

And he made you see all the things you didn't want to see. Made you bring things up out of the depths. He was saying:

'Now that you have remembered, tell me again exactly how you saw the announcement of your wife's marriage.'

Vernon cried out:

'Must we go over it again and again? It was all so horrible. I don't want to think of it any more.'

And then the doctor explained, gravely and kindly, but very impressively. It was because of that desire not to 'think of it any more' that all this had come about. It must be faced now—thrashed out . . . Otherwise the loss of memory might return.

They went all over it again.

And then, when Vernon felt he could bear no more, he was told to lie down on a couch. The doctor touched his forehead and his limbs, told him that he was resting—was rested—that he would become strong and happy again . . .

A feeling of peace came over Vernon.

He closed his eyes . . .

Vernon came down to Abbots Puissants three days later. He came in Sebastian Levinne's car. To the butler he gave his name as Mr Green. Nell was waiting for him in the little white-panelled room where his mother had sat in the mornings. She came forward to meet him, forcing a conventional smile to her lips. The butler shut the door behind him, just in time for her to stop short before offering him her hand.

They looked at each other. Then Vernon said:

'Nell . . .'

She was in his arms. He kissed her—kissed her—kissed her . . .

He let her go at last. They sat down. He was quiet, rather tragic, very restrained, but for that one wild greeting. He'd gone through so much—so much in these last few days . . .

Sometimes he wished they'd left him alone—as George Green. It had been jolly being George Green.

He said stammeringly:

'It's all right, Nell. You mustn't think I blame you. I understand . . . Only it hurts. It hurts like Hell. Naturally.'

She said: 'I didn't mean—'

He interrupted her.

'I *know*, I tell you—I *know*! Don't talk about it. I don't

want to hear about it. I don't want to think about it even
. . .' He added in a different tone: 'They say that's my
trouble. That's how it happened.'

She said, rather eagerly: 'Tell me about it—about
everything.'

'There isn't much to tell.' He spoke without interest,
abstractedly. 'I was taken prisoner. How I got to be reported
killed, I don't know. At least I have a sort of vague idea.
There was a fellow very like me—one of the Huns. I don't
mean a double—or anything of that sort—but just a general
superficial resemblance. My German's pretty rotten but I
heard them commenting on it. They took my kit and my
identification disc. I think the idea was to penetrate
into our lines as me—we were being relieved by Colonial
troops—and they knew it. The fellow would pass muster
for a day or so and would gain the information he wanted.
That's only an idea—but it explains why I wasn't returned
in the list of prisoners and I was sent to a camp that was
practically all French and Belgians. But none of that
matters, does it? I suppose the Hun was killed getting
through our lines and was buried as me. I had a pretty
bad time in Germany—nearly died with some kind of fever
on top of being wounded. Finally I escaped—oh! it's a
long story. I'm not going into all that now. I had the Hell
of a time—without food and water sometimes for days at
a stretch. It was a sort of miracle that I came through—but
I did. I got into Holland. I was exhausted and at the same
time all strung up. And I could only think of one thing—
getting back to you.'

'Yes?'

'And then I saw it—in a beastly illustrated paper. Your marriage. It—it finished me. But I wouldn't face it. I kept on saying that it couldn't be true. I went out—I don't know where I went. Things got all mixed up in my mind.

'There was a whacking great lorry coming down the road. I saw my chance—end it all—get out of it. I stepped out in front of it.'

'Oh, Vernon.' She shuddered.

'And that *was* the end. Of me as Vernon Deyre, I mean. When I came to there was just one name in my head—George. That lucky chap, George. George Green.'

'Why Green?'

'A sort of fancy of mine when I was a child. And then the Dutch girl at the inn had asked me to look up a pal of hers whose name was Green and I'd written it down in a little book.'

'And you didn't remember anything?'

'No.'

'Weren't you very frightened?'

'No—not at all. I didn't seem to be worrying about anything.' He added with lingering regret, 'I was awfully happy and jolly.'

Then he looked across at her.

'But that doesn't matter now. Nothing matters—but you.'

She smiled at him but her smile was flickering and uncertain. He barely noticed it at the moment, but went on.

'It's been rather Hell—getting back. Remembering things. All such beastly things. All the things that—really—I didn't want to face. I seem to have been an awful coward all my life. Always turning away from things I didn't want to look at. Refusing to admit them . . .'

He got up suddenly and came across to her, dropping his head upon her knees.

'Darling Nell—it's all right. I know I come first. I do, don't I?'

She said: 'Of course.'

Why did her voice sound so mechanical in her own ears? He did come first. Just now, with his lips on hers, she had been swept back again to those wonderful days at the beginning of the war. She had never felt about George like that . . . drowned . . . carried away . . .

'You say that so strangely—as though you didn't mean it.'

'Of course I mean it.'

'I'm sorry for Chetwynd—rotten luck for him. How has he taken it? Very hard?'

'I haven't told him.'

'What?'

She was moved to vindicate herself.

'He's away—in Spain—I haven't got his address.'

'Oh, I see . . .'

He paused.

'It'll be rather rotten for you, Nell. But it can't be helped. We'll have each other.'

'Yes.'

Vernon looked round.

'Chetwynd will have this place, anyway. I'm such an ungenerous beggar that I even grudge him that. But, damn it all, it *is* my home. It's been in the family five hundred years. Oh, what does it all matter? Jane told me once that

I couldn't get everything. I've got you—that's all that matters. We'll find some place—even if it's only a couple of rooms, it will do.'

His arms stole up, closing round her. Why did she feel that cold dismay at those words: 'A couple of rooms . . .'

'Damn these things! They get in my way!'

Impetuously—half laughing—he held up the string of pearls she wore. He switched them off—flung them on the floor. Her lovely pearls! She thought: 'Anyway, I suppose I'll have to give them back.' Another cold feeling. All those lovely jewels that George had given her.

What a brute she was to go on thinking of things like that.

He had seen something at last. He was kneeling upright—looking at her.

'Nell—is—is anything the matter?'

'No—of course not.'

She couldn't meet his eyes. She felt too ashamed.

'There is something . . . Tell me.'

She shook her head.

'It's nothing . . .'

She couldn't be poor again—she couldn't—she couldn't . . .

'Nell, you must tell me . . .'

He mustn't know—he must never know what she was really like. She was so ashamed.

'Nell—you do love me, don't you?'

'Oh, yes!' The words came eagerly. *That* at any rate was true.

'Then what is it? I know there's something . . . Ah!'

He got up. His face had gone white. She looked up at him inquiringly.

'Is it that?' he asked in a low voice. 'It must be. You're going to have a child . . .'

She sat as though carved in stone . . . She had never thought of that. If it were true, it solved everything. Vernon would never know . . .

'It *is* that?'

Again it seemed as though hours passed. Thoughts went whirling round in her brain. It was not herself, but something outside herself that at last made her bow her head ever so slightly . . .

He moved a little away. He spoke in a hard dry voice.

'That alters everything . . . My poor Nell . . . You can't—*we* can't . . . Look here, nobody knows—about me, I mean—except the doctor and Sebastian and Jane. They won't split. I was reported dead—I *am* dead . . .'

She made a movement—but he held up a hand to stop her and backed away towards the door.

'Don't say anything—for God's sake, don't say anything. Words will make it worse. I'm going. I daren't touch you or kiss you. I—Goodbye . . .'

She heard the door open—made a movement as if to call out—but no sound came from her throat. The door shut again.

There was still time . . . The car hadn't started . . .

But still she didn't move . . .

She had one moment of searing bitterness when she

looked into herself and thought: 'So that's what I'm really like . . .'

But she made no sound or movement.

Four years of soft living fettered her will, stifled her voice, and paralysed her body . . .

CHAPTER 4

'Miss Harding to see you, madam.'

Nell started. Twenty-four hours had elapsed since her interview with Vernon. She had thought it was finished. And now Jane!

She was afraid of Jane . . .

She might refuse to see her.

She said: 'Show her up here.'

It was more private up here in her own sitting-room . . .

What a long time it was waiting. Had Jane gone away again? No—here she was.

She looked very tall. Nell cowered down on the sofa. Jane had a wicked face—she had always thought so. There was a look on her face now as of an avenging fury.

The butler left the room. Jane stood towering over Nell. Then she flung back her head and laughed.

'Don't forget to ask me to the christening,' she said.

Nell flinched. She said haughtily:

'I don't know what you mean.'

'It's a family secret at present, is it? Nell, you damned little liar—you're not going to have a child. I don't believe you ever will have a child—too much risk and pain. What made you think of telling Vernon such a peculiarly damnable lie?'

Nell said sullenly: 'I never told him. He—he guessed.'

'That's even more damnable.'

'I don't know what you mean coming here and—and saying things like this.'

Her protest sounded weak—spiritless. For the life of her she couldn't put the necessary indignation into it. With anyone else—not with Jane. Jane had always been disagreeably clear-eyed. It was awful! If only Jane would go away.

She rose to her feet, trying to sound decisive.

'I don't know why you have come here. If it is only to make a scene . . .'

'Listen, Nell. You're going to hear the truth. You chucked Vernon once before. He came to me. Yes—to me. He lived with me for three months. He was living with me when you came to my flat that day. Ah! that hurts you . . . You've still got a bit of raw womanhood left in you, I'm glad to see.

'You took him from me then. He went to you and never gave me a thought. He's yours now if you want him. But I tell you this, Nell, if you let him down a second time, he'll come to me again. Oh, yes, he will. You've thought things about me in your mind—turned up your nose at me as "a certain kind of woman". Well, because of that, perhaps, I've got power. I know more about men than you will ever learn. I can get Vernon if I want him. And I do want him. I always have.'

Agatha Christie

Nell shuddered. She turned her face away, digging her nails into the palms of her hands.

'Why do you tell me all this? You're a devil.'

'I tell it you to hurt you! To hurt you like Hell before it's too late. No, you shan't turn your head away. You shan't shrink away from what I'm telling you. You've got to look at me and see—yes, see—with your eyes and your heart and your brain . . . You love Vernon with the last remaining corner of your miserable little soul . . . Think of him in my arms—think of his lips on mine, of his kisses burning my body . . . Yes, you shall think of it . . .

'Soon you won't mind even that. But you mind now . . . Aren't you enough of a woman to jib at handing over the man you love to another woman? To a woman you hate? A present for Jane with love from Nell . . .'

'Go away,' said Nell faintly. 'Go away . . .'

'I'm going. It's not too late . . . You can undo the lie you told.'

'Go away . . . Go away . . .'

'Do it soon—or you'll never do it.' Jane paused at the door, looking back over her shoulder. 'I came for Vernon's sake—not mine. I want him back. And I shall have him . . .' she paused, 'unless . . .'

She went out.

Nell sat with her hands clenched.

She murmured fiercely, 'She shan't have him. She shan't . . .'

She wanted Vernon. She wanted him. He had loved Jane once. He would love her again. What had she said? '. . . his lips on mine . . . his kisses burning my . . .' Oh,

408

God, she couldn't bear it. She started up—moved towards the telephone.

The door opened. She turned slowly. George came in. He looked very normal and cheerful.

'Hullo, sweetheart.' He crossed the room and kissed her. 'Here I am—back again. A nasty crossing. I'd rather have the Atlantic than the Channel any day.'

She had completely forgotten that George was coming home today! She couldn't tell him this minute—it would be too cruel. And besides it was so difficult—to burst in with the tragic news in the middle of a flow of banalities. This evening—later . . . In the meantime she would play her part.

She returned his embrace mechanically, sat down and listened while he talked.

'I've got a present for you, honey. Something that reminded me of you.'

He took a velvet case from his pocket.

Inside, on a bed of white velvet, lay a big rose-coloured diamond—exquisite—flawless, depending from a long chain. Nell gave a little gasp of pleasure.

He lifted the jewel from the case and slipped the chain over her head. She looked down. The exquisite rose-coloured stone blinked up at her from its resting place between her breasts. Something about it hypnotized her.

He led her to the glass. She saw a golden-haired beautiful woman, very calm and elegant. She saw the waved and shingled hair, the manicured hands, the foamy negligee of soft lace, the cobweb silk stockings and little embroidered mules. She saw the hard cold beauty of the rose-coloured diamond.

And behind them she saw George Chetwynd—kindly, generous, deliciously safe . . .

Dear George, she couldn't hurt him . . .

Kisses . . . What, after all, were kisses? You needn't think about them. Better not to think of them . . .

Vernon . . . Jane . . .

She wouldn't think of them. For good or evil she'd made her choice. There would be bad moments sometimes, but on the whole it would be for the best. Better for Vernon too. If she weren't happy she couldn't make him happy . . .

She said gently: 'You are a dear to bring me such a lovely present. Ring for tea. We'll have it up here.'

'That will be fine. But weren't you going to telephone to someone? I interrupted you.'

She shook her head.

'No,' she said, 'I've changed my mind.'

LETTERS FROM VERNON DEYRE TO
SEBASTIAN LEVINNE

MOSCOW.

Dear Sebastian,—

Do you know that there was once a legend in Russia that concerned a 'nameless beast' that was coming?

I mention this not because of any political significance (by the way, the Antichrist hysteria is curious, isn't it?) but because it reminded me of my own terror of 'The Beast'. I've thought about 'The Beast' a great deal since coming to Russia—trying to get at its true significance.

410

Because there's more in it than just being afraid of a piano. The doctor in London opened my eyes to a great many things. I've begun to see that all through my life I've been a coward. I think you've known that, Sebastian. You wouldn't put it in that offensive way, but you hinted as much to me once. I've run away from things . . . Always I've run away from things.

And thinking it all over now, I see The Beast as something symbolical—not a mere piece of furniture composed of wood and wires. Don't mathematicians say that the future exists at the same time as the past—that we travel through time as we travel through space—from a thing that is to another thing that is? Don't some even hold that remembering is a mere habit of the mind—that we could remember forward as well as back if we had only learnt the trick of it? It sounds nonsense when I say it—but I believe there is some theory of that kind.

I believe that there is some part of us that *does* know the future, that is always intimately aware of it.

That explains, doesn't it, why we should shrink sometimes. The burden of our destiny is going to be heavy and we recoil from its shadow . . . I tried to escape from music—but it got me. It got me at that Concert—in the same way that religion got those people at the Salvation Army meeting.

It's a devilish thing—or is it god-like? If so it's an Old Testament jealous God—all the things I've tried to cling on to have been swept away. Abbots Puissants . . . Nell . . .

411

Agatha Christie

And damn it all, what's left? Nothing. Not even the cursed thing itself . . . I've no wish to write music. I hear nothing—feel nothing . . . Will it ever come back? Jane says it will . . . She seems very sure. She sends her love to you by the way.

    Yours,

      Vernon.

                       Moscow.

You're an understanding devil, Sebastian. You don't complain that I ought to have written you a description of samovars, the political situation and life in Russia generally. The country, of course, is in a bloody muddle. What else could it be in? But it's jolly interesting . . . Love from Jane.

      Vernon.

                       Moscow.

Dear Sebastian,—

Jane was right to bring me here. Point No. 1, no one is likely to come across me here and joyously proclaim my resurrection from the dead. Point No. 2, this is about the most interesting place in the world to be from my point of view. A kind of free and easy laboratory where everyone is trying experiments of the most dangerous kind. The whole world seems concerned with Russia from a purely political point of view. Economics, starvation, morals, lack of liberty, diseased and decadent children . . . etc . . .

412

But amazing things are sometimes born out of vice and filth and anarchy. The whole trend of Russian thought in art is extraordinary . . . part of it the most utter childish drivel you ever heard—and yet wonderful gleams peeping through—like shining flesh through a beggar's rags . . .

The 'Nameless Beast' . . . Collective Man . . . Did you ever see that plan for a monument to the Communist Revolution? The Colossus of Iron? I tell you, it stirs the imagination.

Machinery—an Age of Machinery . . . How the Bolsheviks worship anything to do with machinery—and how little they know about it! That's why it's so wonderful to them, I suppose. Imagine a real mechanic of Chicago composing a dynamic poem describing his city as *'built upon a screw! Electro dynamo mechanical city! Spiral shaped—on a steel disc. At every stroke of the hour turning round itself—Five thousand skyscrapers . . .'* Anything more alien from the spirit of America!

And yet—do you ever see a thing when you're too close to it? It's the people who don't know machinery who see its soul and its meaning . . . The 'Nameless Beast' . . . My Beast? . . . I wonder . . .

Collective Man—forming himself in turn into a vast machine . . . The same herd instinct that saved the race of old coming out again in a different form . . .

Life's becoming too difficult—too dangerous—for the individual. What was it Dostoevsky says in one of his books?

The flock will collect again and submit once more, and then it will be for ever, for ever. We will give them a quiet modest happiness.

Herd instinct . . . I wonder . . .

Yours,

Vernon.

MOSCOW.

I have found the other passage in Dostoevsky. I think it is the one you mean.

'*And we alone, we who guard the mystery, we alone shall be unhappy. There will be thousands of millions of happy children and only a hundred thousand martyrs who have taken on themselves the curse of good and evil.*'

You mean, and Dostoevsky meant, that there must always be individualists. It is the individualists who carry on the torch. Men welded into a vast machine must ultimately perish. For the machine is soulless and will end as scrap iron.

Men worshipped stone and built Stonehenge—and today, the men who built it have perished and are unknown and Stonehenge stands. And yet, by a paradox, the men are alive in you and me, their descendants, and Stonehenge and what it stood for, is dead. The things that die, endure, and the things that endure, perish.

It is Man that goes on for ever. (Does he? Isn't that unwarrantable arrogance? Yet we believe it!) And so, there must be individualists behind the Machine. So Dostoevsky says and so you say. But then you're both Russians. As an Englishman I'm more pessimistic.

Do you know what that passage from Dostoevsky reminds me of? My childhood. Mr Green's hundred children—*and* Poodle, Squirrel and Tree. Representatives of the hundred thousand . . .

    Yours,
      Vernon.

                          Moscow.

Dear Sebastian,—

I suppose you're right. I never have thought much before. It seemed to me an unprofitable exercise. In fact, I'm not sure I don't still regard it as such.

The trouble is, you see, that I can't 'say it in Music'. Damn it all, why *can't* I say it in Music? Music's my job. I'm more sure of that than ever. And yet—nothing doing . . .

    It's Hell . . .
      Vernon.

Dear Sebastian,—

Haven't I mentioned Jane? What is there to say about her? She's splendid. We both know that. Why don't you write to her yourself?

    Yours ever,
      Vernon.

Dear Old Sebastian,—

Jane says you may be coming out here. I wish to God you would. I'm sorry I haven't written for six months—I never was one of the world's ready letter writers.

Have you seen anything of Joe? I'm glad Jane and I looked her up passing through Paris. Joe's staunch—she'll never split on us, and I'm glad she at any rate knows. We never write to each other, she and I, we never have . . . But I wondered if you'd heard anything. I didn't think she looked awfully fit . . . Poor old Joe—she's made a mess of things . . .

Have you heard anything of Tatlin's scheme for a monument to the Third International? To consist of a union of three great glass chambers connected by a system of vertical axes and spirals. By means of special machinery they were to be kept in perpetual motion but at different rates of speed.

And inside, I suppose, they'd sing hymns to a Holy Acetylene blowpipe!

Do you remember, one night, we were motoring back to town, and we took the wrong turning somewhere amongst the tram lines of Lewisham, and instead of making for the haunts of civilization we turned up somewhere among the Surrey docks, and through an opening in the frowsy houses we saw a queer kind of Cubist picture of cranes and cloudy steam and iron girders. And immediately your artistic soul bagged it for a drop scene—or whatever the technical term is.

My God, Sebastian! What a magnificent spectacle of machinery you could build up—sheer effects and

lighting—and masses of humans with inhuman faces—
mass—not individuals. You've something of the kind in
mind, haven't you?

The architect, Tatlin, said something that I think good
and yet a lot of nonsense.

'*Only the rhythm of the metropolis, of factories and
machines together with the organization of the masses
can give the impulse to the new art . . .*'

And he goes on to speak of the 'monument of the
machine', the only adequate expression of the present.

You know, of course, all about the modern Russian
Theatre. That's your job. I suppose Mayerhold is as
marvellous as they say he is. But can one mix up Drama
and Propaganda?

All the same, it's exciting to arrive at a theatre and
be compelled at once to join a marching crowd—up
and down—in strict step—till the performance begins—
and the scenery—composed of rocking chairs and
cannons and revolving bays and God knows what! It's
babyish—absurd—and yet one feels that baby has got
hold of a dangerous and rather interesting toy that in
other hands . . .

Your hands, Sebastian . . . You're a Russian. But
thank Heaven and Geography, no Propagandist—just a
Showman pure and simple . . .

The rhythm of the metropolis—made pictorial . . .

My God—if I could give you the Music . . . It's the
Music that's needed.

Lord—their 'Noise Orchestras'—their symphonies
of factory sirens! There was a show at Baku in

1922—batteries of artillery—machine-guns, choirs, naval fog horns. Ridiculous! Yes, but—if they had a composer . . .

No woman ever longed for a child like I long to produce Music . . .

And I'm barren—sterile . . .

Vernon.

Dear Sebastian,—

It seems like a dream your having come and gone . . . Will you really do *The Tale of the Rogue who outwitted Three Other Rogues*, I wonder?

I'm only just beginning to recognize what a howling success you've made of things. I've at last grasped that you're simply IT nowadays. Yes, found your National Opera House—God knows it's time we had one—but what do you want with Opera? It's archaic—dead ridiculous individual love affairs . . .

Music up to now seems to me like a child's drawing of a house—four walls—a door, two windows and a chimney pot. There you are—and what more do you want!

At any rate Feinberg and Prokofiev do more than that.

Do you remember how we used to jeer at the 'Cubists' and 'Futurists'? At least I did—now that I come to think of it I don't believe you agreed.

And then one day—at a cinema—I saw a view of a big city from the air. Spires turning over, buildings bending—everything behaving as one simply knew concrete and steel and iron couldn't behave! And for the

418

first time I got a glimmering of what old Einstein meant when he talked about relativity.

We don't know anything about the shape of music . . . We don't know anything about the shape of anything, for that matter . . . Because there's always one side open to space . . .

Some day you'll know what I mean . . . what Music can mean . . . what I've always known it meant . . .

What a mess that opera of mine was. All opera is a mess. Music was never intended to be representational. To take a story and write descriptive music to it is as wrong as to write a passage of music—in the abstract so to speak—and then find an instrument capable of playing it! When Stravinsky wrote a clarinet passage, you can't even conceive of it as being played by anything else!

Music should be like mathematics—a pure science— untouched by drama, or romanticism, or any emotion other than the pure emotion which is the result of *sound* divorced from ideas.

I've always known that in my heart . . . Music must be Absolute.

Not, of course, that I shall realize my ideal. To create pure sound untouched by ideas is a counsel of perfection.

My music will be the music of machinery. I leave the dressing of it to you. It's an age of choreography, and choreography will reach heights we don't as yet dream of. I can trust you with the visual side of my masterpiece as yet unwritten—and which in all probability never will be written.

Music must be four-dimensional—timbre, pitch, relative speed and periodicity.

I don't think even now we appreciate Schönberg enough. That clean remorseless logic that is the spirit of today. He and he alone had the courage to disregard tradition—to get down to bedrock, and discover Truth.

He's the one man to my mind who matters. Even his scheme of score writing will have to be adopted universally. It's absolutely necessary if scores are going to be intelligible.

The thing I have against him is his scorn of his instruments. He's afraid of being a slave to them. He makes them serve him whether they will or no.

I'm going to glorify my instruments . . . I'm going to give them what they want—what they've always wanted . . .

Damn it all, Sebastian, *what is this strange thing, Music?* I know less and less . . .

Yours,
Vernon.

I know I haven't written. I've been busy. Making experiments. Means of expression for the Nameless Beast. In other words, instrument making. Metals are jolly interesting—I'm working with alloys just at present.

What a fascinating thing sound is . . .

Jane sends her love.

In answer to your question—No, I don't suppose I shall ever leave Russia—not even to attend at your newly planned opera house disguised in my beard!

It's even more barbarous and beautiful now than when you saw it! Full and flowing, the perfect temperamental Slav Beaver!

But in spite of the forest camouflage, here I am and here I stay, till I am exterminated by one of the bands of wild children.

Yours ever,

Vernon.

Telegram from Vernon Deyre to Sebastian Levinne.

'Just heard Joe dangerously ill feared dying stranded in New York Jane and I sailing *Resplendent* hope see you London.'

CHAPTER 5

'Sebastian!'

Joe started up in bed then fell back weakly. She stared unbelievingly. Sebastian, big fur-coated, calm and omniscient, smiled placidly down at her.

There was no sign in his face of the sudden pang her appearance had given him. Joe—poor little Joe.

Her hair had grown—it was arranged in two short plaits one over each shoulder. Her face was horribly thin with a high hectic flush on each cheekbone. The bones of her shoulders showed through her thin nightdress.

She looked like a feverish child. There was something child-like in her surprise, in her pleasure, in her eager questioning. The nurse had left them.

Sebastian sat down by the bed and took Joe's thin hand in his.

'Vernon wired me. I didn't wait for him. I caught the first boat.'

'To come to me?'

'Of course.'

'Dear Sebastian!'

Tears came into her eyes. Sebastian was alarmed and went on hastily:

'Not that I shan't do a bit of business while I am over. I often come over on business and as a matter of fact I can do one or two good deals just now.'

'Don't spoil it.'

'But it's true,' said Sebastian, surprised.

Joe began to laugh—but coughed instead. Sebastian watched anxiously—ready to call the nurse. He had been warned. But the fit passed.

Joe lay there contentedly, her hand creeping into Sebastian's again.

'Mother died this way,' she whispered. 'Poor Mother. I thought I was going to be so much wiser than she was, and I've made such a mess of things—Oh! such a mess of things . . .'

'Poor old Joe.'

'You don't know what a mess I've made of things, Sebastian.'

'I can imagine it,' said Sebastian. 'I always thought you would.'

Joe was silent a minute, then she said:

'You don't know what a comfort it is to see you, Sebastian. I have seen and known so many rotters. I didn't like your being strong and successful and cocksure—it annoyed me—but now—Oh! it's wonderful!'

He squeezed her hand.

'There's no one else in the world who would have come— as you've come—miles—at once. Vernon, of course, but then he's a relation—a kind of brother. But you—'

'I'm just as much a brother—more than a brother. Ever since Abbots Puissants I've been—well, ready to stand by if you wanted me . . .'

'Oh, Sebastian.' Her eyes opened wide—happily. 'I never dreamt—that you'd feel like that still.'

He started ever so slightly. He hadn't meant that exactly. He had meant something that he couldn't explain—not at any rate to Joe. It was a feeling peculiarly and exclusively Jewish. The undying gratitude of the Jew who never forgets a benefit conferred. As a child he had been an outcast and Joe had stood by him— she had been willing to defy her world. The child Sebastian had never forgotten—would never forget. He would, as he had said, have gone to the ends of the earth if she had wanted him.

She went on.

'They moved me into this place—from that horrible ward—Was that you?'

He nodded.

'I cabled.'

Joe sighed.

'You're so terribly efficient, Sebastian.'

'I'm afraid so.'

'But there's nobody like you—nobody. I've thought of you so often lately.'

'Have you?'

He thought of the lonely years—the aching longing— the baffled desire. Why did things always come to you at the wrong time?

She went on.

'I never dreamt you'd still think about me. I always fancied that some day you and Jane—'

A queer pang shot through him. *Jane* . . .

He and Jane . . .

He said gruffly:

'Jane to my mind is one of the finest things God ever made. But she belongs body and soul to Vernon and always will . . .'

'I suppose so. But it's a pity. You and she are the strong ones. You belong together.'

They did, in a curious way. He knew what she meant.

Joe said with a flickering smile:

'This reminds me of the books one reads as a child. Edifying death-bed scenes. Friends and relations gathering round. Wan smiles of heroine.'

Sebastian had made up his mind. Why had he felt this wasn't love? It was. This passion of pure disinterested pity and tenderness—this deep affection lasting through the years. A thousand times better worthwhile than those stormy or tepid affairs that occurred with monotonous regularity—that punctuated his life without ever touching any real depths.

His heart went out to the childish figure. Somehow, he'd bring it off.

He said gently:

'There aren't going to be any death-bed scenes, Joe. You're going to get well and marry me.'

'Darling Sebastian—tie you to a consumptive wife? Of course not.'

'Nonsense. You'll do one of two things—either get well

or die. If you die, you die and there's an end of it. If you get cured, you marry me. And no expense will be spared to cure you.'

'I'm pretty bad, Sebastian dear.'

'Possibly. But nothing is more uncertain than tubercle— any doctor will tell you so. You've been just letting yourself go. I think myself you'll get well. A long weary business but it can be done.'

She looked at him. He saw the colour rising and falling in her thin cheeks. He knew then that she loved him—and a queer little stir of warmth woke round his heart. His mother had died two years ago. Since then no one had really cared.

Joe said in a low voice:

'Sebastian—do you really need me? I—I've made such a mess of things.'

He said with sincerity:

'Need you? I'm the loneliest man on earth.'

And suddenly he broke down. It was a thing he had never done in his life—never thought he would do. He knelt by Joe's bed, his face buried, his shoulders heaving.

Her hand stroked his head. He knew she was happy, her proud spirit appeased. Dear Joe—so impulsive, so warm-hearted, so wrong-headed. She was dearer to him than anyone on earth. They could help one another.

The nurse came in—the visitor had been there long enough. She withdrew again for Sebastian to say goodbye.

'By the way,' he said. 'That French fellow—what's his name—?'

'François? He's dead.'

'That's all right. You could have got a divorce, of course. But being a widow makes it easier.'

'You *do* think I shall get well?'

Pathetic—the way she said that!

'Of course.'

The nurse reappeared and he took his departure. He called on the doctor—had a long talk. The doctor was not hopeful. But he agreed that there was a chance. They decided on Florida.

Sebastian left the home. He walked along the street deep in thought. He saw a placard with 'Terrible disaster to *Resplendent*' on it, but it conveyed nothing to his mind.

He was too busy with his own thoughts. What was really best for Joe? To live or to die? He wondered . . .

She'd had such a rotten life. He wanted the best for her.

He went to bed and slept heavily.

He awoke to a vague uneasiness. There was something—something. For the life of him he couldn't put a name to it . . .

It wasn't Joe. Joe was in the foreground of his mind. This was something in the background—shoved away—something that he hadn't been able to give consideration to at the time.

He thought: 'I shall remember presently . . .' But he didn't.

As he dressed, he thought out the problem of Joe. He was all for moving her to Florida as soon as possible.

Later, perhaps, Switzerland. She was very weak—but not too weak to be moved. As soon as she had seen Vernon and Jane—

They were arriving—when? The *Resplendent*, wasn't it? The *Resplendent* . . .

The razor he was holding dropped from his hand. He'd got it now! Before his eyes rose the vision of a newspaper placard.

The *Resplendent*—Terrible Disaster . . .

Vernon and Jane were on the *Resplendent*.

He rang furiously. A few minutes later he was scanning the morning newspaper. There were now full details to hand. His eyes scanned them rapidly. The *Resplendent* had struck an iceberg—the death-roll, survivors . . .

A list of names . . . survivors. He found the name there of Green, Vernon was alive anyway. Then he searched the other list and found at last what he was looking for—fearing—the name of Jane Harding.

He stood quite still, staring at the newssheet in his hand. Presently he folded it up neatly, laid it on a side table and rang the bell. In a few minutes a curt order given to the bellhop sent his secretary hurrying to him.

'I've got an appointment at ten o'clock I can't break. There are some things you've got to find out for me. Have the information ready for me when I return.'

He detailed the points succinctly. The fullest particulars as to the *Resplendent* were to be collected, and certain radios were to be sent off.

Sebastian telephoned himself to the hospital and warned them that no mention of the *Resplendent* disaster was to be made to the patient. He had a few words with Joe herself which he managed to make normal and commonplace.

He stopped at a florist to send her some flowers and then went off to embark on a long day of meetings and business appointments. It is to be doubted if anyone noticed that the great Sebastian Levinne was unlike himself in the smallest detail. He had never been more shrewd in driving a bargain and his power of getting his own way was never more in evidence.

It was six o'clock when he returned to the Biltmore.

His secretary met him with all the information available. The survivors had been picked up by a Norwegian ship. They would be due in New York in three days' time.

Sebastian nodded, his face unchanged. He gave further instructions.

On the evening of the third day following that, he returned to his hotel to be met by the information that Mr Green had arrived and was installed in the suite adjoining his own.

Sebastian strode there.

Vernon was standing by the window. He turned round.

Sebastian felt something like a shock. In some strange way, he no longer recognized his friend. Something had happened to him.

They stood staring at each other. Sebastian spoke first. He said the thing that all day had been present in his mind.

AgathaChristie

'Jane's dead,' he said.

Vernon nodded—gravely—understandingly.

'Yes,' he said quietly. 'Jane's dead—and I killed her.'

The old unemotional Sebastian revived and protested.

'For God's sake, Vernon, don't take it like that. She came with you—naturally—don't be morbid about it.'

'You don't understand,' said Vernon. 'You don't know what happened.'

He paused and then went on, speaking very quietly and collectedly.

'I can't describe the thing—it happened quite suddenly, you know—in the middle of the night. There was very little time. The boat heeled over, you know, at an appalling angle . . . The two of them came together—slipping—sliding down the deck—they couldn't save themselves.'

'What two?'

'Nell and Jane, of course.'

'What's Nell got to do with it?'

'She was on board—'

'What?'

'Yes. I didn't know. Jane and I were second-class, of course, and I don't think we ever glanced at a passenger list. Yes, Nell and George Chetwynd were on board. That's what I'm telling you if you wouldn't interrupt. It happened—a sort of nightmare—no time for lifebelts or anything. I was hanging on to a stanchion—or whatever you call it—to save myself from falling into the sea.

'And they came drifting along the deck, those two—right by me—slipping—sliding—faster and faster—and the sea waiting for them below.

430

'I'd no idea Nell was on board till I saw her—drifting down to destruction—and crying out "*Vernon*".

'There isn't time to think on these occasions, I tell you. One can just make an instinctive gesture. I could grab on to one or other of them . . . Nell or Jane . . .

'I grabbed Nell and held her, held her like grim death.'

'And Jane?'

Vernon said quietly:

'I can see her face still—looking at me—as she went . . . down into that green swirl . . .'

'My God,' said Sebastian hoarsely.

Then suddenly his impassivity forsook him. His voice rang out bellowing like a bull.

'You saved Nell? You bloody fool! To save Nell—and let Jane drown. Why, Nell isn't worth the tip of Jane's little finger. Damn you!'

'I know that.'

'You know it? Then—'

'I tell you, it isn't what you *know*—it's some blind instinct that takes hold of you . . .'

'Damn you—damn you—'

'I'm damned all right. You needn't worry. I let Jane drown—and I love her.'

'Love her?'

'Yes, I've always loved her . . . I see that now . . . Always, from the beginning, I was afraid of her—because I loved her. I was a coward there, like everywhere else—trying to escape from reality. I fought against her—I was ashamed of the power she had over me—I've taken her through Hell . . .

'And now I want her—I want her—Oh! you'll say that's like me to want a thing as soon as it's out of my reach—perhaps it's true—perhaps I am like that . . .

'I only know that I love Jane—that I love her—and that she's gone from me forever . . .'

He sat down on a chair and said in his normal tone:

'I want to work. Get out of here, Sebastian, there's a good fellow.'

'My God, Vernon, I didn't think I could ever hate you—'

Vernon repeated: 'I want to work . . .'

Sebastian turned on his heel and left the room.

Vernon sat very still.

Jane . . .

Horrible to suffer like this—to want anyone so much . . .

Jane . . . Jane . . .

Yes, he'd always loved her. After that very first meeting he'd been unable to keep away . . . He'd been drawn towards her by something stronger than himself . . .

Fool and coward to be afraid—always afraid. Afraid of any deep reality—of any violent emotion.

And she had known—she had always known—and been unable to help him. What had she said: 'Divided in time?' That first evening at Sebastian's party when she had sung.

'I saw a fairy lady there
With long white hands and drowning hair . . .'

432

Drowning hair . . . no, no, not that. Queer she should have sung that song. And the statue of the drowned woman . . . That was queer, too.

What was the other thing she had sung that night?

'J'ai perdu mon amie—elle est morte
Tout s'en va cette fois pour jamais,
Pour jamais pour toujours elle emporte
Le dernier des amours que j'aimais . . .'

He had lost Abbots Puissants, he had lost Nell . . .

But with Jane, he had indeed lost '*le dernier des amours que j'aimais*'.

For the rest of his life he would be able to see only one woman—Jane.

He loved Jane . . . he loved her . . .

And he'd tortured her, slighted her, finally abandoned her to that green evil sea . . .

The statue in the South Kensington Museum . . .

God—he mustn't think of that . . .

Yes—he'd think of everything . . . This time he wouldn't turn away . . .

Jane . . . Jane . . . Jane . . .

He wanted her . . . Jane . . .

He'd never see her again . . .

He'd lost everything now . . . everything . . .

Those days, months, years in Russia . . . Wasted years . . .

Fool—to live beside her, to hold her body in his arms, and all the time to be afraid . . . Afraid of his passion for her . . .

433

That old terror of The Beast . . .
And suddenly, as he thought of The Beast, he knew . . .
Knew that at last he had come into his heritage . . .

It was like the day he had come back from the Titanic Concert. It was the Vision he had had then. He called it Vision for it seemed more that than sound. Seeing and hearing were one—curves and spirals of sound—ascending, descending, returning.

And now he *knew*—he had the technical knowledge.

He snatched at paper, jotted down brief, scrawled hieroglyphics, a kind of frantic shorthand. There were years of work in front of him, but he knew that he should never again recapture this first freshness and clearness of Vision . . .

It must be so—and so—a whole weight of metal—brass—all the brass in the world.

And those new glass sounds, ringing—clear—

He was happy . . .

An hour passed—two hours . . .

For a moment he came out of his frenzy—remembered—Jane!

He felt sick—ashamed . . . Couldn't he even mourn her for one evening? There was something base, cruel, in the way he was using his sorrow, his desire—transmuting it into terms of sound.

That was what it meant being a creator . . . ruthlessness—using everything . . .

And people like Jane were the victims . . .

Jane . . .

He felt torn in two—agony and wild exultation.

He thought: 'Perhaps women feel like this when they have a child . . .'

Presently he bent again over his sheets of paper, writing frenziedly, flinging them on the floor as he finished them.

When the door opened, he did not hear it. He was deaf to the rustle of a woman's dress. Only when a small frightened voice said: 'Vernon,' did he look up.

With an effort he forced the abstracted look from his face.

'Hallo,' he said. 'Nell.'

She stood there, twisting her hands together—her face white and ravaged. She spoke in breathless gasps.

'Vernon—I found out—they told me—where you were— and I came—'

He nodded.

'Yes,' he said. 'You came?'

Oboes—no, cut out oboes—too soft a note—it must be strident, brazen. But harps, yes, he wanted the liquidness of harps—like water—you wanted water as a source of power.

Bother—Nell was speaking. He'd have to listen.

'Vernon—after that awful escape from death—I knew . . . There's only one thing that matters—love. I've always loved you. I've come back to you—for always.'

'Oh!' he said stupidly.

She had come nearer, was holding out her hands to him.

He looked at her as if from a great distance. Really, Nell was extraordinarily pretty. He could well see why he had fallen in love with her. Queer, that he wasn't the least bit in love with her now. How awkward it all was. He did wish she would go away and let him get on with what he was doing. What about trombones? One could improve on a trombone . . .

'Vernon—' Her voice was sharp—frightened. 'Don't you love me any more?'

It was really best to be truthful. He said with an odd formal politeness:

'I'm awfully sorry. I—I'm afraid I don't. You see I love Jane.'

'You're angry with me—because of that lie—about the—the child—'

'What lie? About what child?'

'Don't you even remember? I said I was going to have a child and it wasn't true . . . Oh, Vernon, forgive me—forgive me—'

'That's quite all right, Nell. Don't you worry. I'm sure everything's for the best. George is an awfully good chap and you're really happiest with him. And now, for God's sake, do go away. I don't want to be rude, but I'm most awfully busy. The whole thing will go if I don't pin it down . . .'

She stared at him.

Then slowly she moved towards the door. She stopped, turned, flung out her hands towards him.

'Vernon—'

It was a last cry of despairing appeal.

He did not even look up, only shook his head impatiently.

She went out, shutting the door behind her.

Vernon gave a sigh of relief.

There was nothing now to come between him and his work . . .

He bent over the table . . .